Papercut

A Series Of Breadcrumbs

Papercut
You Live You Learn
Waiting For The End

Read This Publishing

ISBN 978-0-9877311-1-1

Papercut

A Novel

Book One:
A Series of Breadcrumbs

First Edit By: Melissa Arditti
Second Edit By: Samantha Ross

Shannon Catori

Playlist on iTunes Ping, search Shannon Catori. Playlist title- A Series of Breadcrumbs: Papercut

Read This Publishing
1515 Rebecca St.
PO Box 60039
Oakville, ON
L6L 6R4

This book is a work of fiction. Names, characters, places and incidents either are products of the author's imagination or are used fictitiously. Any resemblance to actual events, locales or persons both living or dead is completely incidental.

All images are fictional representations of artistic works by fictional characters in this book. Images purchased from istock.com

Cover Art by Mark Savoia.
Cover Model: Filipa Jackson as Zahra Roméo-Winters

Copyright © 2012 Shannon Catori. All rights Reserved. Reproduction of the whole or any part of the contents without written permission from the publisher is prohibited.

For information about special discounts for bulk purchases, please contact Read Th!s Publishing at 1-(905) 616-1942 or info@readthispublishing.com

Catori, Shannon 1984, May 25-
　Papercut: a novel / by Shannon Catori.

1. Characters—Fiction. 2. Restaurant—Fiction. 3. Art School—Fiction. 4. Austrian Bakery—Fiction.5. Furniture Store—Fiction.6. High School—Fiction.7. Night Club—Fiction. 8.Chalet—Fiction. 9. Apartment London—Fiction. 10. London Flat-Fiction. 11. Private School/Dorm—12. London Bar-Fiction 13. Art—Fiction.

Read Th!s Publishing

Read Th!s Publishing is the publishing company for Shannon Catori and all of her works.
For more information, book club bookings or guest speaking inquiries please write to the following address:
1515 Rebecca St.
PO Box 60039
Oakville, ON
L6L 6R4
or email info@readthispublishing.com
www.readthispublishing.com
ISBN 978-0-9877311-1-1

Shannon Catori was born in Toronto. She currently lives in Oakville, Ontario with her husband, a handful of pets and a huge stack of books. Accompanied by her little black notebook, she travels around the world collecting inspiration to develop a wide range of fictional and non-fictional works.

Acknowledgements

There are no words to describe the feeling of running my fingers over a page filled with my own words. In a surreal moment like this, even words cease to exist. There has <u>never</u> been a time when I was speechless. I can cross 'speechless' and 'write a book' off my bucket list and for this moment of bucket list-bliss I must thank the very important people in my life who have helped make this all happen. Though it may sound obnoxious, I'd really like to thank myself for following my heart and "giving it a try." I have always loved to write and I've wanted to write professionally for a long time, but never really thought I had what it took, until one day I came across a quote by Author, Toni Morrison who said, "If the book you're looking to read doesn't exist, you must write it." After reading this quote I decided to go for it and I'm really glad I silenced the little critic in my head that told me I couldn't, because I would not be writing this acknowledgement right now! So Toni Morrison, thank you!

I'd like to thank Tamiesha for helping me create Zahra, the most important part of this series. I'd also really like to thank my mom (Louisa) for harvesting my passion for music at such a young age. The twenty years of voice lessons paid off! It's because of you that I have found a way to link a few of my greatest passions; music, lyrics and literature together.

I owe the world to the artists & musicians whose music I've featured either in the book or in my playlist. Your words, your melodies, rhythms and harmonies inspired so many wonderful moments in my life and in the lives of my characters. Your music perfectly captures these characters' highs and lows as they travel this journey we call life.

To my dad (Don) for talking me through much of the process, for meeting with me every weekend to figure out how to get the rights to lyrics and music. For telling me that the book was too long and suggesting that I turn it into a trilogy, instead of deleting half of the story. Duh, why didn't I think of that?

To South St. Burger Co. in Burloak: Thank you, to the wonderful staff who kept our bellies full when I was neck deep in words, sentences and music and couldn't make dinner. Your veggies burgers are the best and your fries, always crispy.

None of this would have been possible without the continuous support of my team. To the best editor, Melissa: You have given me so much inspiration and shared your phenomenal music catalogue with me. Sam, my proofreader, life coach and best friend (or best fuzin), you've always made me feel like I'm the world's best writer. You've picked me up when I was down and forced me to keep going in times when I felt hopeless. You're amazing! And Jonny, my other brain. You've let me run all of my ideas by you time and time again. You've always been such a great support, encouraging me to do what you always knew I could and being honest with me when you knew I was falling short and giving up. What else can I say to you guys except, together we made it!

✌❤♫
S

For Her
For Him
For Us

Author's Note

Hello Reader!

I want to start by thanking you for showing interest in my book and for giving me a bit of your time while you read it. This book is going to be a bit different from others that you may have read in the past, in that there is an accompanying playlist.

Now let me explain why I did this—first and foremost I am a musician and I have been for over fifteen years. In the last few, I opened a music school in the Greater Toronto Area called Mod Music Academy, a place not only to teach, but to inspire rising musicians to find their highest potential. In the school I teach voice and songwriting and I have always taught my students to embrace the lyrics of a song and depict the story with their voice. Sometimes if a student was having trouble grasping the concept of the song I would make up an elaborate story for them and have them act out their part through the lyrics, their tone and in their voice. It was this same idea that led me to write this story, because as we say at Mod Music, *music depicts the journey through life!*

With a playlist to listen to as you read, a sort of movie is created in your head. This "brain movie" is personal, based on how you feel about each character and how you interpret who they are and their role in the story. This theme continues in books two and three of this series. This small ★ (star) married to a footnote, will be your musical guide. In these chapters (where music is featured), the star indicates when to start listening to the song. Further details can be found in the footnotes of the chapters.

Enjoy!

Playlist

1. Hide and Seek-Imogen Heap
2. Let Down-Dead By Sunrise
3. Show Me Love-Robin S., Steve Angello, Laidback Luke
4. Angel-Sarah McLaughlan
5. Feelings Gone-Basement Jaxx
6. Valentine's Day-Linkin Park
7. Heaven (Candlelight Mix)-DJ Sammy ft. Yanou
8. Somewhere I Belong- Linkin Park
9. Ode To A Friend-Jann Arden
10. Krwling-Linkin Park
11. One Step Closer-Linkin Park
12. Loving Me 4 Me-Christina Aguilera
13. Abracadabra-Jessie J
14. We Belong Together-Gavin Degraw
15. Lucky-Bif Naked
16. Little Star-Madonna
17. Never Think-Rob Pattinson
18. Unthinkable-Alicia Keys
19. Wonderwall-Noel Gallagher
20. In the Darkness-Dead By Sunrise
21. Let Me Sign-Rob Pattinson
22. Kissing You-Des'ree
23. Papercut-Linkin Park
24. Give Me Your Name-Dead By Sunrise
25. Superstarr Prt 2 (Babylon Girl)-K-OS
26. For A Pessimist I'm Pretty Optimistic-Paramore
27. Playing God-Paramore
28. When They Come For Me-Linkin Park
29. Airplanes-B.O.B ft Hayley Williams
30. Misguided Ghosts-Paramore
31. Leaving On A Jet Plane-Chantel Kreviazuk
32. Easier To Run-Linkin Park
33. Sanctuary-Global Rhythm

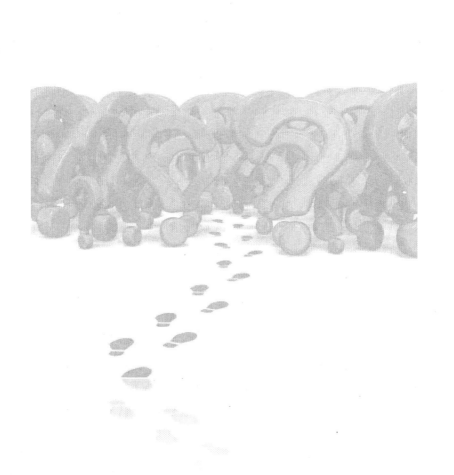

Prologue

(★) [1]My legs were tired. The muscles in my thighs and calves felt like they were on fire, but I had to keep going. Tall totem poles, a rock pond, a long winding ramp, Domestic Arrivals, wrong entrance, instant panic. Signs, signs, signs. Follow the signs, International Departures, *finally*.

My lungs were heavy, my breath heaved in and out of my chest painfully, as I raced toward Check-In at the end of the long hall. Every breath I took felt like I took it through sand as I tried to navigate my way through the crowd of people.

Don't look back. Keep moving forward, Don't look away, keep your eyes on the signs. Don't let them catch you. Keep running, keep pushing, fight through it, make it to the gate.

I came to an abrupt halt, I took my place in line, anxiously tapping my foot on the white porcelain floor. I bit my nails in apprehension, too afraid to look behind me, but waiting to be taken away. I was expecting to be caught. My plan was not a plan at all. This was all impulse. How well can you escape on impulse? The line seemed too long, like I would never make it to the front in time. The pit of my stomach grumbled and churned that it was over for me, that I might as well surrender, there was no hope.

Don't look back, don't look back, don't look back. Please don't be behind me. Line, please hurry up!

This was my time, time to be free, time to run away…
Th-thump, th-thump, th-thump…

Two years ago my life spiralled out of control. This is my story…

---

[1] Hide and Seek-Imogen Heap

Flightpath

Th-thump.

Th-thump.

Th-thump.

My heart raced as I tried my best to race through Check-In. I was already running way too far behind the time that had been clearly pointed out on the trip itinerary. I'm never late, how could I let this happen? The one time it really mattered and there I was seriously pressed for time with the chance of being left behind. I couldn't afford to be left behind, not now, not when I *had* to get away from them. What if they're behind me? What if they followed? I can't turn back, I'll have no place to go, and they'll find me. "Passport and boarding pass please." My ill-fated thoughts were interrupted. I handed the mildly enthusiastic woman my passport and boarding pass hoping that she wouldn't take too long to allow me to enter through the gates.

Th-thump.

Th-thump.

She checked both of my passes and forwarded me to the next check point.

I brought my luggage up to the conveyer belt and struggled to get my first suitcase on the steadily moving apparatus. A kind man hurried to my side and assisted me with my second suitcase and then with my third, "Where are you going anyway?" he asked. "Vienna, for six months, student exchange," I explained, out of breathe and grateful for his help. "Oh! Are you with the White Rock Secondary School group?" He asked. "Yeah," my face contorting, eyeing the man suspiciously, cautiously. He held out his hand for me to shake and told me his name, "Hi, I'm Ruben...Ruben Saka'am, your group's guide for Austria. I'm glad that I'm not the only one running late!" he exhaled loudly, smiling, looked down at me and winked. "Y-yeah," was all I was able to muster out, a bit embarrassed. Ruben had a friendly face, a warm face, a familiar face. I studied it intensely, the sleek line of his jaw, the angle of his nose, the arch of his lips, the smooth skin pulled tight over his face, the gentleness in his eyes. I was trying to figure out where I had possibly seen him before. He was uncomfortable, he shifted his eyes back and forth at our surroundings trying not to make eye contact. He looked Hispanic, maybe Native...maybe even both, I wasn't sure. He had light hazel eyes which stood out against his copper skin. His dark hair was straight and cut very short, just above a buzz cut. He had a few freckles across his nose just slightly visible on his skin. His cheekbones were high and distinct, just like his chin and his eyebrows were perfectly aligned accenting his strong bone structure.

    He fidgeted out from under the lock hold of my stare, "Packed a little heavy, huh?" he asked with an airiness in his voice, as we watched my three large suitcases roll away in the distance, almost completely out of sight on the conveyer belt. He looked at me as though he was waiting for something as we continued down the hall and waited in line to be scanned by the intimidating officer holding the metal detector. I bit down nervously on my bottom lip—these things always made me nervous—when it donned on me that I had been completely rude. I hadn't even introduced myself to him. "Oh right," I clued in, "I'm Zahra. Zahra Roméo-Winters." I stuck out my hand like he had done before, he removed his hand from his jeans pocket and cupped mine. "Sorry, my mind is in another place," I apologized, "yeah, I packed a lot...I didn't know what to take and what to leave behind. I'm not even sure I'll come back here after the six months. I guess I'm just being prepared." I was trying to make light of a very awkward and uncomfortable situation that I really didn't want to talk about. "I know right...? I'm really looking forward to this trip too!" he said, assuming that our much anticipated journey together was the cause of my distraction. "Yeah, I guess..." I replied unconvincingly.

    I could tell that he could sense my discomfort with the thoughts that had just emerged in my mind, he didn't know what to say next. Luckily, he was called through the metal detector and I was given a chance to just breathe and think of something else to say to Ruben so that I wouldn't have to discuss my inner turmoil with my new-found trip adviser. When it was my turn, I walked slowly through the detector, nervous. Not because I feared that I would be called aside and searched, but anxious because as I cleared the door-like space and stepped onto the other side I knew I was free. Free from all the pain and heartache that I left behind. What I feared most was that there was nothing stopping me from leaving everything behind for good and starting over in a new place. Suddenly, Austria didn't seem all that bad.

    I took a deep breath and hurried to catch up with Ruben who was waiting for me just a short distance away. "So have you always lived in White Rock?" I asked. "Just outside," he said. He could see that I was searching for answers and to my surprise, it was Ruben who aired signs of reluctance. Instantly things grew awkward, I looked away. He smiled an unconvincing smile. The left side of his mouth hooked upwards toward his cheek. "I grew up along the bay, on the Semiahmoo Reserve down by the ocean. My family doesn't live there anymore. We all live scattered around

White Rock and Surrey now. I still head down to the reserve from time to time whenever I get my hands on some furniture or other useful item that I think one of those families might need.

"After high school I moved across the border, well the border for most folks, us Aboriginals don't have'em, yeah," he chuckled and paused for laughter…there was none. *"Anyway,* I went to Washington and stayed with some relatives over there. I was going to school, getting into trouble…" he trailed off. "I studied culture in school because I really wanted to travel and I figured going to school and studying something along those lines would help justify my travels to my folks, you know?" he asked, without waiting for my response. "I moved back to the area about a year ago. It's good to be home, to see old familiar faces and of course new ones too," he nudged me with his elbow and smiled a full toothy grin. I smiled back shyly. He had opened up to me without hesitation, his life story poured out like the water at Shannon Falls and I glided along jaggedly beside him, praying that he wouldn't ask me anything about my life, at this point I wouldn't know what to say. Luckily, after walking down a long hallway, we were approaching our gate. I was off the hook for now. I wouldn't have to talk about myself just yet. I still had some time to figure things out, maybe even make something up.

As we walked toward Departures, my heart began to race uncontrollably, the crowd of rowdy teenagers waited anxiously for our flight to board, tied my stomach in a multitude of butterfly knots, small bits of sanity, hanging from the bight.

Th-thump. Th-thump. Th-thump. Th-thump. Th-thump.

"Well, I guess we'll chat a little bit later," Ruben, placing his hand gently on my elbow, headed toward the four teachers who were accompanying us on the trip. "O-okay," I said, with a nervous grin, "see ya!" I called, he was already introducing himself to the faculty. I stood there for a moment, alone, looking at my happy classmates, feeling sorry for myself. Even though I was about to embark on an extraordinary experience, I couldn't completely engage in all the excitement while tortured thoughts ran through my mind like prancing goblins in a spooky story.

"ZAHRA! WHAT TOOK YOU SO LONG?" I snapped out of my nightmare. "We were beginning to worry that you weren't going to make it," Natalie said as she hugged me. "Well, don't look *too* excited," Jason added as he approached me with curious eyes.

Natalie and Jason were my two best friends. I had known them for what seemed like forever. We all went to pre-school together. Each of their parents were significantly younger than mine, but I was mostly looked after by my older sister Jonnæ who was a few years younger than Natalie's and Jason's parents.

Growing up I had many play dates with Nat and Jay in which their moms would mentor my sister, giving her tips on how to manage a small child and a career. Mrs. Naysmith, Natalie's mom, was partner in the family law firm. Jason's mom, Mrs. Anderson-Chen, had been our elementary school principal for a number of years before Ian, Jason's youngest brother was diagnosed with Autism at the age of three. Natalie was an only child, she never experienced the joy in buying a chocolate bar with your weeks-long saved change only to break that bar in half and share it with your brothers like Jason did, but then again, I was so much younger than my sister that I never experienced that either. Instead, Jonnæ would have done anything for me and never hoped for anything in return. I admired my sister Jonnæ. She had always been my back bone, and my confidant. Throughout my life she was very hands on, playing an active role in my development. I can't even begin to imagine what my life would have been like without her, especially because my parents were in their forties when I was born. She helped bridge the gap and was always the voice of reason when anything happened in our household. I loved her for that. I missed her, my wonderful, beautiful sister. My heart tinged with a deep piercing pain as I realized that I would never see her face again. My sister was gone forever.

I tried to mask the pain behind my watery eyes and fought to swallow the massive lump in my throat, *get it together Zar!* I repeated in my head, *this is not the time to cry.* With all of my might, I resisted the urge to rest my head on Natalie's shoulder and take advantage of the trivial hug she had given me to show her relief that I hadn't missed our flight. I didn't want to kill the high that Natalie and Jason were on.

This was supposed to be one of the greatest moments of our lives. "You'll be eighteen by the time you go on this trip Zar and you'll only be eighteen once. You've gotta take life by the horns and just live a little!" was what Jonnæ had said to me last year when I brought the information package home about the student exchange program. I was a bit apprehensive about the whole thing. I didn't really want to go. I had only slightly entertained the thought on the bus ride home that day as I skimmed through the paperwork. *$15,876.62* I said to myself. *Yeah right! There's no way either of my parents were going to go for that, no way in hell!* I shoved the papers into my bag not giving it another thought, realizing how disappointed Jason and Natalie would be. They were first to sign up for the trip, though nothing was set in stone until our five thousand dollar deposits were handed in to Mr. Woods, the teacher who headed the entire project. He thought, "It would be a good idea to allow our students to experience life on the other side of the planet and to gain a bit of perspective." I sighed anxiously at the thought and rang the bell to request my stop. I thanked the bus driver and descended the stairs, swinging my book bag onto my back.

I walked up the narrow, tree-lined road to my front door. The house was close to Crescent Beach where many of our neighbours used their houses as vacation homes, but since we generally had decent weather, we lived in ours all year round. The outside of the house was coloured in sky-blue vertical wood panels with a navy front door and roof. It was a raised bungaloft, a beach house with a walkout balcony from the kitchen at the back of the house overlooking the ocean. At the front, were a dozen stairs leading to the main entrance and over that, was another balcony that led out from Jonnæ's master suite. On the ground level of the house there was a side entrance leading to the den that we rarely used. The house was quite large, too big for just Jonnæ and I.

The floors throughout the house were a natural hardwood colour and the walls were painted a very welcoming beige. There was a dark brown canvas sofa set in the living room surrounding our modern white entertainment unit. This is where we used to watch classic movies and eat gourmet popcorn, popped in Avocado oil and sprinkled with lime salt and parmesan cheese, every Sunday afternoon. The kitchen and small dining area were behind the living room with cabinets that matched the natural wood flooring. It was always an amazing sight, to wake up and step out onto the balcony and watch the sun rise over the ocean. I loved watching children play on the beach in the damp sand as the sun ascended in the sky or watching the locals and tourists alike, waiting patiently on the boarder of large rocks for the tide to change to reveal the sand waiting to be kissed by the sun. At the end of the day, while sipping tea, I would sit on the balcony and watch the children screaming gleefully as the water danced across their feet. And the waves folding over the sand, hurrying back onto the shoreline where it would crash against the rocks as the sun set, putting the sand to sleep for the night beneath the ocean bed, was the perfect scene to capture on a blank canvas.

Below the master bedroom balcony, Jonnæ always parked her eggplant coloured hybrid hatchback car. There was no lawn in front of the house, just a large paved driveway. Jonnæ didn't believe in turf grass, she said watering a lawn was a waste of good drinking water, especially for a plant that wasn't a viable food source for us. Instead, there were flower pots filled abundantly with fresh, organic herbs. Jonnæ didn't have time for flowers and lavish outdoor decoration as she was busy with her restaurant that she so cleverly called…Zahra. I was honoured by the tribute and worked as the host at the front of the restaurant. My job was to greet and seat patrons and stroll around during the evening, making sure that everyone was enjoying themselves. It was always so exciting for newcomers when I introduced myself and when they put two-and-two together realizing the connection between my name and the name of the restaurant. Truth be told, it always made me blush a little.

The restaurant was beautiful and was quickly becoming a hot spot in White Rock, British Columbia. It was situated on the marina in a swanky little district, catering to artists, hipsters, musicians, tourists and naturalists. The outside of the small building was burnt orange stucco with large windows all around and on either side of the glass door so patrons could see the promenade from their tables. The space above the door was adorned with a huge metal cut-out sign that read '*Zahra*' in Jonnæ's artistic handwriting.

Inside, there were dado walls covered with dark brown glass mosaic tiles on the bottom half and the same appetizing orange colour from the outside, on the top, separated by a thin ivory border in between. There were dark wood tables dressed with small floral arrangements set in shiny silver cages and the lighting was soft and warm. There was a small platform stage in one corner of the restaurant where Jonnæ often hosted poetry readings and open mic nights on Thursdays. I loved watching the local talent. The performers always seemed so comfortable, everyone felt at home at Jonnæ's restaurant. I never had the nerve to step onto that stage, I preferred to have my talent showcased on the walls.

There were more than a dozen paintings on the walls. More than half of those were mine, most of the others, belonged to artists I did not know. Along the wall, in the entryway, where customers waited to be seated, were photographs of me growing up in sequential order.

The first was a sepia toned picture of my parents holding me in the hospital nursery, both dressed in casual clothes. My dad in a pair of jeans and a crimson sweater. My mom, in a black and gold Mandarin collared jacket and a pair of jeans, as well. They looked perfect, smiling and content. My mother, Joanne—no hospital gown for her—had said that she was too "old" and had too much dignity to have any pictures taken of her while she was bloated and exhausted after my birth, so she waited until she could freshen up before any official photographs could be taken—because that's what should matter right? Looking perfect, when you've just performed the miracle of childbirth.

Joanne was forty-two when I was born, an unexpected pregnancy by far. Fabién was forty-seven and buried himself heavily into the family business. Both my parents were well respected in our community. My father had worked in his parents' upholstery store and after he took it over it soon became the local hand-crafted furniture store that almost everyone in White Rock trusted. *Winter's Wonderland* was what he called it. I always thought it was kind of cheesy but he was so proud of the name that I couldn't bear to break his heart over it.

My mom had worked alongside my father for the better part of their marriage, but a few years before I was born, she decided to go back to school and become a social worker. After she graduated, she opened a local outreach centre for troubled teens. Within the first year, she found herself primarily dealing with young single mothers between the ages of fifteen to eighteens years old. That's when she decided to focus on these girls by providing school seminars on safe sex—meaning abstinence—as well as support for young mothers who needed guidance and assistance with their new lives. She was viewed by many as a Godsend. She helped so many weary parents talk to their children about the forbidden 'S' word. I guess when she found out that she was pregnant herself, she felt a little bit "awkward" as she put it, whenever I asked about that picture on the wall inside the restaurant. For my entire life, I somehow always felt that she was embarrassed of me, like I was a constant reminder of something gone completely wrong. I was never able to understand the mentality behind this because, after all, she was married and she had another daughter who was sixteen. It wasn't like people were expecting her not to live her life… There were so many things about my mother I just didn't understand.

The second picture was on the same day, the day of my birth, it was of me and Jonnæ. She was smiling with a wide-eyed look on her face, like a proud big sister. She was so happy to have a companion, someone who would understand her and be there for her, even if I was sixteen years younger. She had always wanted a sibling and each year as she got older she realized the prospects of that happening were growing bleak. When she found out that my mother was pregnant, she vowed to do everything she could to lend a helping hand. This really was the moment she had been waiting for and she had always been so proud of me, even if I hadn't done anything to deserve all of her praise.

The third picture was taken when I was six, at a dance recital. I was dressed in a pink tutu, my curly, chocolate brown hair slicked back into a perfect bun at the top of my head. I stood in perfect formation, holding my small plaque, with a gummy smile from ear to ear and one big tooth protruding from the top of my mouth. The memory of the day is quite vague, but I remember sitting on the pier eating gelato with Jonnæ afterwards. My parents had not been so keen on me taking dance lessons, but Jonnæ had convinced them that it was important for me to be able to find a creative outlet to express myself. So, they agreed, as long as she took the reigns because they simply did not have the time.

The fourth frame held a self-portrait that I had painted with water colours in art class. I had finally found my niche. I was fifteen when I painted it and not much about my appearance had changed in three years. In the painting, my hair was long and flowing, thick and curly with golden highlights twisted around chocolate brown strands. My eyes, a soft amber and almond shaped, and my skin a sun-kissed bronze, brown. My lips, soft and full, my nose, thin and rounded at the tip.

I looked like my mom and my sister and nothing like my dad, but I had his intellect, his mind. My mom was a beautiful woman with exotic features. Her mother, Nuri, was from Indonesia and as a teenager, moved to Madagascar with her older brother, Galang. There, she met my grandfather, Antsokotohary Rakoroméotontondra, or as we call him, Antso Roméo, a handsome young Malagasy boy she could not resist. They got married after a short courtship and immigrated to Canada. When they had settled in Prince Rupert, British Columbia, they started a family and had my mom and my two aunts, Miranda and Samantha. My grandfather worked as a fisherman and moved the family to White Rock when my mom was thirteen, Miranda was three and Samantha was just a few month old. My mom attended the same high school as Jonnæ and me, White Rock Secondary School, though Jonnæ spent some time abroad, just like I was about to do as well.

While in high school, my mother met my father, Fabién, both families had made an effort to connect with others from Madagascar, there weren't many in the area. Fabién was several years older but he and Joanne became close, they would hang out together in small groups with mutual friends. Joanne was one of the youngest in the group, but she didn't care as long as she could see Fabién. Fabién had just graduated from University with a philosophy degree, they were always engaged in deep introspective conversations. When around them, Joanne breathed esoteric air, she loved it, still does. When Joanne graduated from high school, Fabién formally asked her on a date, one week later they were engaged, two months after, they were married, eight years later Jonnæ was born.

Before Jonnæ was born my father worked as a professor of Philosophy at the University of British Columbia while my mother studied Anthropology. They lived in Vancouver, close to the University. Within five years Fabien's father grew ill and died. The only wish he ever had was that the family business live on. When Fabién's family immigrated from Madagascar his father, a carpenter, started his business with the few dollars to his name. In time the business flourished and the family was proud. After his father's death Fabién knew he had to fulfill his father's wish. He took my mother back to White Rock and ran the family business. Fabién, though good with wood was not such a skilled carpenter as his father. He began to import handcrafted furniture from around the world as he learned the skills required for excellent carpentry. These imported goods were an instant success. My father had already changed his last name. As a professor, his students had a very difficult time pronouncing Hiverspatrimalasvelonjara, together with my mother they changed their name to Winters, *hivers*, the French equivalent.

When my mom was twenty-six, she gave birth to Jonnæ and adorned her with all the love any parent would give to their first born child. However, Jonnæ says that by the time she was in high school our parents grew tired of her "teenage angst" as they called it. They didn't like the way she shook the barriers of their comfortable, secure walls. Jonnæ was always adventurous and outgoing. She wanted to breathe her own air, experience life on her terms, which was an idea that left my parents vulnerable. Jonnæ would take weekend trips across the border with friends, friends my parents didn't know or care too much for. She spent much of her time down by the water on the beach with the local kids and maybe even experimented with recreational drugs which she would never deny or confirm. Needless to say, her behaviour to me didn't seem all that bad, she was a teenager! But my parents were less than impressed with the disturbance to the family image and let me tell you, my parents—especially my mom—were *all* about images.

The three hour waiting period slipped by quickly as I reminisced on the good parts of my life and before I knew it my class was getting ready to board. As I walked down the aisle of the airplane looking for my seat, I could feel my heart beating uncontrollably. I was so nervous, but not because I was on a plane, or because I was about to spend the next six months of my life with a family I didn't know—I already felt like I'd spent the last eighteen years with a group of people I didn't know at all. I was anxious because I couldn't help but feel like I was leaving that life behind me. I was bit afraid, but very excited for what was waiting for me on the other side. I found my seat and settled in next to a kid from my class that I didn't know very well, I think his name was Justin Walker, maybe. I wasn't the popular one, Natalie and Jason were, I was merely popular by association. I didn't care much for high school social status politics, I much preferred the company of my dearest friend, my sketchbook. I hesitantly smiled at Justin…or Julian, whatever his name was, he barely looked at me, without Natalie attached to my side he had no reason to pretend to want to talk to me. I took out my iPod hoping to block out the world around me, to distract myself from my thoughts. As we prepared for take-off I closed my eyes and counted down from ten… nine… eight… seven…

    I looked out the window and wished Vancouver farewell. Maybe I would be back in time for graduation, but then again, perhaps I wouldn't. It was the middle of November, the air was cool. It was my favourite time of the year. The rain poured frequently, but that was all right with me, I loved it either way. I knew that I would miss the memories of autumn in White Rock. This was my favourite weather, perfect for longboarding. I would get off the local bus a few stops early after school and would coast along the marina to the restaurant to start my shift. The cold wind would pull through my hair and drape across my face like a cool silk cloth and I'd fill my lungs with the briny smell of saltwater. The leaves on the trees were just starting to lose their colour, blurs of lime green, yellow and bright red, surrounded me as I kicked, pushed and coasted on the promenade.

    The temperature in White Rock was much nicer than the mainlands of British Columbia. In the winter, if it snowed, it never lasted. It was never too hot or too cold in White Rock, it was always just right with the sun shining bright in the sky. On the beach, near the promenade, was a large white boulder that was carried by a glacier and broke off during the last glaciation and decided to take up permanent residence on the beach, giving White Rock its name.

The city bordered Semiahmoo Bay and the reserve that Ruben grew up on and was surrounded on three sides by Surrey, British Columbia. The Coast Salish First Nations had a legend that said that the white rock marked the landing spot of a stone that been chucked across the sky by a young Native Chief. The legend said that the young chief and his bride would move from Vancouver Island to wherever the stone had landed and build a home there together. It was their descendants who became the Semiahmoo First Nations—Semiahmoo is the Coast Salish word for 'half-moon,' which describes the shape of the bay.

As the plane ascended higher, I sighed, waving goodbye to Crescent Beach, Vancouver and to White Rock, better known as 'the hole in the sky.'

I woke up startled and confused. I looked around feeling panic-stricken, looking for answers which I soon realized wouldn't be there on the long crowded flight. I glanced over at Justin to see if he was giving me any weird looks. I hoped that I hadn't been talking in my sleep. I'd been so restless, wrapped up in a deep, dark nightmare that was beginning to be all too real, there was no refuge in sleep. Justin was sleeping and so was Kristina Searsly who was sitting on the other side of him.

I was uncomfortable. I was trapped on a long, crowded flight and I desperately needed to feel my feet on solid ground. I longed to be rooted to the earth again. I stretched my legs in front of me, the cramp behind my knees, aching. I arched my back, cranked my neck from side to side, pulled my arms and bent my knees to my chest, restless. Finally, I leaned my head back against the window and closed my eyes hoping to think about anything else that would come to mind. I daydreamed about what Vienna would be like and the new family who I would be living with. Did they live in a big house? Maybe on a farm? Did they have pets or animals? Would I be responsible for milking cows or gathering eggs? Was I being completely ignorant? I concluded that I was being ignorant and interrupted my thoughts to check the time. It was nine at night, which meant in one more hour, we'd be landing in Austria and once again my heart began to race. I put my earphones in and scanned through my music library, hoping to drown out the sound of my heart under a new driving boom of the music. I selected one of my favourite songs.

I sighed as I listened to the lyrics of the song, never realizing how relevant those words were to my life at that very moment. Things were getting the better of me and I was lost without any idea of how to bring it all back, how to make it normal again. I became overwhelmed with emotion as I reflected on my life and I could feel my face becoming hot and tingly. My eyes began to burn and soon the tears were rolling down my face, over my cheeks and collecting at my chin. I quickly wiped the tears away hoping not to wake my classmates sitting beside me. The sadness began to consume me, I felt alone, abandoned. It wasn't until moments later that I heard a voice speaking to me. I jumped, ripping the earphones out from my ears in astonishment. "Hey… Zahra is everything all right?" it was Ruben, he looked concerned. "Oh… hi Ruben," I rubbed my hands across my face trying to compose myself as my seat-mates began to wake up. "What are you doing back here?" I asked, trying to avoid his question. "Just heading to the bathroom. I tried to wait it out but eleven hours is a pretty long time," he said, with his familiar light chuckle trying desperately to lighten the mood. "So are you okay?" he asked again. "Oh yeah, I'm fine," I said, trying to shrug off my previous hysteria. "Just anxious," I looked back and forth from him and my seat-mates, who seemed irritated having been disturbed, with barely convincing eyes. "Okay..." he said, "let me know if you need anything. *Anything,*" he raised an eyebrow and tilted his head, his eyes were stern. "S-sure," I nodded, with my lips pursed into an awkward grin. He walked toward the restroom and I looked down at my iPod quickly changing the song. I put my earphones back in my ears looking up sheepishly through my eyelashes at Justin and Kristina who were already not paying any attention to me, which I was thankful for. It paid to be almost invisible without Nat and Jay, Justin and Kristina weren't any more suspicious of me than they probably already were. I quickly leaned my head against the window and closed my eyes before Ruben returned from the restroom to avoid any further conversation about why I had been crying.

When I opened my eyes again, we had just landed and all the passengers were applauding the safe flight. At that pivotal moment, I decided to enjoy every last minute of this journey because after all it was my journey, my self-discovery, my awakening. I decided that once I stepped off the plane, I would live for the moment. I would push all ill-thoughts of my past behind me. I wouldn't mourn the lose of Jonnæ just yet, I wouldn't think about the betrayal within the four walls of my own home, of Joanne and Fabién, none of them deserved it. For the time being I just needed to be. I needed to ebb and flow like the ocean tide in White Rock. I took a deep breath and stepped off the plane.

Willkommen nach Österreich
(Welcome to Austria)

November 20

The flight was long and exhausting. Maybe it was the eleven hours I had spent on the stuffy plane, with its only slightly bearable seats, or maybe it was that Austria was eight hours ahead and I felt like I had been awake for twenty-four hours. The sun was bright and blazing, on my phone the time read 10:00 p.m., on the large clock in the airport the time said it was six in the morning. Heh, I grunted to myself, I had just begun a new day. How quickly the old day had faded away, it was like magic. With the snap of a finger I was thrusted into new waking hours, thanks to the time change. If only I could have left my suffering back there in Vancouver and started over in Vienna. I told myself that I would. I told myself that it wasn't an option, but how do you turn off your feelings? The day might have changed but my heart still felt the same.

"Okay everyone gather 'round please," Mr. Woods called out over the excited chattering of a group of students ready to take on the world. Slowly all the students from White Rock Secondary School gathered in a clump in front of Mr. Woods, Mrs. Green, Ms. Johnson and Mr. Nazuka. He waited for everyone to unwind before he began to speak again. "Well, ladies, gentlemen, we're here, we made it. Welcome to your new home in Austria! Once we pass through customs you will meet your new families and be taken to your new homes to settle in. Now, I'd like to formally introduce you all to your guide for the next six months, Ruben Saka'am…" With that Ruben stepped forward a little shy, he raised his hand with an apprehensive wave and flashed a side grin. "Hello," he said, addressing the small crowd. He stood in front of the group deciding what to say, he began in a very inviting tone, "Welcome to Austria… this will definitely be an experience for all of you, I know you have lives back home in White Rock, maybe some of you left on a sour note, but I encourage you all to take in these moments, enjoy your time here, take lots of pictures and create lasting memories. Most of all just be happy! Thank you… oh yeah and if you need anything at anytime, someone to talk to, a friend, anything, I'm your guy." He looked directly at me and I felt my face get warm and I couldn't help but think his entire muddled speech was meant for me. I broke free from his gaze and looked down at the floor, embarrassed. "Now we will call out some names, this will be your partner who you will stay with as well as the name of the family you'll be living with. Oh and before I forget," Ruben continued, "the host families are throwing a little party for all of you at a club tonight. Your host family will give you more details once you meet."

"Jason Chen and Martin Brown with Sven Helmfried," Mr. Woods called out. "Natalie Naysmith and Zahra R. Winters with Romy Etzel," he continued. "Ugh," I moaned in disgust, "why does he *refuse* to say my name correctly?" I snapped, as Natalie and I headed over to the conveyor belt to grab our bags. As I struggled to lift my second suitcase off of the belt, I felt a light hand on my shoulder. I looked over my back to see Ruben standing behind me. "Here let me get that," he said, helping me put my bag safely onto the floor. "I'll grab your other suitcase and bring it out to Romy's car okay? There's no way you'll be able to take all three and I'm not sure where you get one of those carts here," he pointed out. "Oh don't worry about it Ruben, thanks though! I'm sure you're really busy now. I'll figure it out," I said. "Really Zahra, it's okay. Natalie won't be able to help you, she's got two bags of her own. It's really no trouble," he reached for my third suitcase that was quickly approaching. "This isn't up for debate. Go meet your host family," he demanded shooing me with his hand. "Fine!" I gave in taking two of my bags, one in each hand and wheeling them away. "See'ya at the car," Ruben called out as I headed toward the exit. *"Bye,"* I sang, looking over my shoulder returning his friendly smile.

"What's up with *Ruben?*" Natalie asked. "Why do you say it like that?" I asked. "Uh, because he's so eager to help you out," Natalie enthused. "He's a nice guy! What's the big deal?" I asked, really not seeing where Natalie was trying to go with this. "Yeah, *really, really* nice!" Natalie said, "And hot!" she concluded. "He's so dark and mysterious, I bet he's got a tormented backstory that he needs help getting over." "Oh geez Natalie, he's… old… well not *old*, but old enough—" I said slightly disgusted. "He's younger than my parents! And definitely younger than yours," she mentioned and instantly my heart sank. Natalie noticed my silence but took it as though I was contemplating Ruben as a possible suitor. "Well, if you don't want him, I'll give it a try," she said. "Good luck Nat. I don't really think he's willing to lose his job for a fling with a minor," I said back. "I'm no minor! We're eighteen now remember?" she reminded.

Our birthdays were just two days apart, Natalie's was first and then there was mine and every year we had a dual birthday party on the day in between. A tradition we upheld for over ten years. "Well, Nat, honestly if you think Ruben will go for it by all means—but I don't want you to do anything you'd regret later and I just don't think he's that type of guy. He's definitely in his late thirties, maybe even early forties and I just don't see him being the kind of guy who'd go for an eighteen year old, especially one who just turned eighteen like two weeks ago." "Details, details Zar. And he's *so* not in his thirties or *forties ew!* You have no perception of age, geez. He's clearly in his twenties Zahra. And how do you figure that you know him so well when you've just met him today?" she asked with a hint of attitude, she didn't like her motives questioned, she was used to getting her way, but it was my job to be her voice of reason, someone had to be. "We talked a little before I met up with you guys before getting on the plane," I explained a bit defensively.

"And you talked about if he'd date a younger woman did you?" "*No.* Okay I'll back off. Have it your way Natalie. Like I said, good luck!" ending the conversation right there. I really didn't want to discuss whether she'd be trying to get Ruben in bed, I didn't want to think of it at all. It was a little unlike Natalie, but I think just like me, she was adopting a new attitude in Austria, an attitude I wasn't sure was going to mesh well with me.

We exited through the opaque glass doors into the Arrivals waiting area. We were greeted by numerous unfamiliar smiling faces. Host families were holding up signs with White Rock Secondary student names. Natalie and I walked down a ramp, as we tugged our luggage behind us. We followed the crowd until we saw a sign that read:

Natalie + Zahra

We walked over with huge smiles on our faces to meet Romy and her family. Romy, even more beautiful in person than was afforded to her in the few pictures she had sent me, had an eccentric kind of beauty, the kind of beauty that leant itself to high fashion runway supermodels over here in Europe. She was taller than me, but then again everyone was. She was probably around 5'8" towering five inches over me. Her hair was dark brown and straight reaching just below her shoulders in precise layers. Her face was heart shaped, her nose and chin pointed and her eyes were large and dark brown. Her frame was thin, with long legs and long arms with a perfectly rounded chest and slender hips. She wore an army green coloured winter coat with a fur rimmed hood that reached almost to her knees, open over a stylish, pleated front, ruby red sweater and dark blue jeans that were tucked into a pair of snow boots. In her hand, she held a black lumber jack hat lined with black fur and a pair of leather mittens. Looking at her, I knew

I was under dressed and not adequately prepared for the cold Austrian winter climate.

Next to Romy stood her mother, Mila, who was an older version of Romy. Their features were exactly the same and behind them both was her father, Fredrik, who Romy looked nothing like at all. I thought that maybe her older brother, Mikael, who was away at University looked like Fredrik. This would have given me some reassurance a few days ago about my own family, as I too looked nothing like my father, Fabién.

Natalie and I greeted Romy and her parents, exchanging hugs, smiles and hellos before we began to continue toward Fredrik's delivery truck. Romy explained in just about perfect English, with no real trace of an accent, that their car wasn't big enough to fit our entire luggage, so her father drove the delivery truck for the family bakery and Romy, Nat and I would follow behind in the family car. We loaded into the car and pulled away from the curb leaving the airport behind and headed toward Romy's house.

The house sat at the top of a small hill and was surrounded by trees. It was a small house with a large open back yard that featured a wooden bridge over a small frozen pond. We pulled up to the house, heading into the driveway and walked up the three shallow steps. Romy unlocked the front door while Fredrik got our bags from the truck. "This will be your home for the next six months," Romy said, as we entered the corridor. The hallway was painted a neutral beige colour that continued throughout the rest of the house. The first door on the left encased Romy's room, a set of bunk beds that had been dismantled was neatly arranged, with one against each wall, separated by a window overlooking the side yard. Two small nightstands were set in the room, one beside each bed. Along the same wall as the door, stood a large built in closest that had been emptied out so that Natalie and I could hang our clothes.

"This is where you two will sleep," Romy said, opening the door. "I'll stay in my brother's room, he's away in University so he won't mind." We nodded and continued to follow her on the rest of the tour of the house. We walked down the hallway past her room and could see the open concept living room and dining room, when we reached the bathroom. We poked our heads in and saw the small glass shower in the corner and beside it a deep set tub. There were towels folded on a shelf beside the shower and adjacent to the shower was a sink and vanity mirror. "Where's the toilet?" Natalie asked. "Here," Romy said, as she opened the door to a small separate area beside the shower room.

Next to the bathroom was an alcove that held the kitchen. There were several floor to ceiling cabinets in a natural oak wood, a lot like the cabinets back home at Jonnæ's house. "Where's the fridge?" Natalie asked, in an almost judging tone. The fridge had the same covering as the cabinets and was therefore disguised. The fridge at Jonnæ's house was the same which struck me as odd. Why would Natalie ask Romy this question when she had been to my house so many times? Had she really never paid attention? Or was she just being rude?

Directly across from the kitchen was the dining room table with six chairs that faced the television of the living room and was against the back of one of the navy blue linen couches, which separated the living room from the dining room. In the living room there was an oval wooden coffee table with a small shelf that housed a few magazines and loose papers. Against the far wall there was a small entertainment unit filled with videos, DVDs and a television and on each side of the coffee table were two more matching navy couches. The living room floor was covered by a soft white rug that almost completely covered the natural blonde hardwood floor. There wasn't any art on display, the walls were bare and so were the table tops. It felt completely different from my home in White Rock. There was also a small hallway beside the kitchen with two more closed doors. We walked to the first one that was closest to the living room and Romy opened the door. "This is my brother's room, where I will be sleeping," she said, as we glanced around the room. It looked just about the same as Romy's except it had one double sized bed in the middle of the room. The bed was dressed with a simple chocolate brown bedspread that matched the wood dresser and had closet doors just like in Romy's room except her closet doors were mirrored and the bedspreads on the two small beds were red. She closed the door behind her and we walked to the last door, her parent's room.

 Their room was a lot like the other two. It wasn't much bigger than Romy's or her brother's. There was a queen-sized bed centred against the wall, covered with a beige floral bedspread and two small nightstands, one on each side of the bed. Next to the window was a single wooden chair and a small table with a few books neatly stacked according to size. Next to the books were two framed pictures, one of Romy and the other of her brother, I was guessing, both as young children. Romy's brother was smiling a wide toothy grin he was missing his front tooth and was holding a fishing rod and his prize fish. The picture of Romy showed her sitting on top of a horse wearing a riding hat and gear on a farm. She looked the same, I thought. Her bone structure was just more defined now. "And that's the whole house," Romy said, concluding our tour. "If you go out the front door and around the back there is a big yard with trees and a pond, but we'll go out there another time," she said, leading us back into the common area. "Your house is beautiful Romy," I said, taking one final quick look around and stopped my gaze on Natalie, who squinted her eyes as if she didn't believe me. Romy unfortunately saw Natalie's expression and I could tell she was hurt by it and I felt terrible. Where were Natalie's manners? Maybe she was expecting something different? Maybe she thought Romy lived more like she did, in a huge house with too many possessions and other useless things. Maybe she figured because Romy's family owned a busy bakery, much like how her family owned a law firm and lived a very lavish lifestyle, that Romy would be the same. This would definitely be a culture shock for Natalie I thought to myself and then I smiled.

✳✳✳

Mila went to the kitchen when she entered the house. She had started to prepare a "welcome home" meal the night before and was putting on the finishing touches as Romy completed the tour. I asked Mila if I could help her set the table and she quickly shooed me out of the kitchen stating that she couldn't accept my help when it was a special brunch for Natalie and I. So I went to my new room to join Romy and Natalie who were sitting on one of the beds, chatting.

"Look who I found," Fredrik announced, as he entered the house after re-salting the driveway and steps. "Hello," the familiar voice rang throughout the house. The three of us girls got to our feet and went to the hallway. Ruben stood in the doorway knocking the little bits of snow from his boots and removing them from his feet. He smiled, "Hey girls," he said, as he took notice of us standing in the bedroom doorway. Natalie, excited and posing flirtatiously, Romy, casual and me rather perplexed. "You didn't wait for me to bring your bag to the car," Ruben said, to me responding to my facial expression. *"Oh yeah,"* I lightly slapped my forehead. "No worries kiddo. I would have brought it tomorrow, but then I remembered you might have something in it that you want to wear when you go out tonight." He lugged my suitcase down the hall to our room. "Thanks Ruben, I really appreciate it!" I said. He placed the bag down in front of us as Romy and Natalie moved out of the way and I dragged the bag further into the room. "See Natalie? He called me *kiddo* do you really think he'll see you any differently?" I whispered with a faint spell of déjà vu. Romy nodded her head in agreement as she assessed the situation. "Well, just because he doesn't see *you* that way, doesn't mean it'll be the same for me, I'm a woman," she sassed. Ruben peered his head into the room before I could respond.

"Food is ready," Mila called from the dining room. She walked down the hall toward Ruben and asked him to join us. He declined politely and was politely forced in return, he joined us. Mila and Fredrik sat at opposite heads of the table and Romy sat on the right facing the living room which I later learned was her usual seat. Ruben moved to the other side and sat diagonally across from Romy. Natalie rushed to Ruben's side before I could even choose a seat and sat down beside him and across from Romy, leaving only the seat next to Romy available. As I sat down next to her, we rolled our eyes at each other and Ruben looked confused at Natalie's insistence to sit beside him.

"This all looks fantastic," Ruben eyed the food on the table. "Thank you Ruben," Mila smiled as she stood and filled each plate with potatoes, cabbage and marinated pieces of steak. "This one is yours sweetling," she said, as she filled my plate with potatoes, two vegetable stuffed cabbage rolls and salad. We ate together like a real family. There wasn't any awkwardness of just meeting these new people for the first time at all. Ruben shared some of his plans of how we would spend the next few weeks as we ate together and when we were done, all of us sat at the table, chatted a little while longer before Ruben thanked the Etzels for a wonderful meal and left to go back to his hotel. He seemed too eager to leave after Natalie had inched closer to him as we ate and leaned in to him as he explained some of the itinerary. He was clearly uncomfortable and as he put on his shoes and coat, he seemed to be a bit more at ease. He wished us a good and safe night with the rest of the school kids and quickly exited the house. Natalie was bummed, huffing and puffing in our room as Romy and I glanced at each other fighting to hold back our laughter.

Ruben

You, My Shadow and Me

Natalie and I decided to spend a few minutes unpacking our suitcases and setting up our room, to be the most practical space for the two of us to share. We chatted happily about the clothes we had packed and all the chic clothes that we were both excited to buy. We couldn't wait to immerse ourselves in European culture and lifestyle. After my clothes were in the closet and my shoes were neatly lining the closet floor I decided to take a nap. So much had happened in such a short span of time and my brain was on overload, I was tired and running on empty. I placed my head down on my pillow and instantly I was asleep, until there was a light tap at the door and Romy asked if she could come in.

"All the students are meeting at eight at Absinthe, it's a club. We planned a little party for our White Rock Secondary friends so we can go anytime you want," she said.

Natalie and I decided to freshen up first and then get ready for our first night out in our new hometown. I took my bag of toiletries to the shower room and turned on the shower faucet to give the water a chance to warm up. As steam filled the air, I stared at my face in the mirror until it was no longer there, hidden by fog, only to remind me that I didn't really know who I was anymore. My heart began to flutter again and I wiped the glass with the palm of my hand, just to make sure that my reflection was still there. I sighed, I must be losing my mind.

I pulled back the glass door and stepped into the hot, blazing shower. The water washed over me and my skin was soon lavished in honey scented soap suds. The shower was refreshing, it was exactly what I needed to help erase the pain of the losses that I had experienced that day, (★)[2] but the solitude of the shower was deceiving. The nightmare that I'd been trying to avoid began to creep up

---

[2] Let Down-Dead By Sunrise

my spine and back into my mind. I tried to scrub the pain away, with repeated circular motions, washing over the same parts of my body, over and over again as tears rolled down my face. I thought about everything I had ever been told or was led to believe about my life and how it had all been a lie. My existence was a lie. I should have known, but how could I? I thought to myself. No! This was in no way my fault, and I couldn't let the guilt of my family's mistakes consume me. I decided again to suppress the feelings, to not allow myself to enter into that dark place, at least not right now. I tilted my head back and let the hot water stream over my face and down my hair. I squeezed a glob of shampoo into my hand and scrubbed my head clean, the same way I had done with my skin. I turned around and bent my head forward under the flowing water. I watched the bubble filled water twirl and wash down the drain, taking all of my pain and guilt away with it, for now anyway. I decided that I wasn't going to be let down anymore, I wasn't going to be taken advantage of, I wasn't going to lied to. This was my one chance to be free, an opportunity at a new life, *my life,* one that only I could define. When I was certain that I had washed all the pain and guilt away, I turned off the water and stepped out into a brand new me.

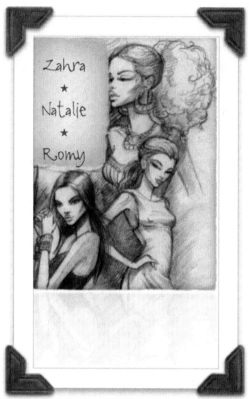

It was already eight-thirty p.m. by the time that we headed out the door. We realized that it would take a bit more coordination to get three girls out of the house in a timely fashion with only one bathroom. We hurried out the door and rushed to catch a taxi, hoping that we weren't missing out on all the fun. As we sat in the taxi, Natalie squealed with excitement at the lively streets of Vienna. I sat quietly contemplating the outcome of tonight's outing, trying to persuade myself to just let loose and have a good time. I had to keep reminding myself that the pain washed away with the soap suds, and that tonight was all about me. However, I couldn't help but still feel selfish. "What's the matter Zahra? Are you not interested in going out? Are you tired?" Romy asked, breaking my fervent train of thought. "What? Oh no, Romy, sorry it's nothing,"

I said, not being able to think of anything else to say. "Do you miss your family back home?" she asked, a bit concerned "No!" I answered too quickly, "I mean yes, I mean…I don't know, I guess I'm still in shock that I'm here that's all," I lied. "Are you sure? We can go back home if you'd like," she said, sympathetically. "WHAT? Back home, no way, I mean sorry Zar if you're not feeling it, but c'mon… let's go have some fun!" Natalie interjected. "I'm not trying to be coldhearted—I just want us to enjoy ourselves, that's all," she reassured. "I know Nat, don't worry about it, really I'm fine," I answered, reaching across Romy to touch Natalie's hand. Natalie smiled at me, and as if she was a volcano about to erupt, she blurted out another squeal and the three of us began to laugh.

As we were laughing, the taxi slowed down and pulled in front of a brightly lit building with some people standing outside whom I recognized and many others that I didn't. We paid the taxi driver and got out of the cab. Instantly, Jason rushed over to greet us with his host partner, Sven, by his side as well as a few of Romy's friends, who were quickly becoming mine. We made small-talk with the new people and together, we walked toward Absinthe, passing by a handful of unfamiliar faces who were gathered outside smoking, drinking and talking. Romy looped her arm in mine, I stumbled and bumped into one of the strangers smoking. "Sorry," I called, not looking behind me. We walked into the club.

The music was loud and obscure, the bass was so heavy that all the glass bottles at the bar rattled against each other at steady repeating intervals. "Do you want a drink?" Jason yelled, using hand gestures so that we would be able to understand him. "OH MY GOD I FORGOT WE CAN DRINK HERE," Natalie shouted in my ear, she was excessively excited, it made me want to go home. She nodded at Jason holding two fingers up pointing back and forth between the two of us. "Oh no, Nat I don't think—" "Oh *please* Zahra, you *so* need a drink. You need to loosen up a little!" she insisted, and she was right. Jason returned in no time. I was surprised at how fast he was able to get all of our drinks. "It's happy hour!" he said, as he handed us each a glass filled with amber coloured liquid. "All the drinks are lined up on the bar, you just have to grab one, they're free!" he informed us, making it clear that he wasn't going to be running to the bar on a frequent basis for us. "Got'cha," Natalie replied, winking. "Well, ladies, here's to us, living it up in Vienna with no regrets...so far," he said. "CHEERS," we answered in unison. We downed our drinks way too quickly, but that didn't stop Natalie from rushing back to the bar to pick up another round. We chugged those too and headed right to the dance floor. (★)³ The music filled the air with a familiar sound, one of my favourite songs, remixed to music I had never heard before. A heavy drum and bass rendition which made the entire club shake with its ultrafast breakbeat, I was definitely in a different place. I raised my arms in the air and cheered, taking Natalie's hand in mine and pulling her further onto the dance floor. I looked over to the DJ and saw Jason pointing at me. He'd requested the song for me knowing that it would instantly get me into party mode.

    I closed my eyes and found my groove letting nothing but the rhythm, the notes, the melody and the vocals fill my head as I enjoyed the surreal moment. For the first time in about forty-eight hours, I was free. When I opened my eyes again, the song had ended, Natalie was gone and I was now dancing by myself amongst my classmates and a crowd of random people. I got up on my toes to look for Natalie and spotted her by the bar, talking to the bartender. Jason was busy trying to sweet talk one of the host girls from Vienna and Romy was nowhere to be found. I didn't know what to

---

³ Show Me Love (Blame Remix)-Robin S., Steve Angello, Laidback Luke

do, or where to go, if I should continue dancing, or should I inconspicuously make my way off the dance floor? I decided on the latter and inconspicuously headed toward a vacant table in the back corner of the club which was just a short distance from the bar. I didn't want Natalie to see me and think she had to ditch her bartender, or Jason or Romy for that matter either. I wanted them to have fun and not worry about me. They were playing it off pretty well and I had a hunch that they knew something was wrong and eventually I would have no choice but to share it with them. I decided that until that time came, I would continue to pretend that my life wasn't spiralling down the drain.

I sat at the little round table and watched all the happy people laughing, wishing that I could truly be one of them. "Hello," a voice said, breaking my silent reverie. I was startled by his presence wondering how long he had been standing there waiting for me to reply. "H-hi," I answered nervously, smoothing my hand over my hair nervously, looking up into the darkness trying to see his face. I was unsuccessful, all I could see were flashing strobe lights behind his head and a faint red light reflection off his face and clothes.

"I bought you this drink," he said, "I just saw you sitting here all alone and thought, well maybe you could use one," he explained.

"One what?" I asked, only half listening to the stranger in front of me.

"…A drink," he replied with a half smile.

"No thanks," I answered a bit too harsh and resistant.

"Oh, okay…may I ask why?"

"WHAT? Are you serious?" I asked starting to get a little irritated.

"Um…yes," he answered truthfully.

"Ughhh…" I sighed with a bit of disgust, "Well if you must know I don't trust you, I don't take drinks from liars," I hissed.

"FROM LIARS?" he asked, shocked, his voice sounding very surprised and slightly offended. "You don't even know me," he continued in a defensive tone.

"Exactly! So…why would I take a drink from you then? Especially when I know you're a liar?" I replied.

"Well, how do you know I'm a liar?" he asked a bit confused and maybe even intrigued, his voice trying to sound less intense.

"It's happy hour," I answered, "all the drinks are free!" I argued.

He sighed, "Yes, you caught me," he chuckled, "the drink *was* free so I guess that makes me a liar," he said, sounding sarcastically defeated. "I just thought it was better than coming over and saying 'hello my name is Jarrett and I brought you a free drink from the bar,'" he said, mocking himself in a goofy sounding voice.

"Jarrett, huh? Well, Jarrett, if that's your real name, I mean how can I be sure when you're a liar and all…" I rambled jokingly. "Coming over here with a free drink instead of a make-belief bought one could have earned you a seat at my table," I stated as-a-matter-of-fact.

"Okay. Well, suit yourself Miss…I just didn't want you to be over here all alone…at a party…by yourself…" he pointed out flashing me a brilliant smile, sparkling white teeth glowing in the darkness. He turned and walked away not giving me a chance to respond.

"IT'S ZAHRA!" I yelled out to him as he began to disappear into the crowd, but he didn't hear me, my voice was swallowed by the music. At first, I thought to just let him go. What difference did it make to me anyway? But then I suddenly remembered the promise I made to myself on the plane and in the shower that I was going to live for the moment. Also, what about the toast Nat, Jay and I made just a few minutes ago? We said no regrets, right? If I let this faceless creature walk away from me and step out of my life, would I regret it later? Or would I regret letting him enter back into it? How would I ever know? I quickly got to my feet and hurried to follow him onto the crowded dance floor. He was almost across the entire club headed toward the front door. Man, was I lucky that I went after him when I did, I thought to myself. I realized that I would have regretted having him walk out of my life before we could even remotely acquaint ourselves. I grabbed his arm and he turned his head to see who was preventing him from exiting the building. His tall frame of 6'1" looked down at my little body of 5'3" and smiled, "It's Zahra," I said, a little out of breath. My heart began to flutter again, but this time it wasn't so bad.

✳✳✳

"Excuse me?" he said, with a sly smile as we stepped outside of the building. "My name. It's Zahra," I replied, "inside you called me Miss…"

"So you followed me outside to tell me your name?"

"Well…err, yes. I didn't want you to go the rest of your life wondering what my name was," I retorted jokingly.
He laughed, "The rest of my life? Wow!"

"I'm not trying to be conceded or anything, but you approached me, remember?" I pointed out.

"Yes, yes I did," he answered nodding his head in agreement while taking a cigarette out of his pocket. My eyes followed as he put the cigarette in his mouth, took out his lighter and lit it. He tilted his head downward to look at me from the corner of his eye.

"Do you want one?" he asked.

"Umm, no thanks…okay maybe," I said.

"Well, which one is it? This time his voice sounded different.

"Hey, you have an accent," I said, almost as a statement but more like a question, feeling ridiculous as soon as the words left my lips. I could feel my face become warm, but thank God my skin was a bit too dark to show that I had blushed. As I waited in agony for him to answer my silly question, he exhaled the smoke up into the sky and chuckled ever so slightly. With a smirk on his face he looked down at me again leaning in just a little and said,

"*Yes*…people from England usually do."

"Sorry," I apologized, "I couldn't hear it inside of there," I said, jerking my head toward the club.

"Well, what about right now in the last few minutes of our conversation?" he pointed out, "clearly, you haven't really been paying attention," he finished.

"I think I'll take that cigarette now," I said embarrassed. He tilted his head back up toward the night sky and laughed loudly with one hand on his stomach. The other people outside of the club stopped to look at him for a brief second before returning to their own conversations. I used those few seconds to examine him. He was slim but definitely built, I could tell through the front of his shirt by the way it hung on his body. His skin was fair and his cheeks were blushed red from the cool night air. His face was gentle but defined, his eyebrows were thick and even, and his eyes were a blueish grey colour, almost like slate. His nose was perfectly straight just ending in a little triangle at the base. He had a mop of messy bronze-brown hair on top of his head that looked naturally styled without any thick, gooey hair products, lightly tossed into the perfect mess. His face was scruffy with a brown beard starting to grow in around his thin, heart shaped lips that were a deep pink colour. His teeth were almost straight with pointy incisors and sparkling white. His voice was smooth and tenor, just like liquid velvet, with a tinge of huskiness probably from all the smoking, I thought. He wore a seafoam green buttoned down dress shirt under a black double breasted wool coat and a beige plaid scarf hung loosely around his neck. He wore straight legged dark blue jeans and black leather loafer that were squared at the tip. He was very well dressed and put together.

"Here," he said, passing me his already lit, half smoked cigarette.

"No thanks," I replied making a face.

"Right—*you don't know me*," he said raising his hands up, palms facing me as if he were surrendering to the police. "I just thought that maybe since you probably haven't smoked before you wouldn't want a whole one, plus it's quite cold out here and you don't have a jacket on and a whole one would take too long for you to smoke, just looking out for you," he said, taking another drag from his cigarette. He was drop dead gorgeous and I could see how girls were easily charmed by him. He wasn't shy, but I could tell that he was a quiet guy, the type to sit alone and read a book in a coffee shop, while sipping black coffee and smoking a cigarette. He wasn't my type at all though, but then again, I didn't really have an ideal kind of guy. I would never have thought I'd be his type either, and there was no indication that he wanted romance from me anyway. He had already pointed out that he felt sorry for me, in nicer words by offering me a drink as I sat alone at the party. This was clearly the place for people to have a good time, did I really look that miserable?

He held the cigarette out to me again, just as it was almost done. His lips pulled apart into a little grin and his right eyebrow raised, asking me silently if I had changed my mind about the cigarette. Live a little, I thought to myself, as I took the cigarette from him and held it between my index finger and thumb. I brought it to my lips and inhaled slowly, choking down the smoke and exhaling it up into the air as he had done before. He laughed, and smiled at me with delight.

"That a girl," he said, letting me take one more drag before handing it back to him. He took one last drag before he dropped it to the street and put out the cigarette under his foot. "Let's go get your jacket," he said, putting his arm around the back of my neck. My heart fluttered a bit, I instantly stiffened, my body became rigid, I didn't know what to make of this moment. I decided not to over think it and just follow the cobblestone steps of my journey. "By the way, you're never smoking one of those again," he said laughing.

We walked over to the coat check and I handed in my ticket. The guy behind the counter handed me my jacket and I began to put it on. "I'm going to go get us some more *free* drinks, to help us stay warm outside," he said. "Wait," I stopped him as I reached for my wallet, "I really didn't like those drinks," I said, twisting my face to make a sour expression. I reached into my wallet and took out some money, "Can you get me something else?" I asked. He smiled, his beautiful smile that I remembered from earlier and said, "Sure, those were quite horrid, weren't they? I guess that's why they were free. Shall I get us two pints?" he asked, not really waiting for a response, but already heading back into the club toward the bar with my money still in my hand.

"Zahra, where have you been? We've been looking all over for you," I could hear Natalie saying as she and Romy hand in hand snaked through a crowd of people. "Where are you going?" Romy asked. "Are you leaving? You can't leave!" Natalie insisted.

"No, I'm not leaving, I was just outside," I answered. "By yourself?" Natalie asked suspiciously. "Here you go love," his sweet sounding voice interrupted. He handed me a beer in one hand and a shot in the other. "Th-thanks," I said, receiving the drinks with both hands. Natalie and Romy looked utterly shocked, waiting for me to answer their silent, unspoken questions. "I'm going back outside with my friend Jarrett," I said, pointing at him with my elbow. He smiled his brilliant smile at them and I could see my friends start to melt. "Err… Jarrett, Natalie. Natalie, Jarrett. Jarrett, Romy. Romy, Jarrett," I said, introducing them all to each other pointing them out by name with my elbow, hands filled with drinks.

"Hi," both Natalie and Romy said just seconds apart.

"Hello," he said, charmingly nodding his head slightly. "We were just going back outside for a bit. To talk," he answered, "it's a bit too loud in here, so loud that Zahra apparently couldn't hear my accent!" he teased, nudging me with his elbow.

"Oh okay," Natalie said, "we'll be in here…dancing," she finished, shooting me a little wink. I smiled with embarrassment and looked down at the ground. I could feel his eyes on me and I didn't want to meet his gaze, I was already over heating as it was. "Bye…" Natalie called as she and Romy headed back inside of the main dance area, waving. With a smile in his voice, he said, "C'mon," and we headed back toward the front door. Just before we exited the building, he stopped and faced me. He held his shot glass filled with a clear alcohol out toward me and I raised mine to meet his hanging in the space between us. "Cheers," he said, "Cheers," I answered as we clinked our glasses together and drank the shot, chasing it with a swig of beer. I could feel that I was starting to spin a little out of control, but at that point, I didn't care. I wanted to forget all the troubles from the last forty-eight hours and this was the perfect time to do just that.

We stepped outside with beers in our hands and leaned against the small ledge of the front window of Absinthe. "So Zahra, your friends seem nice," he said. "Yeah they're pretty great," I answered "I actually just met Romy today," I continued. "Really," he replied generally intrigued. "Well, what brings you to Austria then?" he asked.

I took a moment to think, pushing my sadness back down, not allowing it to gurgle back up from the shower drain where I left it and simply said, "Student exchange, we're here for six months, Natalie and I are staying with Romy's family, there's a group of us here. What brings you to Austria?" I asked trying to deter him from asking more questions. "Modelling gig," he replied. I looked up at his face to see if he was lying. He looked back at me with his perfect delicious, toothy smile. "Are you lying?" I asked suspiciously, my eyes squinted.

"I thought you were a master lie detector," he joked.

"I am," I confirmed. "But my mind is a little foggy right now," I confessed. "Oh is it, maybe I should get you a few more drinks and you'll bare your soul to me then," he said laughing, but I couldn't bring myself to join him. I couldn't even bring myself to look at him, I could only look straight ahead with eyes that were glazed over looking vaguely into the distance. He looked at me straight faced "Touchy subject, your soul?" he asked. "Yeah," I answered trying to dismiss the subject, I quickly said, "So are you really a model?" "Yes, sort of." "What does that mean? Sort of?" I asked. "I do little gigs here and there in between school. I was flown out with a two other guys and a few girls to do a shoot up in the mountains. Winter gear, coats, hats, that sort of thing," he answered. "Wow, I've never met a model before," I said fairly interested, "I guess today's my lucky day," I managed to smile. "Mine too," he smiled, leaning sideways nudging me slightly with his body.

I swayed. "Sure if you think so," I said not convinced. "Well, you're wrong!" he protested. "And I'm entitled to think what I think and know what I know, so there," he insisted. "So what will it take besides a couple of drinks to get you to bare your soul to me? To tell me why you're really here," he said finally after a few moments of awkward silence, he was studying me.

 I could feel my heart begin its uneven dance inside of my chest and my stomach began to churn, I knew that I wasn't ready to face the moment. I had been denying my reality almost successfully and with his petition, I was unravelling at the seams. I ran over to the side of the building, braced myself, using my hand against the brick wall for support, bent over and released my anxiety, my pain and the torment of my memories and felt the nightmare attack me with full force. He ran over to my side at once asking me if I was all right. I was overcome with embarrassment, I couldn't believe I had just thrown up, this was turning out to be the worst night of my life, probably one filled with regret which I had feared all along. "Maybe the shot and the pint were too much for you," he said, clearly feeling guilty.

 "No, it's not that, I'm fine it's just—" I stopped myself.

 "It's just what?" he asked, reaching into his pocket for a napkin. He handed me a very fancy cloth handkerchief that was soft and a pale blue-green just like his shirt, with the letters *AJS* stitched into the corner.

 "No thanks," I said pushing it away. "Please, take it, it's the least I can do," he answered. "I don't want to ruin it. It's too nice." "Don't worry about it, I have others," he replied, pushing the napkin closer to me. I took it and blotted my teary eyes and wiped my mouth avoiding all forms of eye contact with him. I wanted so badly to be able to crawl into a dark hole and just die. This was ten times worse than crying on the plane and being caught by Ruben.

It was worse than Natalie throwing herself at him too. I could feel Jarrett's eyes scanning me, searching for some answers.

"It's what? He asked sincerely.

"Pardon?" I asked, still bracing myself with my hand on the brick wall. "…You didn't finish what you were going to say," he said fidgeting with his hands. It seemed like he was debating placing a hand on my back or my shoulder and ultimately decided against it. "Umm…it's just personal," I answered, turning to lean my back against the wall so that I could face him. "Okay…" he said, still a bit confused, playing back our conversation before I abruptly ran off to the side of the club. "About your soul? Baring your soul?" he asked a little unsure. His hands were on my shoulders now trying to force me to look at him. Tears welled up in my eyes uncontrollably as I tried not to blink, forcing them back down, hoping they wouldn't spill over onto my cheeks. I was unsuccessful in my attempt and immediately the tears rolled down my face, landing with the weight of the world on the cold frozen ground. He pulled me in close, almost like an instinctual response and held me tightly as I cried uncontrollably into his wool coat, which I used as a muzzle to hide the hysteria in my voice. He placed one hand on my back and the other on the back of my head and stroked my hair without saying a word. We stayed like that for what seemed like hours—but was indeed only minutes—in silence except for my sobs and occasional bursts of hysteria.

When I had finally released all of my pain into the atmosphere, in the silence of that pivotal moment I asked, "What does the A and S stand for anyway?"

"What?" he asked, almost in a whisper, leaning down to speak into my hair.

"What's the A and S for?" I asked again. "Your napkin has A.J.S stitched into it," I whispered into his wool coat, breathing in his scent. It was wonderful, he smelled fresh, clean like soap. He had a smell that I could get used to.

"My name is actually Adrian Jarrett Scott, but my friends all call me Jarrett..."

"Why?" I asked. He was silent for a minute, contemplating his answer.

"You know, I really don't know...I s'ppose because we used to hang out with another Adrian, but he's long gone now."

"Well, I think I'll call you Adrian," I assessed.

"How come?"

"...To be different," I answered. He laughed a little.

"Sure! You can call me whatever you want," he said, with a smile I could hear in his voice. I repeated his name to myself under my breath, closed my eyes and took another deep breath, inhaling all of him, gripping onto the lapels of his jacket and pulling him in a little closer to me. I wished the moment would last forever. (★)[4] I felt safe, warm, and at home in the arms of a stranger. I wanted to taste every moment and savour each flavour so that when the moment had passed, I would remember it vividly and it would bring me peace. For a few moments my mind was clear and I was free.

I wondered if I was what he was looking for, because he was everything that I needed. I wondered if I had worn something else, would he have approached me at my table? Would he think I was too plain? When I was getting ready in my room at Romy's, I decided to step outside of myself. I always believed that I had great style, which was never the problem. But at times I found myself wanting to add in an extra punch of colour, pattern or texture, but never followed through because I thought that I would just end up looking ridiculous. For the past few years I'd been wearing my hair

---

[4] Angel-Sarah McLachlan

straight, pressed out flat and sleek. I usually wore jeans or leggings with a long flowing shirt knocked off one shoulder and my shoes varied to whatever felt best that day.

For Absinthe, I chose to wear something sort of similar. I wore a long sleeved hot pink cardigan that I borrowed from Romy that almost reached down to my knees because I was so much shorter than her. I left it open over an ivory strapless top. My legs were covered with tight black jeans tucked into my tall black leather riding boots. I covered my neck with layers of silver chains adorned with different charms of hearts, stars, four leafed clovers and shimmery peace signs. My hair was wild and curly and pulled back into a ponytail. I had taken too long trying to scrub away all of my sorrows and bad memories in the shower that I ran out of time to flat iron it, plus I didn't have a European adapter for my plug. My makeup looked attractive. I dressed up my eyes with dark grey and black sparkly eyeshadow and painted my lips a glossy hot pink. On any other day, I wore very little makeup just mascara and neutral gloss on my lips.

Would he consider that beautiful? Did he even think I was beautiful? What the hell was he doing here with me? And why the hell was I crying all over his jacket? He rested his cheek on top of my head and asked, "What's your last name?" snapping me back into reality. "I don't have one," I replied in between sobs. "What do you mean?" he asked confused. "I left that person behind in the 'hole in the sky,'" I said, "now I'm just Zahra."

"What's 'the hole in the sky?'"

"White Rock, British Columbia, in Canada. It's a nickname for back home."

"Oh. Well, Zahra *Holeinthesky* what was your name back there, before you got to here?"

"Ro-may-o Win-Ter-sss," I said, stressing each part of who I used to be, bitterly. "It's nice, I like it," said Adrian, taking hold of my shoulders and shaking life back into me. "Yeah well she's dead, along with my sister, and my entire family actually," I said, with a small bit of disgust. "WHAT? What happened?" he asked waiting patiently for me to answer, maybe expecting me to start crying again. "I don't want to talk about it, I don't want to burden you with my mess," I said, trying to pull away from him without any real success. He held me tighter so that I could not escape and said, "Tell me only if you want to, but I asked because I want to know." I sighed, "Okay, but not here," I said, "I don't want anyone from my school to overhear us." "Okay, we'll walk…" he decided. (★)[5] He wiped a stray tear from my cheek with his thumb and flashed me the smile that I had now completely fallen for. Just then the song that once had me in tears on the plane popped back into my head, I smiled back at him, as he took my hand and we began to walk.

---

[5] Feelings Gone-Basement Jaxx

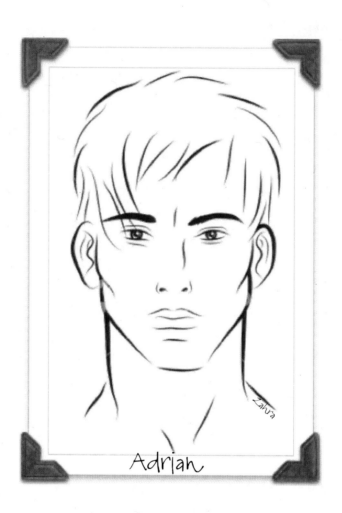

They Say The Truth Will Set You Free...
Who Are "They" Anyway?

We walked in silence for about five minutes as he waited patiently for me to expose my hidden secrets and to unleash my inner nightmare. I took a deep breath and exhaled my hot breath into the cold frozen air. We stopped for a moment so that he could light a cigarette, it seemed like he had sensed that he would need it to help ease the tension of the weight my story was about to bestow upon him. As he lit it and took in his first drag I said, "You know you really don't have to get involved in this, I mean you hardly know me and it just isn't your burden to bear. I already feel like a terrible person for breaking down in front of you, it was totally uncalled for and unnecessary. I'm sorry about that, I just needed some air, so thanks for the walk, but we can head back now." I started to turn around and head back toward the club. He grabbed my wrist, "Not so fast Miss," he said. "I want to know. Seriously, but only if you want to tell me," he reassured, "I think you're about over due for a chat." He showed me the wet spot on his jacket where my tears had soaked in. "Have you spoken to a... Nnn...Natasha about this?" he asked trying to remember her name. "Natalie," I corrected. I quickly shook my head, looking down at the ground. "She's been so excited about this trip, I didn't want to ruin it with my problems," I said honestly. "But she's your friend! Who would you have told if you never met me?" he asked taking another drag from his cigarette. I shrugged my shoulders, I really didn't know, "No one I guess," I said defeated. "Yeah well that's not healthy, now is it?" he pointed out. I put my hand out for him to pass me the cigarette, he handed it to me smiling and I inhaled the thick smoke, coughing out my story as the grey smoke entered the atmosphere.

"My family has been lying to me for my entire life," I blurted out, handing back the cigarette. "Oh..." he said, waiting for me to continue. "Now they're all dead, the mother and father I used to know, my sister Jonnæ, they're all gone." I closed my eyes for a minute thinking back to that inevitable day, it seemed so far away, nothing like it was just yesterday. We were leaning on trees facing each other in a small park just off of the sidewalk. I allowed the tree to bear my weight as I inhaled and exhaled trying to calm my heart. "They're dead?" he asked shocked. "Figuratively," I started to explain. I took one last drag of the cigarette and began to explain what happened.

✳✳✳

    The sun was not as bright as I thought it would have been, maybe it's going to rain, I thought, as I rolled over onto my side to check the time on my alarm clock. But the forecast called for bright skies, I remembered, as my eyes adjusted to the red lights blinking from the clock. It read 5:00 a.m. I was sleeping a light, dreamless sleep, anxiously awaiting the scheduled five-thirty alarm. I would have had exactly one hour to get ready and into my sister's car to head to the airport. There I'd meet up with the rest of my class, hop on a plane and finish the rest of my high school life in Austria. I was so excited I could hardly contain myself. I had been looking forward to this trip for a year, marking my departure date on my calendar. After three-hundred and sixty-five x's, the circled date had finally arrived and I couldn't be more ready to take this huge step in my life. As the clock ticked to 5:01, I realized what had woken me, no, my alarm clock didn't go off early. The sound of outraged voices streamed up the stairs from the den and was flooding into my room through the spaces underneath the door. The angry voices belonged to my parents, they were arguing with my sister Jonnæ.

    "YOU HAVE NO RIGHT Jonnæ! NO RIGHT AT ALL," my mother yelled in and out of a whisper. "YES, I DO MOTHER,

I HAVE EVERY RIGHT, *SHE* HAS EVERY RIGHT," Jonnæ fought back. They were clearly talking about me. At first I thought they were arguing over my trip to Austria. Jonnæ and I knew our parents wouldn't be thrilled with the expense of the trip so Jonnæ decided to cover the costs on her own and I saved all of my paycheques for spending money in Austria. Jonnæ really wanted me to go on this trip. It was like I had no choice, she was going to make sure that I was overseas one way or another. She said it was important and I got the feeling that she needed me out of the house, so I agreed to go to get her off my back about it. She was acting so weird that I figured it would just be best to agree to go. Jonnæ said she would take care of discussing it with our parents, but I never thought she would wait till the morning I was leaving to inform them of my pending journey. My parents never discussed it with me either, but that was usually their way of dealing with things they didn't agree with. They just wouldn't talk about it until it was no longer avoidable, but the morning of? I was so confused.

When I heard them fighting downstairs in the den, the room that Jonnæ and I never used, I *knew* it was serious. Yeah, I figured they'd be displeased about the trip, but to leave any discussion about it until just hours before my plane departed seemed quite uncharacteristic. The air was filled with something that reeked of pandemonium. Something was wrong and they were hiding it from me. I quietly got out of bed so I could hear what they were saying, but it was all murmurs from my room. I snuck out of the room and into the hallway, tucked into the shadows of one of the walls. "SHE *WILL NOT* GO ON THIS TRIP, IT'S NOT GOING TO HAPPEN," my father yelled, I could here the tension in his voice. My father never yelled, he was always so quiet and reserved. It was totally unlike him. "IT'S TOO LATE DAD, SHE'S LEAVING IN LIKE THREE HOURS, WHAT ARE YOU GOING TO SAY

TO HER? HUH? HOW ARE YOU GOING TO EXPLAIN TO HER THAT SHE CAN'T GO?"

"IT'S NOT MY RESPONSIBILITY TO FIGURE THAT OUT Jonnæ, IT'S JUST…*not right*," he stressed.

"THINK ABOUT *HER!* THINK ABOUT WHAT THIS WILL DO TO HER, HAVE YOU THOUGHT *AT ALL* ABOUT ZAHRA? God, Jonnæ, how can you be so selfish?" my mother spat.

Selfish? Jonnæ had always been the most selfless person when it came to me. I had always thought that my parents were the selfish ones. They always left everything up to Jonnæ, they never got involved with me when I was younger, they never seemed to care, now they wanted to stop me from experiencing something completely amazing? How dare they, I thought. I was disgusted with my parents, I wanted to march downstairs and defend Jonnæ, tell my parents to get out and never to come back to our home. I mean I lived with *Jonnæ* for heaven's sake. They we're 'having trouble keeping up with my schedule' as they put. Two years ago I moved in with Jonnæ to make things easier on my parents. Nice right? I wanted to tell them to leave Jonnæ and I alone. I wanted to yell at them and tell them just how terrible I had been feeling my entire life, because of them. They left me feeling unloved and like a burden, like I wasn't good enough and somehow no matter what I did I couldn't measure up. I sat on the floor in the shadows of the wall, cradling my arms around my knees. What are they fighting for? I wondered, what are we *all* always fighting for? I questioned.

My family had disagreements before, but nothing ever like this. I didn't understand what was going on. Why was there so much anger about a trip to Austria? I was going to be back by the end of May, I was still going to attend class and would be graduating in June and I'd be back in White Rock with the rest of my classmates, I just didn't get it. They continued to argue, but I missed much of what was said, I was trying to calm myself down. I tuned back in and heard my mom yelling, "Jonnæ, YOU HAVE NO RIGHTS! DID YOU FORGET THAT YOU SIGNED OVER THOSE RIGHTS WHEN SHE WAS BORN? We've done you a courtesy all these years, letting you be involved in her life."

"YEAH, WELL, I REGRET THAT DECISION *EVERY-DAY MOM*. I MEAN GOD, I GAVE HER TO YOU BECAUSE *YOU* CONVINCED ME SHE WOULD HAVE A BETTER LIFE! But either way *I* still raised her! Only… she never called *me* mommy. Do you know how much that killed me? And for what? For who? IT SAVED YOUR STUPID IMAGE. YOU NEVER HAD TO WORRY ABOUT ANYONE *FINDING OUT OUR DIRTY LITTLE SECRET* RIGHT? WASN'T THAT WHAT WAS MOST IMPORTANT?

"YOU *LIED* TO ME, IT WAS NEVER ABOUT *HER* OR *ME*, IT HAS ALWAYS BEEN ABOUT YOU, THIS NEIGHBOURHOOD, *THESE PEOPLE*," Jonnæ cried, sobbing uncontrollably, screaming with all kinds of hysteria in her voice.

"OH GET A GRIP Jonnæ," my "mom" exploded, clearly irritated, disgust in her voice.

"I—I SHOULD HAVE RAISED HER MYSELF, AS *MY* DAUGHTER… AND NO MATTER WHAT YOU SAY SHE'S NEVER STOPPED BEING *MY* DAUGHTER," Jonnæ sobbed, defeated.

"No Jonnæ, she's your *sister*, and as long as we all live she will continue to believe this to be true, got it?" my "father" insisted. "And keep your voice down for the love of God, you'll wake her up. She'll hear you," he demanded.

My mind spiralled out of control, the room spinning all around me, my life flipped upside down. Heavy air pushed and pulled its way in and out of my body, everything crumbled around me. "NO!" I shrieked with pure terror. The tremble in my hands creeping up my arms cascading throughout my whole body. My life had just come crashing down right in front of me.

My sister was really my mother?
                        Jonnæ? But...
*My parents were biologically my grandparents?...*That meant my grandparents were actually my great-grandparents, my aunts, my cousins...

    My toes began to tingle, it crawled up my legs, my spine, my stomach, my neck, enclosed my face and spread to the tips of my fingers like tiny microscopic enzymes eating away at me with a million needle pricks. I felt sick to my stomach, I stumbled to my feet, heavy footsteps pounded up the stairs, as I ran to the bathroom slamming the door behind me. I rushing to the toilet and releasing everything I had just absorbed. As I lay with my face on the cold tile floor in a state of shock, (★)[6] I realized that my life as I knew it, was over. The Zahra I had once been had died and I was no one, I was empty, I was broken, I was ash.

    Joanne, Fabién and Jonnæ were banging on the bathroom door. They were begging me to let them in, they were begging for a chance to explain, their voices were distant, trapped in a world that I didn't belong to, I belonged nowhere. The other side of the door was a million miles away, their voices muddled with lies and deceit. My family as I knew it dissolved right before my eyes and I had instantly become a motherless child, a fatherless child, a sister-less child. I was no one. I couldn't move, I was glued to the bathroom floor, the death of my family had begun to sink in.

    The pain was raw, the wound still fresh, there was no way to

---

[6] Valentine's Day-Linkin Park

protect myself from those emotions and I was lost. I had lost direction, my path was unclear, my path had dissolved. One minute I was walking along the road, on Zahra Ave, about to meet the intersection of Austria and Graduation and the next minute, a great fog prowled in, clouded over the road and closed itself around me, everything disappeared and I was alone. My sister was dead. My parents were dead. She was gone, they were gone and I was alone.

I don't know how long my body lay lifeless on the floor. I was outside of myself looking down at my pile of skin and bones and tears. Jonnæ's voice echoed eerily through the door, she was crying, apologizing for all of her mistakes. Joanne and Fabién, tried to convince me that they did what was best for me, but Joanne still wore her pride like a designer handbag, I could hear it in her voice, it said she did what was best for her.

I splashed cold water on my face, cupped in my hands. Maybe I was hoping that it would wake me from this nightmare, I don't know. It didn't work. I stared at the stranger in the mirror, she looked like me, tilted her head like me, wiped the tears from her eyes like me, but she wasn't me. I opened my mouth to speak, the voices on the other side of the door were ringing in my ears, like a microphone to a speaker, my head throbbed, my tear-sore eyes squinted away from the light. No sound came out of my mouth, my throat burned, the acid in my chest churned. "Please leave me alone, please just go away," I begged, my voice foreign. "No Zahra, we're not leaving. It isn't what's best right now," Joanne reached for sympathy, irritation was her undertone. "GET. AWAY. FROM. THE. DOOR," I yelled. I slammed my hand against it, the door shook, I jumped in surprise. My heart was pounding, eyes burning, head throbbing, and ears ringing. There was no reply, they grew silent. I unlocked the door, turned the knob slowly and stepped out into the hallway. As I walked to my room three silhouettes lined the wall in the dark hallway, they said nothing, neither did I.

I entered my room and locked the door behind me. I could hear Fabién recommending that they wait for me downstairs. "Well I guess it's safe to say she'll be staying in the country, *thank God,*" Joanne assumed victorious air. "Yeah, you would like that wouldn't you," said Jonnæ. "Well do you think she's in any condition to be going anywhere? She won't even want to go," Joanne insisted. "I can't believe you would even play with the idea that she'd be going away with the state she's in now, *thanks to you by the way*. She needs counselling, we all do," Joanne rambled. "We'll leave her here for now, but tomorrow, I'm moving her things back into our house," she finished as an afterthought.

Fabién barked at them and forced them downstairs. I couldn't believe that after everything that just happened, they were still playing the *Who's Right Or Wrong* game. I was revolted, I hated them, I wanted to spit in their faces, the same way they had spat in mine. I checked the time, it was close to seven a.m. and I had to be at the airport by eight o'clock. I had fifteen minutes before seven arrived and it would take me forty-five minutes to get to the Vancouver Airport. I didn't feel like going to Austria anymore, but I knew there was no other choice. I couldn't stay with Jonnæ, I surely didn't want to stay with Fabién and Joanne. I didn't want to go to family therapy, I didn't want to be told how to feel, I didn't want to keep smiling outside and dying on the inside so that the Roméo-Winters image could be upheld. I didn't care. I had already separated myself from them. It was then that I realized my only option was to get away.

I dressed as quickly as I could in the clothes I had set out the night before. Everything was already in place, my suitcases in Jonnæ's car, my carryon bag hanging from my bedpost. I impulsively snuck into Jonnæ's room and stole another small suitcase from her closet and rushed it to my room. I opened my drawers and emptied them into the piece of luggage. I didn't want to think about coming back. I had never run away before, I was terrified, but packing all of my things made me feel better. After I had zipped the suitcase closed, all I had left to figure out was my escape.

  I took a few long breaths and steadied my heart, there was no time for crying, there was no looking back, it was time to go. I slowly opened my bedroom door, cautiously and crept quietly across the hallway, down the three steps and into the common area of the dark house. As I passed through the loft hallway, I could see *them* sitting in den on the lower level, talking among themselves still as self-absorbed as ever, probably trying to figure out what to do with me next. I grabbed my keys off of the island in the kitchen and hurried to the front door. I quietly unhitched the lock and slowly turned the knob. The door flew open and I ran down the handful of stairs dragging my extra suitcase behind me, swinging my messenger bag over my shoulder., toting my carryon in my free hand.

  As I approached the final few steps, I pressed the unlock button on the car remote, instantly regretting it. The car lights flashed through the windows of den on the lower level and through the curtains I could see the silhouettes begin to stir in a frenzy, racing to the side door off of the den. Fabién, Joanne and Jonnæ ran outside onto the driveway, their lies trailing them like green sulphuric gas. I had already thrown the car into reverse and was backing out of the driveway, onto my quiet street. My neighbour walking his dog stopped to let me pass, he smile and waved, I looked through him. His smile faded, he hurried along. Jonnæ ran down the driveway after me, crying, pleading. Fabién at her side, pulling her back. Joanne stood with her hands balled into fists at her side, shoulders hunched, face scowled. She looked from side to side to see if anyone was watching. Fabién held Jonnæ in his arms, he tried to calm her. He said something to Joanne. She looped her arm through Jonnæ's who had collapsed to the ground, hunched over herself. Joanne rolled her eyes and pulled Jonnae up, she was beckoning for me to come back with her hand, she couldn't plead too loud of course, she didn't want to stir the neighbours. The two of them looked like a pitiful pair. Where was Fabién? As I threw the car into drive, Fabién appeared, fumbling with something in his hand, keys. I gasped. I pressed hard on the gas and never looked back.

    I looked up from my intense gaze on the ground, my eyes had long blurred over, I stared out of focus. I searched to find Adrian's eyes in the darkness that surrounded us in the little park. The only lights were from street lamps on the sidewalk. He was staring wide-eyed at me, he was speechless. He reached out and took my forearm, guiding me to a bench that was close by and we sat down. He shimmied over so that the distance between us became non-existent. He placed his arm around my shoulders and pulled me in so that my weight had shifted and I was leaning into him. "I am so, so sorry," he said finally, with complete sincerity. "I can't believe this has happened to you…" he sighed, frustrated. "I wish I knew what else to say, I don't know…like something that could make it better," he confessed. "You've done enough just by being here with me, thank you for listening, that's all I can ask for." I smiled weakly, instantly I had become very tired.

    I sighed a loud sigh of relief. I didn't know how much longer I could have kept all of that bottled up. I was like a rattled bottle of cola, the fizz spasming from within, whirling around in confusion, working itself into a fit, clawing at the surface, begging to be released, exploding at the slightest bit of exposure. "Can we just sit here for a little while longer?" I asked, leaning my head on his shoulder, I felt dizzy, my head was spinning insatiably. I looked up at his face, he looked down at mine, his lips only inches away. I wanted to kiss him, there must be something wrong with me, in a moment like this I was thinking about my first kiss. I was more of a mess than I realized. We were so close that I could feel his warm breath on my face. It smelled of old cigarettes and alcohol, but it didn't deter me, it was strangely comforting. He broke the tension with his velvety voice, "We can stay here as long as you like, or at least until your friends come looking for you." It was cold outside, the chill nipped at my fingers and my toe, but it didn't matter, for once everything was perfect.

We sat on the bench for what felt like the better part of an hour, mostly in silence. We watched the people walking by, the dead leaves blowing across the frozen ground and the tiny snowflakes that whispered across the sky. There were so many questions I wanted to ask him, but I didn't know where to begin. They were simple questions really, but somehow I was never able to let the words roll off my tongue and through my lips. I was more concerned about whether I'd see him again after tonight. I knew our time together was drawing close to an end and I was nervous about what would happen next. Would he just bid me good luck and farewell? Would I thank him for his time and then we'd go our separate ways?

My eyes were closed, my head resting on his shoulder, his left arm wrapped around me. I don't know how long I was sleeping for. His cold hand brushed against my face. "Hey, your friends are looking for you," he said softly. In the short distance I could hear Natalie, Romy and Jason calling out my name with a hint of panic. We were only about twenty feet away, but because the little park was off to the left of the sidewalk there was no way that they would have ever seen me.

I rose, groggy, my head still spinning. "Wait," he said, before I was completely upright, he pulled me back down to sit beside him and handed me a little piece of paper. "Here," he said. I took the folded paper and opened it. "It's so you can call me... if you'd like... I don't know like maybe tomorrow, or something..." he sighed, "the ball's in your court, you call me if you need to... if you *want* to..." he stammered aimlessly. I looked up from the paper at him, even in the dark night I could see that his face was flushed. He was nervous, for the first time that evening I had seen his vulnerable side, he was unsure of himself. It was odd, he had been so calm and forward with me all night, now at the end he was more nervous then I was.

I held the piece of paper in both of my hands looking down at his number, shocked that he would even want to nurse the idea of speaking to me again. I felt so pathetic, I mean, I didn't even know this person and he had become my chaise lounger and my therapist all in one. I felt guilty, like maybe he felt pressured, like he had to continue to be there for me in my fragile state. But this wasn't his burden to bear. We both knew that. I sighed, "Look, Adrian... I appreciate *everything* you've done for me here tonight but—" "N— no don't worry about it Zahra, I understand really...I just thought...ugh," he sighed, a little lost for words, conflicted. "Wait. Adrian, listen to me, it's not that I don't *want* to talk to you, I just shouldn't. It was wrong for me to lay all of this on you. You don't have to worry about me, I'll get through this. You should just enjoy your time here in Vienna, you know? Go out and see things, do things whatever, y—you shouldn't be worrying about me." "Zahra understand," he was shaking his head, "I want you to call me, I want to spend more time with you... I know you're going through stuff right now, but that doesn't mean you should have to go through it alone." He raked his fingers through his hair and blew hot air into his cold fists. I watched him silently, my eyes followed his every move. He had such a good heart and I didn't know how I became so lucky to have met him that night. He was the greatest person that I had come to know, with all of his quirks and nerves, he was perfect.

I placed my hand lightly on his leg, in the distance I could hear Natalie's voice becoming frantic and I knew my time with him was up. "Thank you," I hugged him. He was stunned by my quick advance and it took him a second to respond. He wrapped his arms around me, "It's going to be okay," he whispered, "I promise, but we better get you back to your friends, Nadia sounds like she's about to send out a search party." "Yeah I guess you're right…" I was disappointed that the night was coming to an end. He laughed, "It's okay love, just call me tomorrow," said Adrian. "When?" we left the bench and the park behind, we walked back toward the club.

"Call me when you wake up."

"When I wake up? What if you're still sleeping?"

"I won't be, I'll probably be at my photo shoot, maybe we can do something afterwards."

"Like what?"

"Whatever you want to do… Does your friend from Austria have something planned for tomorrow? I'll come along, if that's okay."

"I'm sure it'll be fine…I'll call you and let you know," I reassured. "Good," he smiled. He put his cold hands deep into the pockets of his jacket and bumped me with his hip as we approached my frantic friends.

"*OH GOD*, ZAHRA! I was just dialling your parents' number, I was going to tell them that you disappeared! WHERE THE

HELL WERE YOU?" Natalie threatened. "DON'T CALL THEM, NEVER call them, or Jonnæ either," I insisted, motioning with my hand for her to stop. "O-okay," Natalie answered, confused. "I…ah…just…umm…don't need them worrying about me, you know how they get!" I lied. "I'm fine anyway, sorry to make you worry, guys…really…I mean it, it was stupid of me to have walked off." "What were you guys doing? Where did you go?" Romy asked suspiciously. "I think it's pretty obvious," Jason insisted with a dirty smirk. "Jason please!" I interrupted, embarrassed and glad that my back faced Adrian. "We were sitting in the little park over there…" I trailed, pointing in its direction. "We *were* talking," Adrian finished. "*Talking…right,*" Jason teased, he was not convinced. "We were *Jason*, not that it's any of your business," I chided and even more embarrassed that Adrian was witnessing our childish behaviour. "Well, sorry to break up this little love-fest, but… I think it's about time to say goodnight," Adrian interrupted. A hot flash seized through my body, he *did* think my friends were childish. I shot Jason a nasty look, he played innocent. I looked at Adrian with panic-stricken eyes, searching his face for answers. Was this the end? I didn't want to let him go. I swallowed hard against the lump in my throat and opened my mouth waiting for the sound to come out, nothing did.

"It's okay," he placed his hand ever so gently on my back, I almost couldn't feel it, and rubbed, "you'll call me when you wake up remember?"

I nodded, words still would not form. He wrapped his arm around my shoulders, embraced me casually. The smell of soap and winter lifted in the air, I inhaled his scent fully. I could feel the rhythm of his heart through his jacket, it beat steadily against mine that beat out of control. "Sleep well love, have a good night okay, we'll talk in the morning." "All right," I answered, using all of my effort to control my emotions. "Well, many thanks, delighted to meet all of you," he said to my friends, clapping his hands together and bowing. He turned and walked away toward his two friends, the other models he mentioned earlier who were waiting for him outside of the club by the front door. He took out a cigarette and lit it as he approached them and the three of them continued to walk away into the darkness. He looked over his shoulder, smiling, winked and then he was gone.

Long Ride Back Up The Hill

"Would you like to tell me what that was all about," Natalie demanded, sounding very parental. "What?" I was standoffish. "What were you two doing over there?" she prodded, a little insulted that I hadn't offered the juicy details. "Nothing happened Nat, I promise, we just…sat in that park over there," I pointed back to it again "…and talked." "Yeah, you keep saying that. Well, what did you talk about?" she asked as we got into a taxi. I sat in between her and Romy so that they could both hear everything I was saying, hoping that I would finally spill my guts. "I don't know, Nat—he was just asking me about my life, my family, where I'm from that kinda stuff, you know, the basics." I tried my best to sound nonchalant. "Okay, well it seems like you two really hit it off," Romy interjected. "Yeah, you two seemed really chummy, you looked like you were about to cry when he walked away! Why all the emotion if it was nothing?" Natalie pried. "Oh and he called you *'love'* by the way," Romy grinned with a raised eyebrow. "He's British, they call *everybody* love," Natalie interrupted. "I know guys…" I sighed, "We just connected I guess," I said sheepishly, I knew I was blushing, there was nothing I could do it hide it. "*Ohhhh you like him don't you?*" Romy teased, nudging me with her shoulder. "Ha!" I exhaled with an embarrassing chuckle, "it's not like that guys…he's just…a really nice person, that's all…I think he'll be a good friend. Oh and by the way, his name is Adrian. His middle name is Jarrett…but I like Adrian better," I concluded. "P-phh," Natalie grunted "Friends. *Right!* ANYWAY since you were too busy with the *mysterious English-*

man," Natalie said teasingly, "you didn't see me totally flirting with the hot bartender, I got his number," she was extremely proud of herself. "Oh yeah?" I wanted to sound enthusiastic, even though I really didn't care. I didn't quite like this new Natalie, she was similar to the old one in many ways, but she was talking differently, she sounded ditzy now, even though she was one of the smartest people I knew. Natalie had straight A's, pending scholarships, the works. Now she was acting like all she had going for her was her body. "When are you going to call him?" I asked. "I don't know, in a couple of days I guess," Natalie tried to pretend like it was no big deal, but I knew she was fighting the urge to dial his number on Romy's cell phone at that very moment.

"The real question is, when are *you* going to call *him?*" Romy eyed me sharply. *"I mean since you're calling him Adrian and all!"* she teased. "What?" I played dumb. "Oh c'mon don't give me that, I heard him tell you to call him when you woke up! What's going on?" Romy asked excited. "Oh...yeah..." I rolled my eyes. "He wanted me to ask if he could join us tomorrow, if you had any plans for us or something, but later...he has a modelling shoot first up in the mountains in the morning," I looked at my watch, "well like in a few hours I guess." "HOLD UP," Natalie shouted, "HE'S A MODEL?" she was shocked and a little upset that she had to settle for the bartender while I snagged the model. "Why are you yelling?" I asked, plugging my ears. "Do you want to go up to the mountains tomorrow then? Do you think he'll mind?" Romy asked excited. "I don't really know...I guess I could ask," I was unsure. "I'm sure he'd love to have you there Zahra, he seems to really like you," Romy placed her hand on top of mine. "Yeah, but it's not like that Romy..." I couldn't help but think about the blissful moment Adrian and I shared in the park. We were so close to a first kiss but he didn't pursue it and I was convinced that he wanted nothing more from me than my friendship or maybe even just to make sure I wasn't unstable or on the verge of a total breakdown. I felt pathetic, like I was a project he was working on, it made my head hurt. Either way, I was thankful for whatever time he was willing to give me. I couldn't help but think that my feelings for him were different from what he felt for me. I was still really confused by the way I felt inside. I didn't know if my feelings toward Adrian were genuine or if I liked the comfort and relief that he provided when I was with him. I couldn't think about it anymore, I was too tired, the day had been too long and too many things had happened. I let it all go, regardless, I had never felt that way before and nothing else seemed to matter.

My thoughts were interrupted by Natalie, "So... Zar...if 'it's not like that' as you put it...do you think *I'd* be his type?" "NATALIE!" Romy reached across me and slapped Natalie's arm. "*What?*" Natalie snarled, rubbing her arm, "I'm just asking. He's not even Zahra's type! She likes nerdy guys, guys who wear graphic t-shirts with comic book heros on them and greasy hair, for some strange reason, she's not into sophistication." "*Excuse me?* Graphic tees and one day old hair hardly describes a nerd! There is absolutely no reason that you have to wash your hair every single day, it's bad for you...and the environment!" I argued. "And I don't know Natalie, I don't know what Adrian's type is, maybe you should ask him," I scowling at her. I stared ahead out of the windshield with my jaw clenched in disbelief. How could Natalie say that? I'm not into sophistication? What does that mean? I started to wonder what the future held for my friendship with Natalie, at that moment the prospects didn't seem so great. We had never fought over a guy, it's true, our tastes were different. We had never really fought over anything for that matter, but I was starting to feel like this trip was changing her. Maybe she sensed that I was holding something back and she was lashing out at me, but either way I was starting to feel uncomfortable around her. My mind pirouetted to Adrian, the image of him walking away, turning, winking, smiling, danced across my mind. I began to panic, *was* Natalie his type? Would Adrian fall for Natalie with her long flowing blonde hair, her button nose, big green eyes and pale, fair skin? She could be a model herself, if she wanted and it was inevitable. Her comment meant that she *would* try to put the moves on Adrian whether or not I agreed and I wasn't going to fight with her over a guy, I had more self respect than that. She could have him if he obliged, but either way I knew this would probably be the end of our friendship. It made me sad to think that something so trivial would come between us.

I knew Natalie wouldn't openly pursue him, but she would spend an extra few minutes getting ready tomorrow before everybody was going to meet. It made me sick that the only reason she showed any interest in Adrian was because I said he was a model. How fickle, how sad. Was Natalie really this person? Then I thought, how would she have responded if I told her the truth about what was really going on in my life right now. Would she help me? Would she turn away from me because I was putting a damper on all her fun? Would she honestly tell me that she couldn't deal with the situation? Would she even be able to keep my secret? Or would she talk behind my back to my other classmates on this trip? She needed to stay on top of the social ladder, would this be her stepping stone? A shiver ran down my spine as different prospects ran through my mind. Romy placed her arm around my shoulder reassuring me that everything would be fine between Adrian and I and that Natalie was nothing to worry about, not realizing that it was the least of my worries. I rested my head on her shoulder and blocked out any lingering thoughts of Natalie for the rest of the trip home.

We walked into the house, the clock on the wall read 3:43 a.m. I was exhausted, I quickly changed into a pair of shorts and a tank top and fixed my hair into a messy bun. Natalie changed as well, looking at me in silence. I could feel her eyes on me, but I never looked over to meet her gaze. "If you like him Zahra I won't go after him," she said, breaking the silence. "Mm-hmm," I hummed, still not meeting her eyes. I grabbed my bag of toiletries and headed to the bathroom. As if he's yours to take, I thought, as if he's even mine! And what happened to *Ruben?* Or *that bartender?* I met Romy in there washing her face, when she rinsed and looked up in to the mirror, she gave me her friendly grin, "Stop worrying about it," she told me, "what time do you think I should wake you, to call him?" "Oh I don't know…" "Well, don't you think he'll start shooting early? Plus it will take us some time to get up to the mountain, we should probably leave here by nine a.m.," she planned happily. "Nine?" I asked surprised. "That's like…" I began counting on my fingers, "A few hours away," I retorted. "Yes, it's like five and half hours, you can sleep in the car, it will take like two hours to get to the mountain," she explained. "I'll wake you at eight and you can call him then okay?" she squeezed my crossed arms. "*Goodnight!*" she sang as she exited the bathroom. I quickly washed my face and brushed my teeth. I took a second to examine my face in the mirror, could this be the face of someone *he'd* be interested in?

My thoughts were interrupted, Natalie entered the bathroom to wash up before bed. I looked at her reflection in the mirror, finally meeting her eyes with mine. She looked sad. Good. I took my bag and pushed past her and went back to our room. I pulled back the sheets and crawled into bed, I rested my head against my pillow and closed my eyes. I fell asleep instantly and dreamt of somewhere sweet on the other side of the rainbow.

Heart Palpitations, Twenty Questions and So-called competition...

Why Are Girls So catty?
November 21

I woke from my heavy sleep to the light grip of Romy's hand shaking my shoulder. "Zahra," she whispered, "Zahra it's eight." She held her cell phone out to me. "Mmmm," I groaned turning over onto my back. "Okay, Thanks Romy, do you mind passing my jacket?" I asked, in a crackly morning voice. "Sure," she said, halfway out the bedroom and into the hallway. She tossed my jacket on my bed lifting *his* scent of soap, and breeze and imaginary swirls of ocean blue danced in the air around me. I inhaled deeply, it was the perfect smell to wake up to. I sat up and took the piece of folded paper out of my jacket pocket nervously. "Relax," Romy chuckled, "you're so silly." I looked at her and half grinned, flipping open her phone and carefully dialling the numbers written on the piece of paper.

The phone began to ring and I worried that it was too early and maybe Adrian would still be sleeping. I began to panic and played with the thought of hitting the end button. Just then, the ringing stopped and I heard him fumble with the phone and exhale lightly into the receiver. I was sure I had woken him and felt terrible. Natalie began to stir and once she noticed that I was on the phone, she hopped out of bed and ran to the bathroom almost as though she suffered from a lingering case of food poisoning. We could hear the water running in the shower, she clearly just wanted to be first to get ready so she could preen herself like a peacock. Romy rolled her eyes and shook her head in disbelief. "H-hello?" he mumbled. I didn't respond. He cleared his throat and repeated, "Hello?" Romy motioned with her hand for me to speak. "Umm… hi," I said finally. "Well, good morning sunshine, I didn't think you would be up yet," he said. "Did I wake you?" I asked. "Yes," he answered. "Oh…I'm really sorry, I just thought that maybe you would have been shooting soon so I thought I would call…"

"Did you just wake up?" he asked.

"Yes."

"Well, that's all that matters then, you were supposed to call when you woke up remember?"

"Yes," I answered shortly.

"I'm glad you called actually, I have to get going, I'm going to be late for the shoot. I totally over slept and the other guys too. Oh bollocks! We're going to hear it."

"Okay well I won't keep you then…I can call you later," I said, trying to end the phone call. Romy scowled at me instantly for not asking him about the mountain. "Wait, what are you up to later?" he asked. "Actually, the girls wanted to know if we could… ah…maybe come up to the mountain and hang out there?" I asked in response to his question. "Well, sure. It's not my mountain," he laughed. I didn't know if he was brushing me off or if he was really meaning to be funny, but either way it stung a little. I didn't know what to say and was silent. "Are you there?" he asked after a few moments. "Umm, yeah I'm here." "When would you come up to the mountain?" he asked trying to figure out what went wrong in our conversation. "Um… we were thinking we'd leave here in… like an hour or so… we'd get there by…eleven…" I said, nervously awaiting his response. I felt so stupid having this conversation with him and totally over analyzed every second and every breath he took. "OH," he replied, surprised finally understanding my previous question. "Of course you can up to the mountain, I'd love to have you guys there. Of course. I don't know if they'll let you guys right on the set, but you could stay close by." "Okay, we'll ski or something I guess," I said, a little more lightheartedly. "Or maybe you could hang around the chalet…so I can see you in between takes…maybe…it's just a thought," he stammered. "All right, well you better get going so you're not too late and we'll see you soon," I insisted.

"Can't wait to see you love, bye."

"Bye," I blushed.

Natalie was out of the shower and fully dressed and practically ready to go. I handed Romy her phone back and she squeezed my fingers gently as the phone passed from my hand to hers. "What did he say?" Romy asked, ignoring Natalie's presence. "He said that he was looking forward to seeing us again." "DID HE?" Natalie burst. Both Romy and I looked over at her, in disgust. She had too much makeup on and her hair was perfectly tossed, flowing around her shoulders. So much for not going after him! "Well, I'm pretty sure I heard him say he couldn't wait to see *you*, my dear," Romy said, patting my hand, before rising from her seat on my bed and reaching for my arms, she pulled me out of bed. "You need to go get ready, I'll make us some breakfast and pack some snacks for the ride." Romy had taken advantage of being the first one up, she was dressed and ready as well.

I pulled out some clothes from the closet while Natalie applied more makeup to her face with a hand held mirror on the edge of her bed. I ignored her and went to the bathroom to freshen up.

I turned the water on and stepped into the hot, steamy shower. I remembered my last shower experience here, it was horrific. I remembered crying uncontrollably and trying my best to scrub away my pain. This time the water was a blessing as the warmth of the water washed over my body, and embraced me just like how I had been held last night in *his* arms. I smiled as I remembered his face, his smile, his warmth, but mostly his compassion. I hurried in the shower, the sooner I got ready, the sooner I'd be able to see him. I was clothed in a flash and wrung my hair dry as best as I could with my towel. I dressed my face up with just a little bit of make up, simple eyeliner, mascara, and a hint of blush. I checked myself over in the full length mirror, and for the first time in days I felt good about myself, for a few moments I had forgotten about the pain.

I wore a heavy cream coloured sweater and a pair of straight legged blue jeans. I pulled my hair back into a high ponytail and wore three sets of pearl stud earrings ascending in size in each ear. I planned to wear my furry winter boots Jonnæ bought for me on the reserve for my birthday last month to help stay warm up there on the mountain. I stepped out of the bathroom and walked to the dining area where Romy had set out pastries, jam, boiled eggs, bread, ham and coffee on the table. "That's what you're wearing?" Natalie asked surprised. "What's wrong with it?" Romy asked, "I think she looks great," she insisted. "I didn't want to look like I just came straight from Absinthe last night," I snapped at Natalie, as I sat down at the table.

I hated being so catty, it really wasn't the usual way I handled things, but Natalie was starting to get under my skin. I was defensive when it came to *him*, I felt the urge to protect him, to claim him as mine. I stared at Natalie sitting across from me with pure distaste. I didn't want Adrian to get hurt by Natalie who was only interested in him because he was a model. He was such a nice person with a good heart and the last thing he needed was Natalie sticking her talons in him. I wished she would just stick to her bartender, he would be a better match for her, not Adrian who was modest and reserved, thoughtful and self examining. She needed someone who was loud, almost as boisterous as she was, someone who was reckless with misguided confidence, not someone who would be embarrassed every time she shouted a response, not someone who was well-mannered and sincere. Then again, he wouldn't have been the type of guy I would go for either and yet there I was daydreaming of his face, his velvety voice, his warm breath and his perfect smile. I smiled as I thought of his face and hurried to finish my breakfast.

I fell asleep almost immediately when we pulled out of the driveway. I was exhausted from the night before and I took advantage of the long drive ahead. I was glad that I was awake for the last forty minutes of the trip so that I could take in all the picturesque views of the snow-covered hillsides and the beautiful Alps. We parked the car and got out to stretch our tired, aching muscles. Romy popped the trunk and took out her skis, ready to hit the slopes. She insisted that Natalie ski with her to give Adrian and I some alone time, though I assured her it was not necessary. Natalie, however, completely rejected the idea of leaving Adrian and I alone. She wanted to make up for lost time with him from the night before.

"Maybe you should call Adrian, let him know we're here," Romy suggested. "I CAN CALL…I mean…if you'd like," Natalie offered, stretching out her hand to receive the phone. Romy flashed me worried eyes, I shrugged my shoulders, Romy handed Natalie the phone. I took a few steps forward to hand Natalie the piece of paper with his number on it and she grabbed it from me quickly, flipping open the phone and dialling the long set of numbers. I walked over to Romy to help her carry her gear, while we waited for Adrian to answer the phone.

Natalie started twirling her fingers through her hair, "No it's Natalie," she bubbled into the phone obnoxiously excited. "Hi Adrian…yeah…she's…here," she looked over at me with hollow eyes. "…yeah sure," she said in an almost whisper. She stretched forward and handed me the phone. "He wants to talk to *you*," she snarled, defeated, scowling at me under her breath. "Looks like we know who he's chosen!" Romy sang, she didn't care if Natalie was upset. I took the phone and raised it to my ear, ignoring both of them. "Hi," I said softly, relieved. "Hey love, I was beginning to think you weren't coming anymore when I heard Nicole's voice on the line," he too was relieved. "Where are you now?" he asked. "We're here, just by the car." "Come to the chalet, I'm just having a coffee." "All right, see you in a few, bye."

We headed toward the chalet in the distance and to my dismay the only way to get to the building was to ski down a small hill. Natalie, Romy and I stood at the top of the hill looking down at the chalet. Romy set herself up to put on her skis and Natalie decided to do the same with the spare pair Romy brought with us. She was definitely going to try one last attempt at impressing Adrian, but I was almost certain it wouldn't make a difference to him, he didn't even get her name right…again! I had no other option but to slide down on my sit-bones. Romy and Natalie headed down first, both with much grace and ease. Back home Natalie was enrolled in ski lessons which she attended twice a month in Whistler. I however, had no interest in activities that could cause me bodily harm so skiing definitely was not my thing.

I sat down on the cold snow, trying my best to cover my jeans with my jacket and gave myself a little push. As I slid over the little hump, there he was standing at the bottom of the hill with Natalie and Romy. He was assisting Natalie with her skis, helping her unclip the ski boots from the boards, holding her hand to help stabilize her. I approached the end of the little slope feeling awkward and embarrassed, wishing that he was inside of the chalet and not standing there witnessing my disgraceful display. I came to a stop at his feet, falling over onto my side. He waited there patiently with his perfect smile on his face and laughed lightly as I lost my balance. He extended his arms toward me, bent down slightly and pulled me to my feet. "That a girl," he said, with a huge grin on his face. "Was that fun?" he asked, leaning over me to help brush the snow from the back of my jacket as I wiped the snow from my behind. "Yeah, tons," I replied sarcastically. "Do you not ski?" he asked. "Not a chance!" "So then why'd you tell me you girls would be skiing up here today when I spoke to you earlier?" he enquired. "I meant *they* would ski and I... well I would be doing the something else, like sit in the chalet," I admitted jokingly and very embarrassed. "Well, you look smashing," he complimented, taking my hand like a true gentleman and walking me into the chalet. "Shall I order you a coffee or something?" he asked, "how about you girls? Coffee?" he asked, addressing Natalie and Romy who were trailing in behind us. "Sure," we all answered, we found a restaurant booth while he hailed a waitress. "Well, I guess I'm out of the running," Natalie sneered quietly to herself, she hated to lose at anything. "I guess I'll just have to check out the other models," she said, bouncing back to her normal cheery self immediately. Romy rolled her eyes and I pretended not to hear her.

Adrian joined us at the table and asked what our plans were for the day. Romy said she had intended to ski for a bit and Natalie expressed her desire to meet some of the other models. "I can take you over to the shoot whenever you're ready," Adrian told her and instantly she got to her feet. "What about your coffee?" Romy asked. "Who cares," she barked, throwing a few Euros down on the table. Adrian laughed and rose to his feet, telling us he'd be right back and escorted her out the door. "Well, I think I'll take my coffee to go," Romy insisted, "...give you guys some space," she finished winking at me and with that she was on her feet with her gloves in hand, asking the waitress to put her coffee in a takeaway cup. As she exited the chalet she gave me a thumbs up with a huge smile and disappeared.

A few minutes later, Adrian was back and sat down across from me at the table. "When do you have to return to the set?" I asked. "In about an hour or so, they'll come and get me, we're just about done." "Didn't you just get here?" I asked. "About forty-five minutes ago. There are some other models, some ladies that they want to shoot, so the guys have a short day today," he explained. "What are you modelling," I asked. "Winter coats." "Oh," I replied not knowing what else to say. "Yeah, apparently the coats are so warm you don't even have to wear shirts underneath them," he laughed, I joined him. "There it is." "What?" I asked, "Your smile, I love it," he said, taking a sip of his coffee. My face got warm and I looked down at the table, embarrassed. "So tell me about yourself…" I finally said after a few moments of silence.

"What do you want to know?"

"Hmm, I don't know…what's your favourite colour? What's your family like? Do you have any brothers or sisters? When's your birthday? HOW OLD ARE YOU? For starters."

"Okay…" he chuckled, "blue…but with green…like the ocean…."

"You mean like seafoam green?"

"Yeah that's right. My family—They're all right, yes I have siblings—two older sisters, they're twins, my birthday is February thirteenth, I'll be nineteen in three months, anything else?"

"Yes, what are sisters' names? Their age? Your parents names? What do they do for a living? What do you for fun? What school do you go to?"

"Do I get twenty questions next?" he asked. "No…sorry, not yet," I replied.

"Why not?" he asked stunned.

"'Cause I'm afraid I don't have any answers for you right now…" I said, with sadness written all over my face.

"Of course, I'm sorry love," he apologized taking my hand in his, stopping me from drawing circles on the table with my fingertip. He immediately decided to change the heavy atmosphere. He pushed the dark clouds away and answered my previous questions.

"Emma and Catherine, they're twenty-three and identical," he added in by his own admission. "Patrick and Sophie, dad is a stock broker, mom is a professor, teaches Osteopathy at the British College of Osteopathic Medicine. For fun—I really like to write poetry, is that lame? I play the guitar a bit, self taught though and I play the piano too, classically trained, maybe I'll take some guitar lessons one day. I think I'd like to try my hand at songwriting too, you know, turn some of those poems into songs. I go to a private boarding school called Queen Victoria College, just outside of London, I'm technically finished high school, but I'm taking some prep courses for Uni, it's my way of making my parents happy while I figure out what I want to major in, what else?" he smiled.

"Hmmm," I grinned, I enjoyed learning everything I could about him, he was intriguing, different from others and I wanted to take all of him in. "What's Osteopathy?" I asked. "It's a holistic approach to healing the body by using a range of manual and physical treatments. Did that help?"

"No."

He laughed. "Okay, let's see how else I can explain it. It's most commonly used for musculoskeletal problems like back pain, neck pain, leg pain I guess that sort of thing. My mum teaches that treatment of the bones, muscles and joints facilitate the recuperative powers of one's own body. They can even work on organs too. The goal is to help minimize or manage pain and disease. Understand?"

"Yes…I think. That's really cool."

"She can help mend a broken heart."

"*Can she?* Has she ever done it for you?" I asked.

"She hasn't had to," he winked. "Any other questions?"

"Of course," I said, pondering my next list. "Do you have any pets? Lucky number? Favourite song? Favourite movie? Band? Do you have a car? What's your favourite food? Drink? Do you like chocolate? Favourite outfit? Who's your best friend? *Girlfriend?*

"*GEEZ,* I don't know if I can keep up with all of that," he laughed. "Okay let's see, I have a pet, a Zebra Finch—when I was little I had a strange fascination with Tweety Bird so for one of my birthdays my parents got me a bird, his name is Elliot. Lucky number is four, it's the day of my birthday added together one, three, song—Smooth Criminal-Michael Jackson, movie—Donny Darko, band—The Cure. I have a car, a Renault Megane Coupe, Black. Food—Banoffee Pie, is that cliché? Chocolate's all right. The one you have on."

"What?" I asked confused.

"*You* asked: Favourite outfit—*I* answered, the one you have on," he clarified smiling slyly.

"Fine," I surrendered, "I guess that answer is acceptable. Continue," I said, motioning with my hand for him to finish answering the questions.

"Where was I?" he asked.

"Umm…best friend," I replied.

"Oh yes, hmmm, I don't really have one, there's no one I really open up to, well except for you I guess," he said, looking at me under his long eyelashes, one side of my lips dimpling forming a bashful grin. "…and girlfriend," he continued "well that's yet to be determined, we'll see how that goes…" He said, looking away from me a little embarrassed.

Did he mean me? I wondered to myself, could I ask him to clarify? Or would that make me seem daft? I was too nervous to ask so instead I just smiled a tooth-hidden smile, he wasn't looking at me anyway.

"Anymore?" he finally said breaking the silence.

"Yeah, just one," I responded playing with a packet of sugar, "how much longer do I have with you?" the words were almost painful to say, I couldn't fathom him not being there with me, the reality of it was unbearable. He looked at me with pained eyes and said, "Just another day, I'm leaving Tuesday morning… I'm sorry."

I bit my lip to help fight back the tears that I could feel collecting at the base of my eyes, I looked away. He moved to the empty seat beside me in our chalet booth. "I hope we can stay in touch. Maybe you can visit me in London," he said softly. The lump in my throat was too deep to muster up a vocalized answer. All I could do was nod my head as my face was buried in my hands. I lifted my head and looked at him from the corner of my eye, Adrian was fidgeting with his hands, he didn't know what to do. I had created an awkward moment and quickly needed to mend it. That's when I realized that his cream coloured sweater looked just like mine. "You like my outfit 'cause it's the same as yours don't you?" I asked in between sobs. He cracked a smile and placed a hand on my back while he laughed lightly and said, "Yes. It looks much better on you I have to admit."

"When will I see you again if you're leaving Tuesday morning?" I asked. "I can see you tomorrow, when you're finished class," he suggested. "We don't have any classes tomorrow. I mean we're coming back up here to the mountain. We're not going to any classes for the next two weeks, we're just touring the country," I told him. "What time will you be back on the mountain?" he asked. "Our bus leaves at eight thirty in the morning, we'll probably be here by like ten or eleven," I suggested. "I'm sure Ruben will have the driver take a detour so we can take in some sites along the way," I continued. "Who's Ruben?" Adrian asked. "Oh he's just our tour guide. He came over here with us from White Rock, he's planned all of our excursions while we're here for the six months." "Brill! well I'll be here tomorrow all day finishing up the shoot so I can meet you back here in the chalet since I know you won't be skiing," he suggested. "I would love that," I replied. "Me too sweetheart, me too," he said, placing his arm around my shoulders. I could have died there in his arms with no regrets, and then the moment was over, just as quickly as it had begun. He was called back to the set, and I was left there alone.

A few hours later, after I had placed my head down on the table and fallen asleep, Adrian woke me up and told me that it was time to go. The sun was low which meant it was late afternoon. He helped me up and we walked hand in hand back over the little snow covered hill and to Romy's car. In the near distance, I could see Romy approaching on skis and Natalie hanging off of her new model hunk's arm acting like a complete ditz. I stood facing Adrian who was leaning with his back against the car and rolled my eyes. He could read my expression clearly and smiled. He pulled my arm and I flung forward, he guided me to lean on the car next to him.

"I want you to take this," he said, quickly handing me another small piece of folded paper. "What is it?" I asked. "Look," he insisted. On the paper it read in his neat, careful writing:

Adrian J. Scott
Queen Victoria College
West Chambers room 318
North Yorkshire
Yo28 7SS
AJScott213@gmail.com

"Please write to me soon," he said. He stood in front of me and placed his hands on my shoulders. "Of course," I promised. working to fight back my tears while biting down on my lip a little too hard with full awareness of the slight taste of blood.

"Hey guys," Romy greeted with a smile. "Hey Romy, how were the slopes?" I asked. Trying to push back any of that sadness that I was feeling. "Awesome! How was *your* day?" she asked, I blushed, "Great." "So Adrian, we were wondering if you wanted to come by for dinner tonight?" Romy asked, my eyes widening. She smiled and nodded at me. "I'd love to," he answered. We waited for Natalie and her 'catch of the day' to reach the car and Adrian and I quickly claimed our spots in two of the back seats. We figured Romy would invite Natalie's friend over for dinner as well and since there were only three spots available in the backseat and we weren't going to let them sit together while Adrian and I sat apart. Besides, Natalie would forget all about this guy once he left Austria, I'd be surprised if she even remembered his name right now.

She was definitely angered when she saw us sitting in the back, me curled up in Adrian's arms. She decided to sit in the passenger seat in the front with Romy and her model sat with us in the back directly behind Natalie's seat. Natalie was silent the entire trip home. Adrian told funny stories to help bide the time that it took to get back to Romy's.

We arrived back home at nine-thirty, it was dark outside and Romy's parents had already moved on to their bedroom to retire for the evening, they started work very early in the morning. They owned one of the local bakeries in Vienna, they always left the house by five in the morning so that they could start baking before they opened the doors for business at seven a.m.

Romy and I went to the kitchen to pull out the leftovers while Natalie showed her 'catch' our shared room. We looked at each other and shuddered at the thought of what could be happening behind those closed doors. My 'disturbed' thoughts were interrupted by Adrian, offering to give Romy and I a hand with dinner and I couldn't have been more thankful. Number one, so that my mind would continue to be distracted and number two, because the faster we got the food on the table, the less damage could be done in our room.

We had the food out in no time and Romy lost at 'Rock, Paper, Scissors' so she had to go get Natalie and the model from our room while Adrian and I sat down at the table. He took the seat across from me and I scowled at the empty seat beside me. He laughed lightly and said, "I want a clear view, that's all." "Fine," I retorted. He studied my face intensively and my eyes followed his memorizing every line, dimple, hair, and colour of his face. He sighed, "God, I'm going to miss you," he said wearily, reaching his hand across the table to take mine. I tried my best to fake a smile and placed my hand in his. He lifted both our hands to his lips and kissed my curled fingers. I wanted to lean over the table, grab his face and embrace him, kiss him passionately, relentlessly, but I resisted the urge. That didn't seem to be the basis of whatever kind of relationship this was turning out to be and I didn't want to ruin anything, not with him leaving so soon, there wouldn't be enough time to mend anything.

We all sat down, ate, drank, talked, laughed and got to know each other better. Eventually Romy went off to bed and Natalie and her friend headed back to our bedroom much to my dismay. Soon everyone had disappeared and only Adrian and I remained at the table. With him, there was no need to fill every moment with dialogue. There wasn't any awkward silence anymore, even after just a few days of knowing each other. We were peaceful together, more then content, happy, and I was afraid to find out what the next few days would be like once he was gone. We enjoyed the silence as I knew in my heart that words were not necessary. We had everything we needed.

He stood up slowly extending his hand to me, inviting me to stand and take his. I rose from my seat and walked around the table to join him. He led me to the couch where we sat together. He sat first, I curled up next to him and tucked my legs under myself.

I wanted to embrace him, to reach out and touch him, to kiss him, I mean he was leaving in a day for crying out loud, but I didn't have the guts. He patted his leg, I laid down resting my head on his lap.

"What are you thinking?" he asked.

"Nothing—"

"Now that's a lie, *liar.*"

"Did you just call *me* a liar?"

"Yes. I believe I did love," he laughed.

"That's not very nice."

"Well, it wasn't very nice when you called me one the other day," he pointed out.

"Yeah, but you *were* lying."

"That's not fair. I just wanted to get you a drink. Which, I might point out I eventually did!" he stated as a matter-of-factly. I was glad for the distraction, maybe he'd forget about his first question, I didn't want to tell him what I had been thinking. I felt ridiculous about the whole situation.

"So are you going to tell me what you were thinking?" he asked. Damn it. I shook my head. "Okay then, well if you won't tell me what you're thinking, then I think it's only fair that I get to ask you some other questions."

I froze, my body stiffened like a block of ice laid across his lap. He played with the puff of my curls that came out of my ponytail at the top of my head and pulled the band free allowing my hair to spill out all over his lap. He ran his fingers through my hair in response to my tension. "Relax sweetheart, nothing too personal, but the basics like you asked me, okay?" "Okay," I reluctantly replied in an almost whispered tone.

"Ready? Let's see, favourite colour? Number? Day of the week? Band?"

That's it?"

"For now, I'll let you answer those first."

"My favourite colour is cream, ivory-ish…yeah I know it's boring but I love the warmth of it, the fact that it goes well with everything, the cleanliness it possesses and it's also the colour of a canvas. A clean slate waiting to be dressed with a multitude of colours, you know? My number is nine, I don't know why it just is, what day is today?"

"Sunday."

"Then Sunday is my favourite day," I answered looking upside down at him, smiling gingerly. "And my favourite band…I have a couple…I like this Canadian band called Global Rhythm and this other Canadian rapper called K-OS, I also really like Daft Punk and Basement Jaxx. I think I can handle a few more."

"I like Basement Jaxx, Daft Punk too, you'll have to let me hear this Global Rhythm. I'm glad we have some things in common, and *seafoam green* and ivory are quite complimentary don't you think? Anyway, I noticed at dinner you didn't eat the schnitzel…"

"I'm a vegetarian."

"Really? Well, that's good to know, how come?"

"Why do you eat meat? It's just a lifestyle choice, I've always been one, Jonnæ's a vegetarian and since she's my mo— since she practically raised me I guess she just raised me as a vegetarian too."

"Makes sense. Do you ever desire to eat meat?"

"No, not really. I've wondered what certain things taste like, but I can't miss something I've never had. What else?"

"Yes. Earlier today you asked me if I had a girlfriend, why? Does it matter?"

"Of course it matters!"

"Why?"

"What do you mean why? I'm pretty sure you're girlfriend wouldn't appreciate me laying here like this or you playing with my hair don't'cha think?"

"Yes, I s'ppose you have a point, was that the only reason?"

"Well, no—I—I just—needed-to-know-for-my-own-personal-reasons-that-I-do-not-want-to-discuss-with-you-right-now. Next question, *please!*"

He laughed. "Why are you so uncomfortable talking about this? Don't you think it's important?"

"Yes, I do…I'm just…scared," I admitted. "Of me?" he asked. "Not of you, of the situation I guess, I don't know Adrian, I'm so messed up right now…"

He shifted, forcing me sit up. I turned to face him on the couch and he took my hands in his, looking deep into my eyes.

"Zahra, listen to me, you don't have to worry about anything with me, I know things are difficult for you right now. You need you to know that I'm here for you. You don't have to worry. Okay?" he curled his fingers through mine and smiled, energy sparked between our palms, our fingers, adoration surged through our veins.

"Thank you," I mouthed, overwhelmed, what were these feelings? *Could* this be love? How was it possible to feel like you couldn't live without someone you'd only known for a few hours. How was it possible to fall *so* hard. I wrapped my arms around his neck and hugged him tightly. He wrapped his arms around my waist. How would I make it without him next to me?

"Do you really have to go?" It was a stupid question to ask, I already knew the answer. "Zahra if I could stay believe me I would, but I have to get back to school too." "When will I see you next?" I asked anxiously. "Tomorrow, on the mountain," he chuckled softy, lightening the mood. "We'll work the kinks out later, let's just enjoy every moment we have now," he whispered heavily. We were locked in each other's arms, lost in the moment, caught up in the scent of each other's skin, the texture of each other's hair, the warmth of each other's bodies. It was overwhelmingly perfect…until I yawned.

"I think it's time you got some sleep love," he pulled away slowly. "I know, I don't want you to leave yet," I pleaded. "All right, I'll stay until you fall asleep. I'll go get your blanket, I'm sure you don't want to sleep in your room tonight," he said, making a disgusted face. "Yeah you're right…I forgot about Natalie and—" "Drew," he filled in. "Right. I'm not sure I want *anything* from that room really," I admitted. He laughed nonchalantly, but the tension in his neck betrayed him, said otherwise. He headed to my room. He returned within minutes and reassured me that the couch was my best option. (★)[7] He brought my blanket over and took his place on the couch so I could use his lap as my pillow and I closed my eyes. I drifted away into a deep sleep filled with vivid, colourful dreams about a better life, a happier time. I sighed, he was all I wanted, I was in heaven. Yes, heaven and then as quickly and as vividly as the dreams began, they faded and in my subconscious I knew he was gone.

---

[7] Heaven (Candlelight Mix)- DJ Sammy ft Yanou

Pen Pals?
November 22

I was awoken by the bright light in the kitchen and I heard Romy's parents quietly stirring about, preparing coffee for themselves and breakfast for the three of us girls, before they headed to the bakery. I was laying on my back, on the comfy couch, just looking up at the blank ceiling, feeling blank myself. I needed to make some decisions about my life, but I just wasn't ready to face it. I had a feeling that once Adrian left and went back to London, there would be no more distractions. I quickly closed my eyes and pretended to be sleeping as Mila walked by, she'd only feel awful knowing that she woke me up. I could spare her the guilty conscience.

  Mila and Fredrik were talking amongst themselves, wondering why I was sleeping on the couch. I turned to hide my face, I tried not to purse my lips together, recalling what had transpired in my room just a few hours ago. They saw me move and quickly collected their things and headed out the front door. Minutes later, I slowly rose to my feet, stretching each muscle in my body and crept quietly to my room to grab my towel. I decided that it would be best to avoid as much confusion as possible. It was our first day of school, we needed to make things flow. As I passed by the kitchen, I looked at the clock, it said it was just three minutes past five in morning. It was early, but there was no way that I would be able to fall back asleep, my mind was too alert. Romy and Natalie wouldn't be up for at least another hour, I had plenty of time to get ready.

I showered slowly, got dressed and brushed my wet hair. I wasn't sure what to do with it today, it was my last day with Adrian and I wanted to leave a beautiful image of myself in his mind. I pinned my hair up in all kinds of twists and twirls and then took it out. I put it up in a messy knot at the back of my head, and then took it out smoothing out the kinks. It still wasn't right. I tried a ponytail, no good, then half up half down, which wasn't a bad style and I almost kept it until I thought back to the last few hours when I had been resting my head in his lap. He had pulled the hair-tie out of my hair creating a free flowing mop of curls that graced almost the middle of my back in perfect twirling layers creating a puff of curls, like a lion's mane, with glistening bronze and gold wisps of colour around the top. I knew he'd love whatever I did, but this, this would be perfect.

As I brushed through my hair, flashes of memories rolled through my mind. *You can call me whatever you want*, he said, on the night we met. *I bought you this drink*, was how it all got started. I knew that I would have to hold onto those memories with every fibre of my being. I did not know when I would see him again. I tried to push the crestfallen thoughts down again, it wasn't the time or the place. I had to fight against the forces that wished desperately to drag me into a deep depression. I needed for the sake of my sanity not to dwell on the fact that Adrian was leaving because I knew he wasn't abandoning me. He wasn't my family.

It was not his fault, he hadn't done anything wrong and I knew it wasn't fair to feel the same sort of helplessness I'd felt over the situation back in White Rock. Adrian wasn't like them, he was good and pure and I needed to honour that by enjoying every last second we had today.

It was just five-forty-five in the morning when I was completely ready, I still had at least fifteen minutes before Romy and

Natalie dragged themselves out of bed. It was too early for my body to register that it needed food and I didn't want to eat breakfast without the girls, my sis—err—mo—Jonnæ taught me better than that. I went back over to the couch, folded my blanket and put the couch's ornamental pillows back in place. I was going to watch TV but realized it would be too loud, so I picked up a book that was sitting on the coffee table, it was in German. I put the book down, there was no point in looking through it, the words were just jumbled letters to me.

Under some other books and magazines that there was a notepad sticking out. I shifted the books aside and removed the pad of paper and looked for a pen. Once I had a pen in my possession, I started doodling. It had been three days since I used any sort of drawing material and I was beginning to feel out of touch. My fingers itched to curl around a drawing device, the ink stains fading on my fingertips, the natural colour of my fingertips foreign to me. Art was my release, my freedom, and I wasn't surprised at how quickly I filled the page with abstract images fuelled by my despair. In the centre of the chaos, I drew a single eye, it was a beautiful eye, so alive and so clear, like it was reaching, looking into my soul, seeing me for who I was before and after the storm of confusion that filled my life, passed. It was *his* eye. I flipped the page over and began to write.

Adrian,

You've just left Austria and are obviously back in London now, maybe a day or 2 already. I miss you! Though I'm upset with the forces of nature that our time together was so short, I'm thankful regardless that I had any time with you at all, that I got the chance to know you and that you are now a part of my life.

It's crazy how things happen huh? I never thought I'd ever have a pen pal, I always figured I would be terrible at it, but with you I know it'll be different. Though I know you're just reading this, I know that I've been anxiously waiting for a letter back in the mail from the moment I dropped this one off. I can almost hear you laughing at me as you envision me losing my mind waiting for your reply (it's not funny!!)

Did I mention I miss you? I know you have school, and I have school, and life must go on yada, yada, yada, but—I wish I had the power to stop everything for just a while so that we could extend our time together. I guess I'm just not ready to let you go yet. Maybe in time that will happen, maybe not. I always find it amazing how life works, how you could know someone for what seems like forever and in an instant find out that you really didn't know them at all and then meet someone else and click with them right away, be comfortable with them like you're old souls reuniting after years of separation. I feel that way with you and with Romy. In only a few days I feel like the two of you know me better than probably anyone I know and I'm happy for that.

On another note, a more serious one: If you get back to England and decide that you want nothing to do with me, I totally understand. I'll be the first to admit that my life is a little complicated right now. I honestly wouldn't hold it against you if you felt that way too. I figured it was important to at least be able to thank you for touching my life, if only for a little while. You are truly special and one of a kind and I'm grateful that I had the opportunity to share a little bit of time with you, to know you. If you'd like to stay connected I would love that very much, but I'm leaving the ball in your court this time. I want you to decide with a clear mind if I'm worth it, because right now I sure don't feel like I am. Anyway, I hope you had a safe journey home and that everything remained in well working order in your world while you were in mine. Say hi to Elliot for me!
Always,
Z

I finished my letter and folded it, looking for an envelope. I found one in a drawer in the kitchen and placed the letter inside. The lights in the both bedrooms were on, Natalie and Romy were finally waking up. I slipped the letter into my back pocket and covered it with my shirt. I wasn't in the mood for anything Natalie had to say. I tried to make myself look busy in the kitchen, I filled the percolator with water and coffee grounds, Romy would definitely appreciate this, Natalie too, although I doubt she'd say anything complimentary. I put the pastries that were brought home from the bakery in the toaster oven to warm, as Natalie skipped by flashing me a smile and a nonchalant, "Good morning." "—Morning," I waited for her to close the bathroom door. When I heard the shower faucet turn on I hurried to our room and found the little piece of folded paper, the second piece Adrian had given me, the one with his address on it. I went back to the coffee table in the living room and removed the envelope from my back pocket. I wrote his name and address as elegantly as I could across the front.

"What are doing?" Romy's voice interrupted, peering over the couch, "Oh…" I said startled. "Writing a letter to Adrian, I'm going to send it to him today in the mail." I knew I could be honest with Romy, she didn't have a judgmental or condescending bone in her body. And after several months of written correspondence between the two of us, before I arrived in Austria, I knew she would appreciate the sentiment of a written letter. We had grown so close through those letters, letters that Natalie had opted out of writing, it was no wonder she and Romy were not that close at all.

"Oh well here," Romy said, writing her full address out for me on the pad of paper. "Thanks Roms," I replied with a smile, she was always so understanding. I sealed the letter while Romy found me a stamp and together we finished off the letter to Adrian. I could tell that Romy wanted this just as badly for me as I wanted it for myself.

The three of us ate breakfast, well Romy and I *tried* to eat breakfast while Natalie didn't spare a single detail about her night with Drew, whose name by the way she couldn't remember. I sat across from her, sipping my coffee and picking at the croissant, watching her talk, not listening at all. Her voice was just a murmur in the background and her hands waving around were just a blur as my mind examined her and wondered what happened to the Natalie *I* knew? Where did she go? And when did she get so lost? Was it really only a few days ago or was it some time before and I just hadn't noticed. Maybe *I* was the bad friend. I had been feeling hostility from her but maybe she was simply lashing out at me, for not noticing the turmoil in *her* life because I was so wrapped up in mine.

    After we finished breakfast and quickly tidied the kitchen, we headed out the door to get to school with a bit of time to chat with friends and pick seats on the long bus ride back up to the mountain. We stood outside in the cold early morning frost waiting for the local bus to come and drop us off in front of the school. As we stepped onto the bus and found three seats I started to realize that this was the beginning of my adventure. Being around Romy, her family, even Adrian felt too familiar. But, getting on the public transit bus, figuring out how to pay my fare, finding a seat amongst all the German speaking people, riding through the city, passing all the bus stops, that was where my journey began and when my life was bound to change.

    We arrived at the school at eight o'clock in the morning, giving us thirty minutes of spare time. "I have to run into that store over there," Romy said, pointing in the direction of what looked like a convenient store next to the school. "Okay, would you like us to go with you?" I asked, "No, no I'll just be a second, you guys go and get us good seats on the bus," she insisted. Natalie was already heading toward the school, probably to go and find Jason to claim her seat with him on the bus with the assumption that Romy and I would want to sit together. Before I could turn to follow Natalie, Romy stopped me and asked for my envelope, she took it from me and winked. "Thanks Romy," I said with much gratitude. I hurried to follow Natalie, I wanted to let her know that I hoped to sit with her on the bus. I figured that it would be the perfect opportunity to ask if there was something going on with her that she wanted to talk about. Just because I was going through some emotional issues, didn't mean that I couldn't be there for my friends. I knew that I couldn't do anything without the help of my friends. I needed them just as much as they needed me.

I was too late. Natalie had already teamed up with Jason I'd have to talk to her later. But when? It would be almost impossible once were on the mountain, she'd be tangled up with Drew and I would be with Adrian. Jut outside of the school was coffee hut. I walked over to it and bought two hot chocolates, my peace offering to Natalie. I hoped that we would have a few minutes to at least open up the dialogue between us. I called her over and she came willingly enough. I handed her the hot chocolate, she accepted it graciously. I walked over to a bench a bit away from the crowd of students waiting to get on the bus and Natalie followed. "What's up?" she asked as we sat. "Nothing really...Just wondering how you're doing I guess, you know like if there's anything going on. We haven't really had a chance to talk since we got here." "Are you seriously asking me if there's something wrong with *me*?" she spat back. "Don't you think *I* should be asking *you* that question? We both know you're hiding something Zahra and you won't tell me what it is. We're supposed to be friends remember? Best. Friends."

I was a little taken aback, her attitude toward me and her fight for Adrian who I knew she didn't really have any interest in, had all been fuelled by her hostility toward me over my own tortured existence. "Well, as my friend aren't you supposed to be understanding?" I demanded, trying not to lose my temper. "Aren't you supposed to give me time so that when I'm ready I can come to you? Aren't you supposed to be selfless, I mean this isn't about you Natalie!" I yelled.

"So you admit that something's up then," she said victoriously, clearly feeling like she won the battle, she reminded me of Joanne, Natalie wore her supremacy like the newest shade of lip-gloss. "When you decide to truly be my friend Natalie, maybe then I'll open up to you, but I'm not giving you anything to gossip about," I retaliated, I stood up, knocking the hot chocolate out of her hand, it hit the floor splashing at her feet, I walked away. She was left behind, yelling profanities at me, I didn't turn back to look at her. I walked towards the bus in shock. What had just happened? Did I just turn my closest friend into my biggest enemy?

"Zahra what's wrong?" Romy asked, meeting me half way back toward the bus. She looked over my shoulder at Natalie who was cursing and wiping off her hot chocolate, stained tan suede boots. I felt bad for ruining her boots, it really wasn't my intention. The old Zahra would have insisted on buying Natalie new boots— and Natalie would have gladly taken them—The old Zahra would undoubtably feel guilty every time Natalie wore the new boots. The old Zahra would *never* have knocked the drink out of Natalie's hand in the first place despite anything Natalie had said or done. But the new Zahra told herself that Natalie could easy wash the boots, they needed to be cleaned anyway, covered in old salt stains. The new Zahra was starting to see Natalie for who she really was.

I couldn't believe that this person I had known for fifteen years had become a complete stranger in a matter of days, at some point she'd have to recognize that things couldn't always happen in her favour. Had it always been like this? Had our friendship been based on…well, nothing?—on Natalie and Natalie alone?—What did this mean for Jason and I? I would never want him to choose, that was completely unfair, Jason and I had classic movies, indie bands and longboarding in common. With Natalie he had popularity, designer clothes and girls at his feet. He was one of the most popular guys in our school and she, his equivalent. Guys and girls would line up if they had to, to date Natalie or Jason, they had it all —and just as I had suspected, in the future, Jason would trail off leaving both Natalie and I behind—

"Romy, don't worry about it, it's just Natalie," I said. "She just pissed me off." I tried to smile, my smile failed me. "Oh…" was all Romy could say, without knowing what the argument was about.

She turned to walk back to the bus with me and handed me a small package. "What's this?" "Open it," she insisted. I pulled the simple wrapping back and exposed a stack of antique looking paper, tea-stained, darker around the edges with faint lines for writing. Included was a matching stack of envelopes and a nice black inky pen. "What's this?" I asked surprised. "Well, I know your birthday just passed and I never got you anything so I figured since you're planning to write good old fashioned letters to Adrian you might as well have the tools! I also bought a set for Adrian too," she answered excitedly. "Oh Romy, that's the sweetest thing anyone has done for me, thank you!" I wrapped my arm around her shoulders and pulled her in for a side hug. "But Adrian doesn't know that I sent him a letter, I kind of wanted it to be a surprise…and then if he didn't want to write back he wouldn't have to…" "Are you crazy? Of course he's going to write back," she laughed, "I'll just tell him it's a gift from me to him, no big deal, don't worry about it!" she assured. "Romy, you're the best," I smiled, I had almost forgotten about Natalie.

The paper ignited a new energy within me. I wanted to write another letter to Adrian, to rip up the previous note, the one filled with uncertainty and awkwardness and write a new one filled with unashamed emotion and passion that left him wanting more, waiting impatiently for my antique envelope that would stand out against his other mail…but Romy had already put my mismatched letter in the mail. It was too late. If he wanted to hear from me again, the next letter would be so much better, it would have to be. I couldn't waste such elegant paper on useless mumble jumble. Just then Romy's cell phone rang, and she handed it to me saying, *"It's for you."*

"Hello?" I answered.

"Sleep well?"

"Yes, until you left."

"I'm sorry love, I didn't think Romy's parents would appreciate me sleeping there with you in the morning," he laughed.

"I guess you're right—"

"No phones, time to get on the bus," Ruben interrupted. "Okay, just one minute please," I answered annoyed.

"I won't keep you love, just wondering when you think you'll be on the mountain?"

"We're leaving now so I think we should be there in a couple of hours, like eleven-thirty or twelve."

"Okay. I'll most likely be done around that time so I can meet you at the chalet and we can have lunch. What d'you think?" he asked.

"Sure, AJ, that would be great," I said, with a smile in my voice. Natalie pushed passed me deliberately almost knocking the phone out of my hand as she got onto the bus.

"AJ?" he chuckled in surprise.

"I'm sorry, I just—"

"No, I like it," he said.

"PHONES. NOW!" Mr. Woods snapped. Romy and I were the only two not yet on the bus. "Adrian, I have to go, I'm being yelled at," I said irritated. "Okay *Zar*, I'll see you soon love, bye." "Bye…" I quickly handed the phone back to Romy and we ran onto the bus.

As we reached the top of the stairs, we noticed that all eyes were on us. The teachers were peeved, the students looked annoyed, and of course Natalie looked furious. "Sorry," I said as we stepped into the aisle of the bus. All the seats were taken, everyone had already paired up and the only two seats available were single seats beside the staff in the front. I quickly sat down in the first empty seat and Romy did the same. I sat in the window seat, the aisle seat was occupied by a jacket and a bag. Mr. Nazuka sat down beside Romy after doing a final head count and just before the bus took off Ruben rushed onto the bus, shoving a cell phone into his pant's pocket and sat down in the seat next to me.

"Hey Zahra! Sorry I rushed you off of the phone like that, we just really need to get on the road. Were you talking to your family?" Ruben asked. "No. I was talking to a friend," I said a little bit annoyed. "...And if we're in such a rush, why did *you* get to talk on the phone then? I'm pretty sure I saw you putting *your* phone back into your pocket!" I was a little shocked at my tone, especially since Ruben, in a way, was a figure of authority and he had been so nice to me before.

"Yes, this is true, it was a bit of an emergency from back home," he explained. Instantly I felt terrible, "Oh, sorry," I said with full sincerity. "Is everything all right?" I asked. "Yeah, everything's fine. Nothing to worry about, nothing I'm worrying about anyway," he replied, "so... *A friend* huh? You've managed to make friends already in less than three days? Well, I can't say I'm surprised, you're a lovely girl," he said, with a compassionate smile. "Thanks," I said with a half grin, turning to look out the window. "So, what's the deal with your friend Natalie?" Ruben continued. Oh God, I thought, do I really have to endure this for the next few hours? "Nothing really, she's just pissed at me because she thinks I'm keeping something from her." "And are you?" he asked. "Well—" I didn't want to get into it with him, but I felt the same sort of ease with Ruben that I felt with Adrian, not the passion or the desire for him, but I felt like I could tell Ruben anything, like he actually cared about my well being. "Well, what?" he asked, waiting for me to continue. "Umm…well, it's not that I'm deliberately keeping things from her, I'm just not ready to talk about it with her and I get the feeling like she's just looking for some gossip anyway," I finished. "So it's more serious than what's gossip worthy huh? Anything you want to get off your chest? I promise I won't tell," he said. "No, no thanks," I replied apologetically. "No worries Zahra, just thought I'd ask, remember the offer still stands, if you ever do want to talk about it I'm here and not just for the next six months," he added with a friendly smile. "What I was really asking though, is she like… *into* me or something?" "Oh geez, sorry. I guess I should have realized that's what you were asking. Umm I'm not really sure anymore when it comes to Natalie. She's a bit all over the place. She thinks you're 'hot', her words. She also said that she would 'try' to get you, also her words, but I think she's backed off now. Besides she's already juggling a few guys right now. I don't know if she could handle anymore." "Geez! When did she have time to start juggling?" he asked with a smile. "I'm just glad she'll be leaving me alone. I'd really like to keep my job! The last thing I need is the staff thinking I'm messing around with one of the students," he laughed. I didn't. I nodded my head with an awkward grin.

"So, tell me about your friend, what's her name?" he asked. "Umm, *his* name is Adrian." "OH," he said, surprised and wide eyed. "Where'd you meet?" he asked looking a little uncomfortable. "Why does it matter?" I asked, bothered by Ruben's change of tone. I couldn't help but be defensive when it came to Adrian, he had so quickly become my knight in shining armour and no one was going to discredit that. "Sorry, didn't mean to hit a nerve," he said changing his tone again. "I met him the other night, we've been hanging out ever since." "Oh! That's nice that you've made a friend here," he said not so convincingly. "He's from London, he's going home tomorrow morning," I retorted still unimpressed with

Ruben's attitude toward the situation. "Oh…well," he clearly didn't know what to say and he almost sounded relieved to hear that Adrian was leaving which pissed me off even more. "I'm meeting him on the mountain," I said, intentionally trying to rub it in to make Ruben more uncomfortable, but instantly regretted it as soon as the words left my lips. "Well, I guess I get to meet him then!" Ruben perked up. Sounding triumphant. "Yeah…I guess," I answered, with blood boiling in my veins. "What's he doing up there? Just skiing or something, 'cause not to ruin your fun but this is a school trip so…" "He's doing a modelling shoot up there and he said he'd meet me at the chalet for lunch. I'm allowed to eat with a friend at lunch, aren't I?" I asked, sounding like a stubborn child. "A model huh? Well—" "Well what?" I snapped. "I don't know, I guess I never saw you as the type," he said. Was he trying to offend me? "He's not like that! He's not shallow and full of himself like you'd think. He's thoughtful, insightful…different," I clarified. "I'll take your word for it," he answered. "Sooo…you never answered my question, is it a problem for Adrian to have lunch with me?" I asked again. "No it shouldn't be a problem as long you participate in the class activities," he said, assuming authority. "Well, no offence Ruben but I don't ski so I wouldn't be participating in this activity anyway and tomorrow when Adrian's gone, I'll fully participate in anything you have planned, as long as I won't get hurt," I fought back with force. "Well, I can tell you really care about this guy," Ruben assessed, "…and I like how you think you're making the rules now," he said jokingly. "Yeah well we've become great friends in a short amount of time and I'm not trying to *make rules*, I'm just trying to be fair, what else would I do while other kids ski?" I pointed out. "Okay, well just be careful, I don't want to see you get hurt kiddo," he said with a tone I didn't care for. It made me uncomfortable and I turned my body slightly toward the window and looked out over the vast area of land. "Thanks," I said into the window, making it clear that our conversation was over.

I felt bad for shunning Ruben the way I did, he was such a nice person who clearly had good intentions, but I just didn't want to talk about my complicated situation with Adrian anymore and certainly not with him. I didn't want to have a complicated situation with Adrian at all. Didn't I deserve to have one thing in my life that was just simple? I should have known better that simple just wasn't in the cards it seemed for Adrian and me. He lived in London and I, well I lived here…for now anyway.

✳✳✳

The first hour rolled by slowly. Ruben occasionally got out of his seat to speak into the microphone pointing out different sites and landmarks along the way. At one point the bus stopped and we all got out to view a natural spring, where a lot of bottled water was sourced. Then we took a small hike on a trail before heading back to the bus. My mood had changed a little as we got closer to the mountain and I intended to mend whatever I had broken with Ruben when we got back on the bus. I knew I had to try again with Natalie too, but I wasn't ready to put in the effort at the moment.

I took my seat at the window in the front of the bus and waited for Ruben to check that all the students were on the bus. He made another announcement about being close to the mountain and pumped the students up for skiing before he sat back down. "You really like your job huh?" I asked, trying to show him that I wanted to make amends. "She speaks!" he joked, "I really thought you were never going to speak to me again," he continued. "Ha, ha very funny," I retorted sarcastically and waited for him to answer.

After a moment of silence he replied, "Yes I really do, I find all of these sites fascinating, the history behind them, the significance, you know that kind of stuff," he explained. "So did you come to Austria then, like before this trip?" I asked. "Yeah for sure, I was just here about a month and a half ago checking out all the places I'll be taking you guys to," he answered. "How long were you here for when you came?" I asked. He looked down, he seemed to be deep in thought, shame written across his face and said, "Too long."

  I waited but he didn't say anything more. "Why do you say that?" I asked trying to return the favour of lending a listening ear. "I hurt many people with the things I've done in my life. My family, my friends, even people who don't even realize I've hurt them have been affected by my decisions," he said solemnly. "Well, that doesn't make sense, how can you have hurt people who don't even know they've been hurt?" I asked, skeptical. "I assure you that it's possible Zahra, but that's not what you asked me. I was here for six months just like you'll be. Then I went home to White Rock to tie up some lose ends, visit some old friends that I haven't seen in…I don't know…years and then well you know the rest," he replied, trying to cheer himself and lighten the mood of our conversation. "So Ruben, what's your idea of fun?" I asked, trying to change the subject. "Let's see, I love to paint, mainly nature scenes, I feel like it's my duty to capture the beauty this land possesses. It's important to remember it or what is was before we start tearing down all the trees and ripping up all the open land to build houses and high rise buildings. I've been painting, I don't know…for years now, maybe for like twenty-three years or something," he said. "I paint too!" I chirped. "Oh yeah? Glad to see we have something in common," he said with a smile. "Well, I haven't been painting nearly as long as you…I wasn't even alive twenty-three years ago," I rambled excitedly. "Will you show me some of your work sometime?" he asked.

"Well…I can't really, everything's in White Rock…" I said non-enthusiastically. "You can always show me later, when we get back home," he pointed out, but the expression on my face showed no desire to ever return there and he quickly added "…or you can show me any new stuff that you've been working on." "Yeah…okay…I haven't really worked on anything yet…I need to get some supplies first I guess," I answered awkwardly. "You don't have supplies with you? But what if you get inspired on one of these day trips then what?" he asked. I opened my mouth, but nothing came out. How could I explain that I had fallen asleep with my sketchpad and pencil case on my bed, up sketching late the night before my departure and accidentally left it all behind in the frenzy of my escape. "Here," he said, reaching into his hand crafted brown leather messenger bag. He reached in and pulled out an average sized leather-bound book and handed it to me, his fingers as mine once were, ink stained. I took the book and opened it. Inside were pages of pencil, charcoal and water colour paintings. I scrolled through the pages in awe, Ruben was so talented, all of his pieces were precise and life like. I examined each one over and over, my fingers were careful not to smudge or smear anything.

"You're amazing," I said, handing him back his sketchbook. "No keep it, I have so many, I've packed a bunch of them in my suitcase and you need a book on hand to capture your inspirations," he said, pushing the book back towards me. "Oh Ruben, I can't take your book, you have pieces in here," I reminded him. "Keep them, maybe they'll help you get started," he said with a generous smile. "Thanks Ruben, that's really nice of you, will you teach me what you know sometime and maybe show me some of your other stuff?" I asked. "Of course kiddo, I'd love to work with you. I'm glad you like the book, it's the least I can do," he replied. "What does that mean?" I asked. "What?" he asked confused. *"It's the least you can do,*" I repeated. "… Oh, well I know something's been bothering you. Remember when I saw you crying on the plane? I just think maybe your art will help clear your head a little," he answered honestly.

    I felt my heart skip a beat as hot flashes filled my body and the thought of me crying on the plane resurfaced. I wish he never saw that, but there was no way to go back and change the past. "Well thanks again, I really appreciate it," I said, running my fingers over the picture embossed into the leather cover. "Where'd you get this book?" I asked, "it's beautiful." "It was a gift from my mother, she made it," he answered with a proud smile. "She *made* it?" I repeated. "Yeah, she's a crafty woman! She cut the leather herself and created the images on a press. See, here's the moon that represents my last name—Saka'am—shining over the boulder of White Rock, sitting on the beach," he explained, pointing out each picture with his finger. "See the wave crashing onto the rock?" he asked. "the beach is where my reserve is," he finished. "It's beautiful, the picture looks a lot like the one on my boots," I said, raising my furry mukluk boot to show him the image on the top of the foot area. "Oh yeah," he said, nodding his head slowly, "that's like my mom's signature picture, she most likely made your boots, her or one of my sisters," he answered. "She *made* them? My…Jonnæ… my…I got the boots for my birthday and I was told they were special," I said, flushed, knowing that he had heard me fumble with my words over what to call Jonnæ. I bit my lower lip hoping he wouldn't ask me who Jonnæ was and why I had such a hard time talking about her, but my luck was not that great. "They're special because it takes a long time to craft a pair, a pair with any real quality that is. My mom makes bags, leather books, Turquoise jewellery, dream catchers, boots, you name it, her stuff is very popular in White Rock. Who's Jonnæ?" he asked, "She was my sister, but now she's dead," I answered short, hoping to end the conversation there. It wasn't a lie *per say*, my *sister* Jonnæ was dead to me. She died days ago when I found out she was really my mother. I didn't have a sister, I was an only child. I was alone. "SHE'S DEAD?" he asked dumbfounded. But I didn't answer, I just looked away. "I'm so sorry," he said, "I'm really sorry to hear you say that…that she's dead…and for my reaction too, it just wasn't what I was expecting. I understand why you've been feeling the way you've been feeling then," he reassured, placing his hand on my shoulder. "Thanks. She's not really dead though…just figuratively," I answered looking back down at my new book. Just then we pulled into the familiar parking lot up on the mountain not giving Ruben a chance to prod any further.

 At the far end of the parking lot, there were huge white screens, lights and lots of people. Instantly, I knew it was Adrian and the other models and my heart skipped a few beats. The bus pulled up off to the side to allow the students to get off and I could see Adrian sitting with a beautiful girl on the hood of a very sleek black car. He was sitting up resting his arms on his knees. His hair was perfect, slicked back into a pompadour style and he had a stern expression on his face. Slightly squinted eyes, slightly puckered lips, head turned to the left exposing the right side of his face, his 'good side' I imagined. The bus pulled up and I could see a break in his concentration for just a split second and I laughed a little to myself. He was probably so embarrassed and I knew I would *have* to tease him about it later.

 "Guess that's your friend?" Ruben asked. "Yeah," I blushed, never taking my eyes off of Adrian through the tinted windows of the bus. He wore a grey winter sports jacket, left open exposing his bare chest with an off white coloured heavy scarf loosely around his neck and a pair of dark blue jeans. On his feet were black leather pointed toe boots with buckles and straps. As I watched him intensely, I remembered his joke from the other day about the shoot; *the jackets are so warm you don't even have to wear clothes under them!* I laughed again to myself this time so Ruben wouldn't hear.

The girl sitting with Adrian was lying across the hood of the car in a denim mini skirt, tall winter boots and cream coloured shirt covered by a red sporty winter jacket as well. She had the same expression on her face as Adrian did and I couldn't help but think how ridiculous the whole thing was. No wonder he was so hesitant to talk about his part-time job. "Who're they?" I heard one of the girls further back on the bus say out loud, not really looking for an answer. Everyone on the bus was on their feet preparing to exit the bus when Natalie took the liberty to answer the question, "The guy over there," she pointed at Drew who was waiting for his turn on the car, "that's my boyfriend," she said. I rolled my eyes and Romy shot me an annoyed look. I guess it was better than calling it what it really was. "So is Adrian *your* boyfriend?" Ruben asked mockingly. "*Nooo*, it's not like that," I responded giving him a friendly shove. He was becoming like an older brother to me and I was happy for that. I was getting pretty used to explaining or—not explaining—my relationship with Adrian as I wondered how long this non explanation would last for.

I got off the bus after most of the other students. Many of them were checking out the chalet, others were taking pictures of the mountains and each other, Ruben and the teachers were checking over lists and arranging for ski rentals for the students and about a dozen students were crowded around the photo shoot to get a closer look at the models. I hung back not wanting to get in the way, I was sure the set director would shoo everyone off shortly and I didn't want to be associated with that crowd. I was surprised to see Romy, but not Natalie up there with the small crowd, it just didn't seem like her to get all wrapped up in the hype, and then I noticed what she was doing. Adrian had just got off the hood of the car and was walking toward Romy, smiling. They exchanged a few words that I couldn't hear and she handed him the same package that she had given to me earlier. I could see him opening it and Romy explaining the package with large hand gestures and I tried not to make it obvious that I was watching. I turned my back slightly and started drawing images in the snow with my foot. At first the images were just swirls and then the swirls became the image from my new book and my boot, the image by Ruben's mom. Before I had a chance to realize it, my feet were no longer on the ground. "There you are!" Adrian swooned and picked me up and spun me around, butterflies rose up in my stomach as he put me back down.

When I was sure my feet were securely planted back on the ground, I wrapped my arms around his waist underneath his open jacket and bare stomach. "You're so cold," I shivered as my warm body touched his icy cold skin. "Guess the jacket isn't as great as we thought," I joked. "And I'm guessing you're going to warm me up then?" he asked as I held onto him with no sign of letting go. "Sorry…" I apologized easing up on my death grip. "No don't be, *I like it,*" he smiled slyly. "Don't think that guy likes it all that much though," he said turned us slightly so that I could see who he was talking about. "Ughh, that's Ruben," I sighed pulling away unwillingly from Adrian's icebox body.

"Ruben eh? Should I be jealous?" he asked. "No! Remember the tour guide I was telling you about?" I reminded him. "Oh yes, well he seems awfully protective of you or something," Adrian noticed, "I think he *likes* you," he teased. "Eww, Adrian. It's not like that," I said, quickly covering my mouth in shock at what had just come out of my mouth, eyes bulging. "What is it?" he asked.

"Nothing," I laughed to myself. I was surprised that I used the same four words I had grown accustomed to using whenever someone asked me about Adrian and now I was doing the same thing with Ruben, only this time I really meant it. "Is he coming over here?" Adrian asked a little bit confused. "Oh no…I forgot he said he wanted to meet you…" I frowned. "Meet me? Why…?" Adrian asked nervously. "I don't know…he's kind of taken it upon himself to be like my big brother…he saw me crying on the plane and now he won't leave me alone about it. Don't get me wrong, he's a really nice guy, he gave me this book to draw in and he said he would help me with my art if it helped ease some of the tension, he's just looking out for me. Be nice!" I explained, quickly as Ruben approached us.

I held the book in my hand and started showing Adrian Ruben's paintings and sketches in the black leather book pretending that Adrian and I hadn't noticed Ruben's descent upon us. "Hey guys," Ruben greeted, "what's going on?" he asked as though he hadn't seen anything. "Nothing, just showing Adrian your book," I pretended. "You mean *your* book," Ruben corrected. "Hi, I'm Ruben," Ruben introduced himself and extended his hand to Adrian. "Oh geez, I'm sorry," I said, ruffling my hand in my hair. "Ruben this is Adrian. Adrian, Ruben," I said to both of them. "Nice to meet you," Adrian replied, shaking Ruben's hand. "Likewise," Ruben answered with a friendly smile followed by an awkward silence. I could have sworn there was some tension. Ruben and Adrian were just staring each other in the eyes, jaws clenched. "Well…" Adrian started, breaking the unbearable silence, "I'm going to go get my shirt and put away my gift from Romy. Ruben, it was nice meeting you, Zar, I'll meet you in the chalet for lunch 'kay?" he finished, lightly squeezing my elbow, Ruben's eyes followed Adrian's hand watching it linger on my elbow before he lifted his eyes and smiled a disapproving smile at Adrian. "I'll be right in," I called out to him as he stepped away from the tense situation.

"He seems nice," Ruben concluded. "He is very nice Ruben so please don't patronize me...or him for that matter," I pleaded. He laughed lightly and agreed to back off. We walked together toward the chalet and Ruben called all the students together. The groups were divided into students who wanted to cross-country ski, those who wanted to go downhill and snowboard and the few that opted to hang out in the chalet or use the other facilities at the ski club like the swimming pool and hot tub area. Romy went off to downhill ski, Natalie followed behind Drew like a puppy and I went to find a table in the chalet.

I think about twenty-seven minutes had passed—not that I was counting—before Adrian walked through the door. A few girls stopped him and asked for an autograph, a picture, and phone number which I thought was weird and I could tell he felt the same way about all the attention. He wasn't a celebrity; he was just a guy modelling a winter coat for crying out loud. He blushed and put up his hands defensively as he pushed through the small crowd, embarrassed. Our eyes met briefly and he hurried over to the table and sat down. "Seems like you've got some fans," I teased.

"Yeah...right..." he answered, clearly discombobulated. "It just makes no sense to me, I'm nobody, just some guy sitting on top of a car in the dead of winter with no shirt on and a jacket," he rebutted.

I snorted.

"Did you just snort?" he laughed. I blushed, "I guess I did," I admitted. We both laughed as our coffees arrived. "I took the liberty of ordering you a hot drink," I announced.

"Oh thanks," he said, taking a sip of his black coffee. "...but I thought you were going to do the honours? I mean Ruben's off skiing now," he said, with a mischievous grin. I got up from my seat at 'our booth'—the same one we sat at the day before—and joined him on his side. He was sitting with half of his body leaning against the wall and one leg resting on the booth seat. I nuzzled into the space, sitting the same way that he was, leaning the back of my head against his chest and cupping my coffee in both hands. We sipped in silence paying attention to the rhythm of our synchronized breath and racing hearts.

"Are you ready to order?" the waitress asked, interrupting our perfect moment. It was definitely the most intimate we'd ever been and I was not impressed when it had abruptly ended. We ordered our food and sat upright at the table beside each other. Somehow this seemed to create an open invitation for others to join us. Two of the girls who had bombarded Adrian at the door were now sitting across from us at our table, introducing themselves while spewing a dozen questions at Adrian all at once. He was confused and I was annoyed.

As I watched this monstrosity in disbelief, barely paying attention or listening to the ridiculous questions from Amber and Courtney, I started to wonder what I should do, if anything. The old Zahra would sit quietly and let them ask as many questions as they liked, while silently suffering, nauseous with fear and self doubt while those two pretty girls from the popular crowd batted their lashes at the cute boy who was actually sitting at *my* table. The old Zahra would be fuming inwardly, yelling in my head, wishing those girl would go away, telling them that it was lame to assume that they were welcomed into our space and that they were embarrassing themselves. The old Zahra would stare at them dismally as they questioned Adrian about how we knew each other and in my mind I would be arguing that it was none of their business. I would have silently mocked them, I would have wanted to tell them to gain some self respect. I would have wished I had guts to voice my opinions. And as if a thin sheet of blurred translucent paper, separating me from reality had been lifted from in front of my face, my eyes focused. Amber and Courtney were trying to burn holes into my face with their poisonous glares and Adrian, both dumbfounded and intrigued. I had said these things out loud.

 Amber and Courtney immediately rose from their seats and gave me the ugliest looks they could construe on their faces and walked away mumbling profanities at me as they left the table. When they were out of sight, I could hear them talking about me with Natalie who had just entered the chalet with Drew, "…Oh Zahra, yeah I'm not surprised, she's become a real b—" I blocked the rest of Natalie's comment out. I put my head in my hands and moaned dolefully. I was so embarrassed, but not because I felt bad for telling Amber and Courtney off, but because I *didn't*. Adrian rubbed my back while he laughed about what had just transpired and joked that he should hire me as his body guard in case he ever got into any sort of trouble. I could just tell everyone off and they'd leave him alone for sure. "It's not funny!" I barked. "Oh c'mon you have to admit that it is, just a little," he insisted. "Why are you so upset about it?" he asked, "they deserved it, they were being rude," he pointed out. "I'm not really upset, I just…I feel bad that I don't feel bad," I explained taking my head out of my hands to look at him from the corner of eye. He was smiling, trying to contain his laughter. I joined him and we laughed.

 We ate our food and chatted, enjoying the quiet time we had together now that I had scared everyone else off. He told me about the gift from Romy, apparently she told him that I informed her about his poetry writing and we decided together to encourage him to continue writing by getting him a nice paper set…that just happened to come with envelopes. I didn't say much, I wanted him to find my letter in the mail when he got back home, even if my letter was silly. "You know what we need to do once we're off the mountain?" he asked. "No, what?" I asked, smiling gingerly in between bites of my delicious cheese fondue. "We need to get you a mobile phone," he answered happily. "A cell phone?" I asked. "Yeah, maybe one of those temporary ones to use while you're here, so I can call you in the middle of the night, send you text messages you know? We can't always use Romy's phone forever," he pointed out. "You're right," I replied, "but not a temp phone. I think I'll be here for a long time." I was happy that he really did want to continue to be a part of my life once he was back home, well, at least so it seemed. I still had my doubts. "Okay, so I'll meet you at the school and then we'll go get you a phone," he arranged. "And then you'll come over for dinner again?" I asked. "Of course I will, I'll stay as long as I can, maybe I'll even go get my luggage and bring it to Romy's so I'll leave from her place to the airport. How does that sound?" he planned. "That sounds awesome," I beamed, throwing my arms around him.

Was it possible that I was falling in love with him? I had never been in love before and it had only been a few days! I had been on a few dates, nothing serious though. I had even been on a couple of dates with Jason, but after our third date, we realized that we were much better as friends. We had never held hands, kissed or shared any sort of intimate moment. Our dates were even too casual to be considered 'dates'—unless you consider hanging out at the arcade killing zombies, romance—we knew it just wouldn't work. I wanted to be with Adrian though, but maybe I didn't love him. Was it possible to love someone so soon? Did I even know what it meant to love? I wanted to be able to define what we were, and not so that I could just call him my boyfriend or show him off like a fine piece of jewellery. Besides the term boyfriend just didn't seem to apply to him, he was something more than that. Being with him gave me a feeling I couldn't describe and I knew that if it was to ever work properly, I had to get my life sorted out first. I didn't want to leave room for error with Adrian. Deep down I could sense that there was something significant there.

    We continued to eat, swirling vegetables and pieces of bread around in the rich melted cheese. We drank hot Glühwein and then shared chocolate cake for dessert. We discussed tentative future plans and when we would try to see each other again. We thought about Christmas break, it seemed to have some potential and it was only about five weeks away, but in the end we knew it probably wouldn't work out. Adrian would be visiting with his family and I wouldn't be able to afford flying out to England. The conversation started to put a damper on the mood of the day and we quickly changed the subject and decided to discuss visits once he was back home. For now, we just wanted to enjoy each other's company.

    About three hours had passed and both the skiing and snowboarding groups as well as the pool groups were shuffling into the chalet for lunch. We waved for Romy to come and join us and we told her about our plans to go shopping for a phone, dinner at our place, Adrian's luggage arrangement and the infamous confrontation between Amber, Courtney and I. Romy agreed happily to all of our plans. She really liked Adrian and I together and wanted to do whatever she could to help make it work. She laughed wildly at the situation with Amber and Courtney which eventually erupted and included both Adrian and I. The story had definitely spread into gossip and after a short while everyone was staring at our table as we continued to laugh even harder. It was nice not to care so much for once, the new Zahra didn't pay much attention to what everyone was saying or thinking. The old Zahra was a product of her parents, Joanne and Fabién, who lived their entire lives *keeping up with the Jones'* when they *were the Jones'* they were never satisfied, they were always trying to out due themselves. The new Zahra however, was more carefree and concerned about herself and those closest to her, not the entire community and the general public and the population of White Rock or the customers of the furniture store, the students of White Rock Secondary or Austria as a whole.

After all the students had finished eating a late lunch, it was time to head back to the city. Adrian walked Romy and I to the bus where he pulled me aside and into his arms for a final embrace. He tucked his head down and rested it on mine completely enveloping me in his arms. I closed my eyes just savouring the special moment between us. He kissed the top of my head and whispered, "See you soon," close to my ear. I pulled away from him slowly and turned to get onto the bus, looking back at his beautiful smile as I ascended the stairs. I ignored all the nasty glaring eyes as I walked over to where Romy had saved a seat for me.

When everyone was seated the bus began to pull away from the curb. I looked out the window at Adrian who was still standing there with one hand in his pocket, smiling and waving as the bus drove away. I blew him a kiss that I was sure he couldn't see through the dark tinted glass, but then a few seconds after I had blown the kiss, he caught it and held it to his heart.

Let Me Sign

(★)[8] We arrived back at the school at four-thirty p.m., Natalie told us that she was going to Amber's for dinner. They had clearly formed an alliance against me, and Romy too. I felt bad, Romy didn't deserve to be dragged through my mess with Natalie, but I had to remind myself that I wasn't the one pushing Romy away, Natalie was. She had begun the process before we arrived in Austria when she withheld from replying to Romy's letters. She had said she didn't have the time, she would have preferred to send emails, or chatted through an instant messaging service. Handwritten letters were outdated.

After Natalie took off, Romy and I waited for Adrian. We sat on the same bench that Natalie and I had sat on earlier in the morning, we laughed at the frozen puddle of hot chocolate that I had knocked out of Natalie's hand just hours before, Natalie's shoe prints embedded. "Do you think she'll ever forgive me?" I chipped away at the brown frozen puddle with my foot. "On the surface," Romy answered honestly, and I knew she was right. My relationship with Natalie had definitely been shaken. She was used to me biting my tongue to avoid confrontation, bending over backwards at her command and allowing her to get away with inappropriate behaviour just to save face, to keep a "friendship" that had spanned over fifteen years—you just don't give up on something like that—but I was beginning to wonder whether I should. Natalie wasn't able to accept a change in our relationship, she clearly didn't want to. She liked having the upper hand in our friendship, dictating the rules and treating me like a follower, instead of her equal. I was simply sick and tired of it all. I couldn't continue to live my life passively and it didn't matter if she forgave me or not, I was too exhausted to care. There were so many things that Natalie needed to apologize

---

[8] Somewhere I Belong-Linkin Park

to me for too and I could almost guarantee that that would never happen. She would never apologize for her snide remarks about my style, my taste in music, my art, the books I read, my height, the cleanliness of my room, the boys I thought were cute, my collection of scarves or vintage concert t-shirts. To her, everything she said was justified, she was, as she'd say, "doing me a favour." Fifteen years meant nothing, when you realized that you never really knew that person at all, or yourself for that matter. I needed to try to find myself. If I didn't, how could I be whole again? How would my wounds heal? I couldn't bank on anyone else to do it for me, this was *my* life and I had to find my place in the world, defined by my own terms. I had to breakaway from the old Zahra who didn't exist anymore, I had to breakaway from Natalie, who needed me to pick up her pieces, I had to breakaway from my past, I had to breakaway from my future. I had to be in the moment, find myself within, I had to find a place to belong to, that place was here.

  Adrian arrived with his luggage about forty-five minutes later. Romy and I waited inside of the first set of doors of the school to keep warm until we saw Adrian's taxi pull up. He called us over and Romy instructed the driver of where to go. We got out of the cab on a Graben Street that was filled with dozens of little shops that I couldn't wait to check out. We were further into downtown Vienna then the school was and before we started shopping we stopped in at the family bakery to say a quick hello and to leave Adrian's bags in the back room. Romy's parents were very happy to meet him and gave us some delicious treats to enjoy as we walked around the downtown square.

  The streets were paved in beautiful cobblestone and the buildings were antique, it was like nothing I had ever seen before. We went into a phone store and I picked out a phone. I was one step closer to belonging. I was starting to feel like this place was my home. We strolled around downtown a little while longer, helping Adrian pick out small gifts for his family. I picked up a few trinkets, trying to figure out what I could give to him to commemorate his trip, but I was drawing blanks. I wanted to give him something special, something meaningful and that's when it hit me.

On the bus trip back off of the mountain, I had been inspired, just as Ruben suspected. The image of Adrian catching my imaginary kiss and holding it to his heart burned fiercely in my mind. For the first few minutes I worried that my action had been too forward. I was afraid about putting myself out there, laying it all on the line with the potential for Adrian to squeeze the life out of my tender heart and watch it crumble into a million little pieces of nothingness. There wasn't much more that I could take. My nerves began to consume me and I started to feel nauseous. Romy had just laughed at me and told me that I was ridiculous. I was so unexperienced in the matters of love, I had no clue what I was doing. I needed a handbook, I also needed to distract myself. I reached into my bag and pulled out my new sketchbook. I scanned the pages that Ruben had used and found the first blank sheet. I pulled the pencil attached to the book out of the holder and drew light streaks across the page.

My sketch quickly became the image I had grown accustomed to with my own personal twist. I drew a night sky above two people, a man and a women standing on a cliff, embracing each other, overlooking the vast space of the ocean. The man was chucking a stone into the dark sky. I drew the stone moving across the sky dressed as a shooting star and landing on the sand turning into the big boulder on the beach in White Rock. I had created the legend of the young Native Chief, finding his place in the world with his soul mate by his side. I would give this picture to Adrian, it would indirectly tell him how I felt about him until I was ready to speak the words, but I wouldn't give it to him until he was almost ready to leave for the airport. I would explain the legend to him and hopefully he would sense the significance behind the story as it applied to the two of us and nothing more would need to be said.

We went back to the bakery and got Adrian's bags before hailing another cab and headed back to Romy's home, my home. When we got there, everyone settled in and we played with my new phone. Romy and I went to the kitchen to start dinner and Adrian followed, but we told him to relax. He was our guest, he settled for reading a book that he had in his bag. By the time dinner was ready, Romy's parents were home from work. They asked where Natalie was while setting down their bags and washing up for dinner. We told them that she had other plans for dinner and they didn't seem to mind. The five of us ate dinner happily. We laughed, joked, told funny stories and enjoyed each other's company. After dinner, Romy, Adrian (because he insisted) and I tidied up quickly and then we lounged in the living room. Natalie came home a few hours later at around nine-thirty p.m. and Romy invited her to join us but she resisted, claiming she had other pressing matters to attend to. So Romy decided to excuse herself to try to mend the gap that was developing quickly between the three of us.

Adrian and I lay sprawled out on the couch in each other's arms, filling any silences with small talk. Almost an hour later, Romy announced that she was going to bed, as did everyone else in the house. She hugged Adrian goodbye and promised to keep in touch with him, I knew she would. Adrian and I were alone in the dark house with just the light from the table lamp on the coffee table. I could feel my eyes getting heavy; it had been a long day. I didn't want to sleep though, there were only a few hours to be had with Adrian and I didn't want to waste them sleeping. But he was tired too, we decided to set an alarm and sleep for a few hours. Any time spent together was precious time well spent and sleeping in his arms would be perfect.

At two-o'clock in the morning, the alarm on my phone went off. We woke up slowly, my arms were wrapped around him, my head was resting on his chest. The rhythm of his breath and the beating of his heart had lulled me into the most peaceful slumber that I'd had in days. The alarm announced that our time together was over. I didn't want him to leave, or at least I didn't want him to leave without me, but I knew it was inevitable, I would have to let him go. He rubbed his eyes and ruffled my messy hair with his hand before rolling off the couch and headed toward the bathroom, he tilted his head toward the bathroom, indicating that I should follow. I followed him and stopped in the doorway leaning my head against the frame. I watched him splash water on his face and grab his toothbrush and paste from his small bag, left in the bathroom earlier, he quickly brushed his teeth. When he was done, he turned to me, smiling, and ruffled my hair again, "I love your hair like this, it's so wild and curly, it's so free, liberated. You really should stop brushing it," he slid his hand into mine as he passed through the doorway, we walked back to the living room.

He pulled me onto the couch beside him as he called for a taxi to take him to the airport. I could feel the tears burning in my tired eyes. It felt like bucketfuls of saltwater were welling at the base of my eyelids ready to spill over the edge. He looked at me as he ended the call, sadness swept across his face, "Love, don't cry, *please*," he pleaded, pushing a few loose curls behind my ear. "I'm sorry," I apologized, "...it's just that I'm not ready to let go yet, I knew this day was coming but I'm just not ready," I sobbed. "Shhh," he consoled me. "Zahra, I'm not asking you to let me go, nothing says you have to. Sure, I'm going back to London, but that doesn't change anything, okay?" "Okay," I whispered, "…then disregard anything you may get in the mail in the next few days all right?" I finished. He laughed lightly, "What does that mean?" "It doesn't matter now," I insisted. "All right…" he chuckled. "I have something for you," I got up from the couch and grabbed my sketchbook.

I opened my book and flipped to the page where my drawing waited. I carefully tore the page out of the book and placed the book on the coffee table before handing it to him. He looked at the drawing with thoughtful eyes, taking in each stroke, curve and shade that I had made on the paper.

"The legend of White Rock says that a young Native Chief chucked a stone across the sky and made a home for himself and his bride where the stone landed. I've always loved the story. To me it meant that if two people were made for each other, if they were truly meant to be together then it didn't matter where they were, they'd always have each other. So that even if they were apart, their souls would remain together. I know it's just my own interpretation but—"

"Zahra, it's fantastic, you have the most beautiful explanation and the most beautiful heart and soul. You are by far the most wonderful person I've ever met. These past few days with you have been some of the happiest times in my life and I will carry this picture with me everywhere I go, I promise," he said, hugging me bone-crushingly tight. We were silent, what do you say in a time like this?

After a few moments, we decided it would be best to wait outside for the taxi so that the rest of the house wouldn't be disturbed when it arrived. I put on my jacket and my winter boots and helped Adrian with his bags. We waited outside, the sky was pitch black and cluttered with a million shining stars, like silver confetti.

We huddled close together to keep warm and to stay as close to each other for as long as we were able to. The streets were empty and I was sure that the car lights shining in the distance belonged to the taxi and my heart throbbed painfully, panic stricken. The taxi pulled up and the driver got out and put Adrian's luggage in the trunk. I watched in silence, shivering in the cold. We waited until the last possible second before we pulled away from each other. "I'm sorry love, but I have to go now," he said regrettably. "I know…" I sobbed, trying to catch my breath.

We gazed deeply into each other's eyes, speechless, this was it. He held my hand in his and raised them to his lips. He gently kissed the top of my hand, he hugged me for the final time. It seemed almost impossible for us to let each other go. He pulled away from me reluctantly and moved toward the taxi, I struggled to let go of his hand.

As he opened the taxi door, he reached into his pocket and pulled out a folded piece of paper, one of the sheets that Romy had given him. I smiled. Having a folded piece of paper was becoming his thing and was the reason I had decided to send him a hand written letter in the first place. "I made something for you too," he said, pressing the paper into my hand. "I'll call you when I get home and you can tell me what you think," he said. "Okay…" I cried tears that turned to icicles on my cheeks, as he got into the taxi. "Don't cry Zahra, this is not goodbye, it's just a…'see you soon,' okay?" he begged. I held the piece of paper tightly in my hand. He pulled the door shut and waved. I stood there until the taxi was out of sight.

✳✳✳

I stood in the darkness for as long as I could stand it. It might have been too long. Over the past few days I had grown numb to the cold. I knew he wasn't coming back, but somehow I still had hope. I kept hoping that I'd see his taxi turn back into the driveway, he'd run out to me, we'd kiss, he'd say he couldn't bear to be apart and then the end credits would roll. This was no romance film, like the black and white classics Jonnæ and I used to watch. He was really gone.

    He was probably halfway to the airport by the time I decided to move. It had started to snow, soft white, diacritic flakes from heaven, unconstrained, liberated. It was time for me to go back inside, but I worried that if I left that spot the memory of the moment wouldn't be as vivid or that in the morning it wouldn't feel real and that Adrian was just a dream. I fought to move my feet that felt glued to the pavement and headed back up the walkway with heavy steps that felt weighted by cement blocks, to the front door of the house. I entered as quietly as I could and went back to the couch. I was going to sleep in my bed but the couch still held his scent and it was the closest I could get to him, with him gone.

    My cell phone vibrated gently on the coffee table and I picked it up. Across the screen over the background that held a picture of Adrian and I was a small blue box. Inside of the box read a text message that Adrian had left while I was standing alone outside. It read, `I miss you xoxo`. I smiled as I ran my fingers over the screen as if I was stroking his face as if I could hear his voice and replied, `I miss you too xxoo`. I curled up on the couch and opened the piece of familiar paper. It was a poem, his print was structured, neat and precise just like he was and it looked quite lovely on the special paper.

    After I spent a few moments examining the way his hand crafted each letter, I let my eyes focus on the words and the phrases on the paper.

It was the most beautiful thing I had ever read. Never in my life had anyone written something about me that was so magnificent. He made me seem glorious, like I was extraordinary, like I was unreal or supernatural, a figment of his imagination maybe or something he couldn't live without, something he would fight for, something he would do anything for. I read it over and over again deciphering each line. He clearly had the love handbook, I needed to borrow it. Could this really be how he felt about me? All along I had been feeling like I was laying all my burdens on him and yet in this poem it seem like I was saving him from something, was I? I was fascinated at how different I looked in his eyes.

Through his eyes I was perfect. I was everything he wanted and needed and he knew that I would understand that when I read this poem. Maybe to some it would seem like a bunch of words but to me the story was so vivid, so real. As I read the poem for a third time, I reminisced on each phrase. The night that we first met, I stood leaning against a tree breaking down in tears, opening up to a stranger who was standing in front of me.

I drew him in the minute he laid eyes on me, like I was calling out to him through my sorrow, sitting alone at that table in club. He offered me a drink, I attacked him with my words, but he didn't give up, somehow, I think he knew I would follow him.

He would always gaze so deeply into my eyes, the windows to my soul, seeing the person that I wanted to be, past the person who was lost inside a web of chaos, deceit and lies and every time he wrapped his arms around me I knew that I was safe. He had been able to save me from myself without any words spoken. The second and third parts of his poem had yet to be fulfilled but I knew that one day soon the story would be complete. "Let me sign," I said, quietly to myself, what did he mean? I wondered. I thought about it until I fell asleep and in the morning when Romy woke me, to get ready for school, it came to me. When I had blown him the kiss from the bus and he caught it, he didn't just hold his fist to his heart, he made some sort of gesture across his chest with his index finger. Finally, I understood. I smiled and said, *"Let me sign."*

All The King's Horses And All The King's Men...

November 23

"What does that mean?" Romy asked, folding my blanket. "What?" I asked, snapping back into reality. "Let me...sign?" Romy looked confused. I handed her the folded piece of paper that I had slept with clutched in my hand. She read the poem and looked at me with sappy eyes, "He wrote this for you?" she gushed, "'Zahra, you have completely awakened a creative side of me that I never knew existed. I've written poems before but none like this. This one is different. This one is for you, my muse, love Adrian,'" Romy read aloud, *"Ooh he loves you!"* she teased. "Yeah I don't know about that!" I said, fluffing the couch cushions. "Well it's definitely sweet...and powerful!" she pointed out. "I know. I miss him Roms," I admitted. "It's okay, I have an idea! I was thinking about it when I went to bed. You should work at the bakery after school. I used to work there until you and Natalie got here. We can start whenever you want and Natalie as well, if she wants to. That way, you'll be able to save up the money to visit Adrian sometime!" Romy suggested. She really wanted to help Adrian and I reunite and I was willing to do whatever it took. Without him there, I had all the time in the world and working was just what I needed to take my mind off of the issues that I didn't want to deal with, especially the sadness over Adrian's absence. "Sounds great!" I exclaimed excitedly.

  I hopped into the shower and ecstatically thought about the prospects of working at the bakery and saving up some cash to see Adrian, preferably sooner than later. After we were all ready, we continued on throughout our daily routine. We ate a quick breakfast, mostly in silence and then headed out into the cold winter chill and waited for the local bus. We paid our bus fare, found seats and got off in front of the school. Natalie still wasn't talking to me, she decided to opt out of working at the bakery as well. She claimed that she didn't need the extra money, her parents had sent her with plenty of funds and if she ran into trouble, they would simply send her more.

When we got to the school, Natalie trailed off to find the members of her alliance, Amber and Courtney. Romy and I walked over to some of her friends and chatted until the tour bus pulled up. All the students piled onto the bus and listened to Ruben explain our next destination. We were going to visit the Roman Ruins beneath *Hoher Markt Square*, where the city's famous clock, the *Ankerur*, was located. The ancient ruins dated back to a time when Vienna was part of the Roman Empire, it was very thrilling for everyone to step back in time and visit a piece of history.

After the ruins, we were going to spend the rest of the day on Graben Street, where Romy, Adrian and I bought my cell phone. Graben Street was a popular shopping area in Vienna connected by several pedestrian streets. Ruben said we would be checking out *Michaelerplatz* which was located at the old gates to Imperial Palace. The ancient Roman ruins sat in the centre of this Viennese Square. As much as I missed Adrian, I was excited to see more important sites of the city and I especially liked knowing that I had already been to some of the places before, it all felt familiar and helped this place feel like home.

Romy and I found seats at the back of bus so that I could answer the phone when Adrian called me. His flight left Austria at five in the morning and he was supposed to land at around eight o'clock. It was eight-thirty when we boarded the bus to start our day trip and I knew that sometime within the hour Adrian would call to tell me that he made it home safely. Romy let me sit by the window seat to take in the view and to hide when my phone rang. I was worried that the other students around me would rat me out when I was talking on the phone, but Romy insisted it would be fine. She would pretend like we were having a conversation with each other and somehow it would work out, she was such a schemer. Around nine-thirty my cell phone buzzed. I turned toward the window and curled myself into a ball around it. Romy turned her body toward me and kept an eye out for any observers.

"Hello," I whispered. "'Eh Love." He sounded tired. "Did you sleep all right?" he asked, he was always so concerned about the amount of rest I was getting. "Yes, as best I could I suppose." "I know you're on the bus and I don't want to get you in trouble. I just wanted to tell you I made it back in one piece." "I miss you," I replied, I figured if we were being honest then I was just going to tell him how I was doing. "I know love, I miss you too. I'll call you again after school okay?" "Okay," "bye Zar." "Bye AJ." I quickly ended the call and prepared to put my phone back into my bag when it vibrated again and a text message from Adrian showed up on my screen. I wish we could have talked longer, I barely got to hear your sweet voice… oh well, guess I'll have to wait. By the way, AJ?

I texted him back =) a smiley face and an explanation, Adrian + Jarrett Scott= AJ Scott, yes? No?

He replied, Yes =)

A week had passed and Ruben had taken our class on many adventures throughout Vienna. We visited the *Staatsoper*, the State Opera House that showed some of the world's finest operas and musicals. We also went to St. Stephen's Cathedral, a historical church in Vienna that marked the centre of the city. Every day after the bus returned to the school, Romy and I (and occasionally Natalie) would go to the bakery. Romy and Natalie would work at the front of the bakery, taking orders, chatting with patrons and tidying up the few tables in the front cafe. I worked in the back, helping Mila and Fredrik mix ingredients for loafs, buns, cakes and other pastries that were to be baked the next morning.

    With the extra hands helping out, Mila and Fredrik no longer had to leave the house at five in the morning. They were able to sleep in for an extra hour and still have enough time to bake all of the dough I had prepared the night before, in the convection ovens at the bakery. It was during this week that my first letter from Adrian arrived. The rest of the family was washing up for dinner and I was in the kitchen preparing the salad. After I had placed the salad on the dining room table I went to my room to change into a pair of sweat pants and there it was. Mila must have left it for me. I recognized the antique envelope lying delicately on my bed. I grabbed it hastily knowing that it was a reply to the letter that I wrote when I felt so unsure about where I stood with Adrian, uncertain about if he would want to continue communicating being hours away from each other, living in separate countries, different times zones—even if I was only ahead by one hour. As I peeled open the envelope I wondered why he never mentioned receiving my letter, or that he had replied to it in any of our phone conversations. Thoughts of doubt flooded my mind, my nerves on edge. I hesitated for a moment and then ripped the top open and pulled out the folded paper inside, it said:

November 30

Zahra,

What will I ever do with you? You are crazy! Everything is fine but I'm sure you realize that now. Right? What else do I have to do to convince you?

How's the new job going? Are you enjoying baking? Do you even know how to bake? (I'm just teasing.)

Have things changed at all between you and... Naomi? No wait, is it Navina?

I was thinking...I get two weeks vacation for the winter holiday and I was hoping that maybe we could work something out and I could come back to Austria for a week after visiting with my family for the first. I don't want you to get too excited, I don't know if it'll work for sure. I spoke with my mum today and she said that we might be visiting my granddad and he lives a bit far. If we visit with him we'd have to stay there at his house, so we might stay the entire two weeks, but I'll keep working on it. I promise!

On another note, I understand now why Romy gave me this fancy stack of paper! And there I was actually thinking it was for poetry, I must be daft, ha! Ha! Speaking of which, how did you find the poem? Did you like it? Do you believe me now when I say you have nothing to worry about? I'm here for you always. I don't care that we've in different countries, for now, when its right, we'll be together, I'm sure of it. Isn't that what your picture for me meant? So why don't you believe your own words?

I'm still trying to decipher the abstract drawing on your letter, the one with all the swirls and the eye in the middle, care to explain? Or is it for me to figure out?

> Write back soon love,
> I miss you! xoxo
> -Adrian

    I ate dinner in a rush, I wanted to respond to Adrian's letter right away. I had so much to write to him about. We were both so busy with school and the letters gave us a chance to slip away from reality for a few moments and into a world that was designed for just the two of us. We were still talking on the phone and texting each other but not as often as we would have both liked and I knew that I had to respond as quickly as I could because it would be a few days before he would receive my letter anyway.

    After dinner I quickly washed my dishes and hurried to my room to begin my next letter to Adrian. I knew my time was limited, I had promised Romy and Natalie that we'd watch a movie before I knew the letter came. I couldn't let them down, it wouldn't be fair to renege on our plans to spend the night with a sheet of paper. Romy would understand, but Natalie wouldn't and I didn't want to cause anymore ripples then necessary in the somewhat steady pond right now.

    I entered my room and pulled out one of the sheets of beautiful paper from Romy that I kept in the drawer of my bedside table. I grabbed my expensive inky pen, another gift from Romy and plopped down onto my bed. I placed my heavy calculus textbook on my lap to use as a desk and began to write:

Adrian,

I thought I told you to disregard the letter in the mail! Clearly you do not know how to follow instructions!!

I'm actually really enjoying working at the bakery. I knew how to bake a little before, so that obviously helps. In White Rock, Jonnae owns a restaurant called "Zahra" of course right? How self righteous. Anyway, I worked there as the host (I guess 'cause it was my namesake...) Sometimes I would help out in the kitchen and Jonnae would teach me some culinary tricks. I learned a little about baking then and I guess now it's all paying off. Mila and Fredrik have been teaching me a few more things too and I'm really starting to like it. Maybe if you come in December I'll make you something special.

I really hope you can come. I know you said not to get my hopes up but I can't help but be a little bit excited. You have to admit that it would be perfect! I can ask Mila & Fredrik if you can stay here, maybe on the couch or something to keep costs down. They really like you, I'm sure it won't be too much of a problem.

<u>NATALIE</u>!!!! (how many times do I have to remind you what her name is?) and I have become somewhat cordial I suppose, I'll take whatever I can get. I just don't want to make it too uncomfortable for everyone else in this house. Mila & Fredrik are already secretly stressing about me not taking any calls from

> Johnae, Joanne or Fabien. Oh well, I'll figure something out at some point.
>   Your poem is the most wonderful thing I've ever read!! No one has ever taken so much time or put that much thought into anything for me. You're amazingly talented and you have such a way with words that it's hard to believe that the girl in the poem is me. I read it several times a day, everyday, whenever I think about you, which is often ☺.
>   The picture—I was doodling at first and then you crossed my mind and before I knew it, your eye was staring back at me from the centre of the page.
>
> Write to me when you can.
> I miss you SO, SO much XXOO
> ♥ -Z

I folded the letter and slipped it into the envelope carefully. I sealed it and placed it in my bag, protecting it between the pages of my sketchbook to send out the next morning. I walked out of my room and went to watch the movie with the girls.

✳✳✳

After two weeks of touring the city, the students were finally forced to settle into a proper daily routine of classes at the school. Ruben said that when spring hit, we would tour around some more to see a few of the beautiful gardens in Vienna and Salzburg but until then, we had to work hard at all the same subjects that we would have taken back in White Rock, with the addition of beginner German. Within those two weeks, I had received and sent another two letters to Adrian. We discussed things that we had done during the week and events scheduled for the following weeks as well. We talked on the phone a little bit too but not as much as we both had hoped due to our busy work and school schedules. We were trying to reach our goal of visiting each other in the near future, a sort of *Zahra and Adrian reunion fund*. Adrian knew he could have called his parents to send him more money so that he could book a flight or buy a train ticket but he wanted to do it on his own.

In his last letter, he told me that we would not be able to see each other during the winter break. His family was going to visit his grandfather, who wasn't in the best of health and they feared that he would not see another Christmas so they wanted to have the whole family together for the holidays. I couldn't be mad at something so sad, I would have loved to see him but he deserved to spend time with his family and I was happy for him that he had the opportunity to be with his grandfather during the holidays. I wished that I had the same things to look forward to as well.

December 3

Hey Love,

I've gotta say I LOVE the hearts, nice touch!

You said: "No one has ever taken so much time or put that much thought into anything for me" ← that's simply not true. Didn't you just tell me that Jonnae named her restaurant after you? I think it's safe to say that that's a major gesture of love, don't you think?

Thanks to you my poetry has excelled, I'm actually getting high marks for once in my Creative Writing class! What can I say?

You've got my creative juices flowing. I'm writing so much more these days and I like it. I'm glad I've finally got some real inspiration. I understand now how greats like Beethoven and Schumann were able to create such extraordinary pieces of music for the 'Immortal Beloved' and Clara Wieck, respectively. I'm excited to see where this journey will take me...take us.

Always,
Adrian.

P.S. I never get Nadia's name right because simply, I just don't care! She doesn't matter enough to me to try to remember it. Maybe this sounds terrible, but she's kind of forgettable. I'm big on first impressions, she didn't leave me with a good one. Maybe one day that will change but she's given me no reason to pay her any mind.

December 4

Adrian,

    I don't know if I agree that Jonnæ calling her restaurant 'Zahra' is some great gesture of love, it's a gesture of something but I'm not sure what. And to be honest I don't care too much to spend a lot of time thinking about Jonnæ and what other ridiculous things run through her mind.

    I've heard about Beethoven's 'Immortal Beloved' and Robert Schumann's Clara Wieck and after your last letter I did some more research, can I really be compared? I highly doubt it, but thanks.

    So beginner German... it's a lot harder than I imagined. I can count to ten and write it too—ein, zwei, drei, vier, fünf, sechs, sieben, acht, neun, zehn—

    I got my first paycheque from the bakery today! $532.00 pretty sweet eh? I'll have a ton of spare cash in no time... well if this phone bill wasn't so expensive.

Forever,
Z.

December 5

Where are my hearts? I'm pretty sure I said I loved the hearts!

I don't understand how you don't see the restaurant as a gesture of love, it makes no sense! And of course you can be compared to Clara Wieck and the mysterious Immortal, are you kidding me? It's all relevant. You draw something out of me that is different from anything else I've ever felt or written before and so I think it's safe to say that you are easily my Clara or my Immortal Beloved and not just mine but Jonnae's too. Say what you will, you know it's true.

On another note, one that is less chipper and I apologize in advance—I will not be able to visit you during the winter break unfortunately. My family is going to spend the holidays with my granddad who is quite ill. I don't want to think the worst but he really is in rough shape and this may be one of the last times I get to see him. I'm going to tell him all about you though. He'd love you for sure. Maybe one day you'll get to meet him. I'd really like that.

    I'm going to pitch in for your mobile bill. There must be a better long distance plan you can get. What about calling cards?

Missing you,
AJ.

***

I was starting to really miss my *sister*, Jonnæ as we steadily approached the holidays. It was as though my sister disappeared over night, stripped from my life, it was like she was always there and never really there all at once. In her place was a woman who looked exactly like my sister, but could fill that role again. She was an empty shell, neither sister, nor mother, there was no place for her in my life.

Right about now Jonnæ would be bustling around the restaurant, ensuring that the winter menu was perfect and that customers were completely satisfied. It was in this time that many restaurant reviews would be released in the local paper and her restaurant was always in the top five. Last year, Jonnæ made it to number three and her goal was to make 'Zahra' the number one hot spot for the holiday season in two years. So this year, I knew she'd be aiming to be the runner up. She'd be home every evening a bit early trying out several new recipe ideas, leaving Allison, the manager, to close up at night. Jonnae's food was so eclectic, a mix of Malagasy and Indonesian cuisine—with something else I could never really place—organic, vegan, vegetarian and sometimes raw cuisine. It was different, but a major hit in the community. I missed coming home after school to music blaring over the built in sound system, playing Nina Simone, Jill Scott, Floetry or Erykah Badu. Nina Simone's Remixed and Reimagined was Jonnæ's favourite album, the music would fill every corner of the house. I'd walk in and throw my bag onto the couch and would be greeted by Jonnæ dancing around the kitchen with a wooden spoon in her hand. When she'd notice me, she'd call me over, take my hand and force me to dance with her. After a few moves, we'd laugh and she'd have me taste her new dish. It's hard to believe that all those fond memories happened just last winter and now this winter, every thing had changed.

Natalie, Romy and I had completely settled into a routine. We would take the bus to school in the morning and attend two classes before lunch. Natalie would eat with Amber and Courtney, and sometimes they would join us at our table with Jason, Sven, Jason's host, and a few of Romy's friends including Roze, and a girl named Claudia, Courtney and Amber's host, who Jason was dating. After lunch, we would attend another two classes before the day was done. When out of school, Romy and I would head over to the bakery and Natalie would hang out with her allies. She would eventually make it home for dinner where we'd eat together, make small talk and then do our homework. After completing homework, Romy would either watch TV or read, Natalie would talk on the phone, and I, of course, would write a letter to Adrian. Occasionally Natalie would ask for our help in picking out an outfit for a date with some random guy who only had to show the slightest bit of interest in her. Although recently she was starting to get a bit more serious about the bartender she met on our first night in Austria, the night I met Adrian.

"So what's the deal with you and Adrian anyway? You keep writing all those letters and stuff…is he coming here for the holidays? Are you two *finally* a couple?" Natalie asked, with a hint of impatience in her voice.

"It's not like that Natalie."

"Why not? You've been saying that since the first day you met him. It's obvious he likes you and you like him! You two are practically an item without the label so…what's the problem?"

"Yeah but…I don't know…it's Just. Not. Like. That!

"You keep saying that but what does that even mean? How do you know for sure Zahra?"

"…I don't."

"So why don't you ask him!"

"…'Cause…"

"*Cause what?* What are you afraid of?"

"Rejection!"

"Rejection? Since when have you ever lacked in the confidence department? It's obvious Adrian is so totally your boyfriend. I just don't get it. I really don't. What's been going on with you lately? You've changed…What's going on Zahra?" Natalie asked judgmentally, not really looking for an answer. Her eyes, as cold as ice. She stood in front of the wall length mirror, her head cocked to the side as she sampled a variety of shirts on hangers, held snug against her body. I was hurt, the Natalie I thought I knew, the little glint of hope I was holding onto was definitely gone, just like my mom, dad and sister.

"…Nothing," I answered after a moment's silence. How could I truly talk about something I wasn't ready to admit? "Just have fun on your date with your bartender." I peeled myself off of my bed and headed toward the door to break free from all the tension. "Oh you don't have to worry about *that! And his name is Emil by the way,*" Natalie said with a mischievous smile as I left the room.

I stayed clear of Natalie until she left, I sat on the couch watching TV until I heard the front door close behind her. I got up from my warm cozy seat and went back to my room to start my homework. I opened my calculus textbook which I preferred to start with instead of struggling through my German work. I began to read through the questions when I noticed Romy was standing in the doorway with books in her hand, waiting for me to invite her in. "Can I join you?" she asked, not waiting for a response, she knew that she was always welcome. "I need some help," she said as she sat down and joined me on my bed. She sat down beside me and started to ask me questions about the first few problems. After we mottled through the calculus questions she said, "Now it's my turn to return the favour." Misunderstanding, I told her that she could help me with my German homework, it was her first language after all.

"That's not what I meant," she said looking down at her hands. "Look, Zahra, I know I haven't known you for too long but Natalie's right. Something is definitely wrong. You don't have to tell me what it is, but well…you're like my sister now and I hate to see you suffering alone," she pleaded. "It's nothing Roms," I tried to reassure, unsuccessfully.

"Zahra, I know it's not 'nothing,' something's eating at you…" she trailed off.

"What? What is it?" I asked.

"I don't want you to get mad at me but…I couldn't help but notice that you've been avoiding all calls from your family…" her face turned bright red and so did mine. "…And the other day… when my mom insisted that you called yours, I saw you pick up the phone, not dial any numbers and pretend to talk to someone… Zahra…" she gasped, as though she were about to cry. I felt like the wind had been knocked out of me. How could Romy have been so perceptive while I had only known her a month, and yet my so-called childhood friend still remained oblivious to the apparent denial and pain about everything significant my life. It occurred to me then that Natalie was oblivious because she wanted to be. If she was oblivious then she didn't have to get involved and could continue to take cruel stabs at me whenever she wanted to see my face twist with pain while twisting her dagger deeper into my heart. *How could she!* She enjoyed her snide remarks, she wasn't like that with anyone else. There was something about me that caused her to be cruel. But what?

I placed my head down onto my pillow and turned over on my side, my back facing Romy. I was embarrassed. I was ashamed that I had been caught and I knew that if I was going to tell her what I had been denying all this time, I couldn't look at her. I knew my numb phase would soon end, but I would hold on to the denial for as long as I could. I just wasn't ready to deal with it. To look my truth in the face was harder than it seemed. I didn't think I could handle it, to sink deep into the reality of my situation, to figure things out, to questions motives, to speak to those people who had caused all of this damage and find out why they had ruined my life. I knew in my heart, I just couldn't do it.

(★)[9] I sighed, took a deep breath in and began to tell Romy the same story that I shared with Adrian just one month before. As the details unfolded I began to cry the same pain-filled tears I deserted a month ago. Romy joined me on my pillow. She lay behind me and wrapped her arm around me, holding me close so that I knew I wasn't alone. She didn't say anything at all, she didn't have to. I knew that she was there for me, the way a real friend should be. I closed my eyes and said, "Romy you are best friend, you are the greatest person in my life, thank you."

I woke to the sound of Natalie's voice, a carefree whisper, piercing into the room, cutting through the silence like shattered glass, arguing with Romy. I opened my eyes, but didn't move. The room was dark, the light from the hallway shone in where Natalie had left the door open. I squinted away from the bright light and shifted my eyes to the floor where I noticed all of my books piled neatly, my finished German homework on top. I smiled to myself, Romy was a good friend. She had completed my assignment. My eyes shifted again, I looked over to Natalie and continued to pretend that I was asleep. She was back from her date with the bartender and not impressed with Romy sleeping in her bed.

---

[9] Ode To A Friend-Jann Arden

"We were doing homework…I guess we just fell asleep…" Romy lied, not wanting to tell Natalie that she was afraid to leave me alone in my fragile state even after I had fallen asleep. "Well, I'm home now…" Natalie whispered angrily. "Nat, I'm so tired, just sleep in my bed," groaned Romy, shooing Natalie away sleepily. "FINE!" Natalie exploded, stomping out of the room practically slamming the door behind her.

That was the last night Natalie and I shared a room. Every night she ended up sleeping in Romy's room and soon she was moving all of her stuff out and Romy was moving her stuff in.

"Thanks," I whispered to Romy in the dark after Natalie had made her dramatic exit. "No problem Zee, I figured you wouldn't want to spend the rest of the night with the *ice queen*," she giggled, pointing at the doorway where Natalie had once stood. Romy and I realized that we were more than friends, we were sisters. The next morning started out like any other except Natalie was completely ignoring both Romy and I. We got ready in silence, ate in silence, rode the bus in silence and when the bus stopped in front of the school, Natalie was the first one off. She skipped into the arms of Amber and Courtney and never looked back. Romy and I sighed at each other, we knew we had lost her for good. We walked to our lockers in silence, both pondering the same questions, what now? How would the three of us continue to live under the same roof in harmony when Natalie clearly had no intention of mending any bridges with us? Did we want to try to reach out to her again? What about Jason? Well, that day at lunch he didn't side with Natalie or me, he ignored us both and found a completely new set of friends.

During calculus, I decided to write to Adrian and send something for the holidays to his family. I wanted to make a good impression with them, although we had never met. I had the feeling that we would be in each other's lives for quite some time. His family was tight-knit and I wanted to be able to blend in, to fit, to finish the puzzle.

December 7

HERE ARE YOUR HEARTS!!

Can we agree to disagree on the Jonnæ/restaurant thing? And on the Immortal Beloved thing too?

I would love to meet your grandfather at some point. I'm honoured that you would even consider it, he's obviously very important to you so please don't apologize to me for spending time with him! That's just crazy talk. You know what else is crazy talk? You actually thinking that I'm going to let you contribute to my phone bill. You have a phone bill just the same. It's just a small price to pay to be able to spend some time together... well sorta. I wouldn't have it any other way Adrian.

I wish we would have been able to see each other this month over the holiday but I totally understand the importance of visiting your grandfather. When you do go to see him, try not to treat the time that you have with him as though it might be your last. But in case it is, ask him every question you've ever wanted answered, hug him, take pictures with him & when you leave make sure that you tell him that you love him! That's my only piece of advice, and then later, the loss won't be as difficult, at least you won't have any regrets.

On another less interesting note, Natalie and I completely had it out the other day. She moved out of our room and is now sleeping in Romy's brother's room. ~~She freaked out on me for not knowing.~~ Never mind!

Let's just say she's pissed that I haven't told her what's been going on with me, like with my family, etc. I didn't tell her for her own good, I didn't want her to have to carry that burden, just as I never wanted you to either. Plus as time went on I realized that it would just be gossip to her and I don't want all these people out here knowing my business. I talked to Romy about everything that's going on, she caught me faking a call to Joanne. It's just been building up with Mila, she's really worried about why I haven't spoken to my family in a month. So I picked up the phone and pretended to call "home" and I spoke for a few minutes to the operator. I think Romy thought I was crazy. Ha! Ha! Ha! Needless to say, Romy demanded some answers and I couldn't hide it from her, it's Romy!

A few packages from Joanne, Fabien & Jonnæ came this week, Xmas gifts I'm sure... I'm trying to figure out what to do with them, I'm afraid I'll have to open them on Xmas day with Romy's family, I really don't think I'll be able to find a way around it. I'm nervous...

I made something for your family, just a little Xmas card. Be sure to give it to them when you go home for the holidays...that's if they even know who I am!... you can keep it if you prefer.

~xxoo, Z.

Beside My Own Reflection

December 9

December 9

Zee,

Thank you so much for the card, it's beautiful. I'll definitely pass it along to my family and yes they do know who you are! Remember the other two male models from the shoot? Drew and Adam? Of course you remember Drew...but Adam, well he's my sister Emma's boyfriend so he told her all about you and then my whole family got involved in the 20 Q's!!

So...what were you going to say? About you and <u>Natalie</u>? She "freaked out on you for not knowing..." You scratched out a part...why?

I guess it worked out for the better, not telling Natalie what's been going on but I'm glad you told Romy. You need to start talking about it, dealing with it, you shouldn't keep it all bottled up inside. Zahra I'm worried! I know you've upset about Natalie, I mean she was your friend for 15 years...but think of it this way—if you were in a loveless marriage for 15 years would you continue to stay married to that person for the rest of your life, for another I don't know 15-30 years just 'cause 15 years had already passed? Or would you make a radical decision and start over?

<u>I think you've more of a radical!</u>

You know, sometimes, no matter how long the relationship has lasted for, it's just not worth the constant fight, whether it's the fight to save it or the fight to let go. As you go through stages in your life you'll find that the people in your life change, not all of them but some. Natalie just may be one of those people. Your relationship with her was great until you needed her. She just wasn't capable of stepping up to the plate for whatever reason and maybe she wasn't given much of a chance, but either way, now you've found that in Romy! It's a cycle.

Zahra—you <u>must</u> open those gifts from your family. I know all of this is really hard for you but like I said before, you can't keep everything bottled up. I know you don't really want any reminders of home but you might be surprised of how you feel once you open those gifts. You've totally justified in feeling betrayed by Jonnae, Joanne & Fabien but they still love you.

DON'T GET MAD AT WHAT I'M SAYING! HEAR ME OUT! THEY LOVE YOU!

And deep down, you still love them and at some point you're going to have to call them. Call when you know they're at work or something and just leave a message, tell them that you're ok, that you're alive, they're just worried Zav, you haven't spoken to them since you left White Rock and I think you just need to let them know that you're fine, but that you need some space. They're obviously aware of how you're feeling, but I'm sure the silence is killing them. They just need reassurance.

BREATHE!

On to the next part: (This part won't make you so mad)

Have you been working in your sketchbook a lot lately? You've probably noticed the package attached to my letter, open it! I bought you some art supplies, pastels, water colour paints, pencil crayons, charcoal, everything you need to work more diligently in your book. I was going to get you a new book but I know you've quite fond of the one Ruben gave you and I think this stuff will just help you add to it. It's totally up to you, but I was thinking that maybe you could use your book from Ruben almost like a journal, you know, like you could draw in it but maybe also write in it too. I don't know, just a thought. You've got a brilliant mind and I'm sure you've got lots you could document.

I'm leaving on December 21 to go home to my parents' house and I'll be back in my dorm January 4. I just wanted to let you know in case you send me a letter after I leave. I won't be able to respond until I get back. I just don't want you to worry because I know that you will!

How's work? Romy? Her parents? Is her brother coming home for the holiday? If so, you better keep him out of Natalie's reach, kidding!

I guess that's it for the moment love. **DON'T FORGET TO ANSWER <u>ALLLLLL</u> OF MY QUESTIONS!** I'd really like to know why you didn't finish that sentence about your argument with Natalie.

In the New Year we HAVE to figure out when we'll be able to see each other. The 'Zahra And Adrian Reunion Fund' is definitely growing. We should use it! I'm dying to see you! Let's make it our New Year's resolution.

I miss you,
Happy Christmas
—A.

It was the longest letter I'd ever received from Adrian. We had always been keen on small talk, he'd never really given me such distinct advice and I wasn't too sure how I felt about it. I knew he had my best interest at heart, but I didn't like feeling forced to deal with the situation I left behind in White Rock. Maybe I was being stubborn, but in my defence, it had only been a month since I found out that my whole life, the eighteen years of my existence had all been a lie, a sham, a total pretence. (★)[10] How could I just call them now? Make *them* feel better, when I was hurting so badly. *They* did this to *me* and I didn't owe them anything. I was furious.

Every time the images from that day sauntered into my mind like a sultry vixen in a red, skin tight dress, my stomach twisted into knots. I hated to go back there but somehow I couldn't stay away. And every time the pain resurfaced it felt like the lies were beneath the surface of my skin, crawling through my veins, black ink-stained blood poisoning my soul. Minuscule mites, eating away at my existence, leaving me open. Wounds, unforgiving and relentless with no foreseen future of remedy. The truth is, I was afraid. Afraid to dig into my past, afraid to know the truth, afraid to face it all. I was spiralling like Alice down the rabbit hole. Where was up? What was down? The ground below me tilting on an uneven axis, tossing me from left to right, reality a blur. What once I believed to be fact turned out to be fiction, a falsification of the truth, how do you justify an illusion?

What was I to do? Call them, ask them for some clarity? Listen to them talk circles around the truth? There was no point in calling until they were ready to be honest about the past and that was something I knew Joanne would never agree to. When would I reach the end of the line? I knew I'd only been reacting to the situa-

---

[10] Krwlng (Reanimation Version)-Linkin Park

tion and at some point that would have to change, but I didn't know when that point would come. All I knew was that every time I looked in the mirror I stood beside my own reflection, staring at a person I no longer knew. Zahra Roméo-Winters standing hand-in-hand with 'Nameless, Faceless One,' the empty shell of a girl who once was. A girl who once had a home, a family, friends, a life, a passion for art and music, nature, yoga and skateboarding, now broken, lost, stranded, alone and it haunted me that I couldn't seem to find myself…

(★)[11] Bottling my anxiety was making me lose my mind. The knots in my stomach, gripping, twisting, churning uncontrollably, heaving in my gut, making me ill. Most nights after dinner the food wouldn't stay down. I'd turn the tap on full blast, water rushing from the faucet to build a sound baring wall between me and the rest of the house. The thought of Joanne and Fabién conspiring with Jonnæ, predetermining my life before I was born released a sour taste in my mouth and the only way I knew how to deal with it was to not deal with it at all. I couldn't take it anymore. I was tired of talking about, tired of thinking about it, tired of living it, so I turned it all off and began to live by the motto *ignorance is bliss!* There was solace in avoidance, anymore would take me too close to the edge and I was already at my breaking point.

The misty white fog that grew up around my path parted, leading me to the edge of an unforgiving cliff. I tried to fight against it, it only pushed me closer, rubble breaking off beneath my feet, disappearing in the oblivion, leaving me gasping and clawing at the fog, searching for fresh air. I was overwhelmed. I never thought this kind of thing would happen to me. These were the sorts of stories you watched on morning talk shows or afternoon

---

[11] One Step Closer-Linkin Park

soap operas. These were the types of stories you didn't believe to be true. What do you do when your world comes crashing down around you? Where do you go when there's no redemption in your own home, no sense of security in your own family? Who do you turn to then? When it all falls apart. When does it get better? Why me?

The questions blared in my head, over and over again, like a broken record, keeping me up at night, distracting me from the new life I was trying to create for myself. I fought against it, begging it to stop, pushing it back down, tucking it away in the corners of my mind, avoiding the elephant in the room, pretending it wasn't there. I had become the porcelain doll, the image of painted perfection on the outside, hollow and empty within.

And just as quickly as the black clouds overcast my mind, the thunderstorm moving in around me, the white fog stifling, I pushed it all away and predicted nothing but sunny skies ahead.

Loving Me For Me

I ran my fingers over the supplies that Adrian had sent. The quality was impeccable. I took out the paintbrushes, pastels and pencil crayons and started to draw streaks across a page in my book to test the colours. Adrian was always so thoughtful, but what would I give to him? By now, I knew he didn't care much for gifts with monetary value. He appreciated my art, my mind and my soul and I knew that's why he gave me the art supplies; tools to fuel my self-expression. The best gift that I could give him for the holidays was an explanation of how I really felt. He made it clear in his letter that he wanted some answers and I think he sensed that was the issue between Natalie and I. Clarity.

Adrian was smart and could pick up on things quickly. He could read between the lines and had I not been rushing to write the letter in calculus before getting caught, I would not have made the mistake of starting the sentence that explained the discussion of him. It was time. We had to air this silent relationship that we were both a part of. It didn't have to be defined with labels but I needed to share how I felt about him with *him*. I knew he felt the same way about me, I didn't know what I was so afraid of. Like I said before, I desperately needed that handbook! But really, what *was* I so afraid of? Maybe it was because my mental state was so fragile and I wasn't sure how much more my poor heart could take, whether good or bad. Maybe deep down on some sort of primitive-teenage girl-level I was still afraid of rejection, afraid that whatever was building between us was all in my head. I decided that I would write it in a letter; I would write it the way he would have written it to me, in the same fashion he did when he wrote *Let Me Sign*. I too, would write him a poem.

I tore out a blank sheet from my sketchbook and set out the colours that I planned to use from the water colour paints Adrian had sent me. I grabbed all of my supplies and headed to the dining room table. I filled a small glass with water and slipped three paintbrushes into it. With my large brush, I painted the blank page tan to create the antique look of the lined paper that we used, to exchange letters on. Once the page was dry, I began to paint an elegant array of leaves, swirls and abstract shapes creating a border in seafoam green, the colour of limestone quarries, Adrian's favourite colour and ivory which was mine. I added hints of pink, green and yellow to create wisps from the corners of the page. I left the design to dry as I tried my hand at poetry, an art form foreign to me. I struggled with the words at first, my mind unable to form cohesive phrases, instant frustration. Three, four balls of crumpled paper lay askew on the dining room table. My failed attempts snickered at my unskilled hand from where they rested like large white pellets or uneven snowballs, revelling in their imperfection. All I needed to do was clearly define how I felt about Adrian. Why was that so hard? Defining 'us' didn't mean that we would have anything official, but it would stop us from beating around the bush all the time. It was time to uproot it.

I let out a deep breath, stretched my arms up to the sky, tilted my head back to look up at my hands, soft and bronze, short, square tipped nails, fingertips slightly callused from all the painting, smearing, moulding of clay. Fingerprints outlined by inks and dyes. The hands of an artist. I rubbed my fingers against each other, the images created with these hands were my words, not letters stacked side by side. Somehow, I had to transform those images into sentences. (★)[12] I closed my eyes and thought of Adrian, *swirls of colour rise up around him against the darkness in my mind, he's smiling, his arm outstretched, he's offering me the drink that's in his hand. We're in the club where*

---

[12] Loving Me 4 Me-Christina Aguilera

we first met. We're outside, it's dark and cold, I'm panicked, he's smiling gingerly, dimples hidden beneath his scruffy face. He's looking down at me, amused. I'm choking on cigarette smoke. He's listening to my story, I'm sliding down a small snow covered hill, the sun is high and bright, Adrian stands at the bottom, laughing, his eyes gentle and warm, waiting. I'm embarrassed. He's thrilled. Young Native Chief, arms around his bride, shooting stars stream across the sky. It's night again, the air cooler, the sky black and glittered with stars. Hot steaming air escapes both our lungs, we huddle close together. Car headlights trailing up the hill. Hearts racing, sadness looming, arms twisting around each other. Folded pieces of paper. Let Me Sign.

When I had my thoughts sorted out, I used a black marker and began to eloquently write the words from my heart. When I was finished my poem, I carefully picked it up and laid it on my nightstand to dry. I looked it over, feeling completely vulnerable and exposed. My heart's desires, laid out on a piece of paper that I was about to send to the person who brought me back to life. I sat on my bed feeling a hint of euphoria, suppressed emotions finally aired. Maybe I wasn't ready to deal with my family, but at least I was dealing with this relationship. I lay on my bed, turned the table lamp off and stared into the darkness. My eyes grew heavy, my lids pulling together in long lazy strides, sleep was within reach and Adrian was on my mind, what could be better? I started to think about how wonderful he made me feel. With him I could be myself, broken, wounded, lost. With him I could start to find myself again and figure out who I was. With him I didn't need to try to make myself look pretty. He loved me without any makeup, he loved when my hair was a mess, he loved that at times I was a disaster. He's the definition of honesty. He wanted what was best for me and what was best for me was him. He loved me as I was and I didn't have to try to be anything other, he loved me for me. I smiled and drifted off to sleep.

He Loves Me! He Loves Me... Not?

December 15

Do you love me?

It was December 15, which meant ten days till Christmas, three days till Christmas break, and six long days since I sent Adrian my poem. Mikael—Romy's brother—had returned home for a couple of weeks from University and more gifts were flooding in from Natalie's parents, Joanne, Fabién and Jonnæ. There was a healthy layer of snow on the ground and heavy winter boots were a necessity. We had started waking up earlier in the mornings, the snow had slowed traffic and we had been late to school a few times too many.

It was seven fifty-four in the morning, six fifty-four, in London, when I received the text message on my phone. I was standing, pressed up against two other people on the overcrowded bus. I felt my phone vibrate in my bag on my back, but ignored it, not able to reach behind me to grab it. The bus usually dropped us off in front of the school at eight a.m. but due to the weather, we were arriving closer to eight-twenty. When we got off the bus, we had ten minutes to run to our lockers, change out of our heavy boots and get to first period German. While I removed my coat, gloves, hat and scarf, I pulled my phone out of my bag quickly to check out the mysterious vibrating alert. I never usually heard from Adrian this early in the morning. I held the phone in my hand and turned the screen on and there it was, ceasing my heart, his text message. "Do you love me?" I read out loud, stunned. Clearly he had received my package. I thought he would have written a letter back and most of all I thought I had made myself clear in my poem. Now he was asking me for a yes or no answer and he was waiting for my reply, the clock was ticking. At least with a letter, it's expected to take a few days to get a response, but now almost thirty minutes had passed and I knew he was anxiously waiting to receive a text message back.

I had only five minutes to get to class, I really didn't want to be late again, and honestly, I couldn't afford it. Detention was dangling over my head like a pendulum. At the same time, I couldn't leave Adrian waiting. Text messages had the potential to be convoluted. If I simply replied "yes" would he think my answer was too abrupt? If I didn't reply until lunch when I would have more time, would he think I was stalling? Or would he just think that I was already in class? No, he definitely knew I wasn't in class yet. He had to have known I was on my way to school when he sent the message. But what Adrian didn't know was that the bus had been crowded and I couldn't get to my phone when he first sent the message. So now thirty minutes had passed and he was probably staring at his phone waiting for the screen to light up and there I was about to be late for class, arguing with myself about what do to.

(★)[13] I shut my locker door and hurried to class with my phone still in hand and when I got to German class, I had about one minute to spare. I opened the text message and hit reply. What was I waiting for? I did love him, wasn't that why I sent him the poem? I was just confused why he was asking me now. Class was about to start and I needed to get to my seat before Mr. Strauss began the day's lesson, YES, I typed and quickly turned my phone off.

The day dragged on as I anticipated the bell, indicating the end of the school day. After our fourth period English class, Romy and I headed to our lockers to layer on our winter clothes and head to the bakery. Lately, the bakery was really busy as we approached the holiday season. Romy and I were able to pull in a lot of tips from the customers, my money jar was overflowing. After school, we always took a cab to the bakery so we wouldn't waste time on the bus, we wanted to rake in as much money as possible. I had a

---

[13] Abracadabra-Jessie J

goal, I wanted to save up enough money to be able to visit Adrian at least twice so I had to be able to afford a flight or train ticket plus hotel. I had almost enough for one trip and I would have even settled for that right now.

In the cab ride over to the bakery, I turned my phone on and Romy and I waited to see if there was a message from Adrian. We both waited in silence, holding our breath looking for the phone to light up, but it didn't. I worked frivolously until the bakery closed for the evening and even checked my phone again in the car ride home with Romy and her parents, but still there was nothing. Maybe he never got my message, maybe I should resend it? Romy advised me not to. She said that maybe he was just taking some time to think, and that's what I should have done as well. I panicked, I wasn't normally a nail biter, but I had chewed them all off, wondering what the handbook would have said. Jonnæ was my handbook, without her, I was clueless.

✸✸✸

We came home to a quiet house…too quiet. Mila was confused, she walked around in silence, an eyebrow raised, suspicious. Romy and I tossed our backpacks onto the floor in our room and followed Mila into the common area. Fredrik, outside, salting the steps. Mila scratched her temple, peered into the slightly closed bathroom, looking for…something. Romy and I, right behind her, waiting to wash up for dinner, looked at each other perplexed. We lathered our hands with soap, the warm water running from the faucet. Mila cried out in horror. Romy and I raced to where she was. Mila slammed Mikael's door shut, her hands covering her face, dismayed. She had been looking for Mikael and Natalie because the house seemed empty, and well, she found them! They were wrapped in each other's arms, in a very compromising situation. Mila and Fredrik were outraged and an instant fight ensued among the family. While Fredrik continued to yell at Mikael and Natalie, Mila got on the phone with Mr. Woods. Within the hour Natalie, Mila and Fredrik had left the house and were meeting with our staff to discuss a transfer in boarding for Natalie. Mikael stormed out of the house and Romy followed him. I was left alone.

    I went the kitchen and pulled out some food, deciding that even though I couldn't make an authentic meal by any means, I could at least have something on the table when everyone returned. I put my earphones in and turned on some music from my iPod. I scrolled through my music library and found the Nina Simone: Remixed and Reimagined album. This was the one that Jonnæ always listened to when she was creating new recipes. I pressed play and began to dance around the kitchen just like Jonnæ, while I made pasta, garlic bread and salad. Fond memories of Jonnæ teaching me simple tricks and recipes flooded my mind and for a minute I could feel her there with me, laughing, dancing, talking and I smiled. She would have told me not to worry about Adrian, she would have told me that I was over-thinking things, she would have told me that I did the right thing by being honest. It was the first time that I had smiled at a memory of my family and I was glad that some of my skills would come in handy. I put the pasta in the oven with the bread to keep it warm until the rest of the family returned. I turned off my iPod, and to help the time pass, I pulled out my books and decided to start my homework. I was halfway through my English reading assignment, *Nineteen Eighty-four*, by George Orwell, when my phone rang.

    The sound of the vibration in my bag startled me against the silence that filled the house. My fingers anxiously tore through my bag to find my phone begging to be answered. I was about to miss the call, I quickly pressed the talk button, afraid that it was Romy with some bad news. This situation was tough on the family and I felt completely helpless. Maybe it was Natalie on the line, maybe she needed a friend right now and could I be that for her? I wondered. I had to be.

"H-hello?" I answered in a panic.

"Is everything all right?" the velvet voice asked on the other end. *Adrian.* Panic, different panic.

"Umm…yeah, well n-no," my voice cracked. I cleared my throat.

"What's going on? Is this a bad time?" he asked unsteadily.

"It's fine," I sighed, "Natalie and Mikael were caught—"

"OH," he cut me off before I could finish. "A little bit of *how's your father?* Eh?"

"What? What the heck does that mean?" I asked perplexed.

"You know…"

"No. No I don't know."

"What do you think it means?"

"I have no idea! *How's your father?* What the—?"

"Just tell me what happened?" he insisted.

"Mila caught them—"

"Engaging in a little *how's your father!*"

"That doesn't even make sense!"

"Sure it does!" he confirmed.

"If you say so…anyway, now Romy's parents are in a meeting with our teachers, they want Natalie out…Mikael took off and Romy went after him so I'm just here at the house waiting to hear back from someone, anyone!"

"Blast…that's a mess…I guess I predicted right…I can call back another time, when it's better," he suggested.

"Don't be silly Adrian, now is fine, really," I protested.

"Okay…well I just wanted to talk to you about…your package…and your text message," he said firmly, like he couldn't be swayed otherwise.

"Okay," I gulped, feeling my heart begin to flutter in my chest.

"So you love me?" he asked, jumping straight to the topic. I hated this, I hated having to answer the text message, but now he wanted me to say it right there on the phone? I was embarrassed.

"Yes," I answered quietly, knowing that I had no time to hesitate or decide how I was going to answer. We were in real time now, any hesitations would be extremely awkward.

"Are you nervous?" he asked, surprised.

"…A little," I replied honestly.

"Why?"

"Because," I answered shortly.

He laughed.

"Why do you get to ask all the questions?"

"I'm not," he retorted, "you just asked one right now," he slipped in slyly and chuckled.

"You know what I mean," I argued.

"Okay, ask me something," he recanted.

"Do you. Love. *Me?*" I asked sheepishly.

"Why do you ask it like that? It's like you're expecting me to say no or something. Of course I do, I'm *in* love with you. Do you feel the same?"

"Of course, yes," I answered apprehensively.

"Why don't I believe you then Zahra?" he asked nervously.

"I do Adrian, I…I'm just nervous, this is huge…you know talking about this with you," I explained.

"Why? You shouldn't be nervous talking about it with *me!*

It's about *us*, remember?" he reassured.

"I know…have you done this before?" I asked,

"No, never. I'm just comfortable with you, it's still me Zar, nothing's changed," he finished.

"Adrian I've just been so unsure of everything lately, I don't know I guess I was afraid of screwing things up, I still am…" I assessed. "I've never been in love before."

"Zahra, everything's all right, I promise. Don't you think it'll just be easier for us with things out in the open?" he asked.

I sighed. He was right, it's what I wanted.

"You're right," I agreed, "so now what?"

"Well, now, I get the honour of calling you my girlfriend, if that's something you fancy," he said with a smile behind his voice.

I laughed a little and said, "I guess that makes sense."

"Then why are you laughing," he asked, starting to laugh a little himself.

"It just sounds funny."

"Well, I'm glad our relationship amuses you," he said jokingly.

"It just doesn't seem like enough, it feels like so much more doesn't it?" I asked.

"Yeah you're right babes, but we know what it is right?" he asked.

"Right," I agreed. After a brief moment of silence he said, "Well now that that's settled, what do you think will happen with Nadia?"

Family? Yeah Right!
December 16

That night, I slept surprisingly well for one of the first times in a while, despite the chaos that filled the rest of the house outside of my room. I ate dinner in a daze with Romy, Mila and Fredrik, an eerie silence filled the air, the way it did before something terrible was about to happen. Everyone was on edge, Mikael and Natalie's transgressions still fresh on the mind. Mila, traumatized, Fredrik, disappointed, Romy and I, thankful that our eyes had been spared. Mila chomped slowly on a mouthful of crisp salad greens, looked up at me and smiled weakly. Strands of grey streaked hair falling loose from her bun, tired eyes squinting painfully, red and puffed from hours worth of tears. She reached her arm across the table and placed her hand on top of mine and said, "Thank you dear for dinner, it's wonderful." I smiled meekly and licked a spray of tomato sauce from my knuckle.

    It wasn't until the next morning when Romy and I were getting ready for school that I really noticed Natalie's absence. I hadn't even noticed that she never came back with Mila and Fredrik from the meeting with the teachers, or that Mikael didn't come home with Romy either, I was on too much of an Adrian high.

    On the bus ride to school Romy explained that Natalie was staying with Amber and her host, Claudia's family, for the remainder of the trip or until something else could be arranged. Mikael had spent the night at a friend's house and was planning to go home and pack up his stuff once everyone was out of the house. He was planning to return to his dorm at the University, to give his parents some time to calm down. I also found out that Ruben had stopped by after I had gone to bed early to collect a few things for Natalie. I missed so much and didn't even notice.

The day went by quickly and so did work at the bakery. Now that Adrian and I had clearly defined our relationship, there was more of a drive to work hard so that I could save up enough money to visit him. After work, Romy and I went home, while Mila and Fredrik met with Claudia's parents to discuss the Natalie situation further, they brought the rest of her stuff. Romy pulled out some leftovers from the fridge and we sat on the couch to watch a movie while we ate. We talked for a while and Romy gushed over my development with Adrian, she had been waiting for this to happen even before I had been. We talked until Romy's cell phone rang, it was her brother and he needed to speak with her about any updates with their parents.

I went to our room to give her some privacy and called Adrian. We talked for over an hour, I gave him all the updates on Natalie and my financial status for any upcoming visits. He was right; nothing had changed, well for me at least. We still had the same conversation we would have had the day before yesterday except the only difference was that at the end of our conversation, he told me that he loved me and I said the same. Maybe it was different for Adrian, he had people on his end that he would be able to call me his girlfriend to, I on the other hand had Romy, who already considered Adrian to be my boyfriend from the moment she laid eyes on us together. I could tell Ruben... no thanks!

When I was off the phone with Adrian, Mila and Fredrik were back and talking to Romy about Mikael. I decided that it was best for me to stay in the room to allow them a family discussion with Romy and Mikael who was still on the phone. I lay on my bed staring up at the white ceiling and my mind wandered until it stumbled upon Natalie. Though we were no longer friends I couldn't help but feel bad for her. She must have been so embarrassed. Natalie was almost completely impulsive, very smart but somehow lacked the ability to filter her decisions, I had always been her voice of reason. Without me to pick up the pieces Natalie was forced to face herself for one of the first times in her life. For the first time Natalie couldn't deny that her actions affected a handful of people, people who loved her, people who took care of her and she betrayed them, she betrayed herself.

I sighed. There was nothing I could do, Natalie had to fight this battle on her own. She made her bed, she laid in it, literally. I was bored, the room was silent and I felt helpless. I reached for my sketchbook lying slightly under my bed, the edge of it sticking out awkwardly, and searched for my black calligraphy marker amongst my small tin of supplies. I began to draw simple curved lines. When I was done, it looked perfect, she was perfect. It was Natalie as I had remembered her with long flowing blonde hair that reached below her shoulders, fair skin, bright green eyes, a button nose and soft pink lips. She had a fit physique as she was a fitness fanatic, slender shoulders, and was just as tall as Romy. The Natalie I used to know was dedicated, intelligent, at times a little erratic but strong. This was the Natalie I loved and missed, the Natalie I knew I was never going to get back, it wasn't just Natalie who changed. I knew the only way I could hold onto that Natalie was through memory and that memory was now captured in my book.

***

December 18

The last day of school before the holiday flew by quickly. In all of our classes we barely did any work. We watched Christmas movies in first period German and second period calculus and talked throughout biology and English. I took out my sketchbook during first period German, it was the only class I didn't have with Romy and I wasn't that interested in the movie. My mind was on Adrian, as it often was and I daydreamed about seeing him again. I wondered what it would be like to see him now that our relationship had been defined. I needed desperately to add something else to my book besides Natalie's lonely face. I needed some joy in it. I sketched my drawing roughly with pencil first and filled in the lines with coloured pencils until the image was complete, two hands, one pale, the other copper with fingers entwined creating a heart on the page. *Love.*

***

December 24

The weekend came and went and so did the three days before Christmas Eve. On Christmas Eve, we observed a traditional Austrian Christmas. We had baked carp for dinner and put up the Christmas tree which we lit that night. We carolled with the neighbours who came to the door singing the traditional *Silent Night*. Romy explained that the song was first sung in 1818 in the village church of Oberndorf. She said that on the night of Christmas Eve, the priest of the local church found that the church's organ was out of commission, panicked, he gave organist Franz Bauer a hymn he had written and Bauer quickly composed a tune to accompany the hymn that could easily be played on guitar. Christmas was not Christmas without music! That evening *Silent Night* was born. The Etzels, proud of the song, sang it every year.

After we ate and put up the tree, we gathered around it and opened presents. I was nervous, anticipating my turn to open gifts from White Rock that sat anxiously under the tree. For over a month I had been avoided anything to do with *them* and now I was essentially being forced to confront my family through objects *and* with an audience.

I handed Romy, Mila and Fredrik each a package hoping to stall opening my gifts for as long as I could. Romy opened hers gracefully revealing a silver bracelet with half of a heart charm hanging from it with the word 'sister' inscribed into the metal, adorned with sparkling rhinestones. She smiled and moved toward me with her arms open for an embrace. She thanked me genuinely as I helped her put the bracelet on, showing her that I was already wearing the other half. We were bound by a bond stronger than blood.

Next, I opened my gift from Romy. The small box was beautifully wrapped in gold paper with a deep purple ribbon around it. Inside was a pair of small Opal stud earrings, "Your birthstone," Romy pointed out as I took the earrings out of the box. "I know you weren't here yet in October, but I thought these would help tie in your birthday and Christmas all in one." I put the earrings on and hugged her tightly, thanking her for my gift. Mila and Fredrik opened the gift from Romy and I after I had put the earrings on. They had been talking about taking an evening off from the bakery and attending the opera that had just opened for a limited engagement. Romy and I had put some of our money together and bought her parents tickets to *The Magic Flute* and in addition we would work late at the bakery so that they wouldn't have to close early and lose any potential business. Mila and Fredrik were so happy. They really appreciated the gift and were extremely excited to go to the opera. They said that they hadn't been in almost ten years and really missed a night out together. I was glad that I was able to help make them so happy when they had been lifesavers for me.

I had only one gift left to open before I faced the inevitable, the gifts from my family. Mila handed me a large envelope as Fredrik and Romy looked on with anticipation in their eyes. I looked at them apprehensively, I didn't like surprises. I carefully ripped open the envelope and pulled out a few pages written in German. I looked it over feeling perplexed, there were a few familiar images but my German was nowhere near good enough to read what was written on the page. I handed the papers to Romy, who had her hand out, waiting to receive them with a huge smile on her face. She began to translate the words for me and then quickly summarized the text seeing my restlessness. "Basically what is says is that my parents have reserved a flight for you whenever you want to take it to… GO TO LONDON!" Romy sang, like Oprah announcing giveaways on her holiday specials. "WHAT?" I squealed, like an audience member, on my knees, fighting the urge to jump up and down. "ARE YOU SERIOUS?" I burst, my arms waving wildly in the air. Mila and Fredrik sat on the couch smiling gingerly—possibly frightened—and nodded their heads. Romy was clapping so quickly that it barely looked like her hands were moving. I leapt to my feet and threw my arms around Fredrik and Mila, they jumped in shock, the urges won.

"You've been working so hard at the shop, we just wanted to help you out a little," Mila, sitting at the edge of the couch, eyes glossy. "Now you can use the money you've saved for a fancy place to stay," Fredrik insisted—with the underlying message; *you're not staying with that boy!*—I nodded in agreement. "Are you coming too?" I asked Romy as I hugged her too. *"No,"* she answered. "Why not?" I asked surprised. "Because I figured you would want to spend some time with Adrian without a...what do you call it? Third wheel." Romy looked off into the distance tapping her finger against her chin. "Well, what if someone else is there too? I have a cousin in London, I haven't seen her in years but if I can arrange for her to do some stuff with us then you wouldn't have to feel that way," I insisted. "Really?" Romy asked, not wanting to impose. "Romy of course! You *have* to go with me! *You have to,*" I demanded. "Okay," she agreed hesitantly. "Yes!" I said, grabbing her and hugging her tightly. "Zahra, don't forget you presents from your family," Fredrik reminded instantly, sobering me, elated bubble burst.

Romy looked at me wearily, she knew I didn't want to open the gifts from White Rock and she moved closer to sit beside me, her hand gently on my back as I slowly reached for the first box. My hands trembled nervously as I pulled the large golden ribbon from around the package, my breath held. I carefully unhitched one of the taped corners of the wrapping paper. I suspect to anyone else it looked like my intention was to preserve the paper as best I could, but Romy and I were both aware that it was my attempt at stalling. I could sense Mila and Fredrik's impatience, more Fredrik then Mila, I knew she valued the importance of preserving elegant paper. I carefully pulled at the long seam down the middle of the box. The anticipation was killing me and the several pairs of eyes on me were almost stifling. I freed the box from the paper and Mila ran to the kitchen to get me a knife to cut through the tape holding both sides of the box together. I pulled one flap of the box free and then the other and took a deep breath as I reached inside with both hands. A photo album, large and ivory, almost like a wedding album. The satin fabric billowed like soft clouds, little pearl darts created diamond shaped puffs across the surface. The word *Family* written in Joanne's beautiful writing in the middle of the album's picture frame cover. Creating albums and scrap books had been a hobby of Joanne and Jonnæ's. Fabién would always tease them that they were alike in more ways then one. The most obvious was that their names, the same letters rearranged.

The story was that Joanne had had complications when Jonnæ was born and had expected to have only one child—which in fact turned out to be true now that I was aware that biologically I wasn't Joanne and Fabién's child—so when Jonnæ was born Joanne decided to name her daughter after herself, essentially.

"It's beautiful," Mila said, interrupting my silent torment. "Joanne and Jonnæ made it," I answered. "Your mutter und your schwester?" Fredrik asked questioning my choice of words, reassuring me that he knew who they were. "Yeah…I guess," I said, smiling wryly. "What is inside?" Mila asked, sensing my discomfort at Fredrik's assessment. I didn't want to go any further, I didn't want to have to open it and see whatever they had put inside to try to convince me that nothing had changed. Their visual message left a sour taste in my mouth that made me want to gag. I opened the album slowly trying to prepare my heart—and stomach—I was sure I'd be sick.

The first picture was a family portrait taken just a few months ago for Joanne and Fabién's fortieth wedding anniversary. I sighed, we looked so happy then, we were so happy then, or were we? Joanne and Fabién were definitely happy…maybe just Joanne, the family image had been upheld, Jonnæ was most likely silently suffering over her decision to 'be my sister' and I, at the back of my mind was feeling like my 'parents' didn't really want me. *Family? Yeah Right.* I huffed, slamming the album closed.

In the bottom of the box were a few letters from each one of them, letters I knew I'd probably never read. Romy quickly handed me other packages so that I wouldn't be forced to look any further inside of the album and I flashed her a quick grateful smile. I tore open the other package quickly, from my grandparents—err my great-grandparents I suppose. They always gave me generic gifts, pyjamas, slippers, packages of socks, bath sets and things like that. And like I had expected, a lovely pink pyjama set with robe and slippers waited for me inside of pink tissue paper and it made me wonder if they knew that I was in on the big family secret. Just then I thought about what Adrian had suggested, calling my family to let them know that I was okay. I would call my 'grandparents' the next day to say a quick hello, *they* could let the rest of *them* know how I was doing. I told Mila, Fredrik and Romy about my plan. I assured them that I would call my grandparents in the morning, easing some of Mila's tension. I smiled gingerly, all teeth showing—I'm sure I looked part crazed—*Porcelain doll*. I hurried to change the subject to take the attention off of from me.

I asked Fredrik to tell me some old family stories about Christmases in the Etzel household. It seemed like a good idea at first, but I realized that the stories Fredrik began to tell only made them sad about the way things ended with Mikael. He didn't come home for Christmas. Mila got to her feet and hurried to the kitchen pretending to tidy up, banging pots and pans to mask the sound of her crying. Romy, Fredrik and I looked at each other trying to figure out what to do. Fredrik was about to get out of his seat, but I motioned for him to stay. I got up and followed Mila to the kitchen. It was my duty to console her, it was my idea for purely selfish reasons to reminisce on their past.

I walked up beside her and wrapped my arm around Mila's waist. "Mila, I'm sorry. I should have been more sensitive." "Don't be silly, it's not your fault Zahra," she assured, "I don't know what Mikael was thinking…or Natalie, such disrespect…" she trailed. "I know, but I should never have suggested the stories," I said lightly rubbing her back. "I think you should call him, it's Christmas!" Mila turned and hugged me, "You're a goo*dt* girl," she dabbed her wet eyes with her balled tissue. "I'm very happy to have you here with us. I hope you know you can talk to me *über*… no… *about* anythin*k*, I will always comfort you too, while you are here, I am your Ma. After you are not here, I'm still your Ma," she smiled.

We prepared a pot of hot chocolate and brought it out to Fredrik and Romy. We sipped our drinks and listened to Christmas music while Mila spoke to Mikael on the phone.

Mother Mila

The Lucky Ones

December 25

Romy woke me up early, it was seven in the morning when she entered our room with a tray of pancakes and hot chocolate. "Romy?" I questioned, yawning and stretching my arms above my head. "I figured after last night's gifts from your family you could use a little breakfast." "That's sweet Romy, you really didn't have to...but why seven a.m.?" I asked, confused. "Because in White Rock it's ten p.m., Christmas Eve," she pointed out. "You should call your grandparents *now* and thank them for the gifts," she nudged. "Yeah, right...which grandparents? My real ones or the ones I believed were my grandparents?" I asked sarcastically, getting out of bed. "Which do you think?" she chided. "I was thinking about it last night actually, 'cause at least I won't have to talk to Joanne and Fabién," I said, digging through my bag for my cell phone. "Are you sure you want to use your handy phone?" Romy pointed out. "Hmm, you're right." I walked to the hallway and picked up the house phone and waited for the call to connect.

My heart raced as the phone rang. What if Jonnæ and her parents were still at my great-grandparent's house? What if one of them answered the phone? Maybe my grandparents-err great-grandparents were at Joanne and Fabién's house. Now that would be perfect because then I could just leave a message, which was all I really wanted to do. *"Selamat Hari Natal,* Merry *Crees-tmas,"* Nuri my 'grandmother' sang into the phone with her thick Indonesian accent. "Hi *Nenek,*" I spat out after a brief moment of silence, like someone slapped the words out of me. *"Oh,* Zahra!" she shrieked into the phone. *"Buru-buru (*Hurry) Antso, *jawaban* (answer) the telepon, it's Zahra," I could hear her say in broken English, her voice muffled and distant in the phone, she had pulled her ear away from the phone to speak to my 'grandfather' so I waited until I could hear him pick up the other phone before I continued to speak.

"*Salàma!* (Hello) *Zah-rra,*" my grandfather sang into the phone with his beautiful Malagasy accent. I could feel my heart swell in my chest. I missed *home.* "Hi *Baba*," I said, fighting tears. "I hope I didn't call too late, I just wanted to thank you for the Christmas gift, I really love it," I managed to get out before the first set of tears rolled down my face. "You are very welcome d'harling," my grandfather answered. "We thought you might need some warm stuff there. *Hal ini dingin ya?* (It's cold yes?)," my grandmother asked from the other phone. "Yeah it's cold," I sobbed. "Zahra. Don't cry! We miss you too, *dan cinta kasih banyak* (and love you very much)," my grandmother continued. She wasn't the warmest person but she always tried her best to be comforting, I guess that's where Joanne got her demeanour from.

"Wat *ees* the time d'ere?" my grandfather asked, interrupting my grandmother, he was gentler then she was and his affection was better translated too. "It's seven in the morning, Christmas Day, nine hours ahead," I told him, wiping my eyes with the back of my hand. "*Zah-rra*, Are you ok'ey? Everyt'ing is well over d'ere?" he asked. I knew he was asking so that he could report back to Joanne and the others and at that moment I knew that they were aware of everything that had transpired before I left White Rock. "Yes, I'm fine *Babakoto* everything's fine," I answered. As much as I hated giving any updates to Joanne and Fabién, I couldn't resist my grandparents, my grandfather especially. "So d'en why you no call in ob'ver a mont' Zahra? You make us all worry—" my grandmother snapped at me. "Nuri. Enough!" my grandfather interrupted again. "We are just glad you are ok'ey, get some h'rest d'hear, you sound ti'yard. C'ull us again soon ok'ey," my grandfather said. "Of course," I replied. "When you call?" my grandmother asked and I knew she was scheming to make sure that Joanne or Jonnæ were there to receive the call, she was too transparent, I rolled my eyes. "I. Don't. Know. Grandmother," I said sternly, so that she knew that I knew what she was planning. I never called her Grandmother, always Nenek, the Indonesian equivalent. "C'ull whenev'ah you want *Zah-rra*," my grandfather said, panic in his voice probably fearing that I wouldn't call again. "I will Baba, I'll call again some time, I promise," I said.

"Je t'aime beaucoup, m'appellent n'importe quel jour entre le 19h00 et le 21h00 où Nenek est au Chi de Tai."

(*I love you very much, call me any day between 7:00 p.m. and 9:00 p.m. when Nenek is at Tai Chi.*)

"Je t'aime trop Babakoto, merci beaucoup. Vous êtes un épargnant de vie. Merci pour la compréhension." (*I love you too Babakoto, thank you very much. You are a life saver. Thanks for understanding.*)

My grandfather and I always spoke in French to each other. His two primary languages were Malagasy and French, but I had a hard time learning Malagasy except for a few words like 'hello' and 'grandpa.' I learned to speak French from both him and Fabién and was enrolled in the French Immersion program at White Rock Secondary. French was our special connection. Nuri, Joanne and Jonnæ couldn't understand and so whenever Fabién wasn't around and my grandfather wanted to tell me something special, he would tell me in French. "WAT DID YOU SAY TO HER?" my grandmother demanded. "Not'ing Nuri. I juss told her I love her and d'hat it was good to hear her voice and t'anked her for c'ulling," he lied, every 'r' rolling off his tongue beautifully. "Okay well bye guys, I love you," I said, quickly ending the conversation. "Bye Zah-rra," they said in unison and I hung up the phone.

I took a deep breath, that was intense. "Thanks Romy," I said, as I walked back over to my bed where Romy was sitting with my pancake breakfast. *"That's what sisters are for right!"* she stated. "I guess I wouldn't really know but…yeah you're right," I answered wiping the tears from my eyes. "Oh come on Zahra, until this point Jonnæ was your sister, so you still know what it's like to have one, *I'm* the one who's learning," she teased. I smiled an unconvincing smile and she nudged me with her shoulder. I laughed, it sounded awkward and unnerving, Romy ignored it and handed me a fork and we began to eat our pancakes. "So what do you want to do today?" she asked. "SLEEP," I exaggerated. "No school, no bakery, just some time to relax, at least until tomorrow. I think I'll go to the bakery all day with the parents." "Okay, we can do that," she said as she picked up the empty tray and headed to the kitchen. "Go back to sleep," she said leaving the room, "I'm going to call my brother quick before my parents wake up," she said closing the door behind her. I curled up under my blanket and closed my eyes and I drifted off.

    I awoke suddenly to a familiar, but distant sound. My eyelids, heavy, felt glued together and pulled apart slowly as my brain registered the sound, my cellphone. I sat up swiftly and rushed to the edge of my bed to fish my phone out of my bag that sat on the floor. I rummaged through my bag in a hurry, though I knew if I missed the call I could just call back. I didn't want to risk not being able to talk to Adrian, he was the only one besides Natalie, Romy and the Etzels who had my number. I accepted the call and put the phone to my ear.

    "Hello?"

    "Hi babes, *Merry* Christmas."

    "Merry Christmas Adrian. What time is it?"

    "A little after ten here...for you just after eleven, did I wake you?"

    "Yeah it's okay though, I was up before, I just went back to sleep for a while."

    "I thought you'd be up opening presents or something..."

"That was last night, I was up at seven, I called my grandparents…not Joanne and Fabién, my *pretend* grandparents Nuri and Antso."

"You did? I'm so proud of you! How did it go?"

"Well enough I guess, they want me to call back some time. My grandfather said to call when grandma is at Tai Chi so we can have some privacy, I'll give him a call from time to time. I miss them, my granddad the most. I didn't realize it till he started speaking French to me like we used to."

"You speak French?"

"Fluently."

"Speak to me."

"Adrian Je vous aimera pour toujours et toujours. Tu me manque comme fou et moi ne peut pas attendre pour vous voir, finalement pour vous embrasser et pour être dans des vos bras. Vous êtes mon…"

(Adrian I'll love you forever and always. I miss you like crazy and I can't wait to see you, to finally kiss you and be in your arms. You are my everything, my world and you have no clue what I'm saying…)

"That was beautiful, what did you say?"

"I said 'Adrian Merry Christmas to you and your family,'" I lied. "No you didn't! I know a little bit of French and there was definitely no 'Joyeux Noël' or 'famille' in there, so what did you really say?" he asked. I blushed and somehow he could tell through the phone and said, "Okay you can tell me another time but don't think I'll forgot Miss. You *will* tell me later," he insisted. "Hang on love, I've got someone here who wants to speak with you…"

"Hiya!" she chirped, her voice was sweet and welcoming, her British accent more distinct then Adrian's. "Zahra? I'm Adrian's sister Caty, we've heard so much about you," she started to say. *"Catherine please…"* Adrian pleading in the background. "Just wanted to wish you a Happy Christmas is all," she continued, ignoring Adrian's plea. "Thanks. You too, *h-happy* Christmas?" I answered with question in my voice. *"Okay here,"* Catherine said, her voice distant, there was a loud muffle in the receiver like they were fighting over the phone and than another unfamiliar voice was on the line. "Hello?" this voice had a bit more song to it and her accent was more pronounced than both Catherine's and Adrian's combined. "Hello," I answered. "Hi Zahra, dear. This is Sophie, Adrian's mum. How has your Christmas been?" "Hi Mrs. Scott, my Christmas has been great so far," I said, trying to sound casual and make small talk. "Mrs. Scott? Oh dear, please just call me Sophie," she insisted. "Okay. S-Sophie. How has your Christmas been?" I asked. "Oh just lovely dear, thank you for asking. We're just preparing dinner but I thought I'd take a quick second away from the stove to thank you for the beautiful card you made us, you have a brilliant hand, I'd love to have a few things to hang around the house," she exclaimed. "Thank you! I'm glad you liked it. I just wanted to give your family something, um…nice for Christmas," I answered. "Well, thank you again Zahra and if you ever come across one of your pieces that you're able to part with, send it my way and the bill too of course, we'd be lucky to have one of your masterpieces in our home. Here's Adrian," she said. "Okay, thank you!" I blushed, "Mer—Happy Christmas," I replied. "Happy Christmas love," she said handed Adrian the phone.

"Sorry about that Zar, they insisted on talking to you," he apologized. "No, I'm glad I finally got a chance to…meet them, sort of…I guess." "You're right I suppose. So what did you get for Christmas?" he asked. "Well…Mila and Fredrik got me a ticket to London!" "Really?" he asked excitedly, "when will you come?" he continued. "Oh I don't know yet, we'll have to figure something out. The ticket's open-ended, I can pick the date myself, the next available time really is March Break but that's so far away…" "Yeah it is…you're right, we'll have to figure something out," he replied. *"Yes dad? All right…"* I could hear him say away from the phone. "Do you have to go now?" I asked when I was sure he was back. "Yeah, unfortunately I do. I have to help set the table before the rest of my family arrives for dinner. Sorry love, I wish I could talk to you all day…" "It's okay AJ, enjoy your Christmas with your family! We can talk again later, or tomorrow 'kay," I reassured him. "Yeah all right, *Merry* Christmas babes, I'll talk to you soon."

"*Happy* Christmas Adrian, Bye."

I slowly stretched and pulled myself out of bed. I drew back the curtains to let the midday light in. I grabbed my new pyjamas out of the box. I slipped on my new robe and stepped into my new pink slippers and headed toward the bathroom. I was in much need of a hot shower. As I entered the common area I could see Romy on the computer, Mila was watching TV, German Soaps, and Fredrik was reading a book next to her on the couch. Fredrik looked up from his book and I smiled and said good morning before entering the bathroom. I turned the water on to let the shower warm up and as hot steam filled the air I placed my new pyjamas on the stool in the bathroom. Today was a day for lounging, I intended to change from one pair of pyjamas to another. I slipped off my robe and stepped out of my slippers, into the hot shower and melted.

After I had bathed, washed my hair and slipped into my new pair of pyjamas from my grandparents, I threw my robe onto my bed and went to the living room to join Romy at the computer. "What are you doing?" I asked, pulling up a chair beside her. "Checking out flight packages for London," she answered. "Oh really? Anything good?" I asked. "I was thinking we could go in a few days, maybe like on the thirtieth and spend New Year's Eve in London and come back on the second, the Saturday just a few days before school starts back on the Monday the fourth. It will be a short trip but at least it's sooner than later. What do you think?" she asked. I couldn't believe my ears. Could I really be seeing Adrian in just five days? I was so ecstatic that I could hardly breathe. "Romy it's perfect," I chirped, "let me just confirm it with Adrian later and then we'll book our flight."

The hours ticked by slowly as I waited for Adrian to call, hoping that Adrian *would* call. We never really defined whether we'd have another conversation that day. We'd leave it up to how busy he was with his family and as badly as I wanted to talk to him, I knew it would be wrong and completely selfish of me to call him. I just wasn't willing to do that to him and so I would wait.

The day rolled on and Romy and I watched a series of movies while eating popcorn, chips and drinking hot chocolate. During the movies, we talked about what things we'd like to do in London and by the time we finished watching all three movies it was close to seven in the evening and Mila had just placed our late dinner on the table. We sat and ate, chatting about our plans to travel to London in a few days. Talking about seeing Adrian in such a short amount of time was euphoric, I was on a complete high that no one could bring me down from. I floated around the rest of the evening and after Mila and Fredrik headed off to bed, I was able to persuade Romy to stay up with me a little while longer.

With sleeping in until eleven that morning, I wasn't quite ready for bed twelve hours later. Romy and I stayed up talking and fantasying about London, what we would wear, where we would go, places we'd eat, finding a hot guy for Romy, maybe one of Adrian's friends perhaps. We chatted for about forty-five minutes before I could tell that Romy was getting tired. I wanted to let her sleep but I was enjoying my time with her too much. In the last couple of days we had become so close, so much closer than Natalie and I had ever been in over fifteen years of friendship. I asked Romy to wait for just another few moments before heading off to bed and I hurried to our room and grabbed my sketchbook, I felt a strong desire to capture Romy on paper. She had such a good heart and was one of the nicest people I had come to know and I really wanted to have a picture of her in my journal because she was definitely an integral part of my journey.

"I promise I'll be quick, I just want to get a basic sketch done," I said.

"I don't know if I like this Zahra, I'm not a good person to draw, you should find someone else. Someone beautiful," Romy complained. "*Oh shut up* Romy! You *are* beautiful. You know the first time I saw you I thought you looked like a high fashion model?" "High fashion model? Are you crazy?" she asked. "Shh—" I quieted her. "Sit still or I'll draw you with an extra arm or something," I teased. "How do you want me to sit? What should I do? Do I look at you?" she asked panicked. "Romy, you're fine just like that. You can look where ever you want. I just want a picture of you to have always. This is no art exhibit," I said trying to reassure her. "Then why can't you just take a picture with your camera?" She whined, "…maybe it's no art exhibit in a gallery but it will be on exhibit in your book!" she pointed out. "Yes, that may be so *Romy*, but I still want you to sit still. So don't move!" I protested. She made a stern face and found a position that was suitable for her and motioned with her hand for me to begin.

I took a few moments to examine Romy's face structure and body frame which I could tell made her understandably uncomfortable, I tried to capture her image in my mind quickly. I put my pencil to the paper and began to unfold a simple sketch of Romy's face and body, sitting on the arm of the sofa and leaning casually against the back cushion. When I had the basic sketch finished, I told her she could go to bed and I would finish the picture and show it to her in the morning. She took a quick peek at what I had done, hugged me and headed to our room to get some sleep.

 I sat on the couch with my feet on the cushions, using my legs as a table. I took my time with my picture, it needed to be perfect and something that Romy would be proud of, but I didn't want to over work it at the same time. It had to be simple enough to focus only on Romy and her intense eyes and distinct features. Two hours had passed and finally I was finished. I left the book open on the page to allow the lead to set on the paper so that the picture wouldn't smudge. It was close to one in the morning and my eyes were beginning to burn, heavy from focusing on the paper for so long.

 I stood up to stretch my cramped legs and as I worked out the knots in my legs, I heard my phone vibrate twice on the coffee table beside my sketchbook. I reached forward and grabbed it, elated that Adrian had actually called again, but he had hung up before I had a chance to answer. Did he mistakenly call me? Was he still busy? Should I call him back? I decided I would call him back and see what was going on.

 I opened my phone and pressed redial and I sat on the couch waiting for him to answer, if anything I would just leave a message and talk to him in the morning.

 "Zar, did I wake you?" he answered the phone almost immediately.

 "No, I was up," I yawned.

 "You're lying. Go back to bed," he insisted.

 "No really I was up, I swear! The yawn was just bad timing," I said rubbing my eye.

"Are you sure? That's why I hung up before. I forgot how late it was there I was hoping the call didn't connect. I didn't want to wake you is all."

"I promise I was up. I was finishing a picture of Romy I started."

"*Oh,* is Romy there, tell her I say 'hi.'"

"No, she went to bed like two hours ago. It's just me."

"*Perfect.* So I have you all to myself then?"

"Yes'ir."

He chuckled.

"So what are you wearing?" he asked.

"Adrian!" I protested in the phone.

"I'm just kidding," he laughed.

"Yeah right!" I said, not the least convinced.

"I swear! I just wanted to see what you'd say," he continued, still laughing lightly into the phone. "Imagine how amazing it would be if we lived together. We would just be able to be together always and I wouldn't have to ask you what you are wearing, I'd already know. I guess I can dream right?" he continued.

I pulled the phone away from my ear and looked at it, expecting answers. "… Adrian. Are you drunk?"

"No. Not drunk, not completely," he admitted.

"So you're *not* drunk dialling me? Maybe you should get some rest and we'll talk in the morning."

"It is the morning silly, *and* you never answered my question," he stammered.

"What question? I don't think you really asked me one…"

"Yes I did, I asked you if you'd like to live with me."

"Well you didn't *really* ask…but I think that's something we should talk about when you're sober AJ."

"We can talk about it more then, sure, but you still haven't answered," he insisted.

I sighed. "Adrian I would love to live with you. It would be amazing because right now you'd be sleeping off your drunk and there would be no need to ask me these questions," I said.

"Well, I don't know about the talking part…" he slurred, chucking into the phone.

"Okay, *goodnight Adrian.*"

"All right I'll stop. I promise," he said trying to control himself.

"So how was your dinner?" I asked changing the subject.

"It was good. It was great to see my aunts and uncles, some cousins. It's been a while. I passed around my phone, showed them all pictures of you."

"WHAT? WHY?" I whispered sternly into the phone trying not to wake the family.

"Because they asked," he stated simply. "They all gushed about how beautiful you are, asked me how I got so lucky and to be honest, I really don't know. I guess I've got a horseshoe up my ass," he said.

I laughed.

I'd never heard Adrian talk like that. He was usually so refined, such a gentleman, careful with his words, making sure not to offend, not that he wasn't a gentleman now, he was just different with a little liquor in him, or maybe a lot of liquor… His accent was thick and prominent and he was a more relaxed version of himself and I liked it. I felt like this was the Adrian I would come to know and love with time, once we were more comfortable with each other and I couldn't wait, not for the drunk Adrian, but the relaxed one. He was even more fun than the Adrian I loved at that point.

"Well, I don't know about *lucky*," I answered.

(★)¹⁴ "Oh Zahra, come off it! You *know* you're the best thing that's ever happened to me even with everything that's going on in your life. That'll never change. I was meant to meet you and if it wasn't in Austria, then it would have been somewhere else, I'm sure of it. But in Austria the time was right. You needed me and I was there for you. Still am. Always will be. That's what happens when two people are made for each other. What good is it to live your life without someone with whom to share? To marvel in the beauty of the moon, to hold the honour of being the other half of that pair...

"We were walking our own paths of this journey and at some point our paths would have crossed bringing us together and I think that your tragedy jump started the cross, it let us bypass some time. I think that's why I knew I loved you right away, you know? And why I felt so drawn to you in the club, how I knew you were there and that you needed me, how I knew where to find you among all of those people that night.

"You know, you bumped into me outside of the club on your way in, you barely noticed, but I did. Your shoulder brushed my arm and I can't explain it, it was like I was defibrillated. I was jolted to life and for the first time, my eyes were open and I was seeing the world in a whole new light. You gave that to me. And then you were gone, disappeared into the crowd. You could have been any one of those girls but my heart was my compass, it led me right to you.

"I know this all sounds crazy, but I swear it, one minute I was standing outside with my friends having a drink and a smoke and the next, I was being pulled inside by this strong, overwhelming

---

[14] We Belong Together-Gavin DeGraw

force. I was looking around for you and I couldn't find you, I was so nervous and then there you were, sitting all alone at that table, your friends, all doing their own thing. You looked so sad, I just couldn't resist. And even when you brushed me off and I walked away, I knew you'd follow, I knew you felt it too, there's an energy between us...

"We're meant to be together. Just like the sun and the moon we're bound to one another by the forces of nature. Everyone has a soulmate, don't you think?" he asked, "and if ever you're lonely and this bliss has passed, if you're ever lost in a world filled with emptiness I hope you remember this."

(★)[15] I didn't know what to say. I had never had this kind of conversation with anyone and no one had ever felt this way about me before. I had never felt it before either. Is this what it's like to find your soulmate? I never really gave much thought to whether I believed that there was such a thing as a soulmate or 'the one.' I think I believed more in 'the one *for now*,' the person who was right for you at that moment in your life. But after meeting Adrian I understood that it was possible to grow *with* someone. The two of us could grow together and there was no way I could ever imagine myself with anyone else. He was everything I didn't even know I needed, it was one of those 'aha!' moments when all the pieces come together and everything makes sense.

"Do you always speak in verse?" I asked, *(please, someone give me the handbook. I'm begging!)* I was so moved by his words, words that streamed fluidly off his lips like silk, I didn't know how to respond. I couldn't form elegant phrases the way he could. My thoughts were scattered like marbles all over the floor, the words jerked out of my mouth like a child first learning how to ice-skate, choppy, uncoordi-

---

[15] Lucky-Bif Naked

nated. But I knew how I felt, it couldn't be described. I was complete. I was selflessly in love.

"Only when I'm liquored up," he laughed, "it's kismet," he decided.

"It's kismet," I agreed.

"I love you so much Zahra, and don't think it's the drink that had me say all of those things. I just had an insightful conversation with me mum tonight about life and love and you. Us. I needed to tell you," he said.

What could I say to him except, "I love you, Adrian," when I'd totally give my life for his.

"I love you so much Adrian and *I'm* the one with the horseshoe, *I'm* the lucky one to have you in my life. You've taken me as I am, broken, wounded, fragile and you've loved me for who I am today and I guess who you know I'll be in time, so like I said, I'm the lucky one…

"I don't mean to change the subject," I continued, "but I have some news…Romy and I were thinking of joining you in London for New Year's Eve. I know you're still at home with your family and not at your flat but if it's all right with you we'll just stay in a hotel somewhere close to your parent's house. What do you think?"

"That sounds amazing, why didn't we think of that earlier? When can I expect you?" he asked elated.

"On the thirtieth and we'll stay until the second, I know it's not much. It'll be a short trip for now but it's better than nothing right?"

"I'll gladly take whatever I can get, I can't wait. I'm sure my parents won't have a problem with you girls staying at our place in the guest room. I can't stand not seeing you any longer," he confessed.

"I know, me too, I've been counting down the days, just four left, it's officially the twenty-sixth," I yawned.

"Okay sleepy, get some rest and I'll talk to you in a few hours. I'm going to go sleep off my drunk," he said.

"Ah ha, so you admit it! Will you remember any of this conversation in the morning?" I asked.

"Of course I will. There's nothing about you I could ever forget. I love you Zahra."

"I love you too Adrian. And, I am the lucky one."

"No love," he started, "together, we're the lucky ones."

When It All Falls Down
December 26

I woke up after just a few short hours of sleep at eight-thirty a.m. Romy was in the shower and Mila and Fredrik were at the bakery. I intended to spend much of the day packing and getting ready to go London, then work all day at the bakery for the next two days before our flight. As Romy showered, I prepared some breakfast for us. Romy was growing quite fond of scrambled eggs in the morning and Adrian's black coffee with two sugars had grown on me. I prepared our favourites and waited at the dining room table for Romy to get dressed. I told her that Adrian was looking forward to having us join him in London and she said she would look into some flight information once we were finished eating. We still needed confirmation that we could stay at Adrian's house, we figured it would be best to wait to book until I heard from Adrian again.

  Once we cleared the table, I headed to the bathroom to freshen up for the day while Romy sat down at the computer. After I had showered and dressed, I checked my phone to make sure I hadn't missed any calls although I knew it would be a while until Adrian called, he was trying to sober up from the night before. I had missed a call however, from a local number. It was a number I did not recognize and I resisted calling it back. There were very few people who had this cell phone number and all of those numbers were programmed into my phonebook. With Natalie in a new home I had no number for her in my contacts. It had to have been her but why would she be calling me now? What did she possibly want from me? She was living with her *'real'* friends, Amber and Courtney. What was there left to say to each other.

I put my phone into my jeans pocket and pulled out my smaller piece of luggage and laid it open on the bedroom floor. I started opening my drawers taking out socks and underwear and packing them into my suitcase. I walked over to the closet and pulled out several outfits and placed them on my bed trying to figure out what to take, when my phone rang again.

I pulled the phone out of my back pocket expecting it to be Adrian but it was the same local number from the call I had missed before. Could it really be Natalie calling from Claudia's house? Did something serious happen? It couldn't have been that important, she never left a message the first time she called. The call ended and again no message was left, but as I was putting the phone back in my pocket it rang again and I was extremely agitated.

"Hello!" I barked into the phone. "Oh. Hello Zahra? Did I catch'ya at a bad time?" it was Ruben. *"Ruben?"* "Yes, it's me," he replied. "How'd you get my number?" I asked. "From Natalie. She asked me to call. Do you have a few minutes to chat?" he asked. "I guess. What is this about?" I asked only half concerned. After fifteen years of friendship Natalie couldn't even call me herself. *How pathetic.* I decided I needed to give Ruben a chance, he was innocent in this situation, he was just the messenger and I was taught never to shot the messenger, he was only doing his job. "Okay, yeah what's up?" "I'm not far from your place can I drop by for a second?" "Umm, can't you just tell me now?" I asked, trying to figure out why Ruben wanted to stop by. "I could, but I'd rather tell you in person. Also, I have a little something for your family, a 'thanks for dinner' that first night when we arrived." "OH. Well okay." "Great. I'll be there in twenty," he said before ending the conversation.

I walked to the living room where Romy was on the computer. "Do you think you could maybe just call Adrian? I know he's still sleeping but I've found a really great package, if we can't stay at his house," Romy explained. "All right, I'll call him, but Ruben's on his way over now, something about *Natalie*…"

"*Natalie?*"

"Yeah I don't know…"

"Okay, well I'll go get some more coffee and some cake, Ruben really likes mom's cake," Romy said walking to the kitchen. "I'll help," I joined her. I put a couple of mugs and plates out on the coffee table in the living room as Romy sliced the spiced cake.

Within no time Ruben was ringing the door bell and Romy was letting him in. "Hey girls, Merry belated Christmas," he said. "Hey Ruben, same to you," I stepped into the hallway to greet him. As he kicked off his boots and stepped further into the hallway he glanced into our room and saw my open suitcase on the floor. "Going somewhere?" he asked casually. "We're going to London in a few days—" Romy explained. "For New Year's Eve," I interrupted, hoping he wouldn't put two and two together and realize we were going to see Adrian. I knew he would probably object. For some reason he wasn't too fond of Adrian. "To see Andre?" he asked. "*Adrian!*" I corrected sharply. "Sorry, my mistake," Ruben said, hands up defensively. He walked past our room and into the living room and took a seat on the end of the couch. Romy and I followed. Romy sat on the couch across from Ruben and I curled up on the other end of the couch he was sitting on.

After a brief moment of silence, I decided to ask what was going on with Natalie. Both Romy and I were dying to know and to get it out of the way, but Romy was still really pissed about the whole situation with her brother and I knew she wouldn't be the one to ask. "Well. Her parents have decided that she will no longer continue on this trip, she has been sent home. She left early this morning on a six a.m. flight," Ruben explained. "Oh," Romy was shocked. "Is that it?" I asked. "What do you mean?" he asked. "That's it? That's all you had to say? I thought something bad happened to her or…" "Or what? Were you hoping maybe for a letter? Or a phone call?" Ruben asked. "…I don't know. I guess I kinda just figured she would tell us herself. I mean what's the big deal?" I asked. Romy nodded in agreement. "Hmm, I think she's just embarrassed so I told her I would let you two know after I dropped her off at the airport," he said. "Oh *you* dropped her? How was *that?*" Romy asked suspicious. "It wasn't as bad as you may think Romy, she was too embarrassed to really speak, it went better than expected," he said with a smile. "So, she didn't try to jump you?" Romy asked teasingly. "Nope. Thank the gods! The Creator has my back!" Ruben said laughing. I was completely unsatisfied. Something didn't seem right.

"Anyway, here are a few gifts for Christmas," he said taking a few packages out of his messenger bag. He handed one package to Romy and one to me placing the last gift for Mila and Fredrik on the coffee table. "Thanks Ruben," we both said individually as we began to open our prospective gifts. Romy opened her package and was happy to receive a book about ancient tribal tattoos. She was very interested in the markings of ancient civilizations and the book kept her busy for hours as she researched the findings found in her perfect gift. I opened my gift next, it was another sketchbook. Completely brand new and unused. The leather was ivory and the same familiar image was stained with different colours to match the scene. The sky was a dark blue almost black with tiny white dots representing stars, the rock was white, the land was green and the water a peaceful blue. I ran my fingers over the perfect book in awe.

"Did your—"

"Yes, my mom made it. I called in a favour and she made it just for you," he explained.

"It's perfect. Ivory is my favourite colour, how'd you know?"

"You told me, remember?"

To be honest, I didn't. But I had been living in a foggy haze for the past few weeks and I was certain that I said a lot of things to people with no recollection. "Thank you Ruben. I really love it. I'll start in it when I've used up all the pages of my other book," I said moving toward him for a hug, which he gladly welcomed. He held me tightly and we lingered there for a few moments. It was an embrace that I was a bit uncomfortable with which he quickly sensed and let me go. "How's the work coming along in the other book anyway?" he asked, hurrying to change the subject. "It's coming," I replied. "Can I take a look?" he asked. "Umm, sure," I said, getting up to get my book from my room. Romy followed my lead and went to the kitchen to grab the coffee she had brewed, leaving Ruben by himself for a few minutes.

Romy poured us all a cup of coffee and handed Ruben a slice of cake. He smiled delightedly as he took the plate and forked a huge piece of cake, shoving it into his mouth. I sat down beside him and handed him my book, the cake was done in four large bites. He scrolled the pages taking in all the images on each page, my technique, my structure and I was nervous. "These are amazing Zahra, you really have a gift. What a great hand," he commented. I blushed. "Thanks. There were a few more pieces but I sent them to Adrian, I need to fill the pages up a bit more." "You captured Romy perfectly, wow. I'm really impressed! When I was teaching art back in White Rock, some of my students weren't even close to what you've got here," he said. "Let me see that," Romy insisted getting out of her seat and leaning over Ruben's shoulder to see the portrait I had done of her. "Zahra, this is amazing! You made me look perfect, so pretty," Romy gushed. "What are you talking about Romy? That's exactly how you look," I pointed out laughing lightly. She shrugged her shoulders and took her seat again sipping her coffee. "I'd love to start working with you on different techniques soon if you're still interested," Ruben informed. "Yeah for sure, I'd love that," I replied. "Shall we start tomorrow?" he asked. "I'm working all day for the next two days, then one day off and then London," I explained. "Hmm, okay how about your day off? Or would you rather wait till you get back?" he asked looking a little disappointed. Ruben was so interested in my talent that I felt bad to resist, I really did want his help.

    I was interested in learning about oil paints and even doing some abstract pieces using different materials and textures so I couldn't simply brush him off until I got back from London. I knew I had to seize the opportunity, he was giving me free lessons, lessons I knew were extremely expensive back in British Columbia—He said he taught art classes in White Rock, I wonder where he taught? Could it be possible that he taught at the school I attended almost every summer? Maybe that's why he seemed so familiar—I hadn't yet decided what I wanted to do after high school. I hadn't applied to any Colleges or Universities, which peeved Joanne and Fabién, but it didn't make sense to waste their money taking a bunch of general classes while I decided what I wanted to do with my life. To me, it made the most sense to figure it out and then go when I was ready, if I ever would be. Of course this didn't work for the family image, but I never really cared much for upholding an invisible standard. With Ruben's enthusiasm, I was starting to feel like I might like to major in art, art culture or something, if there was such a thing. I didn't really know what kind of job that would land me, but I really didn't care. I just wanted to learn.

    "My day off sounds good. Can we do oils?" I asked. He

smiled. "Of course we can. We can do whatever you want. I'll come back here, we'll start simple, maybe paint the landscape out the back of the house or something," he said. "Okay. That's sounds like a plan," I said returning the smile.

Ruben left shortly after our plan was set and Romy and I continued to pack. I heard from Adrian too. He told me that his parents were really looking forward to us coming and he would pick us up at the airport. We booked our flight for London for December 30 on the eight a.m. flight arriving at ten a.m. London time. I was so excited that the next two days flew by like a blur. Romy and I worked all day trying to pull in as many tips as we could, treating all the customers in the small cafe section of the bakery with extreme generosity to maximize our spending money for our upcoming trip. I could hardly contain myself, within hours, I would be with Adrian. But, unfortunately, as Murphy's Law goes, anything that could go wrong went wrong. I started breaking out, something that I was thankfully never prone to, except for now of course. On my last day of work, I burned my arm on the oven, nothing serious but definitely painful and was sent home early losing out on the extra tips. I needed to take my mind off of the trip that was quickly approaching, I was thankful for my painting session with Ruben.

Romy

    I woke up that morning, skipped the shower and piled on layers of clothing. Just the thought of a hot shower followed by hours outside, made me cold. I ate a quick breakfast and drank a tall cup of hot tea. It was ten in the morning when Ruben called and said he was on his way and would be there in about thirty minutes. I gathered all of my supplies and threw on my hat, scarf and gloves and pulled on the fury boots. We would be working outside and I needed to stay warm. He knocked on the door at exactly ten-thirty. I was starting to realize that it was unlike him to ever be late or held back unless there was good reason.

    We walked outside and around to the back of the house. The backyard was beautiful. All the trees were thickly covered with sheets of heavy white snow and the small pond was frozen, a silvery grey ice. The sky was bright and blue and the sun was burning an intense gold, high in the sky. We walked over to a small clearing and put down our supplies. Ruben had brought with him two small stools for us to sit on so we could capture the scenery. He opened an easel that he bought from a local art store and placed on it a large thin canvas for me to practice on. He began to demonstrate how to apply the paint to the canvas forming different textures with the paint layers and how to create definition amongst the white trees and thick billowing hills of snow.

"So, I take this liner sable brush, you want one with a long narrow tip, hold the handle up and just drag the brush across the canvas. You want to make sure that you go in the direction that tree branches grow or it won't look right. Perfect leafless trees." He wiped the extra paint off the bristles with a rag and picked up a fan brush.

"Evergreens. Pull your fan brush through the paint, wiggle it a little, fill up the bristles. Load the brush with lots of dark blue, black and sap green, you can add a little linseed oil to the paint if you want to thin it down, but we're not gonna do that. Okay, now, make a thin, vertical line, the tree trunk. Next, hold your brush on an angle, so it's diagonal in your hand and just tap the corner of the brush on the canvas, moving down the vertical line. Perfect evergreen. You try."

When it was my turn, I did as Ruben instructed, the tree was all right, but it looked more like diagonal lines on a canvas, than an evergreen tree, I wasn't satisfied. I swivelled on my stool and took the easel with me. I applied another layer of colour from my new angle, but I still wasn't satisfied. I sighed. "Be patient Zahra, let it come to you," Ruben, standing behind me, looking over my shoulder, placed his hand on my back. "I *am letting it come to me*, but my brain isn't connecting the image in my head, to my hand, to the canvas," I was frustrated. Ruben spun me around on the swivel stool so that I was facing him. "Okay, close your eyes," he began, "take a minute, take all of this in. Breathe in the landscape, feel the scenery in your fingertips, feel the cold snow all around you, be one with the universe..." he soothed, meditatively with mocking undertones. With my eyes closed I couldn't tell if he was joking or not, I envisioned his words anyway.

I gasped, "Ruben that's amazing, I can feel it... I can feel every aspect of the snow." The cool, sharp ting of the snow, the complexity of hot and cold combined, on my skin. I opened my eyes slowly, a small mountain of snow piled up in the palms of Ruben's gloved hands. I blinked away the piercing sunlight, my eyes adjusting, Ruben stood facing me, blew the light gossamer flakes, they parachuted in the breeze, landing numbly on my face.

I laughed in surprise, "You tricked me!" I grabbed a handful of snow and threw it at him, running. He guarded himself defensively and in one swift motion, balled a handful of the tiny white flakes and threw it in my direction. I turned my back, the snowball hitting the back of my shoulder. I pulled my hat off my head and quickly filled it with cold, white goodness, charging toward Ruben who was ducking side to side, blocking my tackle. Arms tangled, snow flying everywhere.

"Okay, okay, I surrender. Let's get back to work." Ruben hunched over, his hands on his knees, breathless. "You give up old man?" I swayed from side to side, enticing an attack. *"Old man? Those are fighting words."* He swooped down, covered his fingers with snow, flicked it in my direction. "C'mon kiddo, we should get at least one tree on this canvas." He threw his arm around my shoulder, we walk back to our stools and easel. "Put your hat back on," he demanded. "I can't, it's got snow in it." "Take mine. You'll catch a cold," he pulled his black toque off his head and tugged it onto mine. I could not refuse.

I picked up my supplies, my graffitied canvas pencil case and my stool, Ruben grabbed the easel, canvas and extra seat. "Is that your graffiti?" he asked. I nodded my head. "It's pretty sweet," he said. "You got any pieces?" he asked. I shook my head. "I'm not the kind to sneak around at night, defacing the sides of convenient stores."

"Well we gotta change that, next time I do a piece, we'll share it," Ruben concluded. I looked at him wide eyed.

"All legal! None of that midnight, hiding in the shadows, hoping not to get caught, kind of stuff. It's all through art programs, you'd love it. You could say, I'm all-city-legal," he said proudly. *"You're, all-city,"* I said, skeptical. "What? You don't believe me? I am!" Ruben rebutted. "Okay, where would I see your work?" "All over the place, duh," he stated the obvious. I glared sarcastically. "Fine. What do you write?" "Spukani." *"You're Spukani? You're like famous!"*

He laughed, "I'm not famous Zahra, I'm all-city."

"Same thing!"

"Different world. You use Montana paint?" he asked. "Of course." "Good girl," he smiled, pleased. "Where are we going?" he asked, as he followed my lead across the snowy tundra. "I need a better view." We trekked through the snow, like a empty wilderness, stopping now and then to assess the angles, Ruben trailing behind. I found it, the perfect spot. I rushed toward it, inspired. Though he was joking, Ruben was right, it needed to come to me, the image lucid in my head. I raced to it, the frozen pond. The silvery, grey ice, deceptive. Ruben hurried forward, the stool, easel and canvas discarded, making deep impressions in the snow, arms waving violently. His voice a distant echo. My name echoing off the trees. I motioned him forward, he was moving with great speed. I stepped further out on the frozen perfection, the sun casting a golden blur on the ice. I looked around at my settings, it was magical. Ice and snow and trees and sun, perfect. Ruben, raced, tuffets of snow flying. "Ben, hurry up," I yelled, vigorously motioning with my hand. "I found the perfect spot!"

A loud crack, the ice shifted, parting beneath me. I jerked my head sharply to look at Ruben, terrified, struggling through the snow, his arm outstretched, still too far away. My feet came out from under me, I crashed down hard on my ankle shooting pain up my leg. I opened my mouth to scream, my lungs filled with frigid liquid. I could not breathe. I gasped viciously. I struggled to keep my head above the numbing water, the weight of my clothes steadily pulled me down. The tightening in my lungs made it impossible to breath. My heart contracting in my chest. I released my hands, the stool and art supplies sinking, as I frantically tried to grab ahold of the ice around me, vainly. My arms, unyielding poles of ice, numb, deadened by the cold. I tried to kick my feet to tread water, but fiery pain shot up from my ankle into the thigh.

I cried and screamed trying to keep myself alive, was this the end? Within seconds I could hear Ruben screaming for help, his voice quickly approaching. He slid across the ice scuffing snow in the air as he landed.

"ZAHRA, STAY WITH ME, HOLD ON. I'M GOING TO PULL YOU OUT OKAY, KIDDO? JUST HANG ON. *PLEASE.*

"HEEELLLPPPPP!"

Ruben shouted, lying stomach down on the ice with his face only inches from mine. His eyes were wet and filled with tears as he reached into the black watery hole that was threatening to take my life.

"Please Ben," I cried, "I can't feel my legs, they're so cold," I sobbed, "my ankle…" I wailed uncontrollably. Everything seemed to be moving in slow motion and despite the chaos that surrounded me the world seemed to be so still and unchanged. I was fighting for my life and the birds were still singing. I was fighting for my life and the sun was still shining. I was fighting for my life and I couldn't help but notice how beautiful the trees looked all covered with snow. The spot still perfect.

"I KNOW HONEY. I KNOW, JUST HOLD ONTO ME, I'M GOING TO GET YOU OUT OF THERE, ARE YOU READY?" he shouted frantically.

"Okay. I'm ready," I cried.

"ON THE COUNT OF THREE, ONE, TWO," Ruben reached in and wrapped his arms around my body and pulled me out with all of his strength. I screamed in immense pain as my ankle—that I was sure was broken—hit the solid ice. He cloaked himself around me, rocked us back and forth, sobbing. He rubbed my arms frantically trying to keep me warm, but the cold was too deep, penetrating my bones, aching in my muscles, suffocating, closing off the oxygen to my lungs spreading throughout my body like a thick black fog that I could not overcome. "Stay with me Zahra…

"…Stay with…

"Look…

"…Please…

"… at me…" Ruben, his voice thick. He tried to shake life back into me. I swayed back and forth, drunken, the cold intoxicating, everything in slow motion. Images flashed behind my eyelids at lightening speed. Is this the end? Memories of *tutus, ballet recitals, Jonnæ smiling, waving, taking pictures, pink and white sneakers…red lights in the soles, flowers, tears, Jonnæ, sadness, an embrace, walking away, looking back, gelato on the pier.*

Sketching at the podium…Jonnæ's restaurant, summertime, art school, graffiti workshops, Montana aerosol cans, swirls of colour, painting my room, tanning on the beach, waves, ocean, Natalie, longboarding on the boardwalk,

Jason.

Trip to Austria, signing paperwork, buying luggage, calendar marks, the house, Joanne, Fabién, Jonnæ, fighting.

Running, heart pounding, fog, darkness, rain, escape, airport, Ruben, smiling, plane, take off, landing, Romy, Mila, Fredrik.

Soft blue eyes, light brown hair, perfect smile, embroidered cloth napkin, Adrian…

The beautiful still world around me was quickly fading, My eyes glossed over, images blurred and as hard as I tried, I could not focus, I could not stay and then everything went black.

Trapped

January 1

I don't know how long I was out for. My brain became alert before the rest of my body did. My eyes were still shut and no matter how hard I tried, I could not open them. The sound of machines beeping was all I could hear and whispers, unfamiliar voices, nurses maybe, doctors even, I don't know and then it was silent.

I drifted.

I drifted to a place that was peaceful and quiet, a place where I could just rest, a much needed rest, something I had been missing since that morning back in White Rock. In that place, White Rock didn't exist, nor did Austria or the people I left behind.

"Do you think she can hear us?" a familiar voice shocked me out of my peaceful repose. My eyes still wouldn't open and my lips wouldn't move, I fought desperately against my eyelids and my sealed lips, I wanted to yell and tell her to get out and to stay away from me. Jonnæ was talking to Ruben. "I think so Miss…her heart monitor just increased at the sound of your voice." He sounded tired. "When do you think she'll open her eyes? It's been three days," she said.

THREE DAYS? *Oh no, I missed the London trip* I thought instantly wanting to cry.

"She's crying," Jonnæ pointed out.

Great.

"Look, there's a tear running down her face," she continued.

Thanks for stating the obvious.

"I really think we should leave her alone, her heart monitor is going wild," I could hear Ruben say. "He's right, Jonnæ, I also think we shouldn't be here when she *does* wake up." A voice in the distance.

Fabién? Perfect. They're all here. Leave it to me to fall through some ice and bring the people I've been avoiding, out.

"EXCUSE ME? You're not serious are you?" Jonnæ said in disgust. "Your father's right Jonnæ, seeing us here will be too stressful for her," Joanne assessed.

Yeah ya'think! Please leave. Please go back to your useless lives in White Rock and leave me alone. I don't need your comfort, I don't need your pity, I just need for all of you to go away.

"How do you know that? She might be really happy to have us," Jonnæ said.

Fat chance.

"Plus she can't *see* anything!" Jonnæ rebuked.

"I know you'd like that, but Jonnæ I don't think that'll be the case," Fabién said sincerely.

Yes that's right, listen to your father Jonnæ, leave...

Jonnæ began to cry and I wondered if Ruben was still in the room. I wondered what he was thinking, he didn't know why I had been so upset, but I'm sure by this point he could somewhat figure it out.

"Excuse me, I don't mean to interrupt, but the nurses are saying that Zahra needs to be alone now, that there's too much activity with her heart monitor and she needs to calm down," Ruben said, muddled chatter flooding in around him. His voice sounded distant like he was outside of the room, in the doorway maybe and timid, unlike himself. "Yes of course," Joanne said formally, her voice cold as she addressed Ruben. "Thank you," she said dismissively. "We'll go back to the hotel and back to White on the next flight in the morning," Joanne stated. "I WON'T LEAVE HER, NOT WHEN SHE'S LIKE THIS!" Jonnæ fumed.

Pathetic

"Keep your voice down Jonnæ. No need to be so dramatic. Do you want them to kick you out?" Joanne asked, not looking for

an answer. "We're leaving. NOW!" she barked at Jonnæ
Thank God!

(★)¹⁶ "Okay, just give me one minute, *please*," Jonnæ begged, sobbing. I felt her warm hand take mine, her warm breath on my face. It smelled like it always did, cinnamon or a cup of chai tea and as much as I hated her, I missed her, she was my—Jonnæ. She rubbed my hand lightly and sobbed uncontrollably. She exhaled a few times, followed by short gasps like she was trying to figure out what to say, but was lost for words and then she started to sing.

She sang the lullaby that she wrote for me when I was a child and now listening to it in this sort of sleep state it all made sense. I was too young to understand the lyrics back then, but now it was clear, it was right there in front of me from the moment I was born. If I had only been able to understand, I would have known she was my mother…

Jonnæ wasn't by any means musically gifted, I mean she was no quacking duck, but she was no cherub either. Her voice was average, like mine, she could hold a tune, but either way I had always loved the song growing up, preferring it over any bedtime story. It had been years since I had heard it, not since Jonnæ had moved out of "our" parents' house and into her own. When I eventually moved in with her I was too old for lullabies, the song was locked away.

"Zahra, baby, if you can hear me. I want you to know that I love you. I love you so much. We all do and I'm *so* sorry about all of this. I will do anything to make this better. Come back to me okay. I miss you pretty girl," she cried, sounding so much like a mother, a

---

[16] Little Star-Madonna *(Read to the end of the paragraph with the ★ then listen to the song in its entirety before beginning the next paragraph)*

sound that was so alien to me coming from her mouth. I wanted to curl up in her arms like I did when I was a child. I wanted her to stroke my head and tell me it would get better.

Tear drops fell from her eyes, burned like acid, onto my hand that she held up to her cheek. I wanted to pull my hand away, but I wanted to keep it there forever too. For a moment I was conflicted.

DON'T TOUCH ME!

She kissed my hand and laid it back down at my side, the smell of cinnamon in the air, she was gone.

"Hi kiddo."

Ruben.

After Jonnæ left, the room was silent, I didn't hear when Ruben entered. He was sitting beside my bed I was sure. His familiar scent of sandalwood and pine filled the room and I was so happy to have him there. I felt safe and comfortable with Ruben, grateful that he had gotten rid of my unwelcome visitors.

He sobbed.

"Zahra, I'm so sorry I got you in this mess. I should have never let you go out there on the pond by yourself. What was I thinking? You were just…so happy and I couldn't deny you that. They'll never forgive me, your family. I was supposed to protect you…" he trailed off mumbling to himself words that were inaudible to me.

Who cares what they think? I sure don't. It's not your fault Ruben! I can't believe you're blaming yourself for this. I bet Joanne is. Isn't she?

… Supposed to protect me?…

"I promise when you wake up, I'll keep a better eye out for you. Nothing will ever happen to you again. I promise. I promise."

But Ruben you can't promise that nothing will ever happen…that's just not how life works! And I assure you, you don't need to keep more of an eye on me. You're already doing way too much, but I appreciate it. It's nice to just have someone on my side. Please don't be sad Ruben. Don't blame yourself for this. It's my fault, really.

"Okay. I won't keep your friends any longer. They've been dying to see you now that you're responding to sound. I'll be back in a bit." I could smell his scent waft into the air as he got out of his seat and called my friends in.

"Come on in guys, she's waiting," I could hear Ruben say. Quiet footsteps entered the room. I wasn't sure how many there were, two maybe, three pairs of feet.

Romy? Jason? Natalie? Oh Jason I've missed you. Natalie, we can work things out.

"Hi Zahra, it's me Roms. I hope you can hear me, they say that maybe you can and that today your heart rate has been changing when someone talks to you so maybe that means you know I'm here." My heart monitor pulsed. There was a moment of silence. "I'm just glad that I heard Ruben screaming for help and that I was able to call for an ambulance, that we got you here in time," she started to cry. "I'm sorry Zar, I don't want you to hear me like this. I'll come back soon when I can keep it together," she promised and kissed my forehead. The scent of vanilla draped over my face and trailed behind her as she left the room.

Wait! Romy, come back! Don't leave yet… thank you for saving my life…don't go Romy, not yet…

I drifted back into my wistful rest after Romy left the room. I'm not sure how long I was out for, time was irrelevant where I was, it had no meaning as I waited impatiently for my eyes to open. My mind focused on the world around me again, wakened by the sound of my heart monitor beeping loudly, the pace increased. It was a steady beat, but one slightly escalated. My hand, the same hand that Jonnæ had held and cried on, held between two warm hands. My cold fingers tingling, heat returning quickly. Soft lips pressed firm, then gentle on my forehead, soap and crisp and ocean-fresh scent, swept over my body as he sat back into his seat. *Adrian.* I breathed.

"Well hello to you too." His voice filling each corner of the room. "You look even more beautiful than you did yesterday and way more rested than you did the day before that," he said, faint strain in his tone.

You've been here that long? I've been here that long?

"Zar, look. I know everyone's been saying 'hurry and open your eyes, we miss you et cetera, et cetera. And the truth is, yeah, we do miss you, and yeah, we do want you to open your eyes, but I'm telling you this, do it only when you're ready. The doctors say you're not in a coma, but that because you've survived a near death experience, your body just needs some time, so take it. We're not going anywhere. *I'm* not going anywhere. I promise. I'll be here when you open your eyes so don't rush it, take your time love."

No, there's no time, Adrian. I need to open my eyes right now. I wish I could see you. C'mon eyes, OPEN! JUST OPEN. PLEASE.

"So...I met your family, that was...interesting," he sighed. "I thought your twenty questions was rough," he laughed. "Jonnæ. She's something. She asked me so many questions about myself, about the two of us. Wow! She's super protective of you. Can't say I blame her. You're quite special."

Adrian, why is this happening? We should be sightseeing in London right now.

"Don't hate me for saying this but—you remind me a lot of her. I see so much of Jonnæ in you now that I know her..." he trailed off.

Adrian, forgive me, but SHUT UP! I don't want to hear this right now. Why are you wasting our time together talking about Jonnæ? Who cares about Jonnæ.

"Sorry babes, I won't bring her up again." It was like he could read my thoughts, like he was completely in tune with me. We stayed in silence, me almost lifeless and he, well I'm not sure what he was doing, but I was sure his eyes were on me as he held my hand in his.

"Tonight's my night with you, it's our second night together," he laughed a tired laugh, "…I can't say this is how I expected our first nights together to be. I'm sure you feel the same."
What are you talking about?

"I stayed here with you on New Year's Eve. There's a small couch beside your bed and I slept on it the first night. Ruben stayed last night and I'm here now. We've been switching off each night. Everyone loves you Zar. No one wants to leave you alone," he said.

"New Year's Eve was great. I wish you could have been awake for it. It was you, me, Romy, Ruben and Jonnae. We had a little party. The nurses let us stay past visiting hours and we rang in the New Year together. Is Jonnæ into younger men?"
Younger men?

"Romy called me when they got you to the hospital and I just picked up and left. My dad drove me home to grab my passport and then to the airport right away and I booked the first flight I could get on," he said. "I actually had to go buy some clothes and stuff when Ruben stayed the other night, I didn't even think to take any clothes," he laughed. "I bought a new guitar too, I found it for a great price. It's much nicer than the one I have at home. Anyway, on New Year's Eve the four of us sat here with you, we watched the event on the tele and celebrated together. I don't think you were aware of us yet so you probably don't remember any of it. It was fun. I didn't kiss you at midnight, I really wanted to, but that'll have to wait till you're better, plus your mother was watching!" he laughed.

Ugh.

He sighed. He sounded exhausted. I wanted him to just go back to Romy's and get some real sleep. I wanted him to stop worrying about me because I wasn't sure when I was going to open my eyes again and I didn't want him wasting his time sitting helplessly by my bed.

"Visiting hours are almost over so I'm going to let the nurses set you up for the night, I'll be back in a minute or two. I love you." He kissed the palm of my hand, folded my fingers around it, "Something you can hold on to." He walked away, I drifted back into my familiar resting place for the night.

Still...Trapped...

January 2

I remained in my restful bliss for...well I don't really know how long, maybe it was until the next day. After hearing Adrian's voice, I was able to rest undisturbed for many hours and I was unaware of anything for the better part of day. I didn't know if Adrian was still there, or maybe it was Romy, all I knew is that I was somewhere else.

"Your heart monitors have remained unchanging so I guess you've slipped away again." I could hear his smooth, even voice close by. He was most likely sitting on the chair that had remained unmoved from my bedside. "Oh wait. I think you're coming back to me, there's a bit more activity now," I could feel his hand pass on top of my head and through my hair. "Hey kiddo," he whispered. "It's nice to have you back for a while."

Ruben. I smiled in my mind.

"I'm going to brush your hair okay? Your nurse put it in a braid not too long ago, but I can't imagine it's very comfortable on the back of your head like that. So I'm going to take it out and brush through your hair so it doesn't get tangled," he said. I could feel my head lifted gently and held securely in his large hands. He cradled it like a baby, as he released the long braid that went down the back of my neck and shoulders.

"You know, I used to have long hair myself. For a long time actually, since I was a teenager I started growing it out and I never really cut it until about a month before this trip," he explained, brushing through my curly hair. "They're afraid that your hair will be completely matted when you wake up, it's so curly, but I'll take care of it. I'll brush it everyday until that day comes," he said, in the softest, gentlest voice I'd ever heard Ruben use. "You're a very special young lady, kid, any mom or dad would be so lucky to have you. Don't think they don't know it and whatever they've done to make you turn away from them—I assure you they're regretting it now."

Dad? Oh my God...I don't have one. I DON'T HAVE A FATHER! WHO'S MY FATHER?

It was the first time I had ever thought about it or realized that I didn't know who my father was. I was so caught up in everything else that I never stopped to think about the underlying layers of that truth. I never remembered Jonnæ ever having a boyfriend, but then again she probably wouldn't have still been with that guy once she gave me up to Joanne and Fabién. Maybe that's why she gave me up in the first place. Did she have an affair with a married man? Was I a *love child*? No, that didn't seem like her, then again I knew nothing about Jonnæ, not the truth anyway. Was he just some teenage kid like her? Did he even know that he fathered a child eighteen years ago?

Think Zahra, THINK!

At the realization that my life was even more of a mess than I had been aware of, a brand new hurt, a new gap in my heart, evolved. *How can this be happening to me? Why is this happening to me? I hate you Jonnæ, how could you do this to me? No wonder I don't really look like any of them. It all makes sense now. I look like 'him.' I've spent years staring back at a face in the mirror that I don't recognize, it's the face of a person that I don't even know, that I may never know. I was so close to the stranger and yet so far away.*

(★)[17] I knew that I looked like Jonnæ, even Joanne a bit, but I just figured all the girls looked the same and if there had been a son, he'd look like Fabién. Just like Mikael and Fredrik.

"Hey kid, why are you crying? What's wrong Zahra? Did I say something?" Ruben asked quietly, dabbing my stray tears with

---

[17] Let Down-Dead By Sunrise (Revisited)

some sort of cloth. My heart monitor beeped wildly as I laid there dying inside. I wanted to know him, I wanted him to look me in the face and tell me why I wasn't good enough for him to stay with me, to love me and take care of me. I wanted him to tell me why Jonnæ had to give me up, I wanted him to tell me what was so goddamn important that he couldn't be there for me like he should have been. I wanted the truth, but could I handle it?

The thought of *'him'* cut deep within my skin. The wound was torn open and new skin tried to pull tight across a damaged, broken vessel. The porcelain doll destroyed, her face shattered on the floor, arms, legs, torso left behind, faceless. Months ago, I told myself that I wasn't going to be let down anymore, well that blew out the window!

Who was this faceless man who helped give me life? What was his name? What did he look like? Did he have a wife? *A husband?* Kids? Was he alive? Were there sisters and brothers I knew nothing about? Did he even know I existed? Why didn't he ever try to contact me? Or did he? Why didn't he fight for me? Why didn't he love me?

Anxiety built up within me, I was trapped in my own body, trapped with my sullen thoughts without any escape, the escape I always turned to. Unable to say or do anything, but lie there stuck on that bed helpless, was psychologically ripping at my insides and I was overcome with despair. I could hear the nurses storming into the room, chaos unfolding, pushing Ruben aside. Everything was hazy, my heart monitor a slow distant pulse, unwinding like dying batteries in a musical toy. "I'm sorry," Ruben's voice, deep, slurred, unnatural. I drifted into a forced abyss.

So Hold On...

January 3

(★)¹⁸ I heard the soft strumming on a guitar, playing a sweet sounding melody that was slow and peaceful, without structure and yet with guidance, echoing throughout the room. The undertones of the melody were sad and as he played I floated in and out of the spaces between the real world and my own gilded reality. It was the perfect backdrop to wherever I was and was one of the most serene moments I had had while I waited for my eyes to open and then he began to sing.

It was the first time I'd ever heard Adrian sing. His voice was raw and untrained and possessed a sort of mystical beauty. He sounded so unlike himself and I wouldn't have known it was him if he hadn't told me that he bought a guitar and for the familiar velvety texture in his voice. His song was amazing and pleasantly unexpected. I knew that he wanted to try to turn some of his poems into songs and with this song, he had done it effortlessly, but was this song about me? How could it be? It was so sad.

What does this mean? I could never hate you, That's impossible Adrian! What are you talking about? I wish I could just wake up, I want to wake up, I'm fighting to wake up, but I'm right here, right here with you. I just can't open my eyes…

I would never, COULD NEVER lie to you. Please. What are saying? Hold off from what? From you? No way! Why are you putting your coat on? WHERE ARE YOU GOING? YOU SAID YOU WOULD NEVER LEAVE ME! I AM in love. I'm in love with you. I thought we already sorted all of this out… Save my soul? WHY ARE YOU DOUBTING ME? WITHOUT YOU I HAVE NOTHING! Without you I have nothing…. I don't understand…please… Adrian...

---

[18] Never Think-Rob Pattinson *(Take your time as you read this chapter, let the music float in and out around the words.)*

I was so confused by his song, it was beautiful and peaceful, but sad, confusing and tortured, like he was lost. It was nothing like Let Me Sign, it was the complete opposite, like we had fallen apart, like he had forgotten about being the lucky ones, or kismet, belonging together. And what about that whole 'save your soul' thing? Was I damned? Had he given up on me? Had everyone given up? Where was Romy? Where was Jonnæ? Natalie? Jason? Ruben? Was I never going to wake up? How long had I been out for? Had it been weeks? Months? Was I dying?

I panicked.

My heart monitor rang out, the frenzy erupted, metal banging upon metal, darkness spreading, emptiness around me, spinning, slurred, heavy words trailing, "I'm sorry Zahra…" fading into the shadows, he was gone and so was I.

Holding On
January 4

The light was piercing. It was the brightest light I had ever seen and I was sure that I was dead. No human light could ever shine so bright. It was like a condensed ball of burning flames shining a direct path for me to follow. It shone so bright that I had to bring my hands up, to shade my eyes, but that was no help. The luminescence still burned and with my eyes closed all I could see was red behind my eyelids. I closed my eyes tightly, hoping for relief. How was I to follow the effulgence if I couldn't open my eyes to see it?

I must open my eyes. I must follow the light. No matter how much it burns, I must follow the light. I slowly peeled my eyelids apart so that I could focus on the glow and follow the path to where ever it would take me. My head began to spin and my eyes ached at the pressure from the exuberant light that shone intensely above me. I closed my eyes again, the pain was too unbearable and after a few moments rest, I tried again.

I slowly opened my eyes and attempted to focus as best I could to stop my head from spinning. This time I was more successful. I squinted my eyes to filter the power of the piercing light and soon my eyes focused on what was white and speckled black above me, the drop ceiling. I tilted my head slightly to the left and realized that the bright burning light I had been following in my mind was the sun, shining in through my window, hanging high in the sky directly across from my bed as if it was telling me it was time to wake up.

I'M AWAKE!

"I'm awake," I said, out loud.

How strange it was to hear my voice for the first time in—I don't know how long. As I slowly began to drift back into reality, I suddenly became aware of everything around me. My body ached, my throat was painfully dry and I was stiff, but not as stiff as I expected to be. I suppose Ruben, Adrian, Romy or one of the nurses had been moving my limbs, just as Ruben had been brushing my hair, Romy had been reading to me and Adrian had been singing.

Adrian.

He sang that sad song, the song about me lying or being better off without him or something.

I panicked.

"Adrian," I whispered. My throat, dry, my voice hoarse. There was no response. "Adrian?" I said again a bit louder, as loud as my body would allow.

Silence.

I used all of my energy to try to turn my head toward the couch that Adrian had described was somewhere beside my bed that he had been sleeping on. With much effort, I was able to turn my head and shift my body a little bit, but the effort was unwarranted, Adrian wasn't there. Nothing was there, no pillow, no blanket, just a vacant dark green leather couch attached to the wall.

Instantly I began to panic. What did his song mean? How long was I out for after they sedated me? Where did he go and was he ever coming back? What was going on? My heart monitor blared, announcing my panic to the nurses who came rushing in. Again, but this time I was able to see their faces. I think they were expecting to shoo a visitor out of the room, they were both shocked to see me lying there alone in my room with scared, tired eyes staring back at them.

"You're awake!" the one with blonde hair, pulled back into a bun, said. Her voice was thick with a German accent and she moved to my side to take a look at my face. "Such pretty eyes! We've been waiting a long time to see those eyes," she said, placing her hand on mine smiling warmly. "How long?" I whispered. "Six days," the other nurse, with dark brown hair laced with grey, said as she prepared a syringe. "WAIT!" I whispered as loudly as I could. "Please don't. I just woke up," I begged. "I know *schatzi*, but we need to calm your heart," she explained. "Please. I'll calm down. I was just afraid when I woke up and no one was here," I explained. "*Oh. The boy,*" the blonde nurse at my side smiled. "Such a nice song," the brunette said. "It was sad, no? He's sad," the blonde assessed. "Why?" I asked. "You tell me," she said. "Where'd he go?" I asked. "I don't know, he left early, earlier than usual," she began, "he took his things," she explained. "Will he come back?" I asked. "Oh *schatzi*, just rest now. Don't worry about these things. You need to worry only about getting better. Agnes, give her something for the pain," she continued. "What pain? I'm not in pain," I fought, and then the pain was present and I was fully aware of my broken ankle. "Not too much. I don't want to sleep anymore, please!" I begged again. "Okay, just a little to take off the edge, yes?" Agnes said. "Yes," I answered closing my eyes, indicating that I wanted to be left alone. "Can you move your arms?" the blonde asked. I opened my eyes and looked at her, peeved that she hadn't picked up my hint. I tried to move my arms with much effort and was rewarded with a little bit of movement. They were heavy and I was weak. "Goodt. Now try again," she said. I clenched my jaw annoyed and slowly lifted my arms a little, again. "Goodt enough," she said, setting up my bed table. Agnes fluffed my pillow under my head and cranked my bed into an upright position so that I was sitting.

The blonde, Hilda, placed a few rolled up pillows under my knees and adjusted the pillows propping up my broken ankle. I looked down at my foot hidden inside of a thick white plaster cast that reached halfway to my knee showing only my five toes, four of which were painted a sparkly silver. I was confused. *Great* I thought. *How long will I have to keep this thing on for? Why are only four of my toes painted?* Hilda followed my eyes and said, "You will need to wear the cast for about five more weeks. Your friend painted your toes, Dr. Arnulf needs the big toe clear so that we can check your circulation." "Oh," was all I could say.

"Okay Zahra, here is the remote, let's find something you like," she said, turning on the television and flipping through the channels. She stopped on a soap opera, clearly something she liked, she watched, fixated, for a few moments and commented to herself in German about the two characters on the screen. She obviously was not impressed with what they were doing. "I bring you some food, okay. Soon!" she patted my hand before shuffling out of the room. Everything was happening so fast, so fast that it was hard for me to keep up. In my silent world of dreams and darkness everything moved at a slow steady pace, floating along in space. Here, everything was rushing and for a moment I missed my quiet world of nothingness.

I stared blankly at the screen, withering away wondering what day it was, what time it was, where Romy was, where Ruben was and…Adrian…I tried my best not to think of him. I didn't want my monitor to go off again. I had just bargained my way out of sedation and I would have done anything to avoid that again. I was bored and I didn't want to sleep anymore, I had slept enough, I was wide awake, though drowsy, my head spinning from the pull of gravity.

I don't know how long it was, my perception of time was completely off, but after some time Agnes came back with a tray of food and placed it on the table over my bed. She opened the lid and left the room before I could tell her that I didn't eat meat. I didn't want the schnitzel.

The smell of the food was intoxicating, hunger pangs stabbed in my stomach, churning and gurgling at the sight and smell. I fought with my weak, aching muscles to pick up my fork. My fingers, stiff, my wrists locked and popping away tension. I was breathlessly holding the fork, scooping mashed potatoes, like a baby with its first experience of independence, struggling to bring the fork to my mouth.

"DO NOT PUT THAT IN YOUR MOUTH, drop the fork."

I did. Startled. Concentrated on the task at hand.

"What. Were you going to eat the schnitzel?" he asked. He moved the tray from the table and wiped the splattered mash potatoes off my chest with his napkin and picked up the fork from my bed.

"You scared me," I croaked, my voice hoarse. My throat sore.

"*You* scared *me!* Your first meal was about to be hospital food…and schnitzel. Think about how sick you'd be."

"I wasn't going to eat it! Just the potatoes…and how do you know it wouldn't be any good?"

"Nine years old, tonsils removed, trust me, I know."

"What are you doing here anyway?" I asked.

"What d'you mean? I haven't left, not for more than a couple of hours," he said, sitting down in the seat beside my bed, ripping open a paper bag, displaying a cheese sandwich, placing half of it on my table. "Do you want some?" he asked.
I nodded my head.

"Then you'll have to reach for it love."
I turned my head to look at him and gave him the most helpless look I could, "Please, I'm *so* hungry," I pleaded.

"And weak," he took a bite out of his half. "How will you ever be able to leave this place, if you can barely lift your arms?" he asked. "Maybe I don't want to," I said. "What's that?" "…Leave this place," I answered. "Why the hell not?" he asked, surprised. "Because then you'll leave me," I whispered, fighting back tears unsuccessfully. "Why are crying Zahra?" "Because you think I'm a liar? And because you weren't here when I opened my eyes," I explained. My heart monitor increasing.

"You need to calm down, they'll come in here and make me leave," he said. "D'you know how many times I've been shooed? And the last time I was, Agnes pinched my butt, I'm sure of it!" He took another bite of the sandwich, I watched begrudgingly. "I just stepped out to go to Romy's, take a shower, shave, do some laundry, make a sandwich…and then I got here and Agnes winked at me and smiled…I thought it was because she pinched my butt… Then I came in here and you were engaged, arms deep, in an epic battle with your fork and your fork was clearly winning!" he explained. "What's this about a liar?" he asked confused, leaning forward to wipe my tears with his napkin.

"In your song…" I started to say out of breath and tired.

"Oh. Eat first. You really should get some real food inside of you. You can't just survive off of Intravenous Parenteral Nutrition forever," he said.

"What?"

He pointed toward at the IV pouch attached to my arm.

"But—"

"EAT," he interrupted.

He was right, I was starving and my throat was extremely dry. I reached for the sandwich on my table, but wasn't able to grab it. He watched me intrigued, holding the other half of the sandwich in his hand. "C'mon, it's *good*," he took another bite, "it's got that fresh cheese you love so much! Tomatoes, some lettuce, fresh homemade mayo and a bit of dijon…" he licked the excess mayo off his thumb, making my stomach churn. I used all of my energy to try to lean forward and only moved about an inch. I was tired and breathless and completely frustrated. I leaned back against my bed defeated and upset. He popped the last bite of his half into his mouth and pushed my half closer to me so that it was almost at the edge of the table. I exhaled and heaved myself forward, grabbed the sandwich and smiled.

✸✸✸

"I want to get out of bed," I said, when we had finished eating our sandwich and drinking almost an entire pitcher of water.

"Is that so? You've been awake for what? Like an hour?"

"I need to get out of this bed Adrian," I ignored him.

"All right, where would you like to go?" he asked.

"I don't know…do you think I'd be allowed to leave the room?" I asked.

"Probably not, you've only just opened your eyes. I'm sure your doctor will be in to see you shortly," he replied. "How about I bring you over to the couch for now?" he asked. "Okay," I agreed.

He moved the table from over my bed and put the bed rails down. He slipped his left arm under my legs and his right arm behind my back and slid me across the bed, cautious not to tangle or pull my IV or my heart monitor cords, and raised me in his arms moving slowly toward the couch.

I rested my head on his shoulder, he sat down on the couch with me on his lap. He grabbed the pillow and blanket sitting neatly on a chair across from the couch —that I had failed to notice before in my state of panic— and propped the pillow under my leg and covered me with the blanket. My head was heavy, spinning dizzily, nausea stirring in my stomach. I should have stayed in bed.

"Are you okay, love? You look greenish."

I closed my eyes and groaned. He gently raked my hair with his fingers and kissed the top of my head. "You'll be all right, promise." He rested his head on mine and breathed loudly.

"Ew, don't smell my hair, it hasn't been washed in six days," I pointed out.

"I don't care. It smells like you." He folded his arms tightly around me. My heart ached. I missed him so much and then I remembered.

"Tell me about the song," I demanded.

"Not now babes, just rest," he breathed steadily, as if he had been sleeping.

"No more excuses Adrian. Tell me what's going on."

"It doesn't really matter Zah—"

"Adrian!" I snapped.

"Okay," he said, "I met your… Jonnæ, Joanne and Fabién," he started.

"I know."

"I spoke with Joanne for a while after Jonnæ hounded me for answers about myself and about us, our relationship. Then Joanne came over and sat with me, she started talking about how you never really had any boyfriends back home, but that you went on a couple of dates with your friend Jason some time back and how it didn't work out. She always thought that you would end up with him because the two of you had always been so close, closer than you and Natalie.

"Then she told me that she was surprised that you and I were together because I wasn't your type and that she never thought you'd date a smoker and she wondered what else I could be in to and worried that I would be a bad influence... She said you preferred clean cut guys, no face scruff and that kind of thing. Then she said that you had some guy waiting for you in White Rock..."

"A bad influence? Clean cut? You know who likes clean cut and preppy? Joanne! And what guy in White Rock? I don't even know who she's talking about... Oh, Austin?" I asked.

"Sure. I can't say I really tried to remember the chap's name," Adrian admitted.

"Adrian. You can't listen to *anything* Joanne says. She doesn't know me at all. I haven't lived in her house for a couple of years now and we've never been close. Ever. Isn't that obvious, if she thought that I was going to end up with Jason? Jason and I went on maybe three 'dates' to the arcade, *when we were fifteen!* And, if Jason and I *were so close*, wouldn't he have stopped by the hospital? And he wouldn't have stopped talking to me when Natalie and I started fighting. She knows nothing.

"Yeah, you're my first boyfriend and no, I've never really had a type. I haven't had enough experience to have a type. I can say that honestly. But stuck up, preppy and Joanne approved, definitely doesn't do it for me, and Austin, he's all of those things. He's the son of one of Joanne's colleagues, a work related, match made in heaven. I was forced to go out with him, he was such a tool. I showed up on a skateboard! Can you imagine how that went? The second time we were supposed to get together, I never showed up *and* that was last year. I don't understand why she doesn't want me to be happy," I fumed.

"Well, she saw me smoking outside which I know she didn't like, she didn't know who I was, nor did I know who she was either when they were walking into the hospital, but when I came upstairs and started talking to Ruben and Romy about any updates, she gave me the nastiest look and wrinkled her nose of course. I came back into your room and sat with you for a few moments alone, talked to you a bit, told you how much I loved you, you know the usual and when I left to give Jonnæ some privacy with you, that's when Joanne laid in on me and told me it would never work once you were back in White Rock and I was still in London. She said that you just needed me for now, but the distance between us would be too much and we'd drift apart. Maybe she's right." His arms around me, lax, but his chest was tight and his breathing altered.

"Adrian, you're not allowed to let Joanne get under your skin. Remember, she knows *nothing* about me. You're doing exactly what she hoped for. She's worried that I won't go back to White Rock as long as you're in my life. I know *her* better than *she* thinks. She's only trying to get you to end things with me now, so that when this trip is over I'll just go back and she won't have to worry about making up stories for the neighbours, about my absence."

"So you don't think you'll go back?" he asked.

"I don't know, I haven't thought about it at all. I don't think so, not right away. I'm not ready to face them yet. It was bad enough hearing their voices while I was out of it… I can't imagine it would be any different back in White Rock. Can we not worry about that now?"

"Okay," he said, unsatisfied.

The door opened, my doctor and two nurses entered the room. Adrian carried me back to bed so that I could be examined and he stepped out to call Ruben, to let him know that I was awake. Ruben and Romy were back at school, the Christmas break was over.

"How are you feeling?" Dr. Arnulf asked. "I'm okay," I answered. "Well, you were out for quite a number of days do you know what day it is today?"

"Monday I think, maybe Tuesday."

"Monday. Good! And the date?"

"January something…"

"January fourth. Well done. You must be feeling a bit weak? Do you have much pain?" "Yes. I am weak and no, not much pain," I replied. "You suffered from hypothermia and as you see a broken ankle. Your body was in shock and needed some time to recuperate. I'm glad to see that you're awake now. We will want to try to get you out of the hospital soon and back to your home. So tomorrow we will try to get you up on your feet and see if you can slowly start to move around on your own, with the aid of crutches, of course. I want you to try some light weight bearing, but not all day. You must still take it easy and use only your left leg for the most part, for another week. After that you can start with full weight and a boot cast and when you feel ready you can discard the crutches Okay?" he explained. "Your vitals look good and once you have some strength then you can leave this place, sound good?" he asked.

"Yes, that would be nice," I answered. "Good. Well, I will go get your friend and Agnes will remove the intravenous. Maybe later you can try to get up, we'll find you a wheelchair so you can have a change of scenery. See you soon," he said, smiling, before leaving the room. Agnes lifted my left hand and untaped the tubes. She slowly pulled out the intravenous therapy tube from the top of my hand, my stomach churned, it made me feel queasy, she covered the small hole with a bandage. She turned the heart monitor off and peeled the sticky pads off of my chest and wiped the gel off my skin. "There you go," she said and left the room.

Later that afternoon, when school had ended, Ruben and Romy stopped by. It was nice to finally see their faces again. I had missed them and grew tired of only hearing their voices. "Zahra!" Romy squealed, hurrying to my bedside and wrapped her arms around me. "I'm so happy you're awake Zar, I missed you so much," she continued, chocked up. "Don't cry Roms, please," I begged, hugging her.

"Hey kiddo," Ruben said, walking up to my bed with his hands in his pockets. "Hey Ruben," I smiled, extending my arms for a hug. He smiled nervously, bent forward and hugged me awkwardly. "I come bearing gifts," Ruben said, breaking the weird tension between us. "What'cha got?" I asked, peering over the edge of my bed rails. He walked back to the door and picked up two bags he had rested on the floor by the doorway and brought them over to my bed. "First, I got my mom to send a new pair of boots, your family brought them from White Rock. Your other pair was well… ruined," he said. "Ruben. Thank you!" I looked at the new pair of boots in awe. They were perfect and exactly the same as my old pair and I was extremely happy to have them.

"I also have this for you," he said, pulling a new paint set out of the second bag. "Your other set is at the bottom of Romy's pond and I figured you'd need this, once you started painting again," he said. "I was also thinking that I could make something out of that cast for you," he offered. "If you want…" he finished. "You want to paint my cast?" I asked. "Yeah, I was just thinking that it was so plain, just white plaster and you're more vibrant than that," he answered. "That would be totally wicked Ruben," I piped. "I can start now," he offered, and I agreed. Romy and Adrian decided to go back to Romy's and pick up some dinner while Ruben painted my cast. Romy insisted that I eat as many home cooked meals as possible and vowed to bring me dinner every night until I was released from the hospital and Adrian, with his grudge against hospital food, absolutely agreed.

Ruben pulled the bedside chair toward my leg and peeled the blanket back. He placed the paint set on my table over my bed and opened the set revealing an array of water colour and oil paints, pastels, permanent markers, pencil crayons and sketching pencils. He pulled out several permanent markers, paint pens and a pencil and sketched out a design on my cast. When his sketch was done he outlined it with a thick black marker and then continued to colour it all in with an array of colours.

"So, why did you cut your hair?" I asked, breaking the silence. I wasn't sure if I should speak, he looked so focused and I didn't want to break his concentration. "Excuse me?" he asked, making me instantly regret my question. He looked up, waiting for me to answer. "You said… You used to have long hair…" "Oh when you were…'out'… So you *could* hear us," he said, with a smile. "Only sometimes," I told him. "Well like I said, I always had long hair, it went down my back. It was black and wavy, I took such pride in it, grew it for like nineteen years. I usually wore it down, just brushed back, sometimes in a braid or ponytail. I took really good care of my hair, my twin sister would always say, 'it's a Native thing' I don't know, I guess…"

"You have a twin sister?"

"Yeah, her name is Na-tur-ee, spelled like the word Nature."

"That's such a unique name."

"Yeah she hates it though, 'cause everyone always calls her Nature when they see it, which is fair, that's how it's spelled, right!"

"It sounds kind of like my middle name, it's Nayeli, nay-eh-lee," I said, pronouncing it for him.

"It's beautiful, do you know what it means?"

"No," I answered.

"I love you," he whispered, looking down at the ground conflicted.

"What?" I asked, blushing, *what was he saying?* My heart was racing, my mouth became dry, deep inside of me somewhere, I knew I felt the same. The love I had for Ruben felt natural, like it had always been there, waiting to be discovered, hidden beneath a false bottom, easy to avoid and pretend didn't exist. Was this really happening? Was I about to tell him I loved him too? I was glad my heart monitor was gone.

"It means, I love you, it's a Zapotec phrase." "Oh. Wow! I didn't know that," I said, relieved that Ruben wasn't professing his love for me and embarrassed that I even thought that he would, sad that he didn't feel as I did, cover the false bottom, never to be exposed.

"Anyway," he began, quickly changing the subject. "I decided it was just time to cut it, my hair. They say, whoever *they* are, that cutting your hair is a symbol of new beginnings, starting over. I needed to let go, to release a lot of pent up baggage," he said.

"What kind of baggage?" I asked, "I mean, if you want to talk about it." I didn't want to pry, but I wanted Ruben to know that as his friend and part of my makeshift family, I was there for him just like he was there for me.

"I just hurt many people with some of my decisions. Growing up I was careless with my actions and my family paid the consequence. I never thought about them when I was acting out and in the end they were hurting as much as I was," he explained, looking at me. I couldn't help but look confused, I had no clue what he was talking about. He sighed. I could tell he was trying to figure out what to say next. "I'm the only son my parents ever had, the youngest of seven. My dad died when I was young and I always felt like there was so much expected of me being the only boy and when he died I became responsible for all of my sisters and my mother.

"For a long time I hated my family, my mother, my father the most. I felt like he abandoned me, left me to do his job and I hated my mom for burdening me with it all and so I thought I *had* to rebel. I lashed out, I did what I wanted. I was disrespectful, I took off. I didn't talk to them for a long time, much like you now, with your family, but unlike your family, mine did nothing to deserve it.

"While I was away, I realized that my mother, not even my father when he was alive, expected anything from me besides being their son. I had placed all of these stipulations and expectations on myself, *I* had caused *myself* so much pain, so much anguish and for what? *I* hurt them all. *I* hurt myself, my friends, and the love of my life. I left her because I felt like she had abandoned me, or maybe that she wanted more from me than I was able to give her. Looking back, now I see that she too, expected nothing. She just wanted me however I came. She wanted me to be happy, she wanted to ease my self inflicted burdens and I punished her for that.

"I screwed up bad… and eventually when I came around my family, they forgave me, my friends too, but my girl, gone…and so after realizing that I was to blame for all of my downfalls I forgave myself and I needed to start over. I cut my hair after I went back to White Rock and apologized to the people I felt I needed to apologize to."

"Wow, Ruben…I…where did your girlfriend go? Were you able to apologize to her too?" I asked. "No," he answered short. "I never apologized. I resented her for years. I don't think I've ever really got over it, still. She did hurt me, bad—but I hurt her too," he assessed. "What did she do?" I asked, sympathizing with him and his story. "I loved her so much Zahra, she was the first girlfriend I ever had and she was my world and I would have given up everything to be with her. Then one day, she just didn't show up for our trip to Seattle. It was just maybe three weeks after her birthday and we had planned to go for the weekend. We were so excited, it was our first real trip together and we had made all kinds of plans," he sighed to himself, smiling as he reminisced.

"We were so young, just seventeen, we thought we had everything figured out, all these plans to be together forever…" "And then what happened?" I asked. "Like I said, she just never showed up at my house. I waited and waited. At first I thought she was running late, but an hour passed, then two and three and she never showed. I called her house, no one answered. I called so many times that night and no one ever answered. Like a week passed before I heard anything, her parents told me she had left, just moved on, moved to somewhere in Ontario and I never heard from her again," he finished. "So that's it?" I asked. "That's it," he said. "Do you still love her?" I asked. "You know Zar, I don't know…I've been pushing her out of my head for all these years, forcing myself not to think of her, what she's doing now, if she's married, had kids, what her life is like where ever she is, but I know it's only a matter of time before I have to face my demons and just inwardly forgive her and myself, if I never get the chance to say it face to face," he said.

"But why did she leave?" I asked. "I don't really know, I guess she thought she would end up being another burden to me and that's my fault. I treated everyone I loved the most like that, and she was trying to spare me I suppose. *I pushed her away*," he said, colouring in a swirl on my cast. "I made her feel like she was only going to be a problem in the end, instead of showing her how much I cherished her. Maybe if I did, our lives would have been a lot different," he concluded, mournfully. He looked at me with regret, searching for… something, reassurance, maybe.

There was nothing I could say, nothing I could do that would aid the situation. What and if are two words non-threatening on their own, but put together they can unleash a world of pain and suffering, Ruben's what-ifs just made his pain deeper. His old scars scraped clean, made new. His what-ifs had him tread-milling, never moving forward, never healing from his past. He was stuck, just as I was, I couldn't help him when I couldn't even help myself.

We were silent for some time as Ruben concentrated on my cast and when he was finished he looked at me and smiled. "There," he said, closing the cap of the marker. I looked down at my once white cast and saw the most beautiful and elaborate design, full of swirls and abstract shapes in bright pinks, purples, yellows, bright blues and black. It looked just like the pattern I had painted on my bedroom wall in White Rock, rising up from the corner, behind my bed. I had taken a class two summers ago in a local art school and learned to paint with aerosol cans. The style had intrigued me. *Spukani* murals lined pathways in tunnels and underpass roadways. Murals of landscapes, buildings in grey and black, swirls and arrows all around in bright colours, '*Spukani*' barely legible, letters twisted abstractly. I immediately bought myself several spray paint supplies and large canvases to practice on and I was terrible. When I saw the ad in the paper about the six week graffiti program at Palette, the local art school, I signed up right away. The class was taught by a member of *Spukani's* crew, a guy who called himself Fly. He taught us a bunch of different styles, Wildstyle, Old School, Landscape, Block, Cartoon and Ignorant. The classes were three hours a day, five days a week and I spent the rest of the summer practicing my graffiti. When I felt I was good enough, I pulled everything out of my room and started on my wall. I used the black can first and sprayed large outlined swirls from the base of the wall, upward and painted in the outlines with hot pink, turquoise, light purple and lime green, growing from the corner and spreading out on top of the two walls and around my window. It was the first time I really saw myself as an artist and knew it was something I wanted to pursue in the long run. I had been inspired by the mysterious *Spukani*. Fly had explained that Spukani had travelled around the world learning different styles, popular to certain cultures, he'd brought back and mastered Ignorant style, I fell in love with it myself. At the end of the program, Fly said that we should find an artist whose style we liked the most and study it until we were more confident on our own. I choose Spukani and now Spukani had just painted my cast.

"You know you're my favourite artist, right?" I said, smiling at Ruben, surprised at how similar his design was to my own masterpiece in White Rock. "This is my first, acquired, piece of original art *and* it's a Spukani piece!" I stated proudly. "We'll trade, you have to give me one of your graffiti pieces. What do you write?" "Nccæo," "Nccæo? That's interesting…" "Do you think it's terrible? I couldn't think of anything in class, Fly gave it to me, I thought it sounded cool, do you know what it means?" I asked.

"No, sorry…but I like it! And I'm glad you like the cast," he said, putting all the markers back into the case, "…cause otherwise you'd be stuck with it for the next month or so," he laughed. "Ugh, don't say it like that, 'next month or so' that just makes it seem so much longer," I said, wrinkling my nose, he slid his chair beside me. "Sorry kiddo," he passed his hand through my hair and lightly patting my head. "So now what?" I asked. "What's up?" he asked. "I'm just bored I guess, this place is a complete drag…" "Hmm, okay. Well then tell me something," he replied. "Like what?" "Anything you want," he insisted. I thought about what I could tell him. What did I really have to say that was interesting? I needed to think of something that would help the time pass until Romy and Adrian returned.

"My sister, Jonnæ who you met a few days ago, she's really my mother," I looked directly at him waiting for a reaction. Surprisingly he didn't react the way I had thought he would. He was calm and unmoved and my pause was unnecessary. "She had me when she was sixteen and gave me up for adoption to her parents and we were raised as sisters. I just found this all out the day I left White Rock, I overheard them fighting about me taking this trip. For whatever reason Joanne and Fabién really didn't want me to be here right now and Jonnæ was protesting and then they said that she gave up her rights when she signed me over to them and that's how I found out. If I didn't hear them, they would have never told me."

"I kind of figured something like that was going on, Jonnæ was so protective of you, she seemed more connected to you then your…Joanne, besides you look so much like Jonnæ," he said. "Is it really that obvious?" I asked. "Um, not really, Romy's parents didn't seem to notice anything odd, but I'm just a perceptive person," he explained. "So…where are you at with the whole situation?" he asked. "I don't really know yet. I haven't thought about it at all, I really don't want to at this point. I'm still angry, I feel betrayed... and I deserve some answers, but I don't really want them, you know? I don't really want to ask the questions because it just means that there will be more questions that follow and I don't know if I can handle hearing the things I would hear," I finished.

"Like what?"

"Well, I never thought about it before, I guess because I haven't thought about the situation at all, but the other day when I was still 'out' you were talking about how lucky my parents were, my mom and my...dad... I guess my two official questions would be who's my father? And then just...why?" I trailed. I inwardly fought with myself, holding back tears and the feeling of desperation. I think I was trying to be strong for both me and for Ruben, we were dealing with our own troubled pasts and were finding a sense of security in each other. I couldn't very well fall apart now, breaking whatever it was that we had just built.

"'Why?' I think that's the hardest question to answer and maybe the hardest answer for you to hear. Maybe the answer will never be enough. Before you ask that one, you've really got to be sure that you can handle it. I'm not saying that it has to be a bad answer, but it just may not be a good enough one for you. Maybe it's not even a good enough answer for Jonnæ herself, but at the time it was, and now that she's grown up and she has a better perspective on life and she's seen how it all turned out the 'why' may not seem so well worth it," he said. Ruben was so wise, so insightful, he made it easy to open up to him and tell him everything I was thinking and feeling. He seemed to know how to make it better with his words, to see all sides of the spectrum, to force me to see things not just through my fury enraged eyes, but through the eyes of Jonnæ, but what about my mysterious father?

"And about your dad…well you're just going to have to ask," he said, making a face. "That means…" I started. "…You're going to have to call," he finished. "I know, but I just can't yet. I'll have to wait on that question for now," I decided. "Everything in time kiddo, everything in time."

5'3" And Yet So Tall

January 5

The next morning I woke up early, the sun was just starting to show its face and I was eager to try my hand at moving around by myself. Usually, as I had been told, Ruben would have stayed with me the night before, but because school was back in session, Ruben had to go back to work and since Adrian was taking a bit of time away from classes, they decided it was best if Adrian stayed each night, until I was released from the hospital.

The room was silent, the insistent beep of the heart monitor, gone. I turned, shifting my weight onto my left side and watched Adrian, sleeping on the couch. He looked so funny, I smiled. His long body, curled up uncomfortably on the couch, his head buried in his pillow, the blanket tangled between his legs, his feet hitched on the arm rest of the couch. I didn't want to disturb him. I knew he was exhausted and I couldn't wait till I could leave the hospital so that he could start getting a good night's rest. *That'll mean he goes back to London.* He had to get back to his life and I would have to get back to mine. I wished I could have had more time with him, it seemed like every time we were together it was always so limited. Adrian had been there with me for over a week, but I had only been awake for a day to enjoy it and within the next few, I'd be going home and so would he.

I pushed the button that called for help and Hilda came shuffling into the room. "What can I do for you?" she asked quietly.

"I need to go to the bathroom," I whispered. She grabbed a bed pan and walked over to my bed, drawing the curtain between the couch and the bed for some privacy. "No. I want to get up," I said embarrassed that Adrian was just on the other side of the curtain. "I want to walk to the bathroom," I continued. "Walk there?" Hilda asked shocked. "Yes, I'd like to try," I said. "Okay," she answered.

She removed the pillows from under my leg and cranked my bed up into a seated position and swung my body around so that my legs were hanging down below me. She held my brightly decorated casted leg and strapped on the boot so that I could walk and told me to try to shimmy my way to the edge of the bed. After a few tries, I was able to shift my weight and I was sitting at the edge. My legs tingled and blood rushed back down to my toes and for a moment I felt lightheaded. "Are you ready?" Hilda asked. "I think so," I said. I placed one hand on her shoulder and grabbed onto her extended hand. I hoisted myself up as she pulled my arm and then I was standing.

Even though I was only 5'3" I felt so tall, like I was towering over everything in my room, having been flat on my back for several days. I stood there for a while, getting my bearings, before I was able to try to take a step. The cast was awkward and I didn't know how to move with it. Hilda quickly explained which foot to step with first and how to move around with the cast. I was nervous and afraid that stepping down on my foot would cause immense pain, but I really had to go to the bathroom and so I had to face my fear.

Hilda handed me my crutches and I slowly took my first step and to my surprise it was almost completely painless. Hilda moved along beside me as I slowly pulled my left leg through and completed the step. I stopped. I lifted my booted right leg again, muscles trembling with fatigue and stepped down lightly, as instructed by Dr. Arnulf, stopping short and pulling my left leg through again. After some practice, I was able to make it to the bathroom with Hilda's help. I was proud of myself and was determined to continue moving around as much as I could that day.

When I was done I asked Hilda for a toothbrush and was happy to be able to wash my face and brush my teeth. "Can I take a shower?" I asked. "You are ambitious!" Hilda commented. I shrugged my shoulders. It was just nice to be up and I was starting to feel like myself again. "Okay. We will make a deal," Hilda started, "you can take a shower, but you must be sitting, plus you must not get the cast wet, so we will put a stool in the shower and you will keep the leg out okay?" "Thank you," I gushed.

I sat in the wheelchair that had been stationed outside of my room and Hilda wheeled me down the hall and into the shower room. She set up the stall with a small bench and helped me onto it and left me alone to shower. It was great to shower, to feel the hot water wash over my body and ease all of my aches and pains away. It was nice to be able to do something by myself for a change.

I washed my hair with the hospital shampoo, it was nothing special, just antibacterial and clean smelling, the body wash smelled the same leaving that 'hospital smell' on my hair and skin. I enjoyed every minute of my shower and could have stayed there all day if given the opportunity, but it was cut short by Hilda who came back into the bathroom with a fresh pair of grey sweats and a turquoise tank top that Romy had packed in a bag for me. She helped me dress and wrapped my hair in a towel before helping me into a wheelchair and wheeling me back to my room. When we were just a room away from mine, I asked Hilda if I could get out of the wheelchair and try to walk the rest of the way. She stopped pushing the chair and put on the brakes. She helped me to my feet and I slowly began to take a few steps, this time using only one crutch. I shifted my weight onto my left side, holding the crutch firmly and rounded the corner of the door and entered my room.

"*Look at you!*" Adrian cheered, standing up from his makeshift bed. I smiled. He walked toward me and put out his hand for me to take, which I accepted. He walked me over to my bed as I hobbled on my feet. Hilda left the room figuring that I would be fine with Adrian. She was going to get the breakfast tray. Adrian helped me back into bed and unwrapped my hair from the towel. He squeezed the excess water out and ruffled my hair in the towel before grabbing my brush, from my overnight bag. He sat behind me on my bed and began to brush through my wet hair. "Do you want to try it yourself?" he asked, I could feel his warm minty breath on the back of my neck sending shivers down my spine and goose bumps on my skin.

"No," my voice cracked, I blushed. He continued to brush in silence. When he was done, he put the brush down on the bedside table and wrapped his right arm around my shoulders, pulling me against his chest and kissed the top of my head. "I'm so glad you're getting back to yourself," he said quietly. The hairs on the back of my neck stood on end. "Mmm, hospital scent," he joked, breaking the tension, I laughed. "It's a bit different from my milk and honey body wash, huh?" I laughed, nonchalantly. A laugh that sounded nervous and awkward, instantly I blushed. "Just a bit," he laughed too. "They'll be back in seconds with your tray so I think I should move," he whispered, he sat in the chair beside my bed. My heart sank and it was written all over my face. Dr. Arnulf entered the room and I could feel my face get warm. Adrian had picked the right time to move, I was thankful. I looked at him wide eyed and he simply smiled and winked as if saying, "I told you so."

Dr. Arnulf checked my vitals and talked to both Adrian and I about how I had been feeling and all I wanted to say was…*frustrated*. "I'm feeling great," I said instead. "So I hear you've been up already for the day, took a shower that's really good. We're hoping to have you home in the next day or two, so Thursday for the latest if all goes well and you continue to keep up the good work," he assessed. "Okay great," I said with a smile, glad that my voice was back to normal. "Hilda will bring your breakfast now. Have a nice day and I'll check in with you again later," Dr. Arnulf said, exiting the room.

Hilda came in about a minute or two later with my breakfast tray. Adrian put up the bed table and Hilda put down the tray, uncovering it and revealing a bowl of porridge topped with fruit and sliced almonds. It looked delicious and I used less effort to pick up my spoon to dig in.

"I can't believe you're eating the hospital food," Adrian frowned. "I'm going to grab some breakfast too, want a coffee?"

I nodded. Wild bouncy curls, began to unfold, bobbed up and down as the warm air in the room dried my hair. The porridge was great, Adrian didn't know what he was talking about. There was nothing wrong with the hospital food.

Adrian returned with a croissant sandwich and two black coffees. I was feeling much better and full of energy after my breakfast and I couldn't wait to get back up and start walking around again. As I waited for Adrian to finish eating, the phone in my room rang and Adrian got up to answer it. "Hello?" he said, with a half-full mouth. "Zahra? Umm she's with the nurse in the shower right now," Adrian lied. I could only imagine who he was talking to and I really wasn't interested in finding out. "Yes, this is Adrian, I'm fine thank you, and yourself?" he asked. "Well that's lovely to hear given the circumstances," he continued. He was awfully polite so I knew he was talking to someone he didn't know very well and I guessed it was probably one of three people from White Rock, considering he lied. "Yes she woke up yesterday actually and now she's trying to get up and move around so she can go back ho—to Romy's house," he corrected himself. "Right. Well the doctor said her vitals were great, and as long as she keeps up the good work, in a few days, she'll be out. Yes, of course no problem, you're very welcome. I will tell her that you called. Bye now," he hung up the phone. "Jonnæ," he said walking around the bed to sit back down in his seat, but before he could the phone rang again. "You've got to be kidding me," he said, turning to walk back to the phone. "Let me guess this time it will be Joanne who *hates me!* I'm sure she'll be thrilled to hear *my* voice," he mocked. I made a funny face.

"Hello?" he said again, "oh hey Ruben. Yeah she's here, she just finished breakfast would you like to speak to her?" he asked. "Okay one moment," he said, bringing the phone over and placing it on my bed table. I took the receiver from him and put it to my ear. "Hi Ruben," I said, in a soft voice. My heart pulsed. He asked how I was feeling, "I'm doing much better that's for sure," I said. I told him I had porridge for breakfast and was able to feed myself and that Dr. Arnulf said that if I keep up the good work, I'd be out of the hospital within a few days, two at the most. He told me that after school he and Romy would stop by for a bit and the four of us, Adrian included would go down to the food court and have dinner so that I could have a change of scenery. It was something that I was really looking forward to.

"Zahra, look, I need to talk to you about something," Ruben started. "Okay Ruben," I said a bit concerned. Ruben and I had become quite close. He saved my life a week ago. He was completely selfless. He didn't care about how cold the water might have been, or feared that he would have fallen into the pond too, he just grabbed me, plunged his arms into the piercingly cold water and wrapped his arms around me and saved my life. He held me in his arms, he kept me warm and from what I've heard he never left my side when they brought me to the hospital. It was because of him that I had a private room, a sofa for someone to sleep on, a TV and a phone, for when I woke up. He, like Romy and Adrian had become one of my best friends, part of my inner circle and family that I had created for myself, especially after our talk the other day.

"Zahra, I don't know how to say this…" "Just say it Ruben," I said. He sighed. "Okay…well, we haven't really talked about what happened, the accident and well…I just feel awful about it all. I can't help but feel like if I hadn't suggested the oil painting lessons, the landscape thing, you wouldn't be in this mess right now," he started.

"Ruben—"

"Wait. Please let me finish," he interrupted. "I'm going to make it up to you somehow. Joanne called me today and she sure laid into me about it, but she's right. I acted completely irresponsible and I failed to do my job as your travel guide…but that won't happen again. I blurred the boundaries and I shouldn't have told you all of that stuff about me because my *job* is to show you and your classmates around Austria for the next four and a half months not to be hanging out with you and Romy or giving you art lessons or personal chats and so I apologize. I'll come with Romy later today and have dinner like we said, but after that, I'll strictly only see you at school, during school hours. I'm sorry Zahra," he finished, his voice quiet and wavering.

I began to cry, "Ruben. You can't…you just…can't," was all I was able to say. I couldn't believe what I was hearing, that this person I considered to be so important in my life was telling me he was going to take a step back, that he didn't want to be that person anymore, that he regretted opening up to me the day before...I thought we had something special, he didn't feel the same way about me.

Why was Joanne doing this to me? Why was she so determined to strip me of the influential people in my life? Why was she *punishing me?* Was she honestly that mad that I hadn't spoken to them in six weeks? What did she honestly expect? Joanne was probably one of the most selfish people I knew. My life was in shambles because of her, for the sake of her image, and she wanted to take away the only people who were truly looking out for *me*. Why? First Adrian, now Ruben, who next?

"Ruben. Please don't do this. Joanne has no right to say anything to you about your actions. She's just lashing out at you for her faults, she did the same to Adrian. I don't blame you at all for this. *I* took off onto the ice, I wasn't thinking and you, *you saved my life* and I'm lucky to have you in it. That won't change no matter what Joanne or any of them say. So please, don't..." I pleaded.

Joanne's antics were exhausting. All I wanted to do was close the curtains, pull up the blanket over my head and sleep. I had no more fight left in me, maybe I should just pack up and head back to White Rock. Joanne had plucked off all the pawns, knocked down my knight, attacked my bishop, no doubtably my rook was next.

"When did you stop calling her mom?" Ruben asked, catching me off guard. "When I found out that she wasn't," I replied. "When I met you at the airport?" he asked. "Yes, on Friday, November twentieth, that's when I realized I was alone, that I had no family. And now you and Romy and Adrian, Mila and Fredrik... you're my family.

"Ruben look, Joanne's not here and she has no more say in my life than the chick in the room next door to me. You can't possible let her guilt you. All of you pose a threat to her because she's not here to make demands and boss people around. She's used to having her way, to calling the shots. She can't handle not being in control. Screw her," I said.

"Zahra, that's hardly appropriate," Ruben said, all mature like. Sometimes I forgot that he was like twenty-eight or something, that he was older than me by at least ten years. "I don't care…" I replied. "I know you don't," he sighed. "Let's make a deal Zahra," he started, "… I'll stick around as long as you want me to, okay? But you've gotta start working your life out," he said. "Fine," I agreed, though I had no intention of sorting through anything. I handed the phone back to Adrian and he hung it up and placed it on the bedside table.

"What was that about?" Adrian asked. "Joanne's same old, same old, telling Ruben to get lost, the same as you. She clearly hates me," I said. "She doesn't hate you Zar, she just has odd ways of showing she cares…ways that we obviously don't understand." I shuffled over and Adrian squeezed himself onto the bed beside me. I rested my head on his shoulder and we stared at the TV. "Hey AJ?" I said, quietly after a few minutes. "Yes?" he replied softly with his perfect velvet voice and precise English accent moving his head closer to mine to listen. "You never really finished explaining your conversation with Joanne…" "No I didn't," he replied. "Well?" I asked, rigid with fear. "I don't know Zar, I just can't help but think about what happens whenever you *do* go back. I guess Joanne just slapped me with a bit of reality and it makes me sad to know that at some point you'll be even further away from me…and then what?" he said sadly.

"So…what? You're just going to live out the rest of this relationship until I go back and then that'll be it? This relationship is only worth keeping so long as I'm close by?" I asked, annoyed. "*No*

Zar that's not what I'm saying…" he said. "YES IT IS!" I barked. I'll admit I can be a bit of a hothead at times. "You're overreacting Zahra!" "Adrian if that's how you feel then maybe when you go back to London you should just delete my number from your phone or…whatever," I snapped. I struggled to turn my back to him, lifting my heavy casted leg to the side. He tried not to laugh at my uncoordinated display. I was fuming. *"Zahra! Come on,"* he pleaded. I ignored him. "I don't want to fight with you, in fact I never thought I would…"

"Whatever Adrian, I'm tired and I think I just want to take a nap now," I lied.

"Zahra, don't do this, please," he begged.

"ME? I'm not doing anything Adrian. You're the one who thinks our relationship has no future. Whatever happened to 'we belong together,' the planet force, the lucky ones and kismet? Or do you not remember because you were wasted?" I reminded him.
He laughed.

"Adrian this is serious!" I yelled.

"No it's not, you've just gone stir-crazy, you have a bit of cabin fever." He flipped through the channels on the TV. "Listen to me," he said, placing his hand on my shoulder forcing me to lay flat on my back. "It was never my intension to upset you, it's just hard to think of you not always being here with me, or at least closer to me, I guess. But that doesn't mean I don't want you, or will stop loving you because of it. And I wasn't wasted! I haven't forgotten anything I've ever said to you. We don't know what will happen four months from now. I know you don't plan to go back right away, so if you'll forgive me, I promise to take it just one day at a time," he offered.

I was silent, still pretending to ignore him.
He waited.

"You promise?" I asked.

"Absolutely!" he answered.

"Okay then," I gave in, how could I stay mad at him? It was impossible. I buried my face in his thick grey sweater. He wrapped his arm around me. I closed my eyes and fell asleep.

When I opened my eyes again, the sun was hanging lower in the sky and the hospital ward was buzzing. I was alone in my bed and sprawled across the entire space. I turned my head to see if Adrian was still in the room. He was sitting on the couch lost in thought, studying. He was reading a book and taking notes, his grey sweater tossed on the floor. He wore a fitted white T-shirt and a black pair of jeans, his feet were socked with thick wool of red white and grey. His hair was tossed, most likely from running his fingers through it and he wore a pair black thickly framed glasses.

"You wear glasses?" I asked in a sleepy voice. He closed his book, looked up at me and smiled. "Only when I'm reading." "Adrian please. Don't stop, keeping studying," I insisted. "No, no it's all right. I intended to do some work only until you woke up. I've just got to keep on top of things while I'm away from school, I'm used to it," he said. "Because travelling for modelling?" I asked. "That's right," he said. "Are you ready for lunch?" he asked. "No, not yet. What are you studying? What time is it?" I asked trying to sit up. "It's just after one, you slept for about four hours. I was doing some reading for my English literature class," he said. "What would you like to do now?" he asked, leaning over my bed rail smiling. "I'd like to get up and leave this prison for a little while I think," I answered. "You think? Or you know?" he asked. "Why do you always have to be a smart-ass?" I asked. "*Me?* Listen Miss. I just want to be sure that you're sure about your decisions," he said. "I am. I want to get up. I want to walk around. I want to go outside," I decided. *"Outside?"* "Yes. I really need some fresh air." "It's cold out there," he replied. "Do I have a jacket or anything?" I asked, realizing that all of my stuff had probably been ruined. "You do, I bought you one, Ruben bought you your new boots, Mila knitted you a new hat and scarf and Romy got you some really warm mittens, just like hers," he said. "Perfect! Then I can go outside," I assessed. "Well we'll have to ask your nurses first," he left the room to find one of the nurses.

I was given the okay, Agnes returned to the room with Adrian to help me put on my jacket and winter boot, covering my casted foot with a thick wool sock. She helped me stand when I was bundled up and Adrian stood behind my wheelchair. Agnes handed me my crutches as I sat down in the chair. Agnes covered my legs with a blanket and told us to have fun, but to not to leave the hospital premises. Adrian wheeled me out of the room and to the elevator. We rode the elevator down from the ninth floor with a few other people, who smiled as they looked at me and Adrian. I smiled back politely and waited anxiously for the doors to open. When the elevator stopped and we were on the main floor, the other riders insisted that Adrian and I exit first, holding the door open for Adrian to push my wheelchair through. He stopped just short of the hospital exit and asked, "Are you ready?" "Yes," I beamed, nodding my head in case he couldn't hear me over all the noise in the lobby. He pushed me over to the door and pressed the button for the automatic door and wheeled me outside slowly.

The cold winter air came gushing in toward me as we exited the building, instantly chilling me to the bone and giving me flash backs of the day I fell into the frozen pond. I froze in my seat, stiffened by the paralyzing fear and the painful memory from just a few days past. Adrian quickly came around the chair and kneeled down in front of me. "Are you okay?" he asked concerned. I snapped out of my terror and look into his eyes. "I'll be fine, the cold air just…

shocked me, reminded me of…" I trailed off. "This was a bad idea, I'm going to take you back upstairs," he insisted. "No Adrian, *please* I'm fine really, I just needed a minute," I explained. He wheeled me over to a bench and took a seat, parking my wheelchair beside him and took out a cigarette. I watched him as he opened the package, pulled one out, placed it in his mouth and lit it. He looked at me from the corner of his eye and watched me watch him. *"What?"* he asked, exhaling his smoke into the air. "Nothing," I watched the smoke disappear. "It's *not* nothing, that much I know," he replied. I didn't say anything. "You want me to quit don't you?" he asked. I didn't reply. "I just have a new outlook on things," I said finally. "I value my life so much more now, but at the same time I feel like it's too short to live with so many rules or boundaries, but…" "But you would still prefer if I quit right? I guess I fall into the part about the value of life?" he asked. "It's your life AJ," I replied. "But you're in it and I don't want to give you more things to worry about, you've got enough on your plate as it is. I'll try, I'll start by cutting back, how does that sound?" he asked. I smiled. "Only if you want to Adrian, don't do it for me, do it for you," I insisted. "I know," he said, putting his cigarette out in the ashtray beside the bench. "I feel better already," he said smiling. We sat outside for as long as I was able to bear the cold and after about twenty-five minutes we headed back inside. I wasn't ready to go back up to my room yet so Adrian pushed me around the lobby for a while visiting a few of the gift shops. We stayed downstairs for almost two hours heading back to my room at a little after three p.m.

 Ruben and Romy arrived at the hospital at four-thirty. I lounged on my bed with Romy and Ruben, Adrian sat on the couch. We talked about the bakery, school and life outside of the hospital. Romy handed me my homework assignments which I woefully accepted. I forgot about life outside of the hospital walls, about early morning bus rides to school, classes, schoolmates and most of all homework. I had been out of school for over a week and I was sure I had a lot to catch up on. However, Romy told me that she had been doing my German homework which was waiting for me to hand in when I returned to school and that we were doing a group assignment soon in English, presenting a book chosen from a list handed out by the teacher. Romy said that Kristina and Jackie, the two other girls in our group had already selected our book and Romy brought me a copy so that I could start reading it. I flipped through the pages quickly, before resting the book on my bedside table and picked up the list of calculus questions I had to answer and frowned.

Adrian scooped me up in his arms and walked toward my wheelchair where Ruben was waiting behind it. The four of us had decided it was time to head downstairs to the food court to have dinner. "Forget it, we don't need that thing," Adrian said, swooping me up into the air and deciding not to put me in the wheelchair at all. "Grab the crutches Roms," he called out behind him as he exited the room with me still in his arms. We passed the nurses station and saw Hilda and Agnes' shocked faces. Adrian smiled and said, "Good evening ladies, we'll be downstairs having dinner," he walked toward the elevator with Romy and Ruben tagging along behind.

Ruben picked a table and we all sat down in the food court. Adrian placed me on a seat, sat down beside me, elevating my leg on his lap and Romy and Ruben sat down across from us. Ruben took all of our orders and left to get the food. When the food was ready, we all welcomed it happily. Adrian agreed that the hospital food wasn't so bad. We told him the food court didn't count. We sat at the table for another twenty minutes after we finished eating before my ankle started to hurt. Romy and Ruben said goodnight for the evening and Adrian helped me with my crutches as we headed back upstairs.

When we were back in my room and I was in bed with my leg elevated, I took out my calculus and attempted to do some homework. "Can I help?" Adrian asked. "Are you good at calc?" I asked. "Um, not at all," he admitted "So then why would I want your help then?" I asked smiling. "Are you any better?" he asked. "Actually I am!" I stated. "Why?" I asked, "It's not like you're going to need it in University," I pointed out. "I know, but I'm interested…plus it gives me an excuse to sit real close to you," he said, with his charming smile. "You know you don't need an excuse," I pointed out smiling cunningly at him. He wasted no time and climbed into my bed, sitting behind me. "Teach me," he said, looking over my shoulder at my calculus book. "Okay, but you behave," I warned, "I need to get some of this work done," I insisted. "I promise," he said, raising his hands in surrender. "Hey! Your fingers are crossed," I playfully slapped his shoulder. We laughed, he kissed my head.

I surprisingly whipped through my calculus and got myself caught up on what I had missed. Adrian had offered to read my newly acquired book to me and I was happy to accept the offer. He got up from the bed and turned the main light for my room off. Agnes came in to check if there was anything I needed, which I didn't, but after she left I decided that I wanted to change out of my sweats and put on some shorts. Adrian rummaged through my bag and pulled out a pair of black pyjama shorts and tossed them to me on my bed and turned his back to give me some privacy. "Uh Adrian?" I started, "I'm actually going to need your help." "*Oh*. Okay, do you want me to call a nurse?" he asked. "If that would make you more comfortable," I replied. "Um, tell me what you need me to do," he weighed. "I need you to pull my pants off as I sit on the edge of the bed and then slip my right leg through the shorts and then I can take it from there," I explained. "Okay I'll do it," he said blushing. I shimmied my way to the edge of the bed and lifted my right leg off of the pillows with my hands so that I could sit with my legs hanging down. I shifted my weight onto my right side as I sat on the bed and tugged at the waist of my pants and began to pull them down. Adrian, kneeling on the floor looking only at my cast, focused on the patterns and colours Ruben had drawn.

I wiggled my way as best I could out of my sweats until they were hanging limp around my knees. Adrian's face turned bright red as my pants dropped and hung in the balance waiting for him to take them off completely. With his eyes still fixed on my cast, he pulled my sweatpants off and gently lifted my casted leg, slipped it through the right leg of my shorts. I put my left leg through the other side and Adrian pulled the shorts up, his warm hands passing lightly on my legs leaving goose bumps in their path. My heart raced as he touched my legs and I was glad that his eyes were cast down. *Maybe I should have called the nurse.* I didn't realize how awkward this whole situation would be for the two of us and I was starting to regret it. Adrian stopped, the shorts halfway up my thighs, and for the first time looked into my eyes instead of in my lap, the only place his eyes could naturally go.
I stopped breathing.
He did too.

We were transfixed, stiff and staring at each other. I bit my bottom lip hard trying to regain some composure and placed my hands on top of his to grab the top of my shorts so I could pull them up. Adrian leaned in and stopped just inches away from my face. My heart thudded uncontrollably, *th-thump-th-thump-th-thump-*

th-thump-th-thump as I waited for his lips to touch mine. *Maybe he's waiting for me to move in to him. That would make sense, I have to meet him halfway.* I closed my eyes, moved toward him slowly, letting my lips be my guide. He pulled away, jerking back swiftly, exhaling loudly.

Shock written all over my face, rejection settling in. "No," he whispered. "I'm sorry Zahra, just… not like this, not now, not *here*," he said quietly, resting his forehead on mine. I was speechless, I was hurt. The feeling of rejection didn't subside easily. "Please don't be sad Zar, it's not that I don't want you, and it's not that I don't want to kiss you 'cause *God knows, I do*. I just don't want to here, in your hospital room," he whispered.

I wasn't mad at him, I can't even really say I was disappointed. I threw my arms around his neck and hugged him. "Thank you," I whispered. "For what?" he asked, wholeheartedly. "For taking such good care of me," I answered. "It's what I was destined to do," he said. "Kismet," I whispered. He held me tighter and agreed, "Kismet."

Zahra Nayeli
January 6

"Zahra, wake up love," Adrian said softly, interrupting my serene dream of life outside of the hospital. I opened my eyes slowly, groggily and yawned with a full body stretch. I turned my head to the right, looking at Adrian who was sitting on the chair stationed beside my bed. "Your doctor has come by a few times to see you, but each time you've been asleep and now he's waiting outside of your room for you," Adrian explained. "Oh. Okay," I said, shaking the sleep out of myself. "Can you raise my bed?" I asked. "Sure, and then I'll tell Dr. Arnulf you're awake," Adrian said, cranking my bed up into an upright position.

Dr. Arnulf, Adrian and Nurse Hilda entered the room, forming a semicircle around my bed. Hilda checked my temperature, my blood pressure and circulation, she wrote the results on my chart, clipped to her clipboard and then showed it to Dr. Arnulf. I looked at Adrian who stood at the end of my bed with his arms crossed, straight faced. Was something wrong? I looked at him silently asking, his serious face cracked, a grin formed at the corner of his mouth.

"How are you feeling this morning Ms. Nayeli?" Dr. Arnulf asked. I was taken aback by the name he called me, usually he just said my first name, but to address me by my middle name, as if it were my last, was shocking. He recognized the look on my face and said, "Your friend, the other man, he said that your name is Zahra Nayeli, is that correct?" he asked. "Um yes, that is correct," I replied. It was strange to wake up with a new identity. Though Nayeli was my middle name it was like I had become a whole new person over night, having dropped Roméo-Winters, a name I wasn't so sure I belonged to anymore. I liked the sound of my new name, it suited me, it was so different, exotic, free, and freedom was what I was looking for.

"So, how are you feeling?" the doctor asked again, "you've been sleeping for quite some time today, longer than usual," he assessed. "I'm feeling fine, just a bit tired. I was out of bed for most of yesterday, I guess I just needed to sleep," I suggested. "Well, your vitals are all good and so as long as you are feeling fine, I don't see why you can't go home today," he explained. "Really?" I chirped. "Yes, we'll release you today." "When?" I asked. "I can release you now, but you can take your time getting your things together. Go on and have some breakfast, well lunch now, and a shower, if you'd like," he suggested. "Okay thanks!" I said smiling. "I'm glad to see that you're recovering. When you're ready, you can go back to school. Just make sure to take your crutches and while sitting in class, try to remember to keep your leg up on a chair. Sleep with it elevated like you have been and I'll see you in about a month," he said, extending his hand. I reached forward and shook it. He smiled at me and left the room.

"What time is it?" I asked when it was just Adrian and I alone in the room. "Half past twelve," Adrian said, looking at his watch. "Really? I can't believe that I slept so long," I said, turning on the TV. "I can, you had a pretty busy day yesterday," Adrian said, sitting down in the chair. "Do you want to shower?" he asked. "Yeah in a minute, I'm really hungry though," I said. "Did you shower?" I asked. "Yep, but much earlier, around eight this morning. I'll go tell Hilda that you're ready for lunch," he said, getting up and exiting the room.

I ate my lunch quickly and was ready to take my shower. I was determined to get out of the hospital as soon as possible. Hilda came back to help me into the shower and I bathed as long as she permitted me to. When I was done, she helped me dress in the shower room. I put on a purple zipped hooded sweater and a pair of black yoga pants and covered my cast with the same thick wool sock from the day before.

Hilda wheeled me back to my room and I quickly brushed my hair and threw it into a messy knot on the top of my head while Adrian packed my bag. "I called Ruben while you were in the shower, he'll be here soon to bring you home," Adrian said. "Great," I smiled. When Adrian had finished packing my bag, he sat with me and we watched TV until Ruben arrived.

Hilda and Agnes helped me into my wheelchair and they both hugged me goodbye as we exited the room and entered into the hallway. I said my goodbyes and Ruben took over pushing my wheelchair, Adrian carried both his bag and mine. We got into the elevator and headed to the main floor. Once in the lobby of the hospital, we passed by the gift shop, small cafe and finally exited the building into the cold winter air. Ruben parked my wheelchair by the curb and hurried off to get the car. Adrian and I chatted to distract ourselves from the cold and before long Ruben pulled up.

Adrian threw the bags into the trunk and Ruben helped me into the back seat of the car so that I could rest my leg on the back seat. After I was comfortably seated, Adrian climbed into the front passenger seat beside Ruben. As we drove away, Ruben filled me in on what I had missed from school, everything from classes to gossip about other classmates. All the stories made me even more excited to get back to it all.

I took the time to take in the view and to grasp the scenery, as we ascended around the small hill and into the country where

Romy's house was located. We pulled up to the house and Adrian instantly got out and opened my door, reaching for my crutches. Ruben helped me out of the car and Adrian held the crutches and extended them to me. I hobbled to the front door and slowly up the few steps with Ruben and Adrian close behind. "Is Romy home?" I asked, as I reached to top step, waiting for Ruben to unlock the door. "No, not yet. She doesn't know you're home yet. I thought I'd let it be a surprise," he said, turning the key into the lock and pushing the door open. I smiled. "She'll like that," I said, moving along into the house. "Sit here," Adrian said, pointing at the hallway bench that housed shoes, spare hats, scarves and gloves. I used my crutches as a support and sat on the bench.

Adrian kneeled down at my feet and pulled off my boot. "Thanks AJ," I said, ruffling my fingers through his hair, Ruben rolled his eyes. Adrian looked at me with a huge smile on his face and before I knew it, he had scooped me up in his arms and was carrying me into the living room and placing me on the couch. "You know...you're going to have to let her walk at some point Adrian," Ruben pointed out trailing in behind us. "What will she do when you're back in London?" he asked with a slight laugh. My heart sank, the reality of Adrian's time frame set in, Ruben pulled at his collar awkwardly, regretting having said anything, there was a moment of awkward silence.

"Well. I'll let you guys visit, I have to get back to the school. I'll be back later with Romy," Ruben said twisting his toque in his hands. He turned and headed back down the hallway and left the house, closing the door quietly behind him. "Let's read more of that book you've got," Adrian said, changing the mood and avoiding any more upset about his pending departure. He hurried back into the hallway where my bag sat on the floor and reached in, grabbing hold of my book and walked back into the living room.

He sat behind me on the couch. I rested the back of my head on his chest, he opened the book. "Where were we? Chapter four…"

January 7

The phone rang, waking me up from my peaceful sleep. My body was very happy to be back in its own comfy bed. It rang endlessly and no one seemed to be getting up to answer it, I grabbed my crutches and hobbled toward the door of my room. As I pulled it opened, I heard that Ruben had answered the call.

"…No it's not a good time right now, she's sleeping!" he said, sounding irritated. "I can't just wake her up, she needs her rest. Call back later. I won't be here later. Well you can try… yeah I'll be sure to tell her." He hung up the phone without saying goodbye unlike himself in so many ways. "Ruben?" I asked, opening the door wider. He jumped, surprised by my presence. "Oh hey kid, you scared me," he said turning, so that his back was facing the phone, facing me instead. I leaned on my crutches and looked from the phone to him and back to the phone again. The smile on his face faded. "Your…Jonnæ…she's called a few times now. She really wants to talk to you, but I don't want you to feel like you have to do anything you're not ready for. She can wait!" he said, with a kind smile. He placed his hand gently on my head and messed my hair a little. "Thanks Ben," I said sincerely, he helped me dodge a bullet. "I'm sorry you were awoken, do you want to go back to sleep?" he asked. "Not really, what time is it?" I asked. "It's seven forty-five a.m., Romy's in the shower, then I'm going to bring her to school. Adrian's still asleep…" he said, looking around. "Oh…I guess I'll go back to sleep then," I said, there wasn't much else for me to do. I hobbled forward so that I was closer to Ruben, I wrapped my arms around his waist. I could feel his body stiffen at my touch, but then he relaxed and he threw his arms around my shoulders and hugged me back. He petted my head a few times and the steady rhythm of his breathing made me sleepy and as if he could tell, he said, "Go lay down and I'll bring you a cup of tea."

I hopped back into the room and got into bed. Minutes later Ruben returned with a steaming cup of tea. I sat up and Ruben took a seat at the edge. "Here you go kid," he handed me the cup. "Mint with lots of honey and lots of milk," he said smiling. "Mmm, my favourite, how'd you know?" I asked, happily accepting the mug. "I didn't! But that's how I like it too. When I was a kid and I couldn't sleep my dad would always make me a cup. He'd pick the fresh mint leaves from the garden and boil it in a pot of water. Then he'd add a few spoonfuls of honey and lots of milk so that it was creamy. It would always put me right out…it's one of my greatest memories of my dad and even after he died, I still drank his special tea. I wasn't sure if you'd like it, but I thought I'd give it a try," he finished. "Well it's the best I've ever had. I can't drink tea without milk. One day I just tried it, I figured, how bad could it taste and then it was my instant favourite, but you make it the best," I said, sipping the tea. "Thanks kid," he smiled, "get some rest and let Adrian answer the phone."

Romy was almost ready to go and Ruben wanted to let the car warm up before they headed to school. Romy came in to say bye, she was so happy to have her roommate back and I was happy to be back too. I finished my tea and not long after they had left, just as Ruben said, I fell back asleep.

January 8

    "I love you," he said, as he opened the taxi door, a scene that was all too familiar. "If you love me so much then why are you about to leave again without kissing me?" I pestered. He smiled and kissed my head, "'Cause I'm waiting for the right moment," he mocked. "Oh yeah? And when will that be?" I asked sternly, trying my best to cross my arms with crutches lodged in my arm pits. He smiled my favourite crooked smile and said, "When the clock strikes *right* and *moment*. Now go inside! I hate when you watch the cab drive away." He waved at Romy, who stood at the front door, motioning for her to come and help me back into the house. I hardened my face, huffed and puffed in protest. "You'll be fine babes, I'll call you in a couple hours, now get out of the cold!" he insisted already halfway into the cab. I stood there on one leg unchanged with Romy at my side. *"Oh stop,"* he said. I stared at him straight faced. "Always so difficult," he said, under his breath. He stepped back out of the cab and wrapped his arms around me and held me tightly. "I love you so much Zahra and I'm going to miss you like crazy." I let go of one crutch and wrapped my arm around his torso, "I love you too AJ. Thank you for taking care of me, I don't know if I would have gotten through all of this without you." "You know I would do anything for you sweetheart. That'll never change and I'll keep reminding you until you believe it." He slowly pulled away.

    Romy handed me my fallen crutch as Adrian got back into the cab. I waved as he closed the door behind him. He rolled down his window and said, "See you soon," and then in a blink of an eye, he was gone.

D minor seventh, A minor seventh

January 27

The weeks went by slowly. We had the same routine down each morning; Romy would help me get ready and then Ruben would drive us to school and pick us up afterwards. I tried to resume working at the bakery, but Mila and Fredrik restricted my work load to only two hours a day, twice a week. I was stuck sitting on a chair with my foot elevated at all times. Ruben picked us up at the bakery on the days that we worked and brought us back home. He would help Romy prepare dinner as I continued to do nothing but sit with my foot elevated. I didn't have the patience for things like this and quickly I was becoming frustrated with my situation. We had already presented our English project and there wasn't very much to keep me occupied.

On one particular night, as I watched TV alone while Romy and Ruben started dinner, I decided that although I was slightly incapacitated, the TV just wasn't my best option. I was never much of a television watcher, I always opted for sketching in my book, tanning on the beach, working at the restaurant or playing the piano. I wasn't quite ready yet to start sketching again. There were still too many bad memories attached.

I reached for one of my crutches and lifted myself off the

couch. I hobbled over to the unused upright piano, covered by a cloth, used as an ornament display unit. I sat down on the bench. It had been months since I ran my fingers across the keys and I wondered what my first attempt would sound like. I opened the lid and placed my fingers on the keys. I quietly pressed down the notes required to play a D minor seventh chord, followed by an A minor seventh chord. My two favourites.

"Hey look who's back at the piano!" Ruben said, walking over to where I sat, with a plate and towel in his hands. I looked over at him and smiled.

"I didn't know I told you I played the piano," I placed my hands on my lap.

"You don't remember?" he asked surprised. "You did a while back. You said you've been playing since you were a kid," he said, drying the plate.

"Oh…" I tried to think back to that supposed conversation. I really didn't remember the conversation, but a lot of things from the last few months had been a blur, I took his word for it.

"What are you playing?" he asked.

"I don't know yet, I'm just playing around right now," I replied.

He smiled and rubbed my shoulder before heading back to the kitchen. I continued to play around on the piano and eventually started to play one of my favourite pieces, Erik Satie's Gymnopédie No. 1. The house flooded with the sound of soft legato, melodic lines and I could tell Romy and Ruben were enjoying the change in atmosphere and I was happy to contribute in any way that I could.

The following evening as Romy and Ruben fell into their routine, I fell into mine. I sat at the piano and graced the room with another piece of music. We continued like this for a few weeks and soon I was out of songs that I had memorized. I figured I could just repeat the songs, I knew Romy and Ruben wouldn't mind, but somehow it just didn't seem right.

After three and a half weeks of wearing my cast, I had a morning appointment with Dr. Arnulf. Mila took me to my appointment to check the status of my ankle. Everything was healing to the doctor's satisfaction. He informed me that within a few weeks, I could have the cast removed, which was to my delight. Mila dropped me off at home, there was no point in going back to school for less than half of the day. I ensured her that I would be fine on my own for while, before Ruben and Romy were returned.

She brought me a snack and left it on the coffee table and headed back to the bakery. After I had finished eating, I hopped back over to the piano. I had become obsessed with playing again and was determined to find something else to play for my family when they got home.

I sat at the piano with my hands on the keys unable to think of anything. I realized quickly it would be impossible to teach myself something I didn't already know…unless that something was a piece that I created. I had never written a piece of music before, it was something I was actually quite nervous about. I had been accustomed to splashing paint on a canvas, smudging charcoal on paper and sketching faces in my sketchbook. This was a whole new medium for me. I was entering into uncharted territories and I was actually quite apprehensive about it.

I started by playing some basic scales up and down the piano to get my fingers warmed up and to help my mind tune into its creative side. After my scale playing was fulfilled, I decided that I would play whatever came to mind first without over thinking the creative process. My mind instantly went back to my two favourite chords; the D minor seventh and A minor seventh. I played the chords over and over again. I just loved the way they sounded.

They were both dark, but passionate with the perfect amount of dissonance, enough to evoke emotional and magical thoughts in the listener. I loved passionate music and I think that's why pieces by Erik Satie and Claude Debussy spoke to me the most.

I played my two chords again and then added in a C Major chord but the finished product sounded odd together. I went back to my first two original chords. I liked the C chord, but felt something in between was missing.

D minor seventh, A minor seventh, A minor seventh, C Major...no.

D minor seventh, A minor seventh, D minor seventh C Major...no.

D minor seventh, A minor seventh, G Major, C Major...perfect!

I was lost in my work, as I muddled with my chord progressions that I didn't even notice when Romy and Ruben entered the house.

"What are you working on?" Ruben asked, walking over to the piano. I jumped, as his voice brought me back to the real world. "Sorry, I didn't mean to scare you," he said, placing his hand on my shoulder.

"Hey Ben, sorry...I guess I was lost in my own world," I said, taking my hands off of the keys.

"Don't stop," Romy said, coming over to join us. "It's beautiful, what is it?" she asked.

"Just something I'm working on. I've run out of songs to play for you guys," I explained.

"Play it again," Romy said, sitting down on the edge of the bench with me, being extra careful not to hit my ankle.

Ruben sat down on the couch and the two of them waited for me to play. "Okay, but it's not done yet, just a few chords," I said, looking back and forth between the two of them. Romy nodded and Ruben had the most delighted look on his face. I turned to face the piano again and pressed down on the middle pedal, the sostenuto. I wanted the chords to sustain, ring out and blend together in a majestic manner.

I played the chords carefully and slowly, allowing the pedal to build the progression's intensity.

D minor seventh, A minor seventh, G Major, C Major, G Major, A minor seventh, C Major and repeat. "That's all I have so far," I said, as the sound of the chords trailing off, resonated in the air. Ruben was delighted and smiled from ear to ear, clapping lightly when I was done. "Fantastic Zar," he said proudly. "Yeah it's beautiful Zahra," Romy said, rubbing my back. Ruben got up from seat and handed me a piece of paper from the coffee table, "You should write it down so you don't forget it," he said. I took the piece of paper and pencil and thanked him. He encouraged me to continue working on it, while Romy pulled out my German homework and quickly completed the few questions on the page.

I plugged away at the keys, trying out different chord variations and writing down the ones I liked the most until dinner was ready. We ate dinner without Mila and Fredrik. They had plans with some friends, that night, it was just Romy, Ruben and I. We chatted about my composition, the events of the day at school and of Dr. Arnulf's diagnosis of my ankle.

After dinner Romy, Ruben and I watched a movie, an oldie, something Romy had never seen before. It was one of my favourites and not surprisingly one of Ruben's too. It was a good old classic musical featuring some of the greats like Frank Sinatra, Louis Armstrong, Bing Crosby and Grace Kelly. After the movie, Ruben headed home and Romy helped me wash up for bed. It was Friday night and we had no real intention of going to sleep, but it was definitely time for me to get into bed because my ankle was throbbing.

After Romy helped me settle in, she left the room to take a shower and I used the opportunity to call Adrian. We chatted for a bit, but not too long. Adrian had been quite busy over the past few weeks. He had to catch up on all the work that he had missed while he was in Austria with me. He was also preparing for his audition to the University of Salford to obtain a degree in Popular Musicology. We talked whenever we could, but I made a strong effort not to monopolize a lot of his time when he had already sacrificed so much when I was in the hospital. Adrian finally decided what he wanted to major in, which was a great accomplishment and I wanted to be supportive in any way that I could.

I decided not to tell him about my unfinished song. He would only concentrate on that and would neglect preparing his own material for his upcoming audition. I told him about Dr. Arnulf's prognosis and that I would hopefully have my cast off in a couple more weeks. He told me that his audition date had been finalized and was set for March 2nd at eleven fifteen a.m.. I congratulated him on his accomplishments and after another few minutes we said our goodnights and I left him to continue studying for his upcoming exam.

The morning came and I was itching to get back to the piano. I was thankful that it was the weekend and we didn't have anything major to do. Romy had plans to meet with one of her school friends who needed a bit of girl talk and although she invited me, I declined the offer. I wanted Romy to spend quality time with her other friends too. She had a life before I came into the picture and I respected that. I also wanted her to know that she didn't have to spend every waking minute with me. She told me that she would only be gone for an hour or so and I promised her that I would be fine.

I stepped lightly on my casted leg using my crutches for support and sat down at the piano. I opened the lid and smiled at her, reassuring her that she had nothing to worry about. I bid her goodbye and sent my regards to Claudia, who I heard had just broken up with Jason. Honestly, I couldn't really say I was surprised by the news. Jason was a great guy, but sometimes his ego got the best of him. He knew he was good looking. His pale skin, grey, almond shaped eyes and short black hair, were the perfect combination of his Chinese and Danish background.

Once I heard the door close behind her, I placed my fingers on the keys and played my warm-up scales just like I had been taught in my lessons as a child. When I was satisfied with my progress, I immediately started to work on my untitled masterpiece. I started with what I had and played it for myself a few times and worked new chords into the progression.

D minor seventh, C nine…

A minor seventh, E minor seventh, A minor seventh, C Major…

I was extremely satisfied with the chords that I had selected, all I had left to do was arrange them in an order that would be pleasing to my ear. I closed my eyes and played the memorized chords from the beginning, deciding that I would not stop once I got past the part I had completed, rather I would continue to play whatever set of chords from my selection that my fingers naturally migrated to.

After each chord played, I spoke it out loud to myself so that I would remember the order. I was happy with what I had created and quickly wrote down the chords on my piece of paper that I had left by the piano over night. I smiled as I played my song repeatedly to myself. I had never written anything before and for my first attempt, I was very happy with what I had been able to produce. I worked at it for a little over an hour, before I got up to stretch. I made my way into the kitchen and got myself a drink of water, hurrying back to my song. I was addicted to it.

I sat back down at the piano and tried to work out a melody that would suit my dissonant chord progression, which proved harder than I had expected. I settled for playing random trills and arpeggios on the piano to exercise my fingers and to allow my mind to free up some space for creativity to flow. I was starting to take my song too seriously and was losing my artistic flare. I ran my fingers rapidly up and down the keys, fiddling around in the higher register of the piano, playing three and four note quick rhythms. "That's it," I exclaimed to myself. Through my improvisation, I had found the perfect beginning to my climatic part. I continued to let my hands move freely and plunged my fingers down hard on the keys to create a dramatic ending to my fast paced middle section.

D minor nine, C Major, G Major, A minor seventh…

I quickly jotted down the notes I had played on my piece of paper and repeated the song from the top. When I had completed the song, I rubbed my arms over the goose bumps I had given myself. All I needed now was a basic melody for the beginning. I was so close to having it, I could almost taste it, but for some reason I was stuck. I played the first two chords again hoping to gain some inspiration, but nothing came. "You're thinking too much, rushing…" I said to myself. I closed my eyes and took a few deep breaths in. I placed my fingers on the keys with my eyes closed and played three single notes:

D, E, F…

I began the first D minor seventh chord with my left hand as my right hand played the F. It was perfect. I repeated the pattern of single notes over the prewritten chord progressions and seamlessly my melody unraveled, like a spring tulip in May. I had completed my song and it was amazing. I had never been so proud of myself before. I didn't know I had that kind of creativity in me, but there it was; a song, my song. I played it over and over again until I had it memorized. I couldn't wait for Romy to get home so that I could play it for her and so she could see that I kept myself busy while she was out.

Romy returned home shortly after and filled me in on the Jason-Claudia drama. The story goes: Jason had started to grow distant from Claudia, they had started dating the same night I met Adrian and things were looking good for them, but lately, Jason seemed to be unhappy. Romy explained that Claudia saw Jason out with another girl, no one we knew, she wasn't from our school and we had no idea where he had met her. But then again it didn't really matter where he met her. The fact was that he should have been honest with Claudia and ended things with her, instead of allowing her to see him making out with someone else while she was out to dinner with her family. Terrible.

As I listened to the story, I realized that everyone was changing. Natalie had become a totally different person, who made a mess of everything and was sent home for it. Jason, though he was overly confident was always so sweet and caring, making his over zealous ego seem somewhat endearing, but now he had become a coward, his actions, unforgiving. I too was changing; I was becoming someone I didn't know any more than the new Natalie or Jason. What was Austria doing to us? Deep down inside, I knew Austria wasn't to blame. This was the first time the three of us had stepped out on our own and for the first time, we were finally getting to know ourselves and each other. When I think about it, in a way, the three of us had been forced into friendship. All the play dates, birthday parties and outings to the zoo or the beach had been orchestrated by our parents. Our friendships were arranged and the minute we were out from under our parents' wings, we realized that we really had nothing in common. I don't think we even really liked each other all that much either. I mean our friendships fell apart within the first few days of being in Austria, that says a lot.

I felt bad for Claudia, no one deserved that kind of treatment. It wasn't fair that Jason took her for granted and moved on while she hung onto whatever was left of their relationship. I knew I had nothing to do with it, but I still felt guilty by association.

"Enough of that!" Romy said, changing the desolate atmosphere. "How is the song coming?"

"I think I'm done," I said, facing the piano. I placed my hands back on the keys and began to play my song. Romy, who sat beside me on the piano bench, listened with her eyes closed, taking in all of the notes, rhythms and patterns. When I was finished, she opened her eyes and smiled.

"Amazing Zar," she wrapped her arm around my shoulders.

"Thanks Romy," I blushed.

"But it's not done yet, what about the lyrics?" she asked.

"Oh there are no lyrics, just the piano."

"I think... I think it would be really nice with some singing," she contemplated.

"Oh no Romy! I do not sing!" I stated.

"Why not?" she asked, surprised.

"Uh, because I can't!" I protested.

"Well if you ask me..."

"I didn't! RO-MI-NA," I teased.

"Don't call me by my full name!" she smiled, "I think you should try."

"Ugh," I sighed. "I'll think about it," I promised.

Shouldn't We Be Happy?
February 10

I woke up feeling renewed. Five and a half weeks had passed since I had been released from the hospital and after feeling like this day would never come, it crept up effortlessly. I sat up in bed and carefully removed my casted leg off of the pillows. I propped myself up and swung my legs over the edge of my bed. Two weeks ago, my cast had been changed to a plastic boot and now I was able to put more weight down on my ankle. I quietly got out of bed, trying not to wake Romy and limped to the washroom. I sponged myself off and then headed back to my room. Romy was awake and as she saw me entering the room, got out of bed and assisted me in sitting on the edge of mine.

    I slipped on my white tank top and turquoise cardigan, as Romy knelt silently, carefully removed my boot so that I could get my pants on. There was no need for words these days. Helping me in and out of the bath, dressing and undressing me, had become part of Romy's daily routine. When I had my black pair of stretch pants on, Romy skillfully put my boot back on. When she did it, it was almost completely painless, I didn't have that kind of patience. She had truly become the master at it, even better than me. She squeezed my shoulder and left the room to take a shower.

    I limped to the kitchen and boiled some water for the coffee. I knew that Romy and Ruben, when he arrived, would definitely appreciate it. By the time the water had boiled and I had put a few scoops of coffee into the percolator, Ruben was knocking at the door. I hobbled to the door and opened it as Romy finished getting dressed in our room.

Everything was so quiet.

I really thought when this day came, things would be livelier, but instead I found that it was quite the opposite.

Ruben smiled, he stepped into the house. He unlaced his black leather Chuck Taylor's, I watched quietly. When he was done, he looked up at me, ruffled my hair and stepped further into the hallway. I followed silently.

Shouldn't we all be happy? My cast was finally being removed! This was the day I had been begging for, wasn't it the same for them? Romy would no longer have to help me bathe or get dressed in the morning and at night. Ruben wouldn't have to pick us up every morning and bring us to school. Suddenly, as though someone had snapped me out of a hypnotic daze, it hit me. My accident, although tragic had brought us all together. My bond with Romy was tighter than ever, Ruben had become a vital part of the family and so had Adrian, even though he wasn't around these days. This was our new family, this was our routine. As it went, Ruben came by in the mornings and had breakfast with me and Romy before dropping us off at school, he would pick us up afterwards and we'd go to the bakery. While Romy and I worked, Ruben would chat with Mila and Fredrik and even help out around the shop doing odd jobs until Romy and I finished our short shift. He would then take us home where he and Romy would prepare dinner and I would entertain them both on the piano. Some nights I would chat with Adrian for a few minutes before putting him on speakerphone, so everyone could say a quick hello after dinner. This was what was comfortable for all of us now. My cast removal threatened our routine. I guess it seemed like everything would change.

We sat down at the dining room table with our coffees, toast and yogurt-filled fruit cups. Silence had filled the room. I couldn't take it any longer, I figured that I would have to be the one to break the awkward silence between the three of us. The question that plagued me was what I should say? "So…" I spoke. *Yeah that's great Zahra, was that the best you could come up with?* "Huh?" Ruben asked, inviting me to say something else. "Umm…" I trailed, "guys c'mon… we should be happy that my cast is coming off," I begged. "We're happy Zar!" said Romy, half smiling. Ruben joined the smile, but said nothing. "So Ruben, you won't have to come so early tomorrow morning. It won't take me *nearly* as long to get ready," I smiled, finishing my last spoonful of yogurt. I could see both Ruben and Romy light up as my words sunk in. They were happy, I was happy, things were back to normal.

We got into Ruben's car and headed down the hill to the hospital. It was Wednesday morning and we arrived at the hospital minutes to nine. My appointment was nine-thirty a.m. giving me enough time to check in, get x-rayed and wait for Dr. Arnulf in the Outpatient section of the hospital. Both Romy and Ruben stayed with me in the examining room as we waited for Dr. Arnulf to arrive with my x-ray results. We crossed our fingers, the minutes tick-tocked by on the clock, the only source of noise in the room. I had followed all of Dr. Arnulf's instructions, but until the x-rays cleared me, there was still a possibility that I would be stuck wearing the boot cast longer.

"So what will be the first thing you do when your boot is off?" Ruben asked, to bide the time. "Oh I don't know...I'd really like to put on my other winter boot," I assessed looking down at my feet. "Well that's boring!" Romy teased. I made a face at her and thought more about my answer. "I'd like to get a recorder and record myself playing my song for Adrian, for his birthday...I wish I would have paid more attention to the timing...I should have already done it and had it in the mail. His birthday is in a couple of days!" I said, realizing I had missed my opportunity. I felt horrible about it. I was so caught up in writing the song, forming lyrics and resting my ankle that I hadn't paid enough attention to how quickly the time was passing by.

"That sounds like a decent first activity," Ruben said, thoughtfully. "Not really," Romy interjected. "What? Why not?" I asked, surprised. "Because Adrian will never get it in time, there's only two days to get it to him. Well one really, if you think about it. You'd have to record it today and then send it tomorrow...his birthday is on Saturday so even if you sent it express post, he wouldn't get it until at least Tuesday," Romy explained. My heart sank as this harsh reality sunk in. Romy was right there was nothing I could do. There was nothing I could send in time. From the corner of my eye, Ruben pinched Romy on her leg, I guess he could tell that my mood changed instantly and was silently chastising her. "Ouch," Romy said slapping Ruben's hand. "All I was saying," she began, "is that a package in the mail would never make it in time, but you would!" she finished, eyeing me with a sly look on her face. I didn't follow, "I would?" I asked, *"I would!"* I said, understanding.

Ruben rolled his eyes. He was less than impressed with the idea. How odd I thought, he had seemed to become fond of Adrian over the past few weeks after my accident. However, he seemed to have changed his tune. Did Ruben feel threatened by Adrian? He was a hard guy to read. For weeks it seemed that he had been sending mixed signals. After our conversation in the hospital, I didn't know what Ruben wanted. I put the false bottom back on my emotions, I pushed the feelings aside, locked them away. He had saved my life, that was our only bond. Had I been wearing rose-coloured glasses? So many thoughts ran through my mind.

I sighed. "Is everything okay?" Ruben asked, coming to my aid immediately. He placed his hand on my back, I sat in my wheelchair, in the corner of the room, beside the chairs that he and Romy occupied. "I'm fine Ruben," I shrugged his hand away, my tone a little too sharp. He pulled his hand back and placed it in his lap and from beneath my eyelashes I could see that he was hurt. I had hurt Ruben, one of the few people who had put my needs before his own. A man who had devoted so much of his own time to me, without ever asking for anything in return…or was he? What did he want from me? There had to have been something…right?

"Do you not want to go to London?" Romy asked, misunderstanding my sharpness. Should I just ignore Ruben's hurt feelings or do I say something? I wondered. How would I apologize and what was I actually apologizing for?

"Sorry," I said sincerely, looking only at Ruben, he faked a smile. I turned to Romy, "Of course I want to go to London… It's just that last time we planned this trip I ended up in here," I finished, looking around the room with a slight taste of disgust. "I know… that's why I'm planning it so last minute, there will be no time for accidents to happen," Romy said, smiling proudly. "Yeah, unless the plane goes down!" I teased. "That's really not funny Zahra," Ruben inserted, disapprovingly. It was the first time he had spoken in minutes and he clearly wasn't happy with me. Romy locked eyes with me silently commenting on Ruben's disposition and I returned the look, explaining that I didn't know how to fix it.

"Okay we'll work out the details for the trip later," Romy said awkwardly, looking at Ruben from the corner of her eyes. Ruben looked down at his hands. There was nothing worse than the feeling of Ruben's sour vibe, stifling the air and having the blood of his melancholy mood on my hands...

"So Ben, what do you want to have for dinner?" I asked, in a chipper tone trying to change the heavy atmosphere. "I don't know. Whatever you girls want," he said dismally. I sighed loudly, my efforts went forth with no prevail. Ruben was clearly still upset with me. I inched forward in my wheelchair—a hospital requirement—and moved as close to Ruben as I could get without falling out. I sat facing him on the edge of my seat and leaned forward so that my weight fell on to him. It was awkward, I didn't care. I wrapped my arms around his stiff, shock ridden body and hugged him. "Thank you Ruben, for everything you've done for me. For always being there and for being such a good *friend* when I needed it the most," I rested my head on his shoulder, emphasizing the word friend, just enough for it to sink in, but not enough to reoffend. Ruben bent his arms at the elbows, stuck underneath my tight grip, and lightly patted my back. I could feel his tense body release under mine as he quietly said, "I think by now you know I'd do anything for you Zar. There's no need to thank me." I was confused by his response, he sounded so much like Adrian. I thought I had cleared things up by reiterating that we were friends, but maybe I didn't emphasize the word enough.

"Hello, Hello," Dr. Arnulf said interrupting. He entered the room with his eager intern at his heels, holding my x-rays and medical chart in his hand. Ruben pushed me back into my seat as Dr. Arnulf pinned my x-rays up, for all of us to see.

"Good news!" was all he had to say.

Mission (actually) Accomplished
February 12

I woke up with a sense of excitement. I was feeling transformed, my cast was finally off and I was free from crutches, plaster, plastic and pain. I could finally wear a complete pair of shoes. It was Friday and not just any Friday, but the Friday that I had been waiting for, for weeks now. I crawled out of bed, early with a smile on my face. For once in the past few weeks, I was up before Romy. I stepped out of our room and into the hallway as Fredrik and Mila were just about to put on their coats and leave for the bakery. "You're up early," Fredrik said, when I met them on my way to the bathroom. "Excited about your trip?" Mila assessed. "Yeah, I couldn't sleep anymore," I said, trying my best to contain my eagerness. "Well, have fun and we'll see you in a few days, yes!" Mila said, zipping up her coat and kissing me on the cheek. "Make sure you have everything," she continued, as she and Fredrik headed toward the front door. The cold winter air trailed in as the front door opened, instantly chilling me to the bone, I craved the attention of the hot water.

My shower was short, but just long enough to warm me up. I wanted to spend as much time as possible going over the contents of my bag in case there was anything I had forgotten. I went back to our room and woke Romy up and as she showered, I went over my checklist and zipped up my small suitcase. When Romy had showered and we had eaten breakfast, we hulled our bags out into the hallway and waited for the familiar sound of Ruben honking his car horn. We loaded our bags into the trunk of the car and headed down the winding snow covered hills into town and to school. Our classes before lunch passed by quickly and before I knew it, the lunch bell rang and Romy and I headed to our lockers to grab our coats and meet Ruben at the front of the school so that we could check in at the airport.

    Ruben pulled our bags out of his trunk and onto the pavement at our terminal. "Well…have fun," he said, trying to mask any ruse in his voice. I ignored this and got on my toes to hug him. "See you soon Ben," I said sincerely. He held me tightly, unwilling to let me go. Unfortunately, I had to push away, forcing him to release me from his grip. I had really hoped that we were moving forward in our friendship, but Ruben's insistent affections were putting a hold on what we did have and only drew us further apart. "Sorry," he apologized genuinely. "Guess I'm a little edgy now, after everything that's happened to you." I couldn't tell if he was being honest or if he was covering up his true feelings. I didn't want to assume, but Ruben's obscurity was confusing. "At some point Ben you're going to have to let me spread my wings," I said, in the most casual tone I could use. He laughed lightly and put his hands in his jeans pockets like he always did when he was nervous or embarrassed. He quickly turned to Romy, "Roms, have a blast, take lots of pictures!" he instructed as he stretched his arms out to hug her. "Not fair! How come she gets 'have a blast, takes lots of pictures' and I get…well…nothing?" I teased. Ruben shrugged his shoulders and smiled. We grabbed hold of our bags, Ruben opened his car door. He waved as we headed into the airport and drove away once

Romy and I were just two more bodies in a faceless crowd.

We found our seats and clapped excitedly as the plane took off. In three hours, we would be in London. In three hours, I would be with Adrian again, after five weeks of separation. I needed to close my eyes for a few minutes to help calm my nervous heart. Romy put in her earphones and watched the inflight movie to give me some personal space. She understood without me having to say it, that I was feeling a little overwhelmed by everything that had transpired over the last two days, I needed to give my brain a chance to slow down. My cast had finally been removed and though my ankle was still a bit sore and weak, life had pretty much returned to normal.

After we got home from the hospital, I called my cousin, Hannah, in London and asked her if Romy and I could stay at her place. I didn't know Hannah all that well. I had only met her two or three times in the past, but from what I could remember she was generally a nice person, kind and generous enough to let us stay with for the weekend! Hannah was twenty-one years old, older by just a few years. She promised to show us around once we arrived in London.

With my eyes closed, I daydreamed about Adrian's reaction to my birthday surprise. I had spoken with him the night before and told him that a special package would arrive today. I could tell by his voice that he was excited to see what I had sent for him. He promised to call as soon as it arrived and I laughed to myself, as I pictured the shock that would be written all over his face when he saw mine. My mind wandered and I thought about seeing Adrian more often, what if I moved to London? What would it be like to be with him everyday, to wake up in his arms, to eat breakfast across from him and to prepare dinner together every night? The fantasy made me happy, it would be everything I ever wanted, but then, what about Romy, Mila and Fredrik... Ruben... Could I truly bear not seeing Ruben everyday, or Romy? Not likely. I sighed and opened my eyes. We were minutes away from landing. My heart fluttered uncontrollably, so much for remaining calm, I thought to myself.

The movie turned off and Romy removed her earphones. "Ready?" she asked. I smiled from ear to ear, unable to speak. We anxiously waited for the plane to land and eagerly watched the other passengers grab their belongings. Romy and I followed suit and quickly filed off of the plane and into the Arrivals area. I looked around for Hannah, it had been at least seven or eight years since I had seen her last and I couldn't really remember what she looked like. Luckily for me, she looked a lot like my aunt Samantha, Joanne's youngest sister.

My aunt Samantha moved to the UK after working as a flight attendant before I was born. She married my uncle Bryce who worked with her as a pilot for British Airways. Hannah was born a year into their marriage and they tried their best to visit my grandparents often, which had only amounted to two or three times in twenty-two years.

Hannah had my aunt Samantha's face, a face just like Joanne's but Hannah's skin was fairer and her hair was light brown almost blonde, it was probably dyed. She was tall and slim and looked like a fashionista. She wore a thick fur coat that reached just above her waist, I winched in disgust. Under her jacket was a grey vintage sweater and a pair of tight black jeans tucked into a pair of thigh-high, heeled boots. On top of her head was a black beret and on her face was a large pair of designer sunglasses. She stood out against the rest of the crowd and although she was gorgeous, I couldn't help but feel a bit embarrassed as all eyes were solely on her.

She greeted us warmly with a hug and kiss and looped her arm through mine as we walked toward her friend, Avis' car. I could tell that Avis was Hannah's side kick, she was her Romy. She dressed in the same manner as Hannah. Tight black jeans, red leather ankle boots, a leopard print buttoned up winter coat and the same black beret. She casually greeted us, "Hey," was all she said, which made her seem a little bit rude, but I figured this was her nonchalant way of acting cool. I didn't want to waste another minute thinking about it. I was there to see Adrian and so a socialite wannabe wasn't going to damper my good mood.

We pulled up to Hannah's terrace, similar to a townhouse and followed her inside. She quickly showed us around and led us to the spare room that Romy and I would be sharing. The small house was elegantly dressed with posh trimmings that looked very expensive. We dropped our bags in our room and joined Hannah and Avis in the lounge—the living room—"So what's the plan for tonight?" Hannah asked, cracking open a bottle of white wine in the kitchen. She brought four glasses out to us on a tray and even though I didn't want any, I felt inclined to take it. Both Romy and I held the glasses in our hands and looked down into the soft yellow liquid. We didn't want to seem inadequate to Hannah and her friend, we didn't want them to think of us as childish. Peer pressure, I thought. I had never been one to buckle…had I?

I took a small sip of my wine, I could feel everyone's eyes on me, waiting to hear the plans for Adrian's surprise. I had briefly filled them in on the situation on the car ride over to the house. I held my breath and swallowed the cold wine, it wasn't so bad that way, because I couldn't taste it. "Well," I started. "I think I'm going to call Adrian and ask him if he got my package yet. He'll obviously say no and I'll pretend to be surprised. I'll ask him if he's home, he'll respond and if he's not there, I'll ask him casually where he is. Once the location is confirmed, then we'll all show up!" I explained. Romy nodded as she contemplated the plan, I could tell she liked it. "Sneaky girl," Hannah said, smiling, "I love a good scandal," she liked my plan too. Avis seemed impartial, she just looked straight ahead, shrugged her shoulders and continued to drink her wine. Maybe she didn't like us imposing on her kinship with Hannah, or perhaps she couldn't handle interruptions in her day to day life, unless it was a spontaneous shopping excursion at Harrods.

When I had finished my wine, I headed to my room to change my clothes and prepare myself for the surprise. I could hardly believe that I was actually there, it almost seemed impossible. When I was ready, I went back out to the lounge and waited for Hannah and Romy to finish up. Avis had left to pick up some takeout, while the three of us worked out the details of my plan. If Adrian was home, we would drag him out of his house and if he was already out, we would simply join him. I sat down on the couch with my phone in hand and opened my contacts. I was just about to press on Adrian's name when my mind went to Ruben. He was probably sitting on the edge of his seat, biting his nails, just wondering if we made it to London in one piece. I scrolled to Ruben's name and connected the call. I knew that once the Adrian "surprise package" plan was in motion, there would be no time or even thought to call Ruben.

He answered on the first ring. "Hello?" he said, with slight panic in his voice. "Ben, relax! We're here. We made it, safely," I said calmly, trying to ease his fervour through the phone. "I'm glad to hear it," he said, backing off a little. I guess he realized how desperate he sounded. "So what are the plans for tonight?" he asked, clearly fishing for answers. "I'm not quite sure yet, I think we're all going out," I said, offering very little information. "Hmm," was all he replied. "Well Zar, give Romy my best and I'll see you in a few days." I was surprised. I really thought we would have a long dragged out conversation, not that I didn't enjoy talking to him, but I had a top secret mission to tend to.

Ruben's call was out of the way and Adrian's was next. Romy joined me on the couch, curled up in a ball, anxious. Avis had returned with a few Chinese food boxes and was setting them out in the kitchen with Hannah.

"Hi love," Adrian answered the phone giving me instant hot flashes. My heart pounded in my chest, Romy rocked back and forth with excitement.

"Hi AJ, I'm just wondering if you got my package?" I asked, setting the plan in motion.

"No, not yet I'm afraid, but maybe it arrived now. I'll check when I get home," he said.

"Oh!" I said, trying to act surprised, "where are you?" I asked, casually.

"A few of my mates dragged me out for a drink for my birthday. Maybe I'll skip out so I can check if the package arrived," he said.

I panicked, "No, no have fun, don't worry about the package, you'll get it soon," I said.

"Ask for the name of the place he's at," Romy whispered.

"So… where did your friends take you?" I asked, unable to think of any clever way to get the information. Romy shook her head, disappointed.

"This place called, The Hideaway," Adrian offered.

"Sounds cool, well, I won't keep you, call me later when you get home so I know if you got the package okay?" I said, rushing to get him off the phone. I wanted to head out the door, I wanted to complete my mission.

"Okay, well..." I could tell he wasn't ready to let me off the phone which was perfect. "I'll talk to you soon. I promise," he said.

"Yep, I know you will," I said, with a smile in my voice.

I hurried to the kitchen with Romy at my heels. Hannah handed each of us a takeout box and a pair of chopsticks each. As we ate, I told them where Adrian was and luckily we weren't too far from that particular bar. We would be there within fifteen minutes. I took two bites of my noodles and put the box down. My stomach was in knots and there was no possible way I could eat around it. I watched the other girls finish their meals, impatiently. All I wanted to do was see Adrian, not in a minute, or an hour, but now.

We finally piled into Avis' car and headed to our final destination. Avis quickly found a parking spot not too far from the bar. I was happy, not sure how much walking my healing ankle could handle. My heart beat heavily in my chest, I could hear only my pulse in my ears, the world around me mute. As we walked up to the bar I didn't even realize Romy was talking to me until she grabbed my arm, pulling me away from the front door. "Wait. Zahra," she said, her grip tight. "You can't just walk in there," she stated. "Why not?" I asked, as Hannah and Avis reached us. I had walked so far ahead, left everyone trailing behind. "'Cause maybe he's in there with another girl!" Avis interrupted. Romy shot her a disapproving look and Hannah slapped her arm. "What? I was only teasing!" Avis lied with an evil grin on her face. Very nice, I thought in disgust. Avis was clearly becoming someone I knew all too well. I would be keeping my distance, there was no doubt about that.

My heart beat another uncontrollable rhythm, different from the one before. What if he *was* there with another girl? I had never weighed the possibilities. This surprise mission had the potential to be with filled with complete heartache. I wasn't prepared for heartache...*thanks a lot Avis for filling me with doubt!* Despair written on my face sent Romy into safeguard-mode, she took me by the shoulders and shook me back into reality. "You know Adrian!" she reminded, "What I was trying to say is after all the scheming, you should have a better plan than just walking in and right up to him," she reassured. "Romy's right, the plan is kind of weak don't you think?" Hannah piped in, trying to help me forget about Avis' previous comment. "I've got an idea," she continued. She explained the plan to me and the three of us agreed, it was a great. Avis was oblivious to the conversation, she just wanted to get into the bar and have some drinks.

    I took a few deep breathes in and exhaled loudly. I put my hand on the door knob and pulled the door open. I walked into the bar and quickly scanned all the faces to make sure Adrian wouldn't see me. The bar was noisy, the air was filled with music played over hidden speakers, chattering voices and clanking glasses. Then it happened… As if in a dream, there he was and everything stopped. Time stood still, everything around him blurred.

    Adrian had all of my focus. He sat at the bar with his back facing me and though I couldn't see his face, my heart was my compass. He was amongst several friends all with happy faces, cheering and saluting each other, chugging back beers, testing who could drink the fastest like true boys and yet he looked alone. He sat at the end of his four friends, who were all standing with their backs to him. If he hadn't have told me he was out with friends, I would have thought that he was there alone. He sat hunched over a drink, his elbows on the bar ledge, his head resting in his left hand. He looked sad.

    "Is that him?" Hannah asked, following my gaze. I nodded. "Okay I'm going," she said, with a huge smile on her face. She wasn't lying when she said she loved a good scandal, although this entire surprise was hardly anything scandalous. I found a stool at a vacant table while Romy and Avis found another table to sit at and we waited. I watched as Hannah sauntered over to Adrian and pushed herself in between the none-existent space between Adrian and his friends. His friends averted their attention, but only for a second before returning to their drinking game and Adrian was startled by her approach.

He seemed lost in his thoughts and was unaware of her until she lightly placed her hand on his shoulder and swooped her head down to the side of his face. I couldn't hear her, but I mouthed the rehearsed lines along with her. *"Hi. My friend over there bought you this drink,"* she would say holding the gin and tonic in her hand. Adrian only slightly moved his head, not really making any effort to look in my direction. He shook his head, *"No thanks."* Hannah looked at me with widened eyes, she didn't know what to do next. I motioned with my hand for her to continue. She turned back to Adrian and started to talk again. Adrian's body language showed that he was annoyed. I smiled. I tried to read Hannah's lips, *"C'mon, just one drink, she's really cute, I'm sure you'll like her."* Adrian didn't raise his head and continued to look down into his drink. He shook his hand dismissively at her. Hannah grinned slyly. This was the part she was waiting for, the 'scandal.' I knew she was about to use the line we'd come up with in case all else failed, *"...It's just one drink! and unlike you,"* she started, *"she actually paid for this one."*

(★)[19] Adrian's back stiffened, he slowly raised his head. He looked at Hannah for the first time really *seeing* her, he noted the resemblance between her and I. He turned in his seat swiftly and looked directly at me, dazed. He got out of his seat in an instant, walked quickly, with long strides, toward me. I stood up as he drew near and waited for him to stop in front of me. My heart felt as

---

[19] Wonderwall (Live)- Noel Gallagher

though it were about to explode, it banged violently against my chest, trying to break free from its barrier. With each step that Adrian took toward me, passing through people without hesitation, weaving through the crowd, his eyes never left mine. I could hear my breath heavy, my pulse ringing in my ears. Without breaking his stride as if he were almost floating, in one smooth, seamless motion, he cupped my face and kissed me.

My wildly beating heart steadied to a calm, slow rhythm as the fire in his lips and tongue passed through onto mine. My breathing eased, my legs buckled beneath me, I melted under his touch. He scooped me up in his arms, pulling me into his heat. My limp arms sprang up with new life, like a flower blooming under the heat of the sun and I let my fingers tangle through his hair feeling the texture of each strand under my touch.

This was our first kiss, the kiss I had been waiting for from the moment I met Adrian. The kiss I had expected on so many other occasions, but never had the chance to meet and now without warning, when I was totally unprepared, here it was. Our first kiss, *my* first kiss and it was unlike anything I could have ever imagined. The thought of this moment used to make my heart pound irrevocably, but it was completely different. I was calm and floating above myself in this most surreal moment of my entire life.

We stayed locked in that moment for an eternity in my mind and there was nothing that could pull us apart, not the crowded bar, the blaring music or the staring eyes. None of it mattered. I don't know what it was that eventually pulled us apart, but I know it wasn't by our own discretion. He released me. Romy and Hannah were waiting to say hello. Adrian hugged Romy, he was truly happy to see her and properly introduced himself to Hannah. Avis had busied herself with a few other friends she saw enter the bar at some point and really had no interest in what the rest of us were doing.

Adrian introduced us all to his group of friends who hadn't even realized that he had walked away from them. It was the first time I had heard Adrian call me his girlfriend and each time he spoke the words with his arm around my waist, my heart fluttered and the butterflies in my stomach flapped their wings.

After our introductions, Hannah ordered us all a round of drinks. She loved a good scandal, she also loved to celebrate. "So where's Ruben?" Adrian asked, after many rounds of drinks. "Why do you ask?" I was surprised that Adrian had mentioned it. Maybe he didn't feel any of the tension that seemed to be building between the three of us. "I don't know...as far as I'm concerned the four of us were getting along quite well. I guess I just thought he'd come for a visit too," Adrian assessed. Maybe that's why Ruben had acted the way he did, maybe he felt left out. Adrian was right, over the past few months Romy, Ruben, Adrian and I had become very close and it was unfair for Romy and I to not invite Ruben on our trip. It hadn't even crossed my mind that he might have expected an invite. The original trip didn't include him and when Romy and I planned the last minute trip, Ruben joining us didn't come up.

"Ruben's at home. We didn't think of inviting him," I answered, realizing Adrian was waiting for a reply. I looked down into my drink, I felt bad. No matter how much I was trying to change, I couldn't shake the feelings of guilt that often consumed me. "Don't worry about it!" Adrian said, shaking me. "I'm sure it doesn't really matter to him," he tried to reassure. I decided to shake my ill feelings off, there was nothing I could do, we were already in London and I was only going to be there for a few days. I didn't want to waste any time hanging around with the what-ifs.

My stomach groaned, the alcohol I had consumed not settling, reminding me that I had passed on my takeout dinner at Hannah's house. I regretted not eating it when I had the chance, I could picture it sitting on the kitchen counter, rotting, instead of fighting off the hunger pangs in my gut. The pangs quickly travelled down my leg and into my ankle. I used Adrian's arm to brace myself and limped up onto a bar stool.

"Are you okay?"

"I'm fine," I lied, as I sat on the stool.

"Do you want me take you home?"

"No, it's okay, Romy's having such a good time," I said, smiling. We both looked at Romy who was chatting up one of Adrian's friends, Noel.

"You could come to my place and then Romy wouldn't have to leave Noel right now, though I'm sure she wouldn't mind…" *His place*…I hadn't even thought about Adrian's place. He must have seen the hesitation on my face. "We don't have to go there, it was just a suggestion," he reflected casually.

"Is your place far?" I asked.

"No, about a twenty minute walk," he answered.

"You walked? I don't think I can," I said.

"I'll carry you on my back!" he replied.

"They can come get me when they're ready to leave," I assessed.

"Sure, whatever you want," he reassured.
I smiled a nervous smile.
He rubbed my back.

I slipped off of the stool and limped over to Romy, who was so caught up in her conversation with Noel that she didn't even notice me approaching. I decided not to bother her and turned to Hannah instead. I told her of my plan and she told me just to stay the night. I blushed. She laughed. "Relax Zar, he seems like a really nice guy. I'm sure you have nothing to worry about." I limped over to where Adrian waited and took his hand, we headed to the exit.

"Hop on," Adrian said, crouching down. I climbed on his back and laughed as the butterflies in my stomach fluttered, the blood rushing to my head.

"Now I know what it's like to be tall," I teased, as Adrian walked down the street bouncing me along. I could feel a rumble in his chest and I knew he was laughing. I rested my head on his back and closed my eyes as I floated in the midnight air.

I'm Ready

Adrian's dorm looked just as I had expected—like a young, single, man lived there. The walls were a sharp white, cold and uninviting left bare except for a poster of The Cure that hung over the small TV in the open concept living room. There was an old dark brown leather sofa, crimson patches covering where the leather had wrinkled and split. Music magazines, car magazines, books, empty takeout containers and half-drank beer, bottles, littered a glass rectangular coffee table. Adrian quickly rearranged the magazines, stacked them one on top of the other, grabbed the beer bottles in one hand, the takeout boxes in the other and rushed to the kitchen. "Sorry, I wasn't expecting any guests," he blushed.

From the entryway, the kitchen was to the right. It was small, old, but clean, just big enough for no more than two people. It opened to the living room with an island dividing the two spaces. It was a simple kitchen, a stove, sink, a few cupboards. A microwave sat on the counter. To the left of the entryway and down a short, dark hallway, was the bathroom. It was a simple white bathroom with a toilet, sink and vanity mirror surrounded by five large, round lights and a bathtub with a rainfall shower head. Plush turquoise and tan stripped towels hung from hooks on the back of the door, toothpaste left uncapped on the edge of the sink. "It's simple," Adrian said of the room, he shrugged his shoulders, turned off the light.

"This is the last room." At the end of the hallway was Adrian's room, the only room with coloured walls. He turned on the light, the room lit up, a welcoming seafoam green. Under the window, in the corner of the room was a desk, unstained wood with a laptop and white lamp on top. Beside the desk was his queen sized, white framed, bed, rumpled and unfolded. A navy blue, white, grey and seafoam patchwork quilt lay askew, grey and white pinstripe bedsheets revealed. On the floor, under the bed, was a plain navy area rug, as dark as the midnight sky and directly over the bed, hanging on the wall was something all too familiar.

"What is that doing there?" I asked, abashed. "Oh that? I had it blown up and framed. I have the original in safe keeping don't worry," he said smiling. Staring back at me from across the room was the poem I had sent to Adrian, the tan, antique painted paper, the wisps of pink and blue and green, the letters, words, phrases, describing uninhibited love.

"I'm not worried about the original," I pointed out. "I'd like to know *why* it's up *there*, so large and for everyone to see," I stammered, disgust, all over my face. "And just who do you think I have in my room? No one besides me is ever in here. Why wouldn't I frame it? The colours match perfectly, I just *had to,*" he mocked, standing behind me, cupped my shoulders and shook. "Ugh," I sighed. "What?" he asked. "It's embarrassing!" I shrieked. "You are a strange, strange girl. You should never be ashamed about how you feel," he teased, stepping out from behind me to take a better look at the picture.

"Are you hungry?" he asked. He took my hand and led me down the hallway and into the kitchen. "I don't have much, I usually eat out," he said. "That's okay, I'll figure something out," I walked to the fridge and opened it. Inside I found half of a cabbage browning on the edges, one carton of orange juice, a jug of milk, a quarter emptied, three eggs, half a loaf of bread and a small plate with butter on it. Five beers, clanking together, lined the fridge door. I reached in and grabbed the cabbage, "Do you have rice?" I asked. "Yes, actually," he said, opening one of the cupboards and taking out a small half-filled bag, folded shut with an elastic band. "Jasmine, perfect," I took the rice from him. "Do you by chance have vegetable broth or cubes?" "You'd be surprised, I have two cubes, I've had them for...oh I don't know how long... since I moved from my parent's house, I took them, thought they'd come in handy, they never did," standing behind me, he reached into the cupboard once more, searched for the cubes behind a row of canned beans. "What are you making?" he asked, as I looked around for a pot. "Bubur, it's like congee, do you know what that is?" I asked. He shook his head, no. "It's a rice porridge. My grandma...*great-grandma*, she makes it all the time, Jonnæ too, but Jonnæ's is different. Nuri serves it for breakfast, I like it anytime of the day. It reminds me of..." I trailed. "Sounds interesting, I'm willing to try anything at least once," Adrian leaned his back against the counter. I filled the pot up with water and added a few cups of rice and the vegetable stock cubes. "Now it just needs to boil and get really mushy," I sat down on top of the island.

When the rice had boiled for about twenty minutes I chopped up the cabbage and added it to the pot. "Smells delicious," Adrian said, standing by the pot occasionally stirring the mixture. When it was ready Adrian grabbed two bowls and I scooped out the steaming, soft, white pillowy porridge for the both of us. We sat down on the island, we ate in silence, each spoonful knocking out the hunger pangs one by one. Each spoonful reminding me of the things I missed about White Rock, about Nuri and Antso. Nuri's home cooked meals and private French chats with Antso. Jonnæ's special twists to her version of the recipe, perfected with years of practice.

"What time are they picking you up?" Adrian rinsed our emptied bowls in the sink. "They're not..." "Oh! Okay sure... Are you tired?" he asked deceptively casual, the pulse in his neck gave him away. "A bit," I confessed, playing with the hem of my shirt. It was minutes to two in the morning, the effects of the day were starting to catch up with me. "Come with me," he said, lifting me off the island. He extended his hand, I took it and we walked down the hall to his bedroom. "I'll give you a T-shirt to sleep in and you can sleep in here," he said, as we entered the room. "Where will you sleep?" I asked. "On the couch." He pulled out a plain grey T-shirt from his drawer and handed it to me, "Thanks," I shyly took the shirt and walked to the bathroom. "You can use whatever you want in there," he called out as I closed the door behind me.

I slipped out of my sweater and jeans and threw Adrian's shirt on. It was big and long, but not quite long enough, it graced my mid thigh, but somehow I couldn't help but feel naked. I looked myself over a few times in the mirror trying to think positively. I quickly washed my face and swished some mouthwash around in my mouth. When I was done, I took a deep breath, opened the bathroom door and turned off the light. I slowly, padded barefoot back to the room, my folded clothes in one hand, the other, pulling down at the hem on the T-shirt, self-consciously. Adrian, in a pair of blue plaid pyjama bottoms and a white tank top was straightening out the bed, a pillow tossed aside and a neatly folded sheet sat at the edge.

"Hi," I said nervously, he hadn't noticed when I entered. Adrian turned quickly, startled. "Oh hi...i-is that okay?" he asked, observing my efforts with the T-shirt. "Oh yeah, it's fine," I said, quickly moving my hand away from the hem of the shirt. I rushed to his desk and put down my folded clothes and crossed my arms awkwardly across my chest. Adrian smiled. "What?" I asked. "That T-shirt, it hits me right at my waist is all...on you it's like a dress," he smiled.

"A short, unflattering dress!"
He shrugged. "Well, the bed's all ready for you," he moved aside. "Thanks," I climbed in. He bent down and kissed me, my body froze in shock and then remembered, releasing the tension and

melted. "Goodnight," he said, pulling away and walked toward the door. "Night," I yawned, placing my head on the pillow, his scent wafting up around me. He turned off the light as he exited the room. "Adrian. Wait," I sat up in the bed.

"Yes babes?"

"Don't go."

"Zar," he sighed, "I don't think—"

"Please," I interrupted. "Just stay with me," I said, in a half whisper.

He walked back to the bed and sat on the edge. I reached for his hand and took it in mine. His fingers rigid at my touch. The white glow of the moon, cast faint blue light off the pale green-blue walls. Adrian's profile highlighted like a chiaroscuro painting. He sat unmoved, I wasn't even sure he was breathing. "Hey…?" I whispered, leaning forward to see his face. He looked at me, breath returned to his body, his fingers relaxed in mine. "What's wrong?" I asked.

"Nothing's wrong…" he looked at me with warm eyes. "Will you…stay with me?"

"I don't—"

"Adrian please, I want you too…what are you afraid of?"

"I'm not afraid Zahra, I just…you said…you've never had a boyfriend before and I…just…respect that," he was looking at the wall across the room.

(★)[20] "I know you do Adrian…and I love that about you. But what about you? What about your other girlfriends?" I asked.

"There were others, but I wasn't in love with them. I don't want to rush things with you. I don't want things…to…be…ruined."

---

[20] Unthinkable-Alicia Keys

"Ruined?" I asked surprised, "Okay, AJ look. Let's be honest with each other for a moment. Why are we dancing around this? I just want to tell you how I feel.

"Remember you told me that this is exactly how it should feel when two people are meant to be together? So why are we wasting all this time with what-ifs? We've had so many road blocks in our way and now I'm *finally* here… and we should *be* together. You make me feel a way I've never felt before and—"

"Zahra, don't rush, that's not why I brought you here," he interrupted.

"I know that," I replied, "Adrian, this doesn't have to be something that's unthinkable! It could be so beautiful, you and me… All I'm trying to say is if you asked me, I'd say I'm ready…"

Our fingers curled, intertwining with each other's. Adrian sat facing me, one leg hanging off the side of the bed. He racked my face for answers, his eyes flickering in the moonlight, across my face, down to the floor, contemplating. We were silent.

My heart pounded, the silence sweltering, the air thick. I shouldn't have pushed him. I should have just let him leave the room. He should have slept on the couch. I should have invited him without expectations. We could have been lying in each other's arms. Instead we were sitting quietly, barely breathing, awkward and unsure. Had I just ruined his birthday? Had I just ruined this entire trip? I chewed my lower lip nervously, too afraid to make a sound.

He looked up slowly from the floor, into my eyes and said, "I'm ready."

ADRIAN

(★) [21] How can I deny her when she's everything I've ever wanted? I've waited so long to kiss her, to be this close to her and now she's sitting here beside me in my grey T-shirt. Her perfect copper legs crossed over each other, her wild curly hair flowing free around her shoulders. She's looking at me. She's perfect. I want her in every way possible, but I'm willing to wait until the time is right. I don't know if this is it.

She's looking at me with those bright eyes, *those eyes,* long lashes and her perfect pink lips are pursed in apprehension. She lightly presses her teeth into her lower lip, the way she always does when she's nervous. She tells me that she's ready but is she? I listen to her speak, she knows what she wants.

"I'm ready," I say. She's ready too. She won't be my first, I will be hers, but she will be the first girl that I've ever loved.

I cup my hand on the back of her head and pull her in close to me. I've never been in love before, I can't imagine loving anyone else but her. My lips press firmly on hers at first and then soften. I tangle my fingers with hers as I lay her down gently on my bed. And though I feel my skin, on her skin, I don't feel close enough to her.

I feel like I'm on fire, her soft fingers leave a trail of hot streaks behind. My heart burns and aches as it beats uncontrollably. She is my everything and I will give her all of me. She has taught me what it means to live and to love and we are one.

---

[21] In The Darkness-Dead By Sunrise

Kissing You
February 13

I peeled my eyes open as the light from the sun sneaked into the room and reflected off of the wall. The room was still dark and I probably would have been able to fall asleep if the memories of the night before weren't playing on repeat in my mind, I lay with my head resting on Adrian's bare chest. I curled into him and in his sleep he pulled me closer. I closed my eyes enjoying his scent, my favourite scent. Feeling his arm on my back, I couldn't help but think about the way his skin felt on mine, how soft and gentle he was. His soft lips, his soothing voice, how perfectly sculpted his arms, legs and abs were and how beautiful he looked in the moonlight. He was mine completely, and I was his. I smiled and wrapped my left arm around his chest as he stirred a little at my movement. I lay still trying not to wake him completely. He kissed my forehead.

"You awake?" he whispered.

"No," I whispered back. I couldn't hear him laugh, but I could feel the vibration in his chest under my ear. "I'm sorry," I whispered.

"For what?" he yawned.

"For waking you."

"It's okay, I'm glad I'm awake," he said quietly.

"Why?"

"So I can do this," he said, pulling me closer to him and kissing me gently.

"Happy Birthday, AJ," I said, smiling looking down at him.

"Thank you," he smiled back. "What time is it?"

I looked over at the digital clock on top of his bed frame.

"9:51 a.m.," I said.

"Oh crap...I forgot, we have to get up."

"Why?" I whined. "What's going on?"

"Birthday brunch with my family at eleven."

"Oh!" I said, surprised, "then you better get in the shower."

"You mean *we* better get in the shower! You're coming Zahra," he said.

"Oh AJ, I don't know…they weren't expecting me. Plus if I just show up without Romy, I'm sure they're going to figure out what went on here and I really don't need them thinking about that, especially the first time I meet them," I insisted.

"We'll just say I picked you up on the way. If you don't come they'll kill me! They've been dying to meet you. I promise, everything will be fine, you just worry too much, and you're paranoid!" he said, rubbing my back.

"Okay fine. I'll go, but on one condition."

"All right, what is it?" he asked.

"You let me sketch you, real quick, right now."

"Right now?"

"Right now, five minutes, don't move," I said, getting up from the bed. I threw on Adrian's big grey T-shirt and ran out of his bedroom. I grabbed my messenger bag off the couch and hurried back to the bedroom. I sat down at his desk and pulled my sketchbook out of my bag along with a thin black marker.

"What shall I do?" he asked.

"Anything you want," I said, flipping to an empty page.

"Umm," he couldn't decide.

"Okay I know, how about you sit with your back facing me, that will be the easiest and quickest to draw, plus it won't be completely offensive when other people see it," I pointed out.

"*Offensive? When* other people see it?"

"You know what I mean and of course other people are going to see it, it'll be in my sketchbook."

"I don't know how much I like that."

"It'll be fine AJ, I promise. I'll let you see it okay. If you don't like it, I'll scrap it."

"Fine."

He sat up and turned, so that his back was facing me and I began to sketch his form as quickly as I could and within a few minutes I had finished my initial drawing. I decided I would define some of the lines with black water colour paint afterwards. "All done," I said, holding up the sketchbook so that he could see it. He turned around and smiled. "I approve," he said. "Good, 'cause I wasn't really going to scrap it," I joked.

"Okay shower time."

We headed out the door and to Adrian's car. It was sleek, stylish, expense. He clearly took pride in taking care of it, not a single mark or scruff defaced the smooth, shiny surface. He opened the door for me, like a true gentleman and I slide in. The interior was also black. The bucket seats were black and yellow with yellow accents throughout. It was unlike anything I had ever seen before, very European.

We drove for maybe twenty minutes from Westminster to Chelsea, Adrian's hometown. As we drove along, Adrian pointed out various sites. I had my own personal tour guide and I truly loved every minute of it. "That's where Bob Marley wrote I Shot the Sheriff. Oscar Wilde, lived there, Roman Polanski, there," he said, pointing at the different buildings. "Judy Garland, over there, Bram Stoker! *Vampires*. James Whistler, painter—but I'm sure you already knew that—over there," he pointed again, as we turned a corner. "That's Chelsea Physic Park, there. I'm going to take you there for a picnic!" he said, smiling at me.

"A picnic? It's the middle of winter!"

"Not now, in the spring!" he slyly smiled.

"That sounds lovely," I beamed, that was the happiest I

think I had ever been. Adrian laughed lightly at my joy and placed his left hand on my leg. I smiled and put his hand in mine as we continued to drive. We turned the corner and after only three minutes, the car slowed and Adrian parked the car on a side street.

"Where are we going? Where's the restaurant?" I asked, unlatching my seatbelt.

"There's no restaurant," his voice trailed as he stepped out of the car and to the passenger side, opening my door for me. "This is my family home," he finished, pointing at the row of tan coloured brick houses.

"WHAT?" I yelled surprised.

"Shh!" he laughed, placing his index finger on his lips.

"Adrian you never mentioned anything about going to your house. When you said brunch, I assumed it was at a restaurant…"

"You know what they say about assuming…something about making an ass out of one's self."

"It's actually ass out of you and me, so you're included," I corrected.

"I didn't think the location of the brunch mattered."

"It matters because a restaurant would have been less personal, but your family home…your mum will have to make more food for me… Oh AJ this is really bad," I panicked, as he took my hand and led me to the stairs.

"Stop panicking! We have a personal chef. All meals are catered in the Scott residence, so stop freaking out," he insisted, as we walked up the five slate steps to the frosted glass, front door. "Is that a Porsche?" I asked, eyeing the shiny silver luxury vehicle parked in the driveway. "Yeah, it's Dad's," Adrian answered, leading me to the front door. We stopped and Adrian fidgeted with his keys. My heart pounded uncontrollably. Hours ago I was experiencing one of life's milestones with the most amazing man I had ever known, the first man I had ever kissed, the first man I had ever loved and now I was faced with the challenge of meeting his family and the only thing separating us, was a simple glass door.

"Hello?" Adrian called out, as he stepped into the house, securely holding my hand, pulling me through behind him. My heart was pounding and my head, spinning. I had never met the family of a guy I was dating, I never had to, I was overwhelmed. It was quiet except for some soft instrumental jazz music playing throughout the house. We took off our shoes and walked through the hallway, into the lounge.

The walls were white, the couches were white, with sleek modern lines dressed with dark brown and white accent cushions and the floor, chocolate brown hardwood. In the middle of the floor, underneath a dark brown rectangle coffee table was a soft furry white rug. There was a dark brown bookshelf against one wall, opposite the couch and beside a single seat. The walls were lined with black framed pictures of the family, across from a lit fireplace. With no one there I was able to take in the room and steady my heart. Everything was so clean that I didn't feel like my day-old outfit deserved to sit on the couch, I opted to stand. Adrian walked over to a little television screen that was built into the wall beside the fireplace. I followed him with my eyes and wrapped my arms around myself, comforting myself in the open space, with Adrian no longer at my side.

He pushed some buttons on the little screen and the music playing throughout the house went silent. "Hello? Mum? Dad? Em? Caty?" he called out. Within a few seconds I could hear heavy footsteps running above me, loud thumping racing down a dozen or so stairs. My heart raced as the footsteps became louder.

"ADRIAN!" a blonde haired girl squealed with her arms extended, as she ran into his. "Oh Adrian, happy birthday little brother," she said, as she hugged him tightly. She was a few inches shorter than him, as they embraced her face buried in his shoulder. She turned her head to the side and opened her eyes, she looked directly at me. I stood frozen in my place, unable to move.

"BLIMEY! You must be Zahra!" she exclaimed, startling me. She pushed herself off Adrian and in one swift motion had wrapped her arms around me, stifling me with her shirt. "Catherine, I think you're killing her!" Adrian laughed, trying to pull us apart. "Oh. Excuse me, sorry," she said, clearing her throat and brushing off her black pencil skirt. "This is just such a surprise," she smiled. I was speechless, still a little in shock. I nervously smiled back, unable to come up with any words. "C'mon," she said, taking my hand and leading me up another set of steps into a den that looked similar to the living room, but with dark grey couches replacing the white ones. "I'll go tell everyone you two are here. They'll be thrilled to see you, Zahra," she said smiling, cheerfully, clapping her hands before skipping off up a larger set of stairs.

"See, I told you that you had nothing to worry about," Adrian said, pulling me down onto one of the couches. He wrapped his arm around my shoulders forcing me to lean back and sink into the couch. "AJ please," I begged. "What? You'd rather we sit far apart? Don't you think they'd find that a bit odd if I wasn't sitting with my girlfriend, who surprised me on my birthday?" he said, pulling me in closer to him. He had a point, I had to admit, but I was still so nervous that everything seemed wrong.

"*Oh,* Catherine wasn't fibbing! You are here!" Sophie, Adrian's mum said, in a soft gentle voice, as she clipped in pearl earrings. Both Adrian and I rose to our feet as his mum entered the living room. "Zahra! The pictures of you we've seen don't do you any justice. It's so wonderful to finally meet you!" she said, hugging me. "And my dear boy, what a lovely surprise! Why didn't you tell us you'd be bringing a special guest?" she said, warmly hugging her son. "Happy birthday love," she finished. "…Because I too was surprised to see her," Adrian answered his mother. She released her son from her embrace and looked at me for answers. "I…um… surprised Adrian with a visit for his birthday… I'm staying with my cousin, Hannah," I answered, feeling compelled to add that bit at the end just in case she was wondering. Adrian looked at me from the corner of his eye and laughed quietly to himself, shook his head. "What? Am I missing something?" Sophie asked. "No. Nothing mum, I'm just glad I picked Zahra up this morning from Hannah's, so that you could finally meet her," he lied, winking at me. *"Okay,* well come into the dining room. We'll eat in a few minutes."

We followed her down a small hallway and into a formal dining area. The smell of eggs and pancakes filled the air, was intoxicating.

"Mum if everyone is still getting up I'll quickly give Zahra a tour of the house," Adrian suggested. "Okay that sounds like a good idea, you know how your dad and Emma are in the mornings… slow!" she said, walking into the kitchen to check on the food, before heading back upstairs. Adrian took my hand and followed his mum into the kitchen. "Hey Kent." Adrian greeted the chef, responsible for making my stomach growl. "Adrian! Long time no see, man! The prodigal son back, from Uni," said Kent, walking around the counter to hug Adrian. I smiled. It was nice to see so much love exchanged between sister and brother, mother and son, even son and chef, something that was always missing within my own home in White Rock. There was never any physical love exchanged between Joanne, Fabién and me. Not even between Jonnæ, Fabién and Joanne either. There seemed to be that kind of connection between Jonnæ and me and Antso my *great*-grandfather only.

"Who's this?" Kent asked. "This is Zahra, my girlfriend.

She came from Austria last night to surprise me," Adrian placed his hand on the small of my back sending goose bumps across my skin and hot electric volts inside my body. "Zahra, lovely to meet you," Kent stepped forward to hug me. "In this house we hug," he said, embracing me. Kent was tall, like Adrian, he had dark brown curly hair like mine, his, cut short and close to his head. His skin was a soft caramel colour, his light green eyes, vibrant and when he smiled he had two dimples. He looked like he was in his late twenties which suddenly made Ruben seem a lot older.

"I hope it's not too much trouble with me being here," I said. "Trouble? It's no trouble at all! There's plenty of food to go around," Kent said, smiling, as he walked back to the stove. "We'll let you finish, I'm going to show Zahra around the house," Adrian said, taking my hand again. "Hey Kent," Catherine chirped as she skipped into the kitchen. She had changed her outfit from her white tank top and black high waisted pencil skirt, to a short floral sun dress that made me shiver thinking about the cold February air outside. Kent looked over his shoulder and smiled charmingly. He may have even turned a bit red, but with his skin, much like mine it was hard to tell. "Oh, hey Caty," he said, as casually as he could. "Can I offer you a hand?" she asked, lightly passing a hand across his shoulders, twirling her hair with her fingers. "Um, sure…maybe just pass me those eggs," he said, pointing with his spatula.

"So Zahra, this is the kitchen…obviously," Adrian said, drawing my attention away from Catherine and Kent. The kitchen was all white just like the rest of the house, but had a dark chocolate backsplash. There were two built in ovens on one wall side by side and a warming station above the oven on the right. Next to the warming station was a built in espresso machine all stainless steel and shiny. There was a small island in the middle of the kitchen with a sink and a pot of herbs growing on top. Across from the island was a gas stovetop range with eight burners and beside the stovetop was the fridge that blended in, perfectly, with the white kitchen cabinets. As we exited the room we passed a small built in wine fridge that was completely stocked. It was a beautiful kitchen the only other kitchen I had seen that was professional like that one, was Jonnæ's and being in that kitchen made me feel at home.

"What's up with Catherine and Kent?" I asked, as we walked into another hallway. "What d'you mean?" Adrian asked. "They just seem…friendly," I assessed. "You think? I've never noticed," Adrian said, as he led me up a handful of stairs. "Well, Kent's a good guy." Adrian pulled open a sliding door at the top of the stairs. We stepped into a large bedroom that was white, like I had expected. There was a queen sized bed against the wall pointing out into the middle of the room with a gold coloured bedspread on top and a dark brown fur throw, folded at the bottom of the bed. At the end of the bed, there was a low rectangle coffee table, the same as the one in the living room and on top of the table there were a stack of hard covered books, ascending in size. The walls were bare and across from the bed was a fireplace, the same as the one in the first living room, with the white couches. Above the fireplace was a large mirror that was the same width as the fireplace. In the corner of the room, there was a dark grey, padded chair and close to the colossal windows was a large metal telescope.

"This is my room…well…was," Adrian said, after allowing me to look around. "Are you serious?" I asked. The room looked like something out of a magazine, not a room inhabited by a young teenage boy. "Yeah…I guess it still sort of is my room. I sleep here whenever I stay over, holidays that sort of thing," he answered. "Did it always look like this?" I asked. "Pretty much," his hands were in his pockets. "Wow, AJ it's really nice, but what about your toys or…your things?" I asked. "Well I don't have *toys* anymore, and my things were all packed away when I went to prep school. Okay c'mon there's more," he said, taking my hand and led me out of the room. We walked down a short hallway and came to a pair of French doors. Adrian knocked and then proceeded inside when there was no reply. "This is the shower room," he said, as we stepped through the doors.

The walls were white—of course—and the floor was covered in large dark grey tiles. There was a sink and a large mirror on one wall across from a built in dark brown shelf with several white rolled up towels on it. The other end of the room had a large glass wall, I stepped forward to look through it and found that there was a door among the panes of glass. I pushed the door open and carefully stepped inside trying not to get my socks wet. "You could fit you're whole family in here," I said, from behind the glass wall. Adrian laughed and joined me inside the extra large shower. "It's a bit ridiculous if you ask me," he said, putting his hand on my shoulder. "Let's go," he said, quietly and we exited the room.

We continued to walk down the hallway and entered another room. "This is Catherine's room," he said. I took a peak in from the doorway. The same white walls were found in her room with a few framed pieces of art on the walls. The large bed was placed much like Adrian's and was dressed with a shiny brown spread that looked like a pool of melted dark chocolate. There was a dark brown seat against one of the walls at the end of the bed. A plum coloured accent pillow placed delicately, on it. "Okay next," Adrian said, pulling me back down the hall.

He knocked at the door, but there was no reply so he pushed the door open. "This is Emma's room," he said, as I looked in. It was exactly the same as Catherine's except instead of a plum coloured cushion on the chair, the cushion was red.

We walked to the end of the hallway and Adrian opened

that last door. "The guest room," he said. This was the room Romy and I would have stayed in if we had made our trip in December. The room was astonishing, just like all the others and was elegantly decorated with a dark framed pieces of art on the walls, dark brown and white bed coverings and a bookshelf with a few books on it. "Up there is mum and dad's room, their bathroom, office and dressing room," Adrian explained, pointing toward another small set of stairs. "I'm not sure where Emma is..." he said, taking my hand and leading me back down the hallway, down the stairs into the dining room, where Kent and Catherine were busy setting the table. "Can I help?" I asked, not really waiting for an answer. I walked to the kitchen and grabbed a few plates off the island and walked back to the dining room table. Adrian followed, "No way! The man of the hour can't help set the table," Kent said, smiling. "Here you can start with this," he poured Adrian a cup of coffee.

Adrian smiled, accepted the cup and sipped the hot coffee, leaning against the island. "Where's Em?" he asked in between sips. "She went to pick up Adam, his car broke down the other day," Catherine said, as she grabbed a handful of knives and forks. We finished setting the table and joined Adrian in the kitchen for coffee. "*This* is for you," Kent said, handing Catherine a large mug with a little foam on top. From where I stood, the foam looked like it was in the shape of a heart, but I couldn't be sure. I looked at Adrian from the corner of my eye and raised an eyebrow, silently saying *I told you so*. Adrian shrugged and continued to sip his coffee, but neither Kent nor Catherine was paying us any attention.

Patrick and Sophie, Adrian's parents, joined us a few minutes later and I was greeted with the same affection from Patrick as from Catherine and Sophie. Adrian looked a lot like his mother with his angelic, gentle face. Sophie had light blonde hair like Catherine and Emma I supposed. Her hair, a perfect bob, tucked neatly under her chin. Her skin, fair like Adrian's. She was petite, but still taller than me. Patrick was tall like Adrian, maybe even taller, all of his children took after him in height. Patrick had dark brown hair that was lightly lined with silver on the sides, over his temples. His features were very masculine and his nose was shaped almost like Adrian's, but was crooked, like he had broken it at some point in his life.

    We sat down at the long dining room table and made small talk as we waited for Emma and Adam to arrive. They arrived a few minutes later and I reintroduced myself to Adam, in case he didn't remember me from his modelling trip in Austria. I was greeted by Emma with a hug, but with a little less affection than from the rest of the family, I could have been imagining it, though. Adrian didn't lie, Emma and Catherine were splitting images of each other except for a small light brown beauty mark under Catherine's left eye. Emma wore the same black high waisted pencil skirt and white tank top tucked in, a bright red cardigan left open over top that Catherine had been wearing before she changed. Emma made a face at Catherine when she took notice of the outfit change, but no one else seemed to notice except for the three of us.

    Kent served us all, before he sat down and joined the family with a plate of his own. I smiled as he took a seat beside Catherine, like he was truly part of the family. No one batted an eye as he sat down, except Catherine who blushed, as he shuffled his seat a little bit closer to hers. I looked around the table, but no one seemed to notice their small exchange of affection. I smiled again to myself.

    After brunch Adrian's family handed him a few gift bags and large gift wrapped boxes. He blushed as he received each one. A sweater from Catherine, a pair of jeans from Emma, a gift card to a music store from Kent, an electric guitar from his dad, the amp to accompany it from his mom.

We stayed for another hour or so after we had finished eating. I spent a few minutes with Catherine in her room as she showed me a few new outfits she had bought, just days before. I talked to her about Kent and she blushed as she realized I had discovered her secret. I encouraged her tell him how she felt and assured her that I was positive that he felt the same. "Oh I don't know Zahra…he's a bit older than me, he's twenty-seven. I don't know if he'd be interested, maybe he'd prefer someone a bit older," she said, folding up her mauve coloured cocktail dress. "You wanna bet?" I asked, sitting on the edge of her bed. "Put that dress on for a sec," I covered my eyes with my hand. She didn't ask any questions and slipped out of her sun dress and into the fancy cocktail dress. "Okay ready," she said. I got off her bed and took her by the hand, leading her into the hallway and down the stairs. We entered the kitchen, where Adrian and Kent were washing the dishes.

"Hey guys, do you like Caty's dress?" I asked. They both looked up from the sink full of dishes at Caty and me. Adrian shrugged his shoulders and didn't say anything which didn't really matter to me, the question wasn't for him anyway. "Yeah that's a beautiful dress," Kent said, smiling. "What's the occasion?" he asked, as Catherine turned beet red. "Well, see that's the thing. Catherine bought the dress the other day for a fancy dinner party with some friends, but the party got cancelled and now she's thinking of just returning the dress to the store…" I lied. Adrian looked confused. I guess he knew that it wasn't in his sister's nature to return anything, or to buy an outfit for a specific purpose. "No, don't return it, it looks so lovely on you," Kent said, looking only at Catherine. She was too embarrassed to say anything. "That's what I said," I started, "but I'm having a hard time convincing her, do you have any suggestions of where she could go? Or maybe who she could go with? I mean this dress is just too nice to wear out with some casual friends, you know?" I asked, in an exaggerated tone. Adrian saw where I was going and smiled, standing a few steps behind Kent who had absentmindedly taken a few steps closer toward Catherine. "Umm…you could come to Secret," the restaurant Kent was the executive chef of. "I can make you and a friend something special," he continued, facing Catherine. I smiled and then frowned, shooting Kent a disapproving look, which he caught briefly from the corner of his eye. He was nervous. "O-or *you* could just come… I could make you a nice dinner at the restaurant…?" he said, flashing his eyes back and forth between Catherine and me. I smiled and nodded in approval. Kent's squared shoulders relaxed, he started to breath again. "Perfect! Then it's a date!" I said, from behind Catherine. "How about tomorrow night?" I asked. "Tomorrow sounds good," Kent answered. "Tomorrow…" was all Catherine was able to say. I smiled and took her by the hand and dragged her back toward the hallway and up the stairs to her room. As we left the kitchen I could hear Kent say, "Wow! That Zahra is something!" and Adrian replied, "Yeah, she truly is."

※※※

We met up with Romy at Hannah's house after Adrian and Kent had finished the dishes. Together, Adrian and Hannah showed Romy and I around London. We posed for pictures, looked through brochures and bought souvenirs to remember our trip. Later that night Adrian informed us that he and a few of his friends had planned to go to Lucky's, a local bar that had an open mic night every Saturday night. Romy, Hannah and I got ready at Hannah's house and Adrian went back to his dorm to do the same. I decided to wear a black pair of tight jeans and a white tank top with a silver v-neck sweater on top. I tousled some mousse in my curls and put on my pair on flat riding boots. My ankle was still quite sore and I had to pay special attention to it, comfortable shoes were a must.

At around eight that night Adrian arrived at Hannah's and the three of us met him in his car. He reintroduced us to his friend Noel, who Romy seemed to have taken a liking to. The five of us drove to Lucky's, where another group of Adrian's friends were waiting for him to arrive. Inside of Lucky's, Adrian introduced me to all of his friends; Nathan, Afif, Seth, Lacy, Madison, Alice and Jerome who had all said that they had heard so much about me and were dying to meet "the girl that changed Adrian's life." I blushed at their comments and whenever Adrian called me his girlfriend, I was still getting used to hearing him say the words.

We ordered a few drinks and toasted to Adrian and his nineteenth birthday and danced to the music that played over the loud speakers in the bar. Romy, Hannah and I danced with a few of Adrian's friends, Adrian leaned with one elbow on the bar and watched. He didn't like to dance, "It wasn't his thing," he said. I smiled. Adrian was always so confident, nothing seemed to ever really bother him, but I could tell he was too embarrassed to dance with a crowd of people around. I wondered if he would if we were alone.

After a few songs played, my ankle started to hurt and I decided to sit down and give it a rest. I joined Adrian at the bar and told him that I intended to sit for a while. He found me a seat at a vacant table close to the front of the stage where the DJ was spinning the records played over the speakers. Adrian didn't join me though, he told me he would be back in a few minutes and soon Romy was sitting with me instead. Hannah had gone to chat with a few of her friends who she saw at the bar, giving Romy and I a chance to talk alone. I filled her in on the details of our first night in

London and of my breakfast with Adrian's family and she told me about the rest of her night with Hannah and Adrian's friend, Noel. We were both having a fabulous time in London, we were both sad that it would soon end.

The DJ turned down the music and announced that the open mic session was about to start and any performers should get themselves ready to go on stage. We all cheered and whistled as the small stage crew set up a keyboard, drums and microphones. When they were done, the MC came on stage and announced the first performer. A girl named Mandy, walked onto the stage with two guys, one who walked over to the keyboard, the other walked on stage with a guitar strapped around his body. The keyboardist started to play a melody and Mandy began to hum a simple harmony over the piano line. Mandy's band was mediocre, Romy and I paid her full attention, while most of the other bar patrons continued their conversations and various drinking games. Mandy performed unfazed nonetheless, until her sad love song was finished. The crowd applauded and cheered even though most of them hadn't listened to her song at all and when the clapping stopped, she thanked everyone and walked off of the stage. The MC returned and encouraged the crowd to give Mandy one more round of applause, everyone did. He introduced the next act.

The lights dimmed slightly and Adrian walked slowly out onto the stage with his guitar in his hand. He walked over to the mic, plugged his guitar into the amp and sat down on the stool that the stage crew placed while the MC praised Mandy.

"Uh…this is Let Me Sign," Adrian said into the mic as he fixed himself on the stool. I was instantly flushed. From the corner of my eye, I could see Romy looking at me, smiling as she squeezed my hand, but I couldn't take my eyes off of Adrian, to look at her. I was stunned, I had no idea he had been working to put this poem to music. He had sung for me before, written a song for me before, but that song, was sad and full of uncertainty. Let Me Sign was powerful, magnetic, and defined, full of love, respect and desire. It was the poem that made me feel alive, like I found a place I belonged, someone who truly wanted me, who stood for everything I had yet to become, and now it was a song, a song about me, ready to be shared with the world.

He looked at me and winked, smiling, my favourite half smile, showing just a few teeth at the side of his mouth. (★)[22] He looked down at his guitar and turned a knob to distort the sound, creating a drone. The guitar wailed lightly, the sound flooded the bar as he began to strum simple two note sequences. He distorted the sound again creating another drone that harmonized over the first one that was slowly fading. He developed the melody and changed the two note sequence into an ascending and descending simple tune. He played this sequence for almost a minute, continually drawing more listeners in. He closed his eyes and raised his face to the mic. The spotlight shone all over his face, he hummed an accompanying melody over his guitar pattern. The bar was silent as everyone waited and listened to what he would do next. He continued to hum over the haunting sound of the drone and guitar sequence, never opening his eyes. Almost two minutes passed as the crowd waited anxiously, as *I* waited anxiously for Adrian to sing the first line of the song. He opened his eyes and looked directly at me, our eyes met, locked on each other, never shifting.

He sang and my heart fluttered uncontrollably. I would have thought that with his eyes directly on me, I would feel embarrassed or shy, maybe even uncomfortable, but after the initial shock wore

---

[22] Let Me Sign-Rob Pattinson

off, I found myself unable to look anywhere else and I think it was the same for him. It was like we were alone in the room as he sang his song. Everyone around us disappeared and we were the only two left as he wailed his beautiful melody up into the air. He sang with so much conviction, power and emotion that almost made me cry. His words, his voice, his melody, though slightly haunting, expressed so much love and all the desires of his heart, a heart that was mine.

My vision blurred, my surroundings, contorting. Tears collected at the base of my eyelids, my throat ached as I fought against gravity and the tears that were ready to spill over. I bit my lower lip, hard, to focus on something else, distracting the tears, to let them dry by the end of the song. I decided I just wouldn't blink until it happened. Adrian's friend Madison, silently stepped onto the stage with her violin and began playing a soft melody behind Adrian's voice and guitar. As the violin completed the melodic line I blinked, the tears rolled slowly down my cheeks. Romy rubbed my hand and for the first time in almost three minutes Adrian broke our gaze and said, "Thank you. That's all I have for now."

The crowd that was once silent, erupted, whistling and cheering for Adrian who unplugged his guitar and hopped off the stage. I stood to greet him and he wrapped his arm around me pulling me in for a side hug. He kissed the top of my head and rubbed my shoulder. "That was beautiful," I said, as I wiped the fallen tears off my cheeks. *"Adrian,* that was amazing," Romy gushed, as she stepped around our table to hug him. "Thanks Roms," he said, hugging her. "Zahra, don't you think you should give Adrian his birthday present now?" Romy said. "A birthday present? I thought you coming here, surprising me, was the present," he stated. I looked at Romy with terrified eyes. "I don't know what Romy's talking about," I said, trying to dismiss her comment. I tried to sit back down in my chair, but Romy held onto my arm, restricting me. "Romy, please," I begged. "Adrian, sit," she instructed. He did as he was told and Romy dragged me over to the side of the stage. She informed the MC that I wanted to perform and that all I needed was the keyboard, mic and a stool to sit on. The stage crew prepared my requirements as the next act began to perform their song.

"Romy, I really don't want to do this. I really don't think I *can* do this," I pleaded, my heart palpitated in my chest. "You can do anything you want, anything you put your mind to, you can do and I think it would be a very good idea to do *this*," she said, "for Adrian! Think about how much it would mean to him," she finished. I rubbed my forehead vigorously trying to wrap my mind around Romy's suggestion. "I'm not prepared Romy, I really don't know about this," I said, with an unsteady voice. "Okay, don't do it, but you'll have to explain to Adrian what's going on here," she pointed out. I looked at her defeated, I knew I really didn't have much choice and Romy took my silence as my sign of giving in. She nodded her head at the MC who stood a short distance away, listening to the band that wasn't half bad, performing on the stage.

The band finished their song, the crowd cheered and the lights went low again. I stood behind the curtain that separated me from the crowd and waited, with sweaty palms, for my name to be announced. "Next, we have Zahra visiting all the way from Austria, performing an original song," the MC announced. Adrian's friends cheered louder than everyone else as I walked out onto the stage avoiding all eye contact with Adrian. I wasn't as brave as he was by any means.

I sat down at the keyboard and took a few deep breaths to help calm my nerves. I rubbed my palms on my jeans and placed my fingers on the keys. I put my mouth up to the mic and said, "Um…this song is called 'Kissing You'." The room was silent, though I wished it wasn't. I would have preferred the crowd to be talking among themselves not really paying any attention to me on the stage, but of course that would have been too perfect. (★)[23] I pressed down on the keys playing the first two notes of my song and accidentally looked up right at Adrian. This time it was his turn to watch me in awe. He nodded ever so slightly and smiled a gentle smile. I took another deep breath in and continued to play the next set of notes and chords. I closed my eyes and hummed into the microphone as the slow steady chords released themselves under my fingertips.

    I started to sing and as I continued my nerves eased slightly and I was able to let loose a little. I continued to allow the notes of the melody, I had spent so many nights practicing, flow freely from my heart and mind. Romy was right, it felt good to finally be able to perform the song for Adrian, it was much better than a recording sent in the mail. With all the years of piano training I had had, never once had I performed in a recital and I couldn't think of a better first performance, than to share my song with my muse.

    I looked away from Adrian and down at the keyboard. My eyes followed my fingers, as they rapidly played the piano rift that jumped up and down the keyboard, fluctuating between high and low notes. Emulating the fluttering of my heart every time I thought of Adrian, spoke his name, heard his voice, breathed his scent, kissed his lips or felt his touch. I poured my heart and soul into the brief instrumental break. I played with all the passion from the base of my being and played the final chords that wrapped up my musical interlude. I looked up again and moved my face closer to the microphone and quietly began to sing.

    I took my hands off of the keys and placed them in my lap.

---

[23] Kissing You-Des'ree

The crowd went wild, Romy jumped to her feet, cheering and clapping, Hannah cheered and held her beer bottle in air. Adrian sat in his seat with his hands folded in his lap. I stood up and curtsied and was about to head toward stage right, to exit the platform and return to my group. The MC entered from stage left and announced my name again, the crowd cheered louder. Adrian jumped onto the stage and wrapped one arm around my waist, the other sneaked up around the back of my neck, as he pressed his lips against mine. Cat calls rang out from the crowd and Adrian dipped me backwards with his lips still on mine. He hoisted me in his arms and I wrapped my arms around his neck as he carried me backstage and said, "Do you think the gang will notice if we took off?"

We sneaked out the back door of the bar and ran hand in hand down the dark alley until we reached the busy sidewalk. We stopped in front of the bar, out of breath and looked in the window at our group of friends, who hadn't noticed our absence. "See, no problem, let's go," Adrian said, taking my hand. "Wait, our jackets!" I exclaimed, rubbing my arm with my free hand. We laughed. "That plan always seems to work in movies. C'mon let's go back inside," he said, holding open the door. We stepped into the bar, trailing the cold air behind us and walked back to where our friends were gathered unaware of our previous plan.

I took my seat next to Romy who had busied herself with Noel and Adrian pushed his way in between Afif and Jerome who patted him on the back. I looked back at him, he winked at me. I wish our plan would have worked. I sighed. I zoned out for most of the other performances, I couldn't stop thinking about running away with Adrian and then, I felt a light hand on my shoulder. "Do you want to join me outside for a ciggy?" Adrian said, loud enough for the few people around me to hear. I made a face, he knew how I felt about his smoking. "C'mon, join me," he insisted. He already had his jacket on and I reluctantly put on mine. I took his hand and walked outside with him. "Let's go!" he chimed, to my surprise and we laughed as we acted out our movie moment.

Exhibit
February 14

I woke up to the familiar smell of warm pancakes in the air. I rolled over onto my side to where Adrian would have been sleeping. The bed was still warm where he had laid, but he wasn't there, I opened my eyes slowly, "AJ?" called, in a sleepy voice. "Coming," he replied, from outside of the bedroom. He entered the room holding a tray with pancakes and cup of coffee. I smiled. "Happy Valentine's Day," he said, as he walked over to the bed and kissed me. He placed the tray on the bed and took out a wrapped bouquet of flowers from under his arm.

"Valentine's Day?" I said, rubbing my eyes.

"Did you forget?" he asked handing me the flowers.

"I did actually. I've never really been one for Valentine's Day," I said, unwrapping the flowers.

"Me neither, but I thought this time it was perfect, you gave me the greatest gift for my birthday, you, and now I can return the gesture," he smiled, as he sat on the edge of the bed.

"White Lilies," he offered, before I could say anything. "The lady at the store said that they symbolize virginity and purity, but they also mean 'it's heavenly to be with you.' I'm going with 'it's heavenly to be with you'...purity even," he smiled slyly. I smiled sarcastically, jokingly shoved him in the shoulder.

"Thanks AJ. They're perfect," I blushed.

"I knew you'd like the white over any other colour and roses are too cliché," he said, pushing my wild hair behind my ear. "When did you have time to get these flowers?" I asked, handing them back to him so he could place them in the tin can of emptied pork and beans, that he brought with him on the tray.

"I slipped out while you were sleeping, you sleep like a log you know. The store's just around the corner, so is the coffee shop and the pancakes are left over from Kent," he said bashfully. "It's perfect, it's all perfect," I said, taking a sip of my coffee. "Mmm, so that means Catherine and Kent will have a romantic Valentine's Day dinner!" I realized, almost spitting out my coffee. I wiped my lips with my hand. "I think that's why she was blushing so much," Adrian said after taking a big gulp of my coffee. "You'll have to tell me how it goes," I said, smiling through a mouthful of pancakes. "Umphh mmph umphh, what was that? I'm sorry, I didn't understand you over your mouthful of food," he teased. "I'll give you her number and vice versa, you two seem to really hit it off," he said, eating a mouthful of pancakes as well. "I'm sorry, I didn't understand you over—" I started to tease, he grabbed the spare pillow and hit me with it. "Eat your breakfast, you goof, we've got plans today," he stood up and walked to his closet. He unbuttoned his shirt and reached into his closet, hard muscles flexed and released as he pulled a black sweater off a hanger and threw it on. I watched his every move as I ate my pancakes. This was something I could get used to, waking up each morning beside him, eating breakfast in our little apartment, meeting Catherine for coffee, going to work and then coming home to spend time with Adrian. A girl could dream right?

"Hey Adrian," I said, still watching him.

"Yes babes?" he turned his head to look at me.

"I love you."

"Of course you do! Or you wouldn't be here," he smiled cunningly. I rolled my eyes, sarcastically.

He paused.

He walked over to me, moved the tray off of the bed.

"I love you, too. *So much*," he kissed me, pushing me back and wrapped his arms around me. "I could stay like this forever."

"Me too," I whispered.

✳✳✳

After I showered and got dressed, I followed Adrian out to the car. "Where are we going?" I asked, as I got in.

"Sightseeing and then we have some shopping to do."

"What sightseeing?" I asked.

"I'm going to take you to two of my favourite places, the Saatchi Gallery, it's got lots of contemporary art and then, Kings Road Gallery. It has a bunch of pieces by artists who've travelled the world. It's great, you'll love it," he said, excitedly as he pulled out of his parking spot.

"And the shopping?" I asked.

"We need to get you a few supplies, I want a new painting for the flat and a few more things that you'll pick out so that this place is a little bit more you. I want to be at home and think of you, feel you're there with me, like it's our place, not just mine. What d'you think?" he asked. "I think I would love that Adrian," I answered smiling, running my fingers through his hair.

Adrian was right! I loved the Saatchi Gallery. It was filled with all sorts of different art mediums and pieces that were truly inspiring and I couldn't wait to pick up some supplies and get started with a piece of my own.

We went to the closest art supply store, not too far from the gallery where I picked up a few hundred dollars worth of supplies, I was like a kid in a candy store, I wanted everything. We drove back to Adrian's flat and I spread my things out on the coffee table in the living room. I laid out my large canvas, my small jars of paint, four large paintbrushes and got to work. The painting took just over an hour. I didn't want to think too much about it or try to make it perfect. It couldn't be overworked, just a simple first hand try.

My first chiaroscuro abstract, Ruben would be proud, although if he ever asked me what it was, I would lie and say just some lines or the first thing that came to mind. When in fact, I had been inspired by the moonlight, cast across Adrian's face the other night. It was my abstract version of a couple in love, a tender embrace, limbs tangled together. I left it on the coffee table to dry and when it was ready we took it to be framed. Adrian hung it in the living room above the TV, replacing the poster of The Cure where everyone would see it and I was both pleased and embarrassed, conflicted. This place was becoming my own personal exhibit.

We dropped by Hannah's house to pick up Romy, it was time to head home. We had a late night flight arriving in Austria early in the morning. Our plan was to stay in a hotel when we landed and head to school from there. We didn't have much with us, our suitcases were small enough to shove into our lockers. We were like *au courant* jet setters, hopping on planes, taking weekend trips, back just in time to step back into the real world. We wouldn't have it any other way, Romy and I, my partner in crime.

Papercut
February 26

Two weeks had passed since Romy and I had returned from London. I was just starting to come off of my Adrian high and I think it was safe to say the same for Romy in regards to Adrian's friend, Noel. Even though Romy refused to have any sort of formal relationship, she *had* been talking to Noel every night for several hours at a time. Adrian's audition for the music program at the University of Salford was less than two weeks away and no matter how prepared he was, he still felt like it wasn't enough. With Adrian busy and Romy preoccupied with Noel, I had time on my hands to sort through things… It wasn't until I checked my day planner to schedule some art time with Ruben that I realized how quickly my time was running out. I panicked. Three months, three months and then this would all be over… what would I do on May 28? May 28…*dooms day*…

I plopped down on my bed with my planner and a handful of colourful pens, it was time to map things out.

MARCH 1: Oils with Ruben 7:00 p.m.-9:00 p.m.
MARCH 4: Sculpting with Ruben 6:00 p.m.-8:30 p.m.
MARCH 7: "Research"
MARCH 8-12: March Break
MARCH 10: Adrian's audition, 1:00 p.m.
MARCH 13: "Research"

…Research, time to look into my life, my past and decide what my future would hold. The question was tough, was I really going to follow through with it?

Ruben came by for dinner, like he still did most nights and after we had cleaned up, we spread all of our oil paint supplies out on the dining room table. I was excited to start my lessons with Ruben again, but nervous at the same time. The last time I tried to tackle oils with him, I fell through the ice.

I laid my large blank canvas out on the table and waited for Ruben's instructions. When it came to our art lessons, I was quickly starting to learn that Ruben, my friend, stepped out the door and Ruben, the art instructor, invited himself in. After my accident he decided to be all business, he had no time for goofing around. He was determined to help me create my portfolio. In his opinion, I should be studying art in post secondary school. I hadn't applied to any and he was afraid that once we were back in White Rock, Joanne would make it nearly impossible for us to work together. The portfolio had to be completed in Austria.

"Let's try and paint this blue circular object and these other abstract shapes that go along with it," he said, pushing the objects to the centre of the table. "A fruit bowl Ruben?…Really?" I asked, non-enthusiastically. He laughed lightly, "Think of it as more than that Zahra. You know how to do this. Now on your palette, squeeze out a bit of each colour you intend to use and then blend some of your white and blue paints over here on this part of the board," he instructed pointing out what he wanted me to do.

"Good, now that you've got the bowl on the canvas we need to create some texture. Get some of the pure blue on one part of your brush and some white on the other half and follow the crescent shape of the bowl. Yeah like that!" he praised my quick hand.

"Yes! You see that nice white line, that creates definition and see how the paint is thicker here? That's what you're looking for so now when it dries it will stand out on the page and be almost three dimensional." Ruben was very passionate about art. He was completely happy when he was around any sort of visually creative medium and I wondered why he didn't pursue it as a full time thing.

He could have easily been in one of those museums in London. I knew he loved to travel, but he clearly loved art more. Maybe he didn't think there was much of a career in art alone which confused me. Why was he pushing for me to study art in University, if he didn't think it had much stability to offer.

"Hey Ben?" I asked, as I painted an orange. "Yeah, Zar?" "If you love art so much...why didn't you just become a full time artist?" I asked, never taking my eyes off of my painting. He sighed. I looked up. He sounded sad. "I would have liked to...you know? Have some pieces in some famous gallery somewhere, but not everything we want is written in the stars," he said, playing with a tube of yellow paint. "Not in the stars? I don't know if I believe in that. I think sometimes you have to go after what you want, you can't just sit around and wait for it to happen," I said, taking the tube of yellow from him, squeezing some of it out onto my palette. He chuckled to himself, "You sound like someone I know," he said, smiling gently. "Oh yeah? Who?" I asked. He sighed again, *"Me!"* he grinned, solemnly. "So?... Why not pursue your art more seriously then? Maybe because you don't think there is much potential in it!" I said, swirling the yellow paint in with some orange and white. "Not everything is about money Zahra," he took a sip of his water, left over from dinner. "Ah ha! So you *don't* think there's any potential! And I know it's not all about money! I never said that, but I would have to be able to support myself," I said, highlighting my orange on the canvas so that it looked like a sun. "You *would* be able to support yourself. I have no doubt about that at all! You could get in some small gallery to start, a few cafes, Jonnæ's restaurant, she already has a bunch of your stuff on display..."

"How'd you know that?"

"What are you talking about?"

"How'd you know Jonnæ has my art in her restaurant? I'm pretty sure I never told you that," I said suspiciously.

"Because I've been there! Remember you told me that your sister owned a restaurant named Zahra? When I met her while you were in the hospital, I recognized her face, I've been there, I've seen the art and realized that's why you looked so familiar to me…" he answered plainly.

"Why didn't you mention it before?" I asked defensively. "Because I didn't think it really mattered. I didn't think you wanted me to bring up anything about Jonnæ, so I didn't," he said trying to reassure me.

I had a funny feeling about the whole thing, something in the pit of my stomach said otherwise, something told me not to believe him. But I had grown suspicious of everything over the past few months and I had no reason to doubt Ruben, he had done nothing wrong.

"So if you think I have a shot at being somewhat successful at this art thing and you're my mentor, why don't you think you could be too? It makes no sense," I said, changing the subject and the hostility that crept into the room, though I couldn't help but still be a bit argumentative.

"It's not that I don't think I couldn't make a decent living, I wouldn't make enough for a *family* to have a decent living," he said, stopping himself short.

"A family? You have a family to support?" I asked surprised.

"…like my mom…" he said hesitantly.

"I'm pretty sure your mom makes a good living on her own with all of her Native crafts," I put my paintbrush down and turning to face Ruben so I could get some answers.

"Yeah, sure. I know that. That doesn't mean I won't do everything I can to help her," he argued.

"Doesn't this all sound familiar to you Ruben? You're doing the same thing you said that you resented everyone for, when you were younger. You're putting too much responsibility on yourself. I'm sure your mom doesn't expect you to support her and if you decided to pursue art full time, she would be more than happy with your decision! So why are you holding yourself back?" I argued.

"You know Zahra, some things are just a bit more complicated than that! And some things are just a bit over your head!" he got up abruptly and stalked down the hallway. I got to my feet, shocked, I had never seen Ruben angry I never wanted to and I definitely didn't want to be the reason for it either. "Ruben wait!" I begged, as I followed him down the hallway. He had already pulled on his boots and was putting his toque on his head, with the door open. "Lesson's over, good job with the oils. Tell Mila and Fredrik thanks for dinner," he said, stepping out of the house. I chased after him, "Ruben!" I yelled, but it was too late, he never stopped. He got in his car and drove away, I stood in the driveway and watched him go.

March 4th came and passed and I didn't have my sculpting lesson with Ruben. I can't say I was surprised. He never showed up for dinner any of the days in between our argument and he never called to give me directions to his place so that we could sculpt. I had tried to call him several times to apologize, but he never took my calls. I had ruined everything. It seemed that I had that affect on people. I divided families, tore people apart, ruined lives... Why did Jonnæ even bother having me? Maybe by the time she realized she was pregnant it was too late to do anything about it. Why hadn't she just given me up to an anonymous family? She could have gone on with her life and her parents would have been happy and they wouldn't be at odds over me. They'd love each other, they'd sit down and have Sunday dinners together, they would hug and say 'I love you' to one another. I brought bitterness, resentment, shame.

Maybe my real father, whoever he was, didn't want anything to do with Jonnæ when she told him she was pregnant and maybe every time she looked at me, I caused her pain and reminded her of all the disappointment she felt all those years ago.

She should have gotten rid of me when she had the chance in whatever way she found fit. But that would only solve half of my problem. I still would have upset Ruben the way I did…but maybe not. My anonymous family may have taken me away to another country or city and I wouldn't have gone to White Rock Secondary School. And I would never have been on this trip. I would have never met Romy…or Adrian…maybe it would have been better that way. I might only end up hurting them too, in the end…

My father… I looked at myself in the mirror. I clearly had his face, the face of a stranger. I was so close to him, but still a million miles away. There was only one thing to do. I opened my phone and went to settings to block my number and dialled…

The air was thick, I could hardly breathe.
And then the ringing stopped.
The brief moment of silence lasted for an eternity.
"Hello?"
Her voice was the same, but plagued with raggedness.
I said nothing.
"Hello?" she said again, frantically.
I hung up.

When would I be ready to talk to her again? Hearing Jonnæ's voice on the other end of the line, ripped me apart inside.

One hand, my heart swelled, I loved her, but at the same time my jaw clenched, my hands curled into fists, palms cut, where the nails dug in.

Her voice echoing down the line stopped me in time. My brain forgot how to tell my mouth to form words, the air sucked out of my lungs. My stomach was in my throat, like riding a roller coaster, my legs, numb. How was I ever going to get answers about my life, if I couldn't speak to the person who gave it to me?

March 6

Noel arrived from London to visit Romy. Things were progressing in their *non*-relationship and I was happy for Romy. She deserved a good guy and Adrian sang Noel's praises, I felt good about the time they were spending together. I only wished that Adrian was with Noel, in Austria, for the March Break, but his audition was four days away. Mila had agreed to let Noel stay in Mikael's room for the week which absolutely delighted Romy. Noel, was her Adrian, although she would never admit it. She picked him up from the airport and brought him back to the house. Mila came home early from the bakery to make a special dinner, like she always did, when there was a new guest.

I set the table while Mila finished the *Tafelspitz*, an Austrian dish where the beef is simmered with carrots and other root vegetables in a broth and served with roasted potatoes and horseradish. For dessert, I mixed the batter for the *Sachertorte*, a famous Austrian cake. Sweet apricot jam, sandwiched between two dense layers of chocolate cake, covered with rich dark chocolate icing, I thought of Ruben as I stirred the silky mixture, he would have finished a slice in two bites, max. He wouldn't get to taste it, he wasn't around anymore.

"Zahra, come taste this," Mila said, holding up a wooden spoon with my bean goulash on it. "It's fantastic, as always," I managed to smile. "The table is ready," I picked at one of the dumplings, waiting to be eaten with my stew.

"So now that we're alone, tell me. Where is Ruben? I miss him around here," Mila said, plating the chunk of beef. "Umm..." I looked down at my feet. I didn't know what to say...there was nothing for me to say. I had no idea where Ruben was. "He's upset with me. I don't think he'll be around anymore..." "It is not possible for you to upset people. You are too precious," she smiled, pinched my cheek and brought the food to the table. I followed her to the dining room, "You look at me through a mother's eyes. I don't think it's possible for *you* to see otherwise," I folded my arms across my chest, leaning on the wall. "Have you tried calling him? I'm sure if you had a chance to explain yourself, things would be different," she said, squeezing my elbow as she passed me and entered the kitchen. I made a face, did she really think I hadn't already tried that? "I called. Like *nine times* already. He won't answer!" "So try one more time, dear!" "Yeah I guess..." I pushed myself off the wall and shuffled my feet across the floor to my room. I plopped down on my bed, grabbed my phone from my nightstand. I sighed, scrolling through my recent calls and selected Ruben's name. The phone rang only twice before it went to his voicemail, he was *clearly* avoiding me. But instead of hanging up like I had the nine times before, I waited for the beep.

"Hi Ruben, it's me...Zahra...again... Look...Ruben...I'm really sorry. I never meant to make you mad. The last thing I want is for you to hate me... I was just trying to help you... like you've helped me... If you never want to talk to me again, that's fine. I guess I deserve it... No, it's not fine! But... Please, call me back." I wanted to tell him that I loved him, but the words escaped me, they shocked me. I thought I had locked away those feeling, shoved it back under the false bottom, hidden behind a trap door. But there it was, flooding over me, I loved him and my love for him was an obvious betrayal to Adrian, but the love confused me. It wasn't passionate, it was a different kind of love, a deep rooted attachment I felt to Ruben and maybe that was because we shared a special bond, he saved me...

(★)[24] I ended the call and lay down on my bed and listened to the silence that filled my room. I was alone. For the first time in several months, I was truly alone. I closed my eyes, begging for sleep, desperate to push down my emptiness. But sleep could not save me. The weight of my truth..._all_ of my truth sunk in, sitting heavy on my chest in a winning battle for my sanity. Without Ruben, Adrian or Romy's distractions I couldn't hide anymore, there was nowhere else to place my fears, my pain and the anxiety I felt about the chaos that I called my life. I thought of Jonnæ, lying to my face every time she spoke to me. I thought of Joanne and Fabién, revelling in their perfect image, it made me sick. Everything was upside down, backwards and inside out, I questioned everything and I was stuck. The sun sets and the daylight betrays me. The day ends, my nightmare unresolved and I'm forced to face another day.

✸✸✸

It's like a paper cut, a wound so small, but yet so deep. A tiny, little cut that causes so much pain and takes over your life. You tip toe around it, you protect it, you hide it, conceal it with a bandage, hope for it to heal on its own. And when you think it's over,

---

[24] Papercut- Linkin Park

you take off the bandage, when you start to forget about it, the wound reopens and the cut is still just as deep. It only healed on the surface and the pain hurts so much more, worse than it did in beginning, worse than you remember it. It leaves destruction in its path. The pain swells up at the seams, burns and aches, irrevocably, never giving up without a fight, never backing down, forcing you to recognize it until it slowly fades away. And sometimes it leaves a faint scar, so that every time you look at your finger, you remember how quickly and how easily it all happened. Just a tiny crack, an err in judgement, a minor slip up; that scar is proof that you will never be exactly the same. That scar reminds you that you can never step back into the past, the past is behind you, a distant memory, but you keep wishing you could go back because you know if you could, you would prevent it from ever happening. That paper cut changes you, from that day forward you tread cautiously, you live your life around it, trying to avoid a reoccurrence because every time you look at your tiny scar, the memory of the pain is still there. You remember what you were doing, how you slipped up, the moment you were vulnerable and life had its way with you, laughing in your face as you watch the blood slowly well up and spill over the surface…it's like a paper cut…

✳✳✳

I was so caught up in my head, I didn't even hear Romy knocking on the door. She had returned from the airport, with Noel who was setting himself up in Mikael's room. The last thing I wanted was for Romy to be worrying about me and my drama, while Noel, with his dark brown hair tucked behind his ears and pulled into a messy bun at the back of his head, dark brown eyes scruffy face and black thickly framed glasses, that Romy loved so much, was visiting.

"Zahra? What are you doing in here?" she asked, concerned, as she entered the room. "Just resting," I lied. "Are you going to join us for dinner?" she asked, not buying my lie at all. To be honest, I had completely lost my appetite and wasn't sure if I would be able to keep anything down, but Mila had worked so hard on the special meal I couldn't disappoint her, like I had disappointed everyone else. I pulled together a smile; patchwork porcelain, shattered pieces scooped up from the floor, glued back together, flawed, alone on the shelf—no one wants the doll that's broken—rolled off of my bed and walked with her to the dining room.

I greeted Noel, smile plastered to my face, eyes hollow, empty, and sat down at the table to try and enjoy the meal. And like I had expected, I couldn't keep it down…

I splashed cold water on my face and looked at myself in the mirror, horrified. Is there anything worse than running from the dinner table to be sick? I disappointed Mila anyway. Gaunt features stared back from my reflection, pale skin, lifeless body, drained of life's energy. I had nothing left. I faked sick so that I could stay in bed for the rest of the evening and hopefully the next few days. I needed to be alone, the porcelain cracked almost beyond repair. I was successful in my deceit, I was left alone to "rest." Romy checked in too often, she knew there was more going on than an upset stomach, but she had Noel and they only had a week together, I didn't want her worrying about me, worrying wouldn't change anything.

March 7th, 8th and 9th rolled around and again the light betrayed me. I was nowhere closer to a resolution, it wasn't something I could sleep off and sleep was all I wanted to do. I wasn't eating, barely drinking and my clothes were fitting loose. I checked the scale, I had dropped almost eight pounds, I looked frail, my Austrian family was concerned, I continued to play sick.

The house was quiet. Mila and Fredrik were working late at the bakery and Romy and Noel were out. I had the place to myself.. I lay on my bed looking up at the ceiling, the way I had been for days, waiting for something to change. Wasn't time supposed to heal all wounds? I waited…and waited…until my phone rang. The faint light from my phone lit up the room and burned my eyes that had grown accustomed to the darkness. I stretched my arm, heavy and limp, grabbed my phone off of my nightstand and answered. "Ruben?" I croaked. My voice hoarse after hours of silence.

"…No, it's me."

"Adrian…"

"Still no word from Ruben, huh?"

"Nope. I think now, it's officially safe to say that he hates me!"

"Oh babes, I'm sorry… I don't know what to tell you…"

"Don't worry about it, it's my fault. I should learn to keep my mouth shut…stay out of people's business."

"If you ask me, you've done nothing wrong. You were just looking out for the guy. Being a good friend and *he* overreacted!"

"Yeah…but you're biased."

"Maybe. But that's really how I see it. I don't understand what Ruben's problem is. Maybe he's upset with himself for reacting so badly and now he's embarrassed."

"Somehow AJ I doubt that…anyway what's up? I know you didn't call to talk about Ruben! Are you ready for your audition tomorrow?"

"You know sweetheart I think I am! I feel good about my songs. I've practiced all that I can and now I'm just waiting to get it over and done with."

"I'm. *Really* proud of you Adrian and I *know* you're going to be amazing tomorrow. What songs did you decide on?"

"Thanks. I'm going to do two songs you've already heard. Let Me Sign and Never Think—"

"Never Think? Why?"

"I know you're not too fond of that song, but it's one of my favourites, even though it's based on hard times."

"I guess…"

"I have to prepare three songs so I wrote a new one."

"Did you? Can I hear it?"

"Yeah sure. I can play it for you now if you like. I went to a recording studio the other day and made a demo with the three songs. I figured that I should probably also hand in a CD to the panel tomorrow so they can listen to my songs again. They'll have so many people auditioning, how will they remember me if I don't stand out right?"

"Right! That's really smart Adrian. I'm definitely impressed. What's the name of the song you're going to play?"

"It's called Give Me Your Name. Are you ready?"

"I'm ready when you are."

"I'm going to play it from the CD okay. It sounds so much better."

"*Fine!*"

I would have preferred to hear Adrian play the song live over the phone, but it didn't matter either way, I just wanted to hear what else he had written. Distraction was a blessing.

(★)[25] The electric guitar strummed, the beat came in, a wailing melodic line, slid up and down the guitar. It was different from what I had heard from him before. I was used to his acoustic style

---

[25] Give Me Your Name-Dead By Sunrise

paired with strings and sometime drones, like when he performed Let Me Sign, at the open mic night in London. This was different, this song had a full band, drums, guitars, bass, vocals, harmony; progression. Everyone was moving forward, everyone was developing, everyone, except for me.

The music was mellow, layered with harmonies, vocals, echos and mid tempo. I was extremely impressed and I was sure the admission panel would be too. I couldn't help but smile as I listened to all of Adrian pour out in his music.

I was speechless, I listened to his words as though there was only me and his music, in the whole entire world, his voice amplified in my head. I knew how Adrian felt about me, but every time I heard one of his songs, the feelings were brand new, like the first time he said, 'I love you'. Instantly, my eyes welled up with tears, I sobbed as I listened to the rest of the song. How could he love an empty vessel? How could he want the broken porcelain doll, discarded in the clearance pile. How long before he realized I was worthless?

"So what d'you think?" he asked, after the song ended. I tried to pull myself together before that, unsuccessfully. "Oh sweetheart, don't cry!"

"I'm sorry… I just don't understand how you manage to write these songs about me. When are you going to realize that I'm nothing? I don't deserve any of your beautiful music."

"Are you crazy? You're the reason I have beautiful music to write! If it wasn't for you, I wouldn't be auditioning to this school tomorrow. Before I met you, I had never written a song before. Before I met you my poetry was tragically disappointing and uninspired and then you came into my life and everything changed. I always mean every word that I sing about you. *You're my life!*"

"You don't know what you're talking about. You're too good for me, Adrian…" "Zahra, I don't know how to make you see yourself through my eyes…"
I tried to pull myself together. Adrian had other things to focus on.

"I know you're gonna rock it tomorrow." I said, trying to calm my nerves. I hastily wiped my eyes and shrugged away my tears. He sighed softly to himself. "I wish you wouldn't do this to yourself…" he started. "I wish I could hold you right now, until the feeling's gone… I'm a bit jealous of Noel."

"Yeah, me too… " I admitted. It was hard being away from him especially when I was fighting for my emotional sanity. He was my air, he was my calm and he was in another country. I was alone with my misery. My other saving grace was happily spending the week with her boyfriend and my last person of refuge hated me.

I didn't want Adrian to worry about me and blow his audition, so I lied to him which I hated to have to do. I told him that I wasn't feeling well and needed to go back to sleep. He was disappointed, he knew I was lying, but I didn't want to talk to him anymore. "Don't push me away," he whispered, before I ended the call.

If I could, I would have stayed up all night, just listening to him breathe on the other end of line, but I was such a wreck and I would never have been able to live with myself if I ruined something else for another person that I loved so much. Ruining Jonnæ, Joanne, Fabién and now, Ruben's lives was already too much. Adrian had a steady path paved out in front of him. I refused to be a road block.

I turned off my phone, I didn't want to talk to anyone. I went back to what I did best, nothing. I lay on my bed looking up at the dark ceiling, the faint light of the moon cast through my window, I thought of that night, alone with Adrian, chiaroscuro images danced in my head. I thought about my favourite daydream, what it would be like to live with Adrian, to wake up with him in the morning, have a special breakfast before heading to his audition. I dreamed about standing outside of the audition door, listening to him play and hearing what the jurors had to say about his music and then celebrating afterwards. I sighed. I was missing out on so much with Adrian and I would only be missing more, once my time in Austria was over and I was forced to go back to my miserable life in White Rock. I already didn't deserve Adrian, I couldn't force him to stay with me once I was back in British Columbia. He had been right all along. How *would* we make things work?

    Where would I go when I got back there? I couldn't picture myself moving back into my old room at Jonnæ's house. There was no way that would ever work. At first I thought that maybe I could spend some time at Ruben's, maybe rent a room from his mom or something. Granted I had never voiced this idea to him, I figured I still had some time. But there was no way I could ask him now when Ruben wouldn't even take my calls. There was nothing left to do except close my eyes and wait to fall asleep.

Marta?
April 12

The snow had all melted and spring was in the air. Romy and I had spent some time over the weekend buying the latest spring fashions with some of our hard earned money from the bakery. After I showered, I put on my new bright yellow knit sweater over a pair of dark blue straight legged jeans. Ivory coloured feather shaped earrings looped in my ears, my hair, pulled up in a high ponytail. I met Romy in the kitchen for breakfast. We laughed as we looked at each other. We had dressed in the same outfit, different colour. "You look great!" I laughed. She smiled, "I'll go change," she suggested, putting her coffee cup down on the counter. "No way! I don't mind. We'll be twins for the day. I always wanted to be a twin!"

"Breakfast?" she asked, pulling some things out of the fridge. "Oh no, not yet. I don't think I'll be able to eat right now. Maybe I'll take some toast to go," I said, contemplating. "Nervous about seeing Ruben?" she asked, assessing my mood. "Yeah, it's been almost six weeks since…" "I know. I'm sure everything will be fine now, so much time has passed," Romy tried to lie. "Thanks Roms but I doubt it. If everything's fine now than he would have returned at least one of my calls." "Well, There's only one way to get to the bottom of this. Let's go," Romy said, pulling me behind her, I quickly grabbed my toast.

We waited for the bus, I nibbled on my toast, anxiously, thinking about what I would say to Ruben. I needed to find the best way to keep things casual and avoid all awkwardness, if that was at all possible. I finished my toast noisily on the bus, mulling over Ruben's possible reactions to seeing me. It wasn't until Romy looked at me with sarcastically worried eyes that I realized how much noise I had been making. "Sorry…" I said, quickly shoving the rest of my toast into my mouth. "Stop worrying! It won't do you any good.

Just breath we're almost there," said Romy, she requested our stop. We got off the bus and I tried to walk nonchalantly behind her, hoping that her tall stature would hide me. Romy pulled me out from behind her and forced us to walk side by side, gripping onto my arm tightly. She dragged me over to the crowd of students waiting to get onto our bus. We were about to embark on our final set of countrywide tours, now that the weather had changed. We had a number of places to visit before the end of May.

Mr. Nazuka shuffled us all onto the bus and Romy and I looked around for Ruben, but he was nowhere in sight. I hurried onto the bus relieved that I had dodged the bullet for a moment more. Once all the students were seated Mr. Woods walked up and down the aisle doing a head count. The bus doors opened and my heart skipped a beat in anticipation, I held my breath and waited. But instead of Ruben, a middle aged blonde woman walked up the steps and stood at the front of the bus facing us. "Class, this is Marta. She will be our new guide. Please welcome her," Mr. Woods explained, standing as close to Marta as he could. Everyone clapped and Romy and I looked at each other confused. Where was Ruben?

We toured around some Baroque parks including the park at Belvedere Palace and even took a boat tour from Schwedenplatz in the centre of Vienna around the city, but I honestly can't say I took any of it in. My mind was on Ruben: (★)[26]

How could he just leave without saying anything?

Why did he leave?

---

[26] For A Pessimist I'm Pretty Optimistic-Paramore

Was it because of me?
                It had to be because of me!

      Had I really upset him that much that he would quit his job?

Was that too self absorbed? No! I did this! It *was* my fault.

                Had something happened to his mother?

Was there some sort of emergency?

   Wouldn't he have at least told me if there was an emergency?

I thought we were closer than that…despite everything that happened…

How could he just leave me without warning?
      Was it really that easy for him to just forget about me?

                      I thought we were friends…
      I thought he loved me, like I loved him…

    We got home after the long day of sightseeing and working at the bakery. Everything had gone back to the way it used to be except, there was no Ruben. His seat left vacant at the dinner table, an extra plate left empty, on top of a place mat, just in case he showed up. Would I ever see him again? I had absolutely no way of contacting him. I knew he lived down on the beach not far from Jonnæ's house, but I didn't know where and I had no contact information for him besides the local Austrian phone number. Was I supposed to just give up?

On our second day of sightseeing—more parks, some churches et cetera et cetera. Who knows…whatever!—I was still trying to figure out the Ruben situation and even though I knew there was nothing I could do, the more I thought about it the closer I felt to him, like I still had something to hold on to.

Day three

Day four

Day five

Day six

Day seven

The entire week was a blur just like all the pictures of the sights I took, out of focus, colours smeared around the edges. Romy said they were artistic, I said, I didn't even remember taking them.

I was back in class, the week with Marta was over and I had a test in German. I think I studied, if I did nothing stuck and I was completely unprepared. Five months of Romy completing my assignments didn't help either. I had learned nothing. There was no point in pining over spilt milk, I took out my pencil and an eraser and waited for the tests to be handed out. When all the students from White Rock Secondary had their tests in hand and we were told that we could start, I wrote my name on the top of the page and scanned the questions. I quickly answered the ones I knew and tried my hand at the ones I thought I could figure out, all the rest I left blank. I wasn't in the mood to fight with myself for answers I knew I didn't have.

I turned my test over and opened my notebook. I was out of the nice tea stained paper, I had no choice but to settle for the plain white-lined sheets. It had been a few weeks since I had sent Adrian a letter and I missed waiting anxiously for his letters to come in the mail. Writing to him was like writing in my diary and I really needed to get some things off of my chest.

April 19

Adrian,

I'm sure I'll talk to you about it on the phone before you receive this letter, but I miss writing to you and having your words with me in my sketchbook. I've run out of our nice paper so please excuse this plain sheet, it'll just have to do.

So...Ruben's gone. He just...left! He didn't even let me apologize. I guess he didn't want to hear anything I had to say. I guess I just wasn't as important to him as he was to me. We have this new guide, Marta. She's all right, nice enough I suppose, but she's not Ruben! And I can't enjoy anything that we've been doing with her because I keep seeing her as this person who's come in to replace Ruben, but Ruben can't be replaced. He saved my life... but maybe that was just instinctual. I mean it's not like he'd just stand there and watch me drown! Maybe I thought we had more of a connection than we actually did. Maybe he was just doing what was right, he is a good person after all. I guess his absence is a wake up call that everything isn't always as it seems.

I love you!
Z

I did speak to Adrian like I had expected and I filled him in on the Ruben situation and told him to look for my letter in the mail. We spent our time talking about other things instead. Adrian was in the middle of his final exams and was anxiously waiting to hear back from the school about his audition. I felt bad for dampening his mood with my never ending drama, I opted against talking about the end of May and White Rock.

Our conversation was brief, Adrian had to study and I had things to think about. The end of May was steadily approaching and I had no plan, I left White Rock on impulse, would I be returning the same? Where would I go? I tried to call Jonnæ before and failed, would I really be able to go back there? And if I did, would I ever be able to leave again? They wouldn't let me, they'd be watching me closely. What did this mean for me and Adrian? If I went back there I would have less freedom. Joanne would make it her mission to keep the two of us apart, she had already made it clear that she didn't care too much for him, things would only be worse in her territory.

How could I stay in her house? Would I stay locked in my room and only come out when I was sure no one was home? How would this all work? Would we go back to pretending that everything was fine? That our lives were normal? Joanne would like that for sure. I couldn't let that happen. I *could* just stay in Austria! the Etzels would love to keep me…but maybe not forever…and they'd have questions. I'd have to come clean, they'd understand wouldn't they? But I'd feel terrible for putting them in the middle of this ugly situation. I could lie and say that my parents agreed to let me stay a while longer, but what if Joanne and Fabién showed up? I wouldn't put it past them. Then what? I'd just have to deal with that when the time came. This was my home, these people were my family. I wasn't going anywhere.

Marta!

She Must Be Insane!
April 25

April 25th

Hey Love,

The paper doesn't matter, it doesn't change the importance of your words, but because I know it's important to you, I've added a few spare sheets for you in the envelope.

I really liked Ruben, I thought he was a good man, but I don't understand why he would just take off without saying anything to you. Your words couldn't have upset him that much and if they did, he must know that there was no malice in your intention. It's complete rubbish if you ask me and if I could, I'd give him a piece of my mind! He has no right to make you feel the way you feel and I think personally you should stop berating yourself for looking out for your friend. He clearly doesn't appreciate the person that you are and the friendship that you've offered him.

I know it's easier said than done, but you need to let it go, sweetheart. You're not enjoying yourself in Austria anymore and that's no good. Ruben left for whatever reason, like a coward. Maybe something happened in his family or to another one of his friends back home but even so, he should have never left things unfinished between the two of you. Not after everything you two have been through and no he didn't just save your life because it was the right thing to do. He cares about you, obviously! And his actions now, are so ridiculous! He should have called you. There was absolutely no reason for you to find out that he was gone from your teachers. That's unfair, it's cruel. But I know you and I know you'll always feel broken if you don't say what you need to say. In my opinion you have nothing more to apologize for, but I'm not you. You may never really get the opportunity to tell him so I think you should just write it down and let it go. If you want to, you can send it to me or you can just keep it to yourself. Either way, you need to go on living your life just like he's living his.

I love you and I don't want to see you adding more stress to your life. There's already so much going on. Take a deep breath love and exhale.

Always.
A.

Thanks Adrian!
You always know how to make me feel better. If I was to apologize to Ruben this is what I would say:

Ruben,
I'm sorry that I stepped out of line and that I opened my big mouth, I never meant to hurt you with my words. I was only trying to be as good a

friend to you as you have been to me, but maybe I misunderstood and overstepped my boundaries with you. I wasn't trying to say anything bad about your family, about your mother or about you either... I just remembered the things you said to me before about your past and I didn't want to see you get hurt again, like before. But like you said...some things are over my head and I realize now that though you have shared some of your past with me there are obviously a lot of things I don't know that you don't have to tell me because they're none of my business. However, I really don't think it was necessary for you to be so rude. You hurt me Ruben, and maybe that was your intention because I hurt you... but unlike you, I meant you no harm. I see this all clearly now...maybe it's better that we're not friends.

I wish this wasn't true...
Zahra.

May 1

Zahra since you are being completely ridiculous and are refusing to take my calls you've left me no choice, but to resort to such desperate measures as to write a letter, it's quite pathetic if you ask me. Normal people talk to each other!

So now we're into the month of May and your time is running short. I expect you to be on that plane with the rest of your classmates, smiling as you walk through the gates and into the arrivals area. Your father and I will be waiting for you there and you will come home with us and spend as many nights as necessary in your old room, back at our house. You are not to return to Jonnae's until we have sorted some things out.

Both you and your <u>sister</u> have been displaying completely erratic and unacceptable behaviour which will no longer be tolerated by me and your father. This situation will be dealt with in the most respectable manor possible. We will call a family *meeting once you have settled back into your real life here at home, understood?*

We are looking forward to seeing you soon, say hello to the Etzels for us.
Sincerely, Mom

I was expecting a letter from Adrian in response to my apology to Ruben, but instead I opened an identifiable letter that had my name and address printed with computer ink on the envelope. I didn't know what to expect when I opened the letter, but the last thing I ever thought it would be was a letter from Joanne! Reading the letter put a sour taste in my mouth and I literally felt like I was going to be sick. How could she taint the significance of a hand-written letter, when it was something so profound that I shared with Adrian, how could she say it was pathetic? Why did she hate me so much? How did she know I had no intention of returning to White Rock? I guess it was pretty obvious…how could she still lie to herself and pretend that everything that had gone on wasn't that big of a deal…this "situation…" I think it's safe to say it's a bit more than just a situation! And how could she *still* call Jonnæ my *sister?* Was she really in such denial? How could she expect me to pretend like nothing had changed? Like everything was okay, to demand that I move back home and put on a show for everyone outside of our dysfunctional circle. Was she insane?

I thought of just throwing the letter out, there was no way I was going to respond to her ridiculous demands, nor was she looking for a reply. I didn't owe her anything. Instead, I forwarded the letter to Adrian. I thought he'd get a kick out of Joanne's irrationality. He disliked her as much as I did. We hadn't had many conversations in the past few days, he was busy studying, ready to leave prep school behind and I was busy avoiding everything... and everyone.

May 6th

Hey Babes,
This letter is completely asinine! I'm really starting to think Joanne is crazy! Did you reply?

You know so much has been going on, I honestly completely forgot that your time in Austria is running short. What will happen when you go back to White Rock? I feel like once you've back there, things will become really difficult for us. Don't get me wrong, I'm not afraid of difficult things, I'm just worried. I feel like Joanne will try really hard to keep us apart and it'll be harder for us to plan trips to see each other. I already can't stand that I haven't seen you in months and you've not that far away, what'll happen when you've 7577.36 kilometers away from me?

I'm scared Zahra, and there's not much I'm afraid of. I wish we had more time together, I wish things would just slow down so I could hop on a plane and spend some real quality time with you. We haven't even had a chance to discuss our next get-together. This is all happening so fast. My last exam is next week Friday on the 14th if you're not too busy, I'll come for a few days, after that.

I really miss you and I really need to see you soon, especially if you'll be leaving in a couple of weeks. I can't believe this is happening. I always knew the day would come, but I guess I figured if I just didn't dwell on it, it wouldn't be so bad in the end, but I think now it's worse.

You know I'm definitely going to come, even if you're busy, I'll stay out of your way. I just need to be where you are. I'll leave here right after my exam and I'll stay an entire week!

Can't wait to see you,
Adrian.

Superstar

May 14

I wanted to skip school and get ready for Adrian's arrival but I had my final calculus exam and I really wanted to complete the course on a high note. I was never going to have to do another calculus question again. I was never going to have to do another test or exam after today unless I changed my mind about College.

I tried my best to focus on the math problems in front of me as I tapped my pencil anxiously on the side of my desk. I whizzed through the questions and doodled aimlessly on my desk with my pencil. It would be the last time I sat in this seat, the last time I'd be in that class. The following week was Marta's, we'd be back on the bus, driving to each end of this city and everywhere in between.

The bell rang and Romy dragged her feet as she walked toward me. I smiled and wrapped my arm around her shoulders. "I'm sure you did fine!" I reassured her. She shook her head, no, as we headed out of the classroom. We walked to our lockers, I grabbed my grey sweater before we exited the building.

"So you must be totally bursting at the seams for Adrian coming!" Romy said, excitedly. "What time does he arrive?" she asked before I had a chance to answer her first question. "He said his flight comes in at six p.m., I told him we would pick him up from airport if that's okay." We stepped out onto the pavement and into the nice spring air. The tulips that were planted outside of the school were in full bloom. Romy fished the car keys out of her bag and I searched for my sunglasses. We walked toward where we had parked the car; we had been allowed to drive to and from school for the past few days, which was a nice treat from having to wake up so early in the morning. We waved bye to a few friends who were getting on the bus and continued to the parking lot. I wanted to get home quickly so I could clean my room and get Mikael's room ready for Adrian to stay in for the next week.

Romy unlocked the doors and I got into the passenger seat. She started up the engine and put the car into reverse. When the car was in drive, she slowly continued up the street away from the school. We stopped at the stop light and waited for it to turn green.

"WAIT! Romy hold on!" I sat up straight. I watched what was going on behind me from my side mirror and quickly unbuckled my seatbelt and unlocked my door. Before Romy could ask me what was happening, I was already out of the car and running back toward the school. I stopped, a little out of breath and rested my hand on the cab that had pulled up in front of the school. I wasn't completely sure why I had responded so quickly to it, I wasn't even sure who was inside, but I had to take a chance.

The back door opened, a long leg covered in dark blue jeans, a suede beige loafer on the foot stretched out, stepped onto the pavement. I caught my breath and stepped out from behind the cab and waited anxiously for the anonymous person to get out from the back seat. In the few seconds of quiet anticipation I wondered how awkward it would be if some random man stepped out of the cab and I was just standing there on the sidewalk two feet away. What would I say?

The dark figure shifted his weight, slide toward the open door. I took a step back to give him some space and my heart fluttered, the butterflies awakened, taking full flight, rounding circles in my stomach as Adrian appeared in front of me and smiled. He dropped his bag, that hung on his shoulder, to the ground and scooped me up in his arms.

"I thought you weren't coming in till later," I said with pure delight, my arms gripped tightly around his neck.

"I wanted to surprise you. I had intended to be here before you finished for the day, but there was a delay at the airport." I wrapped my legs around his waist and held onto him as tightly as I could. Life beat back into my heart, after weeks of desolation.

"It doesn't matter, I'm just glad you're here." I rested my head on his shoulder. Romy had turned the car around and was pulling up beside us. Adrian put me down and picked his bag up off the ground, threw it into the back seat, he sat down beside it. We drove home.

The ride home was filled with updates about Adrian's family, Mila, Fredrik and Mikael, Noel and Romy's relationship. When we got to the house, Romy headed to the phone to tell Mila and Fredrik that Adrian had arrived. Mila instructed Romy to pick up a few items from the store for dinner and before we knew it Adrian and I were at home alone. Romy would have taken any excuse to give us some space as I had done for her and Noel when he came by for March Break. The four of us had come to truly understand and appreciate the importance of personal time together in long distance relationships. I led Adrian to Mikael's room to show him where he would be staying for the next week. He plopped his bag down on the bed and I took a seat beside it as Adrian looked around the room. I unzipped the bag and began to take the neatly folded clothes out one at a time.

"What are you doing?"

"Getting you unpacked."

"I've only been here two minutes."

"And two minutes have already been wasted! I'm getting you settled in."

"I s'pose that's fair. Can I at least help?"

"You can pass me some hangers," I said, trying to keep things as casual as possible. I knew what happened the last time a boy and girl were alone in this room and if I wanted the Etzels to continue to let me live here, I needed to be on my best behaviour.

We got to the bottom of the bag and there was only one shirt left to hang up. I passed it to Adrian who held the last hanger in his hand.

"What's this?" I asked, taking a few pictures and folded pieces of paper out from the bottom of the bag.

"Come with me and I'll show you," he said, scooping me up in his arms and carrying me out into the living room. It was like he read my mind that we shouldn't be found in the room like Natalie and Mikael, even if nothing was going on. It was hard for me to refrain from letting my fingers softly trace the lines of his face, to grip onto the strong muscles in his back or tangle in his hair the way I wanted them to. We were like two magnets; he was the positive to my negative. We were completely drawn to each other by sheer force.

He dropped me lightly onto the couch, sending butterflies up from the pit of my stomach and into my throat, forcing me to burst out laughing. Adrian smiled, plopped down on the couch next to me, bouncing me up slightly into the air, reminding me that I was so much smaller than he was, almost entire foot.

I looked at the pictures that Adrian had printed from his computer and he took the folded papers from my hand and opened them up.

"Well. I have some good and bad news…"

"Bad news first, always bad news first."

"Okay. I'm moving. I have to…quite far too, three hours north."

"WHY? WHERE?"

"Manchester area. I can't continue to live in my dorm, having applied to Uni. The prep school's kicking me out. The good news is that I got an early acceptance to the University of Salford," he said, nonchalantly.

"YOU WHAT? ADRIAN!" I flew forward and threw my arms around his neck. "Congratulations! That's amazing."

"Thanks love!"

"So why's moving bad news?" I asked, when I was able to think.

"Well. I know how fond you've become of my family, my sister Cate, and now we'll be quite far from them, like I said a bit over three hours."

"*We'll?*"

"That's what these are about," he said, taking the pictures from me. "I've looked into a few flats in the area and I printed these pictures and some information about the ones I thought you'd like the most. I want it to be just as much your place as it is mine. Just like the flat now."

I smiled, it was nice to have a place where I belonged, where I was truly wanted. I looked through the pictures and scanned through the information sheets on each place. "I like this one," I handed the picture and matching information sheet back to him. The place was really nice and modern looking with an open concept main area. The walls in each room were white with dark hardwood floors throughout, just like at Adrian's family home.

The kitchen was white and modern with built in stainless steel appliances, shiny black countertops and a small round bar table with two black bar stools. The living room had a beige suede L-shaped sofa with a short white rectangular coffee table in front of it. On the other side of room, facing the couch was a flat screen television on top of a black entertainment unit. Behind the unit, the walls were completely glass and opened to a balcony that overlooked the buzzing street. In the bedroom there was an ivory coloured cushioned backboard and a large queen sized bed, dressed with white, black and ivory coloured bed coverings and had a small dark wood nightstand next to it. There was a large walk in closet and another balcony that overlooked the River Irwell.

The washroom was modern too, with a large deep set ceramic bowl in the middle of a dark wood abstract shelf, beside it, a wall hung toilet. On the other side of the wall there was a small wet room, an all glass shower with dark slate coloured tiles throughout the room. There was a second bedroom in the flat, with a double sized bed, covered with a white, brown and purple bedspread. It was amazing, a huge improvement from his simple dorm.

"I knew you'd like this one. I already called about it and if you liked it, I'd get the keys next week. I just have to call them back in the next few days to finalize. I didn't want to risk losing it so I gave my deposit just in case," Adrian said, rubbing my back.

"This place is awesome, but that's in part because of the furniture…"

"It's included."

"Oh! How much is it a month? What's a serviced apartment?" I said, reading through the description again.

"It's not much, £799 a month. It's a lot like a hotel, but a flat…so it's set up like a flat but there's a restaurant on the main floor, a spa and it can be rented on a weekly basis instead of monthly if needed."

"Does it have housekeeping? Or room service like a hotel?" He laughed.

"I guess that's something I could find out for you."

"It says that it's in Manchester though, shouldn't you live in Salford, for school?"

"It's really close I promise. Honestly it's three minutes away. Plus, I wanted something that would be fair for both of us. You'll like Manchester. It's more your scene," he explained.

"Okay, but it has to be more right for you than for me! You're the one who'll be there all the time. Whenever I come I'll pitch in for the rent of that month. It's only fair."

"We'll see."

"I'm serious Adrian! Or I won't come!"

"Yes you will. You and Romy. That's why I chose something with a second room, more space! Space for her and Noel. Just give me a final 'yes' and I'll call the landlord right away."

"Okay you have a final yes!" I squealed, throwing my arms around him again. I don't know why I was so excited. It wasn't like I was moving in, but either way it was something to look forward to.

"D'you think it's safe?"

"Is what safe?"

"Safe for me to kiss you for minute. We won't get caught or in trouble?"

I smiled. "I think it's safe," I said. He placed his lips softly on mine and though we had kissed many times before, this kiss was more focused, his fire transferred through his lips onto mine, down my throat and into the pit of my stomach. It shot like fireworks through my arms, down my back and into my legs making me weak all over as I melted into him.

"Okay, I think we should stop before this goes too far," he whispered, he hesitantly pulled his lips away. He rested his forehead against mine and steadied his breathing with his eyes closed and I took the opportunity to do the same. "I love you," he whispered, he kissed my forehead. "I'm going to go call the landlord." He slid off of the couch. I continued to look at the pictures of the new apartment and within a few minutes I heard someone at the front door. I got up from the couch and quickly headed down the hallway and opened the door for Romy who was struggling with several grocery bags. I took a few bags from her and we walked to the kitchen.

"Mom will be home in thirty minutes to start Adrian's *special* dinner," Romy said, rolling her eyes. "What are we having?" I asked, unpacking the bags. "From the looks of it vegetarian lasagna," Romy put the fresh cheese into the fridge. "Where's AJ?" she asked. "Talking to his new landlord. He's moving to Manchester. He got into his school! The flat has two bedrooms for us to visit and Noel too!" "That is awesome! When will we go visit?" "I don't know Roms…he gets the keys next week…but I'm supposed to go back to White Rock at the end of the month…" "But you're not going to right? You're going to stay!" "I don't want to go back, but I haven't asked *Ma* if I can stay yet." I had started calling Mila, Ma after Christmas, when she told me that she would always be there for me. It made her blush each time the word came out of my mouth. "You know she'll say yes! Dad too!" "I know… I'll ask in a few days. I feel kind of bad for lying to them about everything that's going on. If I stay beyond the six months, I'm putting them in the middle of all my chaos," I assessed. "Okay well…I still think you should ask and not worry so much about it. Figure out what you want to say, but make sure you do it soon," Romy said, hugging me before she walked out of the kitchen and into the living room where Adrian was also headed after he finished his phone call.

"So?" I asked as we all sat down in the living room and Romy turned on the TV.

"Got it! I'll pick up the keys when I get back. I have to pack up my few things from the school flat and then I'll head north to get settled in," he said, patting my knee.

"So do we get to help you decorate?" Romy asked, settling on a channel.

"No need. The place comes fully furnished."

"Yeah, but what about all of your stuff?" she asked.

"Yeah? What about the stuff we picked out together? The zebra print rug? The painting I made for you? The poem you enlarged?" I asked.

"That's like three things! Do you guys really want to go all the way to Manchester to put three things in the flat?" he joked.

"Maybe we're just looking for an excuse to come by!" Romy said, throwing one of the couch's accent pillow across the living room, over the coffee table, at Adrian which he caught with little effort, Romy frowned.

"Okay, well you girls know you're always welcome to come whenever you want. But like I said, I won't get the keys until I get back and that's not till the 22nd so let's say I get them on Monday the twenty-fourth…and then I have to pack. I won't get to the flat until like the twenty-eighth…and we all know what happens on the twenty-eighth! I think we have more important things to worry about right now," he said sadly. I looked down at my hands. I couldn't bring myself to make eye contact with either one of them. My pending departure was much too painful to think about.

"Hello? Mom is home!" Mila warned from the doorway. "In here Ma," I called out from the living room, assuring her that nothing was going on. She reached the end of the hallway and stepped into the common area. "Oh," she said, with a sigh of relief. Adrian got to his feet and walked toward her with his hands in his back pockets. "Adrian!" she sang, extending her arms to him. "Mila," he answered, wrapping his arms around her. "It's so good to see you Adrian," she giggled. "I think mom is just as excited to see you as Zahra is! She's totally in love with you," Romy teased, she walked to Mila and Adrian, nudged Mila with her elbow, before heading to the kitchen. "Don't tell him that!" Mila yelled jokingly, she lightly slapped Romy's arm. "Don't go near my kitchen," she said, blocking Romy's entrance. "*Okay!* She wants to take all the credit for the special meal for her *boy toy,*" Romy laughed, she patted Adrian on the shoulder. "Enough out of you!" Mila joked, slapping Romy on the butt with the kitchen towel. Adrian laughed lightly and smiled at Mila, who blushed a little. "Can I help?" he asked, in the smoothest version of his smooth voice that he could manage. Romy and I looked at each other, rolled our eyes. "Okay," she said, turning a deeper shade of red. "You're such a schmooze," I called out from behind him. He turned his head to look at me as he walked into the kitchen, he winked. I jokingly shook my head in disapproval and continued to watch TV with Romy.

When Fredrik had returned home for the evening and had finished washing up, the five of us sat down and ate Mila and Adrian's delicious lasagna, while Adrian told Mila and Fredrik his good news. We all stayed up late to celebrate Adrian's success. Fredrik put on some music and we danced and drank some homemade wine that Mila and Fredrik had made the year before. We must have polished off two bottles easily. Everything after that was a blur and then the morning came.

The weekend rolled by slowly with little excitement. Adrian and I stayed in, watched a handful of old movies, eating all kinds of junk food we found in the kitchen pantry. Romy worked all day at the bakery with Ma and Pa. She said seeing Adrian only pushed her to work harder so she could visit with Noel again.

Monday came and Romy and I were headed back to school for another set of city tours with the very dedicated Marta. Adrian drove us to school in the car and then offered to help out at the bakery for a few hours. He pulled up in front of the school and got out, to see us off. Romy walked ahead to reserve our seats on the bus so I could say bye to Adrian, who was leaning with his back against the car. I wrapped my arms around his waist and buried my face in his chest and inhaled my favourite scent, his. Clean and fresh and soap and *home*.

"Miss you," I said quietly, as he ran his fingers through my hair.

"Me too Zee. I'll be right here at three," he assured.

"Make it two-forty-five just in case," I said.

"Will do. Have a nice trip," he kissed my head before I walked away from him and past the staring eyes that belonged to the same girls who I told off six months ago in the chalet. I climbed on the bus and pretended to pay attention, like I had done every time we were with Marta. Tuesday, Wednesday and Thursday were the same and Adrian was fitting in perfectly as just another member of the family and I was really starting to like having him around on a daily basis. It just felt…right.

Thursday was no different from the few days before it, Adrian dropped us off in the morning, Romy left to reserve our seats on the bus, I hugged Adrian, he kissed my head, "I'll be here at three," said Adrian. "Make it two-forty-five," I began, and before I said 'bye' I said, "I think I'm going to ask Ms. Johnson if she knows what happened to Ruben." "Are you sure that's a good idea?" Adrian asked.

"I don't see why not, she's always been really nice to me. She eats at Jonnæ's restaurant with her fiancé all the time, I'm sure it'll be fine," I explained.

"Are you sure you want to do that? I didn't know this was still bothering you," he sounded slightly offended. Was he jealous?

"I wouldn't say it's bothering me, it's just still on my mind from time to time," I kissed his cheek and walked toward the bus.

"Two-forty-five!" I called out behind me.

"Two-forty-five," he answered. He watched me walk away, arms folded defensively across his chest.

I let Romy in on my plan and she agreed that speaking with Ms. Johnson was a good idea. I waited for what I felt was the right time. We got off of the bus after about two hours of guided tours for a short break. Everyone was stretching their legs. I found my way over to where Ms. Johnson was taking a few pictures of the countryside and cleared my throat to announce my presence. She turned to face me at the sound and I smiled and waved as I stopped in front of her.

"Hello Zahra. Having fun?" she asked.

"Uh, yeah. A blast," I ran my fingers through my hair nervously.

"What can I do for you?" she asked kindly.

"Um…well, I hope this doesn't come across badly and maybe it's out of place to ask, but…I was just wondering what happened to Ruben…" I asked shyly. Her face changed, it hardened and twisted in an expression I couldn't quite place, disgust maybe.

"Don't you think whatever you had going on with Ruben was a bit inappropriate?"

"In-inappropriate? I don't understand…"

"You two were always spending *a lot* of time together, too much time if you ask me. He's much too old to be hanging around with you like that," she stated.

"Like what? He saved my life!—"

"Yeah exactly! Why was he even at your house with you and your host that weekend? Or in general for that matter?" she interrupted.

"WHAT? He was my mentor...my art mentor...he...he was my friend..." I said stammered out of breath. The wind had been knocked out of me. Was it that obvious that I loved him?

"He's not your friend Zahra. He's far too old for that," Ms. Johnson said, putting her camera back into her bag.

"So now there's an age limit on friendship. What's ten year?" I asked, shocked, trying to hide my broken heart.

"Ten years? Ha. Is that what he *told* you?" she asked, laughing in disbelief.

"No...he never told me, I never asked...I just assumed..."

"Honey, try more like twenty!" she placed her hand heavily on my shoulder.

"...Oh...so...you sent him away?" I asked, confused.

"No. I just spoke with him about my concerns regarding your...whatever it was. He left on his own accord, clearly he knew he was acting inappropriately," she answered.

"But...how? How did you know he was at our house the day of the accident? How did you know we had spent any time together?" I asked, confused. I guess the answers were obvious enough, we weren't trying to hide anything, there was nothing *to* hide. Maybe everyone knew that Ruben had spent plenty of time at the Etzel house.

"We were all there at the hospital Zahra, Ruben called the staff. He told us about the art lessons. I didn't think it was that strange at first. I know how much you love art, how talented you are. I've seen your work at your sister's restaurant. And I knew Ruben had a background in art. But your mother, she voiced her concerns to me. She asked me to keep an eye on Ruben..."

We were summoned back onto the bus before Ms. Johnson could continue. She smiled unapologetically and walked back to the bus. I trailed behind her and waited for Romy to catch up with me.

We got on the bus and I told her everything I had learned and she was just as shocked as I was to find out that Ruben was much older than we had thought. We spent the rest of the trip trying to figure out why Ruben never told us that he was close to forty years old. We were shocked that Joanne had him sent away.

What about the fondness, the closeness that had developed between us. Was it all a lie? He hadn't been honest with me about himself, then again I never asked. It was Natalie who planted the first seeds. She said I had no perception of age, I believed her and I was blaming Ruben. When I had the chance to sort through how I felt, I realized that the love I felt for Ruben was in no way close to the feelings I had for Adrian, it was a different kind of love, but had Ruben manipulated that? I was confused, I was angry, the last thing I needed in my life was more answers. I tried to push those feelings away, his age didn't change the Ruben I knew…or did it?

We got back to the school and Adrian was there, waiting by the car faithfully like he had been everyday that week. On the ride back home he insisted on hearing every detail on the Ruben story. A story that revealed a truth I really didn't want to have to think about. I had caused Ruben his job. When I was in the hospital he had tried to take a step back, but I insisted, despite Joanne's threats, that he remain unchanged. We had both been warned, I didn't listen, he paid the price.

It was Adrian's last night in Austria, we needed to celebrate. A handful of my friends, including—unfortunately—the stupid girls from the chalet—invited by association—, decided to go back to Absinthe for old times sake. It was the first time I'd been back there since my first night in Austria, when I met Adrian.

I spent a considerable amount of time getting ready. I wanted to look perfect to relive a perfect moment, against my personal bedlam. The air was just warm enough for a dress. I threw on one of my newest purchases, a brown and ivory coloured, knee-length, zebra print, tube dress with a wide black belt nested under the bust. I put on a pair of new bright pink peep toe heels and a matching pink, three quarter length sleeved cardigan. I left my hair down the way Adrian loved it and dabbed a little bit of orange blossom oil behind my ears.

Romy wore a sparkly silver halter dress that reached above her knee, with matching silver heels. Her hair in a high ponytail, her face perfectly painted. Adrian stepped out of his room and into the living room, where I was waiting on the couch. He wore an olive coloured dress shirt, the sleeves rolled up to his elbows, the first two buttons, undone. He had on a black pair of jeans and his beige shoes that were by the front door. His hair was a perfect mess and he was almost cleaned shaven, but I stopped him before he had the chance to shave his scruff that I loved so much. I stood to greet him.

"You. You look *so* beautiful," he said, wrapping his arm loosely around my waist.

"And you. Are super hot!"

He chuckled quietly.

"Is this a tribute to the good ol' days?" he asked, pinching the shoulder of my sweater. "Looks just like the one you wore on the night we met," he said smiling.

"You can call it that!" I took his hand and headed to the hallway. "The taxi's here," Romy said, grabbing her bag off of the hallway table. We exited the house, got into the cab and headed down the familiar path to Absinthe, the place where it all started.

Adrian took my hand to help me out of the taxi and we walked toward the entrance of the club. He stopped before we could enter the building and whirled me to the side, out of the way so that the others could pass.

"This is where we sat…when you truly decided to let me in, to let me be part of your life," he said, sitting on the ledge of the window sill just like before. He pulled me in so that I was standing in between his legs and he wrapped his arms around my waist, we were almost at eye level with each other. I loosely wrapped my arms around his neck and smiled as I thought back to that day.

He put his fingers to his mouth and took out the gum that he had been chewing and chucked it into the street.

"What's that?" I asked, watching the little white ball skip across the pavement.

"Nicotine gum. I always keep my promises," he said, winking at me. "I only chew it once in a while now, after this pack I think I'll be good and nicotine free," he said smiling.

"I'm really very proud of you babe," I said happily.

"I'm proud of me too. Thanks," he answered, moving his face closer to mine, our eyelashes touched, our lips met.

"You know…you're wrong AJ, I let you in over there," I said, jerking my head to the right, toward the side of the building and the old tree that I had leaned on. "After I threw up," I added.

"Yes, that's where you let me in, over there by that tree, after you threw up and before we sat on the bench in that little park off to the side. But this is where you *decided* to let me in. When I asked you to bare your soul, remember? *Before* you threw up, the way you looked at me…I could see it in your eyes. You trusted me, a complete stranger and you let me in. Happy anniversary sweetheart." He tightened his arms, embraced me.

We kissed each other long and passionately, desperation in the pressure of his lips. We both knew it, after that night, it would be a long time before we saw each other again.

"You've never said anything about anniversaries before. Ever," I said, when we both decided to come up for air.

"Well this one is extra special. It's been six months as of two days ago, since I met you right here in this place. Six months since you completely changed my world Zahra Nayeli." "Six months since you completely changed *mine,*" I replied.

"We don't have to go in, we could just stay out here. It's nice out now. We could just sit on our bench in the little park. What d'you think?" he asked.

"I think that's a much better plan," I pulled him off of the small ledge. He took my hand just as he had that faithful night and we walked past the corner of the building, past the old twisted tree and down the same small path to the bench where I was sure many stories had been told. Adrian took his rightful seat on the left and I took my original seat on the right. He put his arm around my shoulder and we sat without words for a few minutes, enjoying the silence and our own personal memories of that night.

"So you'll come to Manchester, when? Next week some time, maybe? You won't have anymore classes. The rest of your schoolmates would have already returned home. But you're staying right? So you'll have some free time," he said, twirling one of my well defined ringlets through his fingers.

"Maybe AJ, I haven't sorted anything out yet. I don't know what I'm going to do, but I'll figure it out soon. I have to talk with Ma and ask her if I can stay. But I don't want to think about any of that right now…please," I begged.

"Of course. I'm sorry love," he said, combing his fingers through the thick of my hair.

"No apology necessary, I'll figure it all out and when I do, you'll be the first to know I promise."

"You know Zar, you don't have to figure it out on your own. You don't have to keep your fears bottled up inside. I know you've got a few, so don't pretend like you don't, and just because I'll be busy packing, tying up loose ends back home, doesn't mean that I'll be too busy for you. We won't talk about it passed that…but Mila will let you stay for sure," he added in the end quickly.

"I guess…"

"If you stayed what would you be missing at school? You'd still graduate right?"

"I wouldn't be missing much. There'd be a presentation of the trip to the rest of the school and prom."

"You can't miss prom! Isn't that really important to girls?"

"To some more than others…it would be pointless for me to go. Who would I go with? You wouldn't be there with me…and who would I sit with at dinner? No one! That's who. It would be a complete waste of time. Believe me," I said, thankful that I wouldn't have to be subjected to that potentially mortifying night. I had no friends in White Rock. "Okay well there's been too much talk and not enough kissing," I complained. "Don't tell me that you actually brought me over here for a chat!" I teased.

"That's what we did last time!" he stated.

"Yeah and as I recall we almost kissed *last time*, but you turned me down," I reminded him.

"I didn't turn you down. It's not like I didn't want to! What kind of guy would I be if I kissed you after you cried your eyes out and told me the most tragic life story?"

"And after I'd thrown up, right?"

"I didn't care about that at all. I still would have kissed you regardless, if the timing had been right. You kissed me with stale cigarette and beer breath did you not, when you came to visit me? The status of your breath has never been an issue," he teased.

"Oh is that so?" I said, playfully slapping his arm.

"It is so," he laughed cupped the back of my head and moving in for a kiss.

"Is that better?" he asked, with his lips still pressed against mine.

"Mm-hmm," I mumbled. He held onto me tightly and kissed me again which we continued to do for the rest of the night between brief moments of silly banter and casual conversation, until we could hear Romy calling both of our names in the distance. This time, however, I wasn't so eager to get back to my friends. Not that I was eager before, but last time they were worried, I had disappeared, we had only just arrived, already I was lost. This time, there was no panic in Romy's voice. I lingered in Adrian's arms for a while, hugging him for one of the last times before he left Austria.

We hesitantly got up from our bench and walked hand in hand back up the small path to the sidewalk where Romy and the others waited. "The park, I should have known," Romy joked, rolling her eyes at the two of us. "We were…talking," Adrian said, a guilty grin on his face. "*Right.* I'm pretty sure I've heard that one before!" Romy teased with slurred words, "but somehow, this time I *don't* believe you," she laughed to herself, punched Adrian's arm. Amber and Courtney, Adrian's previous admirers stood by with Claudia, Romy's friend and Jason's ex, trying to ignore the two of us, but ever so often I saw them both steal a look at Adrian, gussy themselves up in case he looked in their direction, he never did.

We all piled into the taxi van, it dropped each group off at their final destination. The three of us, Romy, Adrian and I stepped quietly into the house. I helped Romy change into her pyjamas, she was slightly intoxicated and fell asleep immediately as soon as her head hit her pillow. I changed into a pair of grey sweat shorts and a white tank top and walked to the living room to meet Adrian, as we had planned. It was the only way we'd be able to sleep together and he was already setting up the couch with his pillows and his blanket.

"Hey beautiful," he said, with a smile. "How's Romy?" he asked.

"Fast asleep," I said, with a sort of half smile.

"She's pretty sloshed eh?"

"Yeah…she needs to just sleep it off." I climbed under the blanket on the couch and tucked myself into the side of Adrian's body.

"What would you like to do? Do you want to watch a movie?" Adrian asked quietly as I rested my head on his chest. I shook my head, no, slowly, The steady rise and fall of his chest lulled me. "I'm really tired," I said sleepily.

(★)[27] "Okay, we'll sleep then," Adrian said, playing with my hair. I closed my eyes and settled in for the rest of the night. I could hear the sound of his heart beating and the rhythm of his soft, slow breath. Before I totally drifted off to sleep, Adrian quietly began to sing.

---

[27] Superstarr Prt 2 (Babylon Girl)-K-OS

To Do Lists
May 22

I woke up to the sound of Adrian's voice softly in my ear.

"What time is it?" I asked, rubbing my eyes.

"Minutes to ten in the morning," Adrian said, looking at his watch that was resting on the table beside the couch.

"What time's your flight?" I yawning.

"Half past two, unfortunately. I'll have to leave here at noon," he said, solemnly. "This is always the hardest part. I hate leaving you," he said, playing with my hair again, almost as if it was continuous from the night before.

"I know…this is always the worst part. The part I hate the most," I whined, cuddling him. He wrapped his arms tighter around me and I inhaled deeply. "I love the way you smell in the morning," I whispered.

"In the morning? Why? I can't see that being too pleasant," he chuckled to himself.

"I like it…'cause it's when you smell the most like you, no colognes, or scents on your clothes, just…you." I said, inhaling again.

"I've told you right, that you're weird?"

"Whatever!"

"I'm sorry babes, but I have to start getting ready…" he groaned.

"I know…"

He slowly peeled himself off the couch and sleepily walked to his room to grab some clothes. I watched him walk to the wet room and listened for the sound of the water from shower. I got up from the couch, shook the sleep out of me and went to the kitchen to boil some water in the kettle. When it was boiled I made a pot of coffee and poured a cup for Romy. I walked down the hallway and lightly tapped on the door, but there was no response. I slowly opened the door and stepped into the dark room where Romy was still fast asleep, snoring gently. I quietly left the room with the coffee still in my hand. Adrian was in his room getting dressed, I folded the blankets and waited for him on the couch.

"I made some coffee, you can have this cup if you like," I said, unsmiling. He padded over to the couch and sat down beside me. "Black, two sugars," I handed him the mug.

He took it and sipped and said, "Thanks, but that's the way *you* like it. I just like mine straight black," handing it back to me.

"It was for Romy but she's still knocked out…"

"So you pawned it off on me?" he teased.

"I was trying to be nice, but I'll just drink it myself!" I said taking a huge gulp of the coffee.

"Careful! It's hot!" he laughed.

"It's also almost done," I said sarcastically.

"So you burned your throat to prove a point, did you?" he asked, taking the mug out of my hands.

"…Maybe…"

"Pretty lame point, if you ask me!" he joked, finishing the cup of coffee.

"Nobody asked!" I took the empty mug from him and put it in the kitchen sink to wash. Adrian snuck up behind me and wrapped his arms around my waist and crouched down to hug me from behind. He slid his arms down mine and rested his hands on top of my hands that were covered in soap suds and water. He washed the mug with me and when we were done he kissed my cheek.

"You can drive right?" he asked.

"Yeah, why?"

"Would you feel comfortable driving Romy's car?"

"You mean, like to the airport?"

"I was actually thinking we could get a head start, maybe grab some breakfast somewhere. Or we could get some stuff out of the fridge and sit in the park for a while. Then I'll drive to the airport and you'd just have to drive the car back. Romy's nowhere near getting up…"

"I like that idea. Let me see what we've got here. You might as well put your bag in the car, maybe write a little note for Romy," I suggested. Adrian smiled and headed to his room to gather his things. When he had his bag ready and by the door, he tore a piece of paper off of a small note pad on the hallway table, he wrote a note for Romy, to let her know that we had gone to the airport. I met him in the hallway with a plastic bag filled with goodies and handed him the car keys off the hallway table.

We drove down the hill and down a busy street, past several cars and the local bus. We pulled up to the curb, found a place to park and walked hand in hand through Prater Park and found a place to sit off the main artery of the park in a luscious meadow. I pulled out a thermos that I filled with more of the coffee I had made, and a few pastries from the fridge that Ma and Pa brought home every night from the bakery. I also took out some apples, two yogurt cups and some napkins. We instantly started eating and drinking our shared coffee from the thermos cup, black, one sugar, it was a compromise. When we had finished eating, Adrian checked the time and we had thirty minutes to relax. We lay down on the grass; Adrian on his back with his hands behind his head and me, resting my head on his chest. We looked up at the sky, blue and white, vast and clear.

"So…honey…I know you don't really want to talk about it…but…what's you plan? I'm really worried about this," said Adrian, ending a moment of bliss. Reality swept in with the breeze. He was right, I didn't want to talk about it, I had no real plan yet.

"Um…well…I was going to talk to Mila tonight and just tell her that my mom said I could stay for another couple of months… the rest of the year… or something… I know Mila will say it's fine, I'm really not too worried about it," I lied. In reality I was very worried. If Mila said no, or thought I should go home for a while to spend time with my family and come back later, I'd only have enough money to stay in a hostel for about a month and that was pushing it. I'd have no money for food or any other necessities. My plan had several flaws.

"Okay, if you're sure that plan will work…what happens when Joanne calls the house?"

"Mila and Fredrik are hardly home, the time difference is too great they'll never run into each other," I assured him, though I think I was really trying to assure myself.

"Okay," he sighed. "I totally trust that you have this under control," he said, playing with my hair with a false sense of calm, his heart racing in his chest.

"I think it's time to go…" I said, trying to change the subject. Adrian looked at his watch and sighed again.

"You're right," he said, sombrely. I sat up slowly and got to my feet using all of my strength to help heave Adrian off the grass. I brushed myself off, we grabbed our stuff and headed back to the car and within twenty minutes we were at the airport. Adrian parked the car and handed me the keys and together we entered the airport. We sat together in the departure area until he absolutely had to check in. We hugged and we kissed and promised to see each other again soon, all the usual see you later words, but I wasn't sure if I could truly mean them. What would I do after hiding out in a hostel for two weeks, pretending that I had gone back to White Rock? Could I go back to Romy's house and say that I came back from White Rock after only spending two weeks with my "family?"

"I love you sweetheart," Adrian said, bringing me back to reality.

"I love you too Adrian, more than you'll ever know," I hugged him tightly with tears streaming down my face. I couldn't help, but feel like my words were some sort of a final goodbye, heart shattering into a million tiny pieces. He hesitantly pulled himself away from me, the possible finality of our relationship plaguing the air. He walked through to Customs, his head hung low, his fingers pushing through his hair. I stood there, steadfast in that spot where we exchanged goodbyes, until Adrian was completely out of sight and then I stood there even longer. I had no idea what my next move was and time was running out. I had five days left to figure out how to stay and five days left to figure out the anomaly of Ruben.

I walked as slowly as physically possible back to the car, my feet carrying the weight of the world in each prolonged step. I sat in the driver's seat with my head on the wheel, memories orbiting around me. The last time I was behind a steering wheel I was speeding down the highway, racing away from my life, Jonnæ weeping on the driveway, Joanne angry and embarrassed, her pride-clad handbag, scuffed, and Fabién, Fabién somewhere, close on my trail. I darting in between cars, all the way to the airport and when I got there I left the car too. I pulled into the short term parking lot, not wasting anytime looking for a parking spot, I was in the wrong section of the airport, it didn't matter, all that mattered was that I was there. I had made it. I abandoned the car. I don't even remember if I took the keys out of the ignition…

    I sighed, started the car and reversed out of the parking spot. I headed back through the familiar streets and up the hill into the countryside, past the neighbour's farm and into our driveway. I parked the car and walked inside to a silent house. I opened the bedroom door and found Romy, still fast asleep. I checked the time on the digital clock in our room it was already one-thirty in the afternoon. I crept over to where Romy lay almost lifeless and checked to make sure she was still breathing. It was hard to tell in the dark. As I neared, she groaned, a faint grunt escaped through her lips. I smiled and quickly tip toed out of the room and closed the door behind me.

    I sat down at the computer and turned it on. With no one around, I had a prime opportunity to look into a few more affordable hostels if it became necessary for me to stay in one. I jotted down some information in the back of my sketchbook and called for availability information. It was a lot easier than I anticipated, I was left with nothing to do. I got up from the computer and cleaned the living room and headed to Mikael's room to tidy up after Adrian. I was about to strip the bed of its linens, but decided against it. Adrian's scent flew up into the air as I pulled back the blanket. I lay down and absorbed his scent instead. I flipped through my sketchbook that was still in my hand when I entered the room and looked through all the pieces I had completed. It had been so long since I put anything in it besides hostel information. It was hard to draw or paint when every time I opened the book I thought about the night Ruben walked out on me.

I got up from the bed—Adrian's scent would linger for a few more days—and walked back to the computer in the living room. I opened up a new search engine window and tried several different phrases and was unsuccessful in each attempt. "Think, think, think, think, think," I tapped my finger on my head rapidly. "Ruben, Ruben, Ruben…Sakum?" I said, questioning myself. I typed it into the search engine and found nothing. *Coast Salish Native art Sakam*, I typed into the search. It wasn't correct but it did give me several options to choose from. I clicked on the first link and scanned the text on the website. There wasn't much to work with, but my heart still pounded, I was getting closer. I clicked on the second link and scanned it just as I had done with the first.

Handcrafted journals, fury moccasins, dream catchers, leather messenger bags, earrings and necklaces are just some of Yoomee Saka'am's specialities. Yoomee was born on the coast and together with her late husband, raised seven children. Yoomee often displays her arts at local festivals and around Vancouver and has a small shop set up in her home on the beach right by the water. To contact Yoomee please click here, I read, quietly to myself.

My heart raced, I clicked the blue link. An email form popped up, prompting me to fill in my name, email address and comments. I sighed in frustration, but found a local number on the side of the webpage. I quickly copied the number into the back of my sketchbook under all the names and numbers of the local hostels. I turned off the computer and went back to Mikael's room. I sat on the bed and waited a few moments for my nerves to settle. I glanced around the room, huffing, a few hours ago Adrian was there, sleeping in that room, changing in that room, writing a new song that he lulled me to sleep with, in that room and now he had taken everything and he was gone.

I noticed some papers on top of the nightstand and stretched to reach them. I unfolded them and realized that Adrian had left the information about his new place behind. I smiled as I looked over the pictures again and imagined visiting him there one day…someday, hopefully. I refolded the papers and tucked them into my book and flipped back to Yoomee's number. I picked up my phone and punched in the number for my calling card, there were only a few minutes left on it, from all of my phone calls to Adrian. I dialled the number written on my paper and listened as the phone rang. I suddenly remembered the time difference and quickly counted back nine on my fingers. It was five in the evening of the previous day in White Rock, it was still safe to call.

"Hello?"

"Uh-um…hi…"

"Yes?" the calmest voice that sounded like Mother Nature herself, asked.

"Hi…ah…my name is Zahra…"

"Zahra?" she asked, surprised like she knew who I was.

"Umm…yeah?"

"You're…you're one of Ruben's friends. He talks so much about you."

"Talks? As in still does? Or talked," I rambled quietly to myself.

"I'm sorry dear, I'm getting old, can't hear as well these days, can you say that again?" she asked.

"Oh nothing. Sorry," I apologized quickly followed by a moment of awkward silence.

"I'm Yoomee, Ruben's mother," she said, finally with a smile in her voice.

"Oh…well. It's um, nice to speak to you. Thank you for the book…a-and the boots too."

"You're welcome dear. I'm glad you're enjoying them,"

"Mm-hmm…so…I was wondering if Ruben was around actually? If I could maybe speak to him…or if you could give me his number…or tell him that I called," I rambled uncontrollably.

"Oh sure, I'd love to tell him, or let you speak with him, but he's not here," she said, with regret in her voice.

"Oh, okay…can I just leave him a message then?" I asked, returning the regret.

"No dear…I mean, he's gone. He left here two weeks ago and hasn't been back. I'm afraid he didn't say where he was going either…" she sounded very sad and I felt horrible for calling and had no clue what to say next. I had pushed Ruben to repeat his mistakes from the past. He had taken off again without notice, after I berated him about falling into his old traps and Ms. Johnson had wrongfully accused him of inappropriate behaviour. He had returned home and then took off, breaking his mother's heart all over again.

"Oh. I'm really sorry…" was all I could think to say.
"Me too, dear."
"Thank you for your time Mrs. Saka'am…"
"Please. Call me Yehyah, and you can call anytime."
"All right, thanks. Good night," I said.
"And good afternoon to you dear," she said gently.
"Bye."
"Talk you to soon," she said instead.

The rest of the day went by slowly. Eventually Romy rolled out of bed and I filled her in on the updates about Ruben as we ate left over lasagna that Mila had put in the freezer. Adrian called, hours later to let me know that he had made it home safely and I told him everything I knew about Ruben too, he was just as curious as Romy was. The news was too depressing for me to even try to make up a story for Mila and Fredrik, about extending my stay, I retired early and went back to Mikael's room to lay where Adrian had once laid and wrapped myself in his fragrance. It wasn't hard to come up with any excuse for that, Romy spent several hours talking to Noel on the phone in our room, I said I'd give them privacy and took my things and moved temporarily into the other room.

I closed my eyes and envisioned Adrian resting his head on the pillow next to me, gazing into my eyes, smiling his perfect smile, stroking my face and playing with my hair the way he always did. Before I knew it I was in my own perfect world where Adrian and I were happily together, with no distractions, no interruptions.

Sunday rolled in and rolled out. I spent the day configuring multiple strategies for my life. I comprised a list of important things I needed to get done in the next few days.

1. Come up with a story for Ma + Pa
2. Speak with them about staying
3. Call and book a hostel...maybe.
4. Try to sort out when to visit Adrian
5. Start looking for a new job... (possibly)
6. Try to figure out Ruben...
7. FORGET about Ruben!

Some of those things were easier to write down on paper than they were to pursue. I had eighteen hundred dollars saved in my jar. A cheap hostel for two weeks was going to cost me just over four hundred dollars and then I'd have to rebook, the hostels booked on a two week maximum. If I got another room in the cheapest hostel I could find, I would be able to stay there for an entire month with one thousand dollars left over for food, toiletries and a plane ticket to visit Adrian. It seemed like a half decent plan if needed, but it wasn't ideal. I figured my story out and decided that I would talk to Mila and Fredrik about it the following day during dinner after school. The other things on the list would have to wait, and forgetting about Ruben would be last.

Playing God

May 26

Monday came and left and I was too scared to ask Mila and Fredrik if I could stay. Romy and I, along with the rest of our classmates continued our final stretch of our Austrian tours. We were spending two nights in Salzburg and would be returning on Wednesday. Asking Mila and Fredrik if I could stay was not something that could be done over the phone. While we were in Salzburg, we visited the birthplace of Mozart, Mozart Square, a few castles and famous cathedrals. We stayed in hostels there, four people to a room giving me a chance to experience hostel living. I got some information from the front desk before we left the hostel and found out that it was much cheaper than the ones I had researched in Vienna. Romy wondered why I was so interested and I filled her in on my back up plan.

Romy hugged me, hating the idea of me staying in a room with a bunch of strangers, but offered to help me pay for a hostel in Vienna so that I would be closer to her. There was a three hour travel distance between Salzburg and Vienna and even though the hostels in Salzburg were almost ten dollars cheaper, it wasn't worth the distance between us. I thanked her for her generosity, but I didn't feel comfortable placing that burden on her. She wouldn't take no for an answer and so that was that. On the bus ride back to Vienna, I felt better about the prospects of staying in Austria, either way, something would work and I wouldn't have to leave. I could officially wipe White Rock off my radar. We'd be home in time for dinner, it was time to talk it over with Mila and Fredrik. I was ready.

We arrived at the school just minutes after six in the evening and Fredrik waited by the car around the corner with two small bouquets of flowers, instantly making both Romy and I blush.

"For my two girls," he said smiling, as we approached.

"*Dad...*" Romy groaned. "We were only gone two days!"

"Two days too many," he said, handing us each our bouquet and hugging us, kissing the tops of both our heads.

"Thanks Pa," I swooned. I felt better by the second about asking to stay. We drove home and Fredrik told us about our special "welcome home dinner" Mila was busy preparing. "Of course!" Romy joked, nothing less was expected. I couldn't imagine not living there with my family. This was where I belonged, these were the people I loved and who loved me. There was no way I could leave them.

We were welcomed by Mila with hugs and a million kisses, she was so happy to have us home, she even cried a little, Romy and I laughed. Ma was always so dramatic. Fredrik brought in our bags and Mila hurried us to the table where she immediately started serving us food, all of my favourite things that she'd ever made over the last six months. It was sweet, but also a little unsettling. It was time to speak up. "So…Ma I spoke with my…parents today…" I struggled with the words, the lies. "Yes, me too, yesterday," she interrupted. I swallowed hard, almost chocked on my malt bread, the air knocked out of me. "You…what?…You spoke with them…?" I asked, sweat beading on my chest, my shirt clinging to my skin. "Yes, your mom. She called yesterday evening to thank me and Pa for taking such good*t* care of you, my little darlin*k*," Mila cleared her throat, took a moment to compose herself. "She said she and your father were really looking forward to seeing you. She said that life wasn't the same without you and they can't wait for you to be home. I told her that it was completely our pleasure to have you, and that our lives, too, have changed and would never be the same without you here. I told her that it was like we gained another beautiful daughter, and that you were welcome to come back and stay for however long as you liked whenever you wanted," she said.

She placed her hand on top of mine and dabbed her wet eyes with her napkin. My eyes filled with tears just like hers, Joanne had beat me to it. She was smarter than I gave her credit for...or at least I had forgotten how smart she really was. I had been counting on her never catching up the Etzels on the phone because of the time difference, but nine hours would never stop Joanne from getting what she wanted. All she had to do was call at ten or eleven in the morning to catch Mila or Fredrik at six or seven at night. And all she had to do was wait till we went to Salzburg for the two days so that I wasn't around to answer the phone myself and hang up before she could get to speak to Mila "mother" to mother, "heart" to heart. It had totally slipped my mind that our families back in White Rock had a copy of our complete itinerary. Joanne had been playing the same game that I was. She caught me in a checkmate and I had lost, it was over. Romy rubbed my back, reminding me that she was still there. There was still some hope, I had the hostel! I looked at her and tried to smile, she hugged me and whispered, "It's okay, we'll book the hostel tomorrow," in my ear.

After I finished what I realized was a farewell dinner, I headed straight to my room. I had to lie down, my head was whirling, reality buzzing angrily, around me. I curled up on my bed and closed my eyes. Romy came in to see if I wanted company, but could quickly tell that I needed to be alone, she left. Eventually when I got up to brush my teeth, I saw Romy sitting on the couch talking on her phone. "Say hi to Noel for me." "It's not Noel, it's Adrian," she said. My heart stopped, my stomach ached. "You told him?" I barked, my voice unfamiliar. Romy, shocked at my tone and to be honest it shocked me too. "Zar...I just...thought he knew...thought he'd like to help, pitch in for the hostel..." she confessed. I walked into the bathroom and slammed the door behind me, making sure to lock it. I slumped down on the floor, my back against the door and cried. There was no more hiding from the truth. I could no longer pretend that everything was fine. I didn't want Adrian to know that I would be living in a hostel. I didn't want him to know that I wouldn't have a home, come Friday morning. Everything in my life was a disaster, Adrian was my constant. I never wanted the lines between the two to blur. Things were falling apart much too quickly.

Romy knocked on the door, begged me to let her in. I was so embarrassed by my behaviour, I had acted like a child, it was hard to eliminate the distance between us, the bathroom door. I extended my arm to the lock above my head, unhinged the pin, the tumbler released. I turned the knob slowly the door cracked open. Romy slid in and joined me, knees hugged, on the floor. She instantly wrapped her arms around me and apologized. "No Romy, you have nothing to apologize for. *I'm* sorry! I overreacted. You've only been trying to help… I was wrong to snap at you. I didn't tell Adrian because I didn't want him to worry, but that's on me, not you," I cried. "Shh, don't cry Zar, everything is going to work out fine! As much as you don't want him to, Adrian *is* going to help, you'll be able to stay in the hostel, maybe even a hotel for a couple of months and I'll see you everyday and Adrian will come and visit too and then you can come back to the house in a few months and pretend you've just come from White Rock…it will be fine!" Romy whispered and I believed her.

I washed my face, erasing hysteria, erasing despair and met Romy in our room. "Adrian's been calling your cell phone," she said, as I sat down on my bed. I looked at my phone, six missed calls, I sighed. "I'll call him tomorrow, I just need to sleep…" I turned off the lamp that sat on my nightstand. "Okay," said Romy, getting off her bed. "I'm just quickly going to call him back and tell him you've fallen asleep and you'll talk to him tomorrow," she left the room with her phone. I closed my eyes, drowned out the noise in my head and waited for sleep to come.

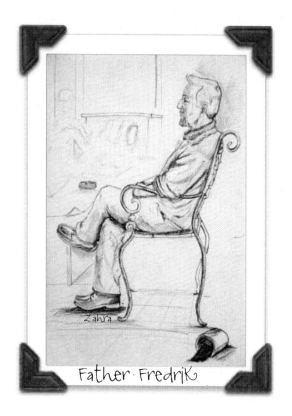

Father Fredrik

May 27

I woke up late on Thursday, our short Salzburg trip was the end of our tours and we were given Thursday to start packing, while our Austrian hosts were off preparing the hall for our farewell party. A small note sat on my nightstand, it said that Romy had pulled out some breakfast for me and left it on the dining room table and that she would be back at around three in the afternoon. It was close to eleven when I rolled out of bed. I padded barefoot down the hall to the dining area, the house, still. I sat by myself at the table, ate my strawberry filled croissant, drank my cup of cold tea, cooled off by the air, set out hours before I had woken, just as Romy had promised—I'm sure she didn't expect me to wake up so late—When I was finished eating, I cleaned up and started to put my things together. As I took my clothes out of the closet, heavy tears burned my painfully, swollen eyes, blurring my vision. Was this really the end? After tomorrow morning, I would no longer wake up in this room with Romy. I'd be waking up by myself in some hostel, somewhere in town with a bunch of strangers. I shouldn't have waited so long to hatch out my plan.

I rolled up all of my clothes into little bundles and placed them in my luggage. I wanted to try to minimize the amount of baggage I had. Romy could keep my other suitcase, even some of my clothes. She could always bring them for me when she came by the hostel. She could even bring some stuff home and wash with her things. Our styles had become interchangeable, Mila wouldn't suspect anything if my clothes were mixed in with Romy's. I smiled, maybe this would actually work. There was a glimmer of hope in this situation. It took me two hours to go through all of my things and decide what I needed right away. I filled one suitcase and my carryon bag and stuffed my messenger bag with as much as possible, never diverting from the plan that was about to be set in motion.

(★)[28] After I was finished packing, I went to the dining room again and sat down at the table with a few sheets of paper and a pen. I had no intention at first of responding to Joanne's letter, but I had to let her know that she had not won this time. I dated the letter for tomorrow's date, for that was when the games ended.

---

[28] Playing God-Paramore

May 28th

Joanne,

    According to you I shouldn't be allowed to make my own decisions. According to you, your word is bond. Maybe you should have tied me up and kept me prisoner in my room so that I couldn't go anywhere you didn't want me to. I know what you're trying to do, it won't work anymore, but be my guest to keep trying... You don't own me, you don't even know me...

    When will you ever come down off of your high horse and realize that you can't keep playing God with my life? When is enough, enough? You don't deserve to have an opinion or a say in my life. You could have at least been more understanding about what I'm going through. But wait... How could you begin to try to understand what this is like for me if the only person you think about is you? Doesn't it get tiring constantly living lies?

    Don't try to put this all on me, this is not my fault. Maybe you should take a look in the mirror, try to see what I see when I look at you. Nothing.

Your granddaughter, Zahra!

I felt good about my letter, maybe it was a bit harsh, but to be honest, I didn't really care. I couldn't care until I felt that Joanne cared about me just half as much as she cared about herself. It was like she refused to see how the truth would affect my life and there was nothing I could do to change that. That was a truth she would have to find on her own and until she did, I wanted nothing to do with her.

I folded my letter and put it in an envelope, addressed it to 'The Joneses' and slipped it into the back of my sketchbook. I walked to the computer with my sketchbook in hand to look over the hostels again. When I found one I was comfortable with, I dialled the number on my cell phone and waited to speak to someone at the front desk. "Hi I'd like to book a private room at your hostel," I said. A man with a thick German accent had answered the phone. "Sure, for how long?" "How long can I stay?" "Maximum two weeks," he said. "Okay, two weeks, please," I said nervously. "Okay your name?" "Name...umm...will you need to check I.D?" I asked. "...Uh yes, of course," the man said confused. Damn! I couldn't give a fake name just in case Joanne got a clue or put any sort of pieces together and started calling around. "Okay...my name is Zahra Nayeli," I said spelling it for him. "Okay Zahra, when can we expect you?" he asked. "Tomorrow." "What time?" he asked with suspicion in his voice. "Time...?" I asked, "I-I'll have to call you back," I said unsurely, hanging up the phone.

And then it hit me, my plan was fatally flawed. Sure I could stay in the hostel, sure Romy and Adrian could help me pay for it, sure Romy could bring me clothes and food, to cut down on expenses, but none of that mattered if I couldn't *get there*. How would I escape Mila and Fredrik driving me to the airport? How would I get away from all the teachers and the students? And even if I had to get on the plane, how would I get back on another one, once I was in White Rock? And if I did, I would have even less to spend on a hostel and most of the burden would be placed on Romy and Adrian and that wasn't fair.

(★)²⁹ I had to come up with a new plan. I opened a new search on the computer and went to a travel site to search the cost of a plane ticket. I typed in my departure and arrival information and checked the time of the most reasonable flight. When we landed in White Rock, there would be so much hype and excitement that I could easily trail behind and get lost in the crowd. We were set to land in White Rock at eleven at night, I could get on the next flight back to Austria leaving at eleven-forty p.m. and no one would be able to stop me. Yes, that could work…couldn't it?

I laughed to myself in an almost sick and twisted way, my new plan forged in my head. There was still a chance that Joanne wouldn't win this round, there was still a chance for me to take control of my life. As I rolled through the blueprint in my mind a sense of optimism draped over my body. I wrote a few notes for myself in the back of my sketchbook, I was lost in my own world. I chuckled to myself again. Try to catch up— "Hello?"

I answered my ringing cell phone, the tribal war drums in my mind subsided. It was Romy, she said she was pulling into the driveway and wanted to know if I was ready to go to the party. She said she was coming into the house for a minute, I quickly closed the screen on the computer. I didn't want her to worry about this. She would make it too obvious that something was up. I left the computer and quickly sat down on the couch and pretended to sketch in my book. "Hey!" I called out casually as she walked into the opening. I closed my sketchbook, got up from the couch and hugged her, leading her away from the living room entirely. "I

---

[29] When They Come For Me-Linkin Park

see...you're all packed up..." she said, apprehensively. I sighed, "Just some stuff. I figured I could leave the rest here and you could bring it bit by bit, when you come by my new place," I said, fighting to growing lump in the back of my throat. "Yeah of course!" she said, with glossy wet eyes. We hugged and I changed the subject.

"So. How does the hall look?" I asked. "It looks great!" she said, trying to cheer up. "You'll be surprised I'm sure! It's going to be a great night. Everyone did a wonderful job getting things ready," she said, wiping her eyes. "You should probably start getting dressed. Dinner starts at five..."

I walked to my room and grabbed one of two outfits I left unpacked. I showered for a long time, running over all the possibilities of my plan, what could go wrong and how to make it go right. I showered until the hot water ran out, disturbing my thoughts and ending the play by play run in my mind. I dressed slowly in somewhat of a trance, until Romy knocked on the door and told me it was time to go. I hadn't even brushed my hair yet. I grabbed a colourful head scarf I bought at the beginning of the season, filled with red, bright blue, black, white and yellow and tied it around my head like a headband, I was going bohemian. Jeans and a loose, white, off-the-shoulder shirt, brown fringe moccasins—that Yoomee made—completed the look. Somehow I thought that they would give me strength, I remembered the power of her voice.

We got in the car and drove silently to the bakery where we picked up Mila and Fredrik who carried boxes full of desserts for the farewell dinner. Once they were in the car we continued to drive in silence, what was there to say? I helped Mila carry the boxes in, while Fredrik parked the car. Romy was right, the place was gorgeous. The theme was 'Arabian Nights.' There were red, orange and fuchsia coloured fabrics draped from the ceilings making the room look like a large tent with white paper lanterns hanging down above us. There were several alcoves in the room with large throw pillows in the same colours as the draped fabrics, gold patterns sewn into them, accenting their hues. They were placed strategically on the floor making small circles around short round tables with lit candles on them. On one side of the room, there were tables set up from dinner, each with a handful of framed pictures of some of the adventures we had all been on over the last six months. On the other side of the room, there was a DJ who had started to spin some lounge music by the dance floor for after dinner.

"Romy this is so amazing! I can't believe you guys did all of this!" We walked across the room to the kitchen, where all the host mothers were busy putting the finishing touches on dinner. "Thanks Zar," Romy smiled warily. I put the boxes down on the kitchen counter and together Romy and I headed back toward the main hall. The rest of the group started flooding in and Romy and I gathered with our usual crowd. We gushed over how exotic everything looked and I noticed that none of the friends in our little group were kids from my own school. I had no friends from White Rock Secondary School anymore. All my friends were people I would miss, if I couldn't make it back.

Mrs. Green called us all to attention and we found places to sit at the tables. Our small group found seats and awaited Mrs. Green to begin. She stood at a podium that had been set up and welcomed us all for the evening. She started to give a speech about the success of our trip and then handed the mic over to Mr. Woods, who continued similarly as she did. All the students cheered as Mr. Woods told jokes and funny stories about the trip and started to show a slideshow of pictures. One of the pictures was of Natalie, Jason and I with our arms around each other smiling at the airport in White Rock, immediately my heart sank. I had started this trip with the two people I would have walked through fire for, I looked over to where Jason sat, he didn't look back at me. Natalie was well…gone. I looked down at my hands and played with my fingers. So much had changed in six months…I missed a few pictures while I looked away and when I had regained composure, blown up on the large screen was a picture of me, Romy and Claudia completely unaware that a picture was being taken, all of us drinking coffee with mittened hands. Romy held my hand, we both smiled without looking at each other. I looked at Claudia and smiled. So did Jason…he looked at her, the girl he had dated for a few months and cheated on, but didn't even look at me, his friend of fifteen years.

Several slides passed, A group of students skiing, another few standing in front of the famous, Von Trapp house. Next was a picture of me, Romy, Claudia, Jason, Sven, Ruben and this nice girl named Melissa, who I didn't really know, from White Rock Secondary and who I regretted not getting to know any better. She seemed like she would have been a great friend. I stood next to her, my arm around her shoulder like we were old souls and Ruben stood next to me smiling, giving a sideways peace sign with his fingers. My heart sank again for not spending more time with some of these people, for being so wrapped up in myself that I hadn't even taken the time to reach out to anyone, like Melissa, for example. I looked so happy standing there with her. I knew just a few things about her, things I had learned that day. She was really into the indie music scene and sometimes got around on a skateboard, like me. She wrote poetry and loved a good deal, she was never short on coupons and was always willing to share them. Then there was Ruben, so smooth, so cool. I imagined that when he was my age, he was one of the cool kids, the guy everyone was proud the say they knew. I missed him.

The slideshow ended and everyone clapped. Some students were even crying as the sad music faded and the last picture washed out off the screen, a group shot of all the students and their hosts in Salzburg at the hostel. I hugged Romy during that very sentimental moment. I wanted to believe that everything was going to work out in my favour, but in the back of my mind, I felt otherwise.

Marta took the stand when the slideshow finished and thanked all the students for welcoming her at the last minute and told us that we were all a special bunch and the best group she had ever worked with. Standard words, I was sure, I rolled my eyes. I felt bad for giving Marta such little credit, she had done nothing wrong, but she was no Ruben and as long as she was there, Ruben wasn't. What did it matter anyway? The trip was done.

"I had the *pleasure* of meeting Ruben months ago..." she continued. I made a face, I didn't like the way she said pleasure. "I actually gave him the tour of Vienna and Salzburg before any of you even got here," she was clearly proud of herself, I fought the urge of clapping for her, "good for you Marta," I would say sarcastically, instead, I balled my hands into fists, digging nails into my palms, painfully. "He's a really great guy and I'm sure an amazing guide and you all loved him very much. I'm sure if Ruben were here right now, he'd have plenty to say...oh wait. *HE IS!*" she cheered into the microphone, a set up for sure. Everyone cheered, whistled and clapped and Romy and I looked at each other, shocked.

My heart jumped up into my throat, as we rose to our feet to see if it was true. I couldn't see over everyone, I was the shortest person on this trip. I climbed onto my chair to get a better view and there he was. He casually walked into the hall, waving at all of us with a huge smile on his face, like he was the prime minister or something.

He looked at all the cheering faces, and mouthed hello to several people as he walked toward the podium. I wanted desperately to get down from the chair, but my shock ridden body was frozen stiff in place. I didn't want him to see me at the back of the room. I was the easiest person in the room to spot now that I towered over everyone, standing on the chair. My eyes followed him as he moved toward the podium in what seemed like slow motion in my mind. In that same slow motion, he looked up and stared directly at me, still smiling, but with a smile that seemed like it was for everyone else except for me. He broke our stare as he reached the podium. He thanked Marta for the great introduction and for doing such a great job taking over for him.

"Well, Did you guys miss me?" he asked, and everyone cheered. "Oh c'mon, give it up for Marta one more time," he said, bobbing his hands, palms up, up and down in the air. Everyone cheered louder. "Okay, okay, everyone sit down," he said, and everyone did, except me, I was still frozen. Romy tugged on my arm quickly, snapping me out of it and I sat down as fast as I could. "Look guys, I'm sorry I took off like that, some stuff came up back home and just so that you know, everything's holding down back in White Rock, but it just isn't the same without you all there," he said, leaning casually on the podium, both hands flopped over the edge of the stand, exposing large tribal tattoos covering his arms. I had never noticed any tattoos before, the weather had been too cold during the winter for rolled up sleeves. The newly discovered tattoos were a symbol of how much I didn't know about him.

His silver thumb ring reflected light off the fabric covered walls and his wrists were covered with leather bracelets. He was wearing a casual black long-sleeved T-shirt, pushed up sleeves and a pair of blue jeans, black, white and red, Chuck Taylor Converse shoes on his feet.

"I must say this was the most fun I've ever had on one of these student exchange trips. I've only done two others myself and you all are a wicked group of people and I'm glad I got to experience Austria with you." His words were more convincing than Marta's, call me biased if you want!

"I'm sure this trip will be something none of you forget. Each one of you will take something different and unique from this experience and it will stick with you for the rest of your lives. I know it! This trip presented a major opportunity for growth, to learn something new about yourselves and about your neighbour. You all had a chance to make some new friends and I think it would be valuable for all of you to keep in touch with each other. Don't let these friendships end, because these are the people you grew with, the people who understand what you experienced here and that is something truly special. I'm sure many of you will be back, I know I sure will be, so this is no goodbye, just, thank you for an awesome six months and see you soon!" he finished his speech and everyone clapped, cheered and hugged their neighbour and then dinner was served.

I could hardly eat, not with knowing that Ruben was so close and that he could come over to my table at any point in the night, but he didn't. Dinner was over and a few kids from our student council thanked our hosts, their families and our faculty from both White Rock and from Austria, for an amazing trip and presented the staff each with a small parting gift and a card that we all signed. Mr. Woods turned the night over to the DJ and everyone started dancing. I tried to sit out, but feared that if I sat alone, I'd be vulnerable to any attempts at an altercation with Ruben so I let Romy and Claudia drag me onto the dance floor and I tucked myself into the middle of our little crowd where I would be hidden by all the giants.

We danced this way for several songs before I was tapped on the shoulder and dragged out of the small crowd and away from the dance floor entirely. My heart raced uncontrollably and everything in front of my eyes patterned in black, I feared I was going to blackout. We moved so quickly that my short legs had a hard time keeping up and I tripped over my feet occasionally as we rushed out of the hall, down a quiet hallway, up the stairs from the basement and finally into a lonely stairwell that didn't have too much of an echo.

"I seriously think there are some words that need to be said, don't you?" Ruben said, speaking to me for the first time since he rushed us out of the hall. It was the first time he even looked at me since dragging me behind him. "So what? Are you insisting that I apologize?" I replied, defensively. This wasn't how I imagined this moment playing out. In fact, in my imagination this situation hardly existed. Ruben and I would speak to each other with no hostility, we'd both apologize and then laugh it off, *Ah ha ha ha!* It was all a big misunderstanding. We would hug and make up and that would be the end of it. That wasn't how this was going and I couldn't rewind and delete the last few seconds, all I *could* do *was* apologize and so I did. I sat down on the stairs and slumped forward holding my face in my hands. I could feel the heat from his body beside me and I turned my face a little to the right to look at him. He hesitantly put his hand on my back and rubbed lightly. "Ruben. I *am* sorry. I'm really truly sorry. I never meant to hurt your feelings or make you feel like I was judging you or your decisions about your life, your money or your family…I was trying to make sure that you were happy, but I never should have said anything that I didn't have the right to say…"

"I know Zahra…I don't blame you for anything. I blame myself entirely. I totally overreacted and I so rude to you…I'm honestly ashamed of myself, I'm embarrassed really. *I'm the one who's sorry and I should be,*" he said, apologetically. "Okay, but I don't understand why you wouldn't take my calls and why you just left without saying goodbye…"

"Like I said, I was so ashamed of myself, I was too embarrassed to even answer your calls…how sad it that? I left because I had a bit of a confrontation with one of your teachers—"

"Ms. Johnson, yeah I know…she told me," I interrupted. "She did? I'm surprised," he said. "I asked her why you left," I admitted. "Yeah…she said that she found it disturbing that I cared too much about you. And I said, 'well I find it disturbing that you actually think someone can be cared *too much* for. She didn't appreciate my comment." We both laughed. "There's that smile," he said placing his hand on the back of my head. I smiled and looked at him searching his face for all my unanswered questions. "I thought you were like twenty-eight," I said casually. "Twenty-eight? I wish!…If I could go back to twenty-eight…man, the things I would do… So would you have not hung out with me if you knew I was older?" he asked, apprehensively. "Not necessarily…I would have respected you more, though," I teased. "Funny!" he answered sarcastically. "Good genes I guess. C'mon we should go back before Ms. Johnson thinks we're being inappropriate in the stairwell," Ruben said, pulling me up from the stairs where I sat. When we were both standing he released my hand and wrapped his arms around me and hugged me inseparably. This was the Ruben I loved, how could I live without him? Maybe White Rock wouldn't be that bad after all…

We walked back slowly to the party and I still had so many questions to ask him, but wasn't sure if I should. "I can't believe Christina…Ms. Johnson…actually thought there was something inapt going on here," he said, pointing back and forth between the two of us. I looked down at the ground ashamed that I had ever thought that Ruben had made advances toward me, or that he felt the same connection to me that I felt to him. He was so causal, I must have been reading too much into our relationship.

"I mean...I guess I *could* see how she might think that. It just never crossed my mind...I think you're a great kid...*sorry!* Young lady and I see so much of myself in you...so much artistic potential I mean...that sort of thing," he said, pulling the banquet door open. I nodded my head and smiled a little, there really wasn't much to say.

"Okay go have fun with your friends! I'll save you a seat on the plane tomorrow, screw Ms. Johnson! What is she gonna do, tell on me? She's already done that!" he laughed. He rubbed my back again, Ms. Johnson, sitting with the teachers at their table, glared at Ruben in the ugliest way possible. He simply waved as he headed over to where Marta stood by the punch bowl. I walked slowly back to where Romy, Claudia and the gang were still dancing.

    Tomorrow…

                On…

                            The…

                                        Plane…

Tomorrow would be my true test.

Would I be able to pull off this plan?

I had to. It was the only way...
The only way I could make this all work...

I knew what had to be done...

Shooting Stars

May 28

(★)³⁰

Romy and I stayed up for as long as we could, reminiscing on every last detail of our time together and to my luck she never asked me how the plan was going to unfold. Maybe she knew that there really was no hope for us. Maybe she knew that we had been playing pretend, or, maybe she actually thought I had it all figured out.

    I would *have* to go back to White Rock now that Ruben was there. There was no way around it, there was no way I could sneak away from the crowd. He was saving me a seat! I couldn't sneak away from Ruben, there was no way. I already knew that he would disapprove of my plan, I couldn't risk telling him. He'd only rat me out. Maybe I could say I needed to use the rest room once we landed and when Ruben was summoned to help do a head count, I could sneak out then and make a mad dash to my departing terminal. I'd have to leave my suitcase behind, but Ruben would take care of it for me...wouldn't he? I'd have the shirt on my back and the few things I shoved into my carryon. That could work... couldn't it?

    Romy fell asleep without realizing it, so much for staying up all night! She was exhausted, though. She had such an early morning, she had been busy all day, setting up the hall, I couldn't blame her for falling asleep. I, however, couldn't sleep. There was too much on my mind. It was three a.m., it made no difference.

    In six hours, I would be heading to the airport, back to hell with no real hope of coming back. I watched Romy sleeping, peacefully, for a while. I would miss her the most out of this place.

---

[30] Airplanes-B.o.B ft. Hayley Williams (Listen to the song in it's entirety before you begin to read the chapter)

She was everything and who knew if I'd ever be allowed to see her again. Joanne would be watching my every move after I took off the way I did. She would never let me anywhere out of her sight, probably for the rest of my life. She definitely wouldn't let me come back to Austria again out of fear that I wouldn't return, which is exactly what would happen.

I would never be allowed to see Adrian again, Adrian who had called me two dozen times already. I really should have called him back…I just couldn't bear it. Maybe I would be able to secretly call him when Joanne retired for the night. She'd probably take my cell phone though and I wouldn't be able to call him at all…

And Ruben…

Maybe I could get a restraining order against Joanne! Yes that could work. I was eighteen! I could live on my own. I was old enough to make my own decisions, I was considered a consenting adult, she couldn't control my life. She'd find a way…

I crept into the living room and quietly turned on the computer, one last internet search. One last chance to make this work…

Perfect!

I looked at my phone…so many missed calls…poor Adrian.

I smiled and made the most important call of the evening. The call I was destined to make. The call I knew I had to make all along.

I took out the few sheets of fancy paper that Adrian had supplied me with and my trusty letter writing pen, just a few loose ends to tie up before my time expired.

May 28th

(★)[31] To my sister, my soul, my friend. Romy. Did you know your name is derived from Rosemary? And did you know that in Greek mythology it is said that rosemary was draped around Aphrodite when she rose from the sea? Can't say I'm surprised—you are the most beautiful person I know both inside and out. The first time I saw you I thought, 'this girl could be a model!' You're perfect in every way, never change. I love you for you and for bringing me back to life. You are an angel! Forgive me, but I have to go away for a while. I'll be back some day I promise, so don't try to stop me.

    I need some time to figure this all out and I don't know if I can do it here. Not with Joanne expecting me in White Rock and with Ma and Pa expecting me to go back there. It just isn't safe here for me right now. Maybe this is a mistake, but we

---

[31] Misguided Ghosts-Paramore

all make them and sometimes we run from them...

    I feel like I'm a vagabond, just a wandering soul, trying to find my place in this world and someday I know I'll find it, but until then I need to create my own path, the one laid out for me has disappeared, I'm on my own now.

    This is life right? And sometimes it hurts and I'm sorry for any pain that this is causing you. I never meant to hurt you, but I have no other choice. Remember that you're someone I know I can rely on so please don't feel useless. You've done everything you could and I expect nothing more.

I love you,
Zahra.

    I folded the letter and wrote Romy's name in script across the back and pulled out my next sheet. Next in line were the two people who felt more like parents to me, in those six months than the people I believed to be my parents for my entire existence.

(★)³² Ma, Pa

You have given me the greatest gift ever, a family. Because of you I know what it means to come together and love each other, the way a family should. I've only ever felt loved by Jonnæ, she did a good job, the best she could, I know that...and maybe this sounds horrible but at some point her best just wasn't good enough, I deserved the truth and not in the way I found out either.

I almost feel like she intended for it to happen the way it did, because why else would she have waited so long to tell Joanne and Fabién that I was coming here out here?

Why would she wait till the morning I was leaving? She had to know there'd be a fight. She had to know things would be said, let out in the open, when people are mad they say angry, hateful things and those things ended up being about my entire exis-

---

[32] Leaving On A Jet Plane-Chantel Kreviazuk

tence. Confused? Ask Romy, she'll fill you in.

Thanks you for everything, really, I mean it from the bottom of my heart and I hate to do this, but I have to... my taxi is here and it's time for me to go. Believe me, I hate to say goodbye like this, but I don't want to wake you and I know you'll only try to stop me. I'm so sorry...I hate to go...

I love you. Don't be sad!
Your daughter, ALWAYS!!
Zahra.

I folded the letter and wrote their names on it the same way I did with Romy's and left it on the kitchen counter. I dried my eyes and quickly composed myself, there was no time for sadness. I stealthily walked down the hallway to my room where Romy slept soundly. I snuck in using the light of my phone to guide my way. I reflected the light off of my shirt and watched Romy sleep for a few seconds. This was harder than I expected. I placed the letter on her nightstand and blew her a kiss as I crept back out the door, closing it softly behind me. I slung my messenger bag around my shoulder and grabbed my carryon in my right hand. I quietly opened the front door and stepped out onto the porch. It was still black outside, rained cried down from the sky, the sun would wake up in about half an hour. The only light to guide my path was that of the taxi I had called and requested to wait for me at the edge of the driveway. I closed the door behind me and was thankful for the automatic lock. I left my key to the house behind, on the table in the hallway. It was not mine to keep.

I ran down the driveway as fast as I could in my pyjamas and my pink slippers from my great-grandparents and flung the back door of the taxi open. "Take me to the airport, please and hurry!" I begged out of breath. The cab driver slowly pulled away out of the driveway and hurried down the street. I stared out my window as my home faded in the distance, I couldn't help but look back anyway, even when it was completely out of sight. It was the saddest day of my life.

"Why in such a rush?" the cab driver asked, as we descended the hill. The hill I might never drive up or down again. "Uh...I don't want to...um...miss my flight," I lied. We drove in silence the rest of the way, I stared blankly out my window, numb to the world around me. And when we pulled up to the airport, I quickly gave the cab driver his money and a generous tip. I hurried out of the cab, slamming the door behind me and ran into the airport without looking back. I looked around hopelessly for a while and finally found the counter I was looking for. I pulled out my money and handed what was needed to the attendant and told her I had no bags to check. She handed me my ticket, my heart about to explode. This was it. I had made it.

"ZAHRA WAIT!" my name sounded foreign to my ears, I had never expected to hear it here. My delight vanished, I slowly turned around to face my killjoy. *I was so close,* just three more steps and I would have been on the other side. I would have been walking through customs, three more steps and I would have been free.

"What are doing? Are you crazy?"

I sighed in frustration. "Ruben? Are you serious?" I looked up at the sky. How could this have happened? I was *so* close. "How did..." I started to ask. "Romy called me. She said she woke up when she heard a horn honk outside of her window, she saw the cab Zahra..." he started, frustrated. So Romy *was* awake...why couldn't she just let me do this? Did she not understand how vital this moment was? "How did you get here so fast," I asked in tears. I had been defeated. I had tried so hard and never gave up and never backed down and yet, I was still defeated. "I'm staying in a hotel right here, figured it made sense since it's one night. Nice place!" he said. "No offence Ruben...but right now I don't care!"

He slumped his shoulders; he knew he couldn't joke us out of this situation.

"Are you going to him...?" he asked.

"Yes."

"So you love him?"

"Completely."

(★)[33] "No Zahra! Stay with *me!* Don't go...stay with me...I love you so much Zahra and I *know* you feel it too, there's a bond here between us. Stay with me."

Tears continued to roll down my face, "I can't Ruben...I'm sorry. I can't go back to White Rock..."

"Yes, you can. You can stay with me and my mom in my house on the beach...there's room for you."

"I appreciate it Ruben but...I just can't. Not now."

"Why not?"

"Because...this is so much easier," I cried.

---

[33] Easier To Run-Linkin Park

Ruben stood in front of me about ten steps away, in a white undershirt and baggy grey sweat pants, he had just rolled out of bed. His hands were in his pockets and tears were running down his face. "Okay, then tell me this...Do you like the way he says your name?"

"What...? Jonnæ always says that...that if you like the way your name sounds rolling off the lips of the one you love than you know you truly love them and were meant to be together...How did you know that?"

"She's right! Those are the lips and the voice that you'll have to hear saying your name everyday...so do you like the way it sounds?"

"Yes. I do! I love the way it sounds...but how did you know that?"

"Great minds, I guess,"

"Jonnæ always says great minds think for themselves! Not alike!"

He chuckled, "Well she's a smart woman!...you better hurry, you don't want to miss your flight then," he sobbed.

"Are you serious? You won't try to stop me?"

"Nahh...When I get back to White Rock I'll just tell Joanne that I couldn't catch up with you."

"Romy?"

"She'll understand."

"And the teachers?"

"That you've been given consent to visit a friend in the UK. I'll work it out, don't worry about it. Okay, give me a hug real quick then," he said, taking a few steps closer to me. I dropped my bags and threw my arms around him. Ruben always had my back through thick and thin. He too, was my angel, my personal guardian angel and I was forever indebted to him for this. "Thanks Ruben. I mean it." "No worries kiddo, keep in touch, it's the least *you* can do," he said, squeezing me tighter. I knew he didn't want to let me go and neither did I. He *did* feel the connection between us, how could I live without him? How could I leave him now? I could still change my plan, I could go back to White Rock, I could stay with Ruben.

He cleared his throat, sniffled and tried to take a few deep breaths, he held on even tighter. "*Nccæo,* it means shooting star. So spread your wings little bird…Fly higher and bolder and freer than all the other birds in the sky. Promise me that you'll never forget who you are, don't lose yourself out there."

I buried my face in Ruben's chest, tears soaking in to his shirt, made translucent, a colourful tattoo covered one side of his chest. A sun, a moon, maybe.

"Shh," he soothed, "don't cry Zahra, everything's going to be *allll…right…*" he whispered.

I was frozen solid, my body turned into a block of ice, I pulled away slowly, sick to my stomach and buzzing all over. And then I saw it.

I picked up my bags, never taking my eyes off him as I slowly began to walk backwards one step at a time.

I panicked. My heart, pounding against my chest bones, aching, begging to be released.

Th-thump Th-thump Th-thump Th-thump Th-thump Th-thump
Th-thump Th-thump Th-thump Th-thump Th-thump Th-thump

I did not know this man. He was not who I thought, I could not trust him.

Ruben dried his wet eyes with his hands, tattoos exposed, It was all so clear. No, I did not love him. No, we did not have a special connection. It had all been a lie, he had manipulated me and I had spent too much time with my eyes wide shut.

    I did not stop walking.

                                                                              Slowly…

                                                   Steadily…

                            Backwards…

                One foot…

    Behind the other…

until I reached the safe zone. I was almost through to the doors to Customs. The stranger in front of me had the same dumbstruck expression on his face, as I had on mine. I never took my eyes off him and somewhere among the haze, the buzzing and the ringing in my ears, I could hear him shouting,

    "ZAHRA!…

                PLEASE…

                              WAIT!…"

-Fin-

Epilogue
May 28

This had to be the place. I looked around to examine my surroundings before entering the building. It was early, everything was quiet and no one was around. I walked past the empty desk and down the lonely hallway and waited for the lift. I watched each floor light up, as the lift descended. My arms trembled, they were tired and weak and my feet felt heavy beneath me. The second floor button, lit up, resting, taunted me while I waited in the lobby.

I knocked on the door in my pyjamas and slippers, bags strapped around each shoulder. I hoped that someone would answer. This trip couldn't be in vain. No one came, no one answered. I knocked again and waited, but still there was no response. I slid down onto the floor with my back leaning against the door and rested my head on my arms, folded on top of my knees. The lack of sleep and the turmoil was catching up to me and it was hard to keep my head up any longer. (★)[34] I had no other option, but to wait and as I waited, I cried. What had I just done?

Let me in
I'm at your door
I'm here but I'm wounded and I need you more…
Take my hand
Tell me you understand
I'm here, but I'm faltered…

Anywhere the wind blows
You find me, you save me
Every time my heart breaks
You're my sign of hope…

---

[34] Sanctuary-Global Rhythm

Epilogue

Anywhere my road leads
You guide me, you guide me
Every time my heart stops
You always bring me back…

I fell asleep in the hallway, head on knees, body aching, giving up. The door opened, my weight shifting backwards, supported by air. I don't know how long I had been waiting there. Time was irrelevant when you had nothing to look forward to. "*Zahra?* What are you doing here?" he crouched down and scooped me off the floor. My sleepy eyes opened, burning from the tears and the glare of the light in the hallway. I looked at him in a daze, confused. What *was* I doing there?

He carried me to the room, laid me gently on the bed. I was drunk with sorrow, anxiety, betrayal, so drunk that I couldn't speak. My glazed eyes watched numbly as he removed my dirty slippers from my feet and tossed them on the floor. He lifted my torso, so that I was sitting and removed my arms from my shirt sleeves and tossed my shirt on the floor. My teeth chattered, my body quivered as he rummaged quickly through his boxes, for a shirt for me to wear.

Hold me close
Don't ever let me go
I'm safe where ever you are
Your touch dries my tears
Erases all my fears
As you fill the room with your fragrance…

Anywhere the wind blows
You find me, you save me
Every time my heart breaks
You're my sign of hope…

Anywhere my road leads
You guide me, you guide me
Every time my heart stops
You always bring me back...

He carefully pulled the shirt over my head, followed by my right and then left arm and he pulled the shirt down around my body, covering me like a large dress. He slipped off my dirty pyjama bottoms and threw them into the pile on the floor. He rummaged through his things and found a pair of socks and slipped them onto my frozen, cold feet, he held them in his hands and massaged life back into my body. I watched expressionless, my head slumped to the side. I was dead inside.

Save me, save me, save me...
I claim sanctuary...
I wanna be lost in you, lost in you, lost in you
Lost in your arms...
Sanctuary...

He never looked directly at me. He never said a word. He pulled the blanket up, from the ruffled bed he had been sleeping in, and covered me with it. He lightly kissed my head, the first personal interaction we had. He had shovelled me off the floor in the hallway and held me casually, there was no sign of affection, we were like strangers. He got up from the corner of the bed where he sat and turned off the bedroom light, before he left the room. He said nothing.

I don't know how long I was sleeping for, but it couldn't have been long. I could hear him on the phone in the next room.

"...I haven't heard from her at all and then she just shows up here...totally unexpected..."

Epilogue

Had I made a mistake in thinking I was welcome here? I thought he'd wanted me, I thought this would be good for us...

"...No, I have no idea...what's going on? Hmm...I see...no I don't know either...no I haven't heard from Ruben...*why?* What's Ruben got to do with it?...You can't get ahold of him?...but I thought you said you called him first...why won't he answer? Okay I'll try, what's his number? Yeah I'll keep you posted..."

No! I yelled inside. Don't call him!

The words escaped me, my mouth bound together by shock.

Don't tell him where you live! I don't want him here. We should have never been so open with him, so trusting...he's not our friend. He's poison, he's deceitful, he's a *liar*. We opened up to him, I let him into my life and he took advantage of it. He played us all...like our lives were a game, like *my* life was a game...

The mayhem made me sick to my stomach, exhausted my brain. Against my will, my eyes closed, heavy and I fell asleep before I could get up and warn them about Ruben. They did not know the truth and I was still finding it hard to believe myself. We got caught up, he rolled the dice, he played the game and I was the loser in the end.

✳✳✳

I woke up to the sound of footsteps coming down the hall and I quickly closed my eyes pretending to be asleep. How long had I been sleeping? Was it Ruben there to take me away?

He entered the room his fragrance wafted around the air and my heart broke. Sad, lonely tears, fell silent and slow from the corner of my eyes. A puddle of saltwater sorrow, under my face, soaking into his pillow where my head rested. He didn't want me here, the tone of his voice as he spoke on the phone, told me so. I was wrong to have come…to force myself on him…to impose. I thought I could have taken refuge, claimed sanctuary in this place, but I was wrong and it felt wrong to wear his shirt and his socks and to lie in his bed.

He entered the room, I lay as still as I could, holding my breath so that he wouldn't hear me cry, my back turned to him. A part of me wished that I was facing him so that I could peek at what he was doing, through tiny slitted eyes, but the other part of me was thankful for the distance, the barrier, my back had created between us. I knew I had no other choice at that point, he was in the room. I could not escape. I would have to spend a few hours there and as uncomfortable as it was, I was grateful for his cozy bed and soft pillow to rest my head on for a little while. I would sleep off my delirium, thank him for the time he allowed me to spend and I would move on and figure out my next strategy from some place else.

He climbed into bed behind me and buried his face in my thick hair at the nape of my neck, inhaled deeply and he kissed the back of my head.

I claim sanctuary in your arms
With you I breathe…

He pulled me in close, cuddling me, wrapped his arm around my waist, so that we were as one, with one heart beat, one pulse, and he whispered, "Shhh…don't cry Zahra, you're safe now, you can breathe."

YOU LIVE
YOU LEARN

Book 2 Preview

ONE
Jonnæ
November 19

"Hi...It's Jonnæ, do you have a minute? Did I call at a bad time? Look—I know you don't want to talk to me, but... Please. Please don't hang up! It's Zahra. She's gone...She knows everything— She overheard me arguing with Joanne and Fabién. She knows that I'm her mother and she left...just took off, snuck out of the house and I'm guessing she's headed to the airport for Austria. I'm just afraid she won't come back...

"What do you mean what did I expect? Yeah I planned on telling her, but I didn't want her to find out like this...I don't know how I wanted it to happen, I was still trying to figure it all out...I thought maybe we could have done it together... This is NOT my fault, how can you say that? I'm pretty sure you had a part in all of this too! Hello? Hello?"

***

I was wild and carefree when I was younger. Joanne and Fabién, my parents, were so strict. They were raised in a time when appearance was everything. Where your life revolved around keeping up with the Jones' or even doing better than them. My mother was conservative, my father more liberated, but in their eyes, I was rebellious. I wouldn't call myself rebellious, I was just born in a different time. We were constantly butting heads. My parents weren't too fond of my

YOU LIVE YOU LEARN

friends either, they were good kids, from good families, we all went to White Rock Secondary, My best friend was a girl named Aubrey, she was such a great person, she would have done anything for anyone that she loved and I always wanted to spend every minute with her. I probably would have been allowed to, had she come from my neighbourhood. I lived in the same house that my parents bought shortly after they got married, the same house that they live in now, on Thrift Ave., Pretty ironic name if you ask me!

    Aubrey lived about ten minutes from us, in an apartment with her mom, grandmother, grandmother's boyfriend and her younger brother. If Joanne had her way I would never have been allowed to play with Aubrey at all. She didn't like Aubrey's family dynamic, she didn't like their neighbourhood, I was never allowed to play at her house.

    I was a pretty smart kid, I skipped a grade and was in the ninth grade, a year before any of my other friends. Aubrey was a year older than me. When I started high school all of my other friends were still in elementary, we all drifted apart. I became close with all of Aubrey's friends, instead and I felt like I fit in with them better too. Sometimes after school we would head down to the beach on nice days, when the sun was high and the sand was warm. The water would be just the right temperature to cool the skin after it had been scorched by the blazing sun.

    Aubrey was dating this guy, he was a few years older, seventeen I think, he went by the name, 'Fly' he really wasn't though, if you ask me, he was quite lame, but at the time we thought he was so cool. He had a car with a decent sound system and he didn't go to school at all, he was badass! He lived free. He lived with his friends in a small basement apartment by the beach that he had rented out from his sister. He worked with this art teacher, kind of like an apprentice. He used to drop by the school at the end of the day, sometimes around lunch and would wait for us with two of his friends whose names I really can't remember now and they'd pick us up, take us away from the confined walls of school and bring us down to the beach. He would park his car right close to the water and we would lie on the sand listening to music, blaring from his stereo and laugh, talk and drink beer. I was always a little weary of drinking and hanging out till the sun went down, but I'd always push those fears aside, convinced that my fears weren't my own, but belonged to my mother. I would stay out as late as I could, stumble home, push past my mother who waited up tirelessly for me and I would pass out fully clothed on my bed.

    I'll never forget the day I met him. He was perfect. At the time I think I was too young to know what love was, but I can definitely say that I loved him, still do. I was afraid of him though, well maybe not of him, but the way I felt when he was around. He started coming around with Fly's gang in the summer. He was taking some art classes where Fly was working. He was the youngest guy accepted into the program and I suppose he and Fly grew close, being the two youngest kids in the class. The first few times he came down to the beach he barely noticed me, I think he said 'hi' to me once. I think the second thing he ever said to me was "thanks," after I walked over to the guys by the car and passed around a container filled with sandwiches. He was so cute...and he didn't even notice me at all.

The third thing he ever said to me was "Hey. Where've you been?" "Just busy," I said, casually, while inside, my mind was racing, my inner voice, cheering, my stomach, churning, my head, spinning. Teenage love is so unpredictable...

You Live You Learn... Coming Soon

Behind this page is Jonnæ's letter to Zahra, enclosed in Zahra's Christmas packaged photo album from chapter 13: Family? Yeah Right!

(★)[35] Zahra,

I never thought I'd be writing a letter like this to you, but it is my fault that I am. You have to know that I've always wanted you to know the truth and that though it sounds cliché, I wanted to give you a better life and I was convinced that by agreeing to this arrangement would give you that better life. I know now that I was wrong. I'm writing this letter not asking for your forgiveness, (forgiveness will come when you are ready) but asking that you just continue reading past this sentence.

Zahra I love you. I love you more than there are words invented to describe it. It is something more committed or deeply rooted than storge love, if that is even possible.

I know you have many questions and all of them I intend to answer if you give me a chance. This is a lot for you to take in and I intend to give you all the time you need, but remember, you don't have to go through this alone.

---

[35] Sade-Babyfather

Fatima-Zahra, that's who you were named after. She was the daughter of the Prophet Muhammad and she was said to be the purest woman alive. They called her "the shining one" because of her magnificence. Your father told me this story the night you were given life, it was my sixteenth birthday, it was the first time he told me that he loved me and it was the greatest moment of my life, apart from the morning you were born. You are my single greatest achievement and the same goes for your father and I confidently speak freely.

Your father loves you. He loves you so much and together we've tried to give you everything that you've needed. It's a shame that we've had to do it at an arm's length and I'm sorry that you do not know him, but he's in your heart and in your soul. He's in your style, he's in your laugh, your demeanor, your eyes. I look at you and I see him, more than I see myself and it has been both a blessing and the most painful thing I've had to face, knowing what I've done.

Your father was my first and only true love. I was a few years younger than you when I met him and even though I was so young I knew there was something very special about him. We were together for two years and those two years were absolutely life changing. He was as amazing then as he is an amazing man now and I wish that things were different and that he was in my life and available for me to love. But just like you, I will never stop loving him, he gave me you. I will love him from a distance for the rest of my life if that is all I'll ever have. I am forever in his debt for the joy he brought to my life—you.

I know this is all very hard for you to understand and I know my words on this page are just empty letters, stacked side by side. Yet, I still feel like I need to say this: We were so young and I knew you, me and your father couldn't survive on love alone so I thought that if Joanne and Fabién raised you, you would have a fighting chance... I think that now I believe that sometimes love is all that is needed, or at least it is the most important ingredient in any recipe and now I'm just trying to reinvent the batter that can hopefully bring us back together.

I want to give you all the answers to all of your questions and I know what most of those questions would be, but telling you in a letter is one above telling you in an email and two above telling you in a text message on your phone. This is a conversation we need to have in person, the three of us; you, me and your father.

He can answer all of the questions you may have about him and his family and I will tell you anything your heart desires about me. You can yell at me, you can hate me, all your feelings are warranted. I am an open book, so is your father, we just want the chance to be able to have an open and honest conversation with you whenever you are ready.

I don't expect that from this letter or from the truths that you are now facing, you will turn about and call me 'mom' or even think of me as your mother. But I think that deep down inside you've always felt a stronger connection to me than to Joanne and that, my love, can never be questioned. You are the flesh of my flesh and if nothing else matters then at least we have that.

Lastly, I want to remind you that though it may not seem, Joanne loves you. She unconditionally loves you, she just has a different way of showing it and a difficult task at that. I'm her daughter and you're mine and somehow she was given the job of moulding the two together and she hasn't mastered it yet and I'm sorry if you've felt slighted by her in any way. Either way she could do better, we all could and I'm so very sorry that you have found out our truth the way you did.

Life isn't the same without you Zahra, the stars don't shine as bright in the sky when you're away. The sun isn't as warm and the ocean breeze isn't as sweet. You are all I live for and whenever you are ready to come home, I will be standing in the driveway where I last saw you, waiting.

I love you so very much my little shooting star. Never forget it.

Jonnæ